THAT MURDER FEELING

THAT MURDER FEELING

A SOUL GARDEN MYSTERY

NEVE MASLAKOVIC

COSMIC TEA PRESS

ISBN: 978-1-7366979-3-1

for the sensitive souls out there

mur·der·ous *(mûr′dər-əs) adj.*
1. Capable of, guilty of, or bent on murder.
2. Violent; deadly; brutal.
3. *Informal.* Difficult, dangerous, or unpleasant: *a murderous deadline.*

"Every murderer is probably somebody's old friend..."
— Agatha Christie, *The Mysterious Affair at Styles* (1920)

CHAPTER ONE

The phone call that would lead to a new entry in my sketchbook, in the M section, came on a Tuesday. The date on the one-a-day calendar on my desk read March 5, 1985—eleven days ago—and I was dealing with a case of identity theft. It was late afternoon and my clients, Wade and Ellie Gackle, sat side by side on the saggy burgundy couch in my office, slightly apart. Someone had been withdrawing money from the Gackles' bank account and using their credit card, so they'd walked in looking to hire a private investigator. Common enough—except for what churned in the vicinity of Wade Gackle's boots. I moved my briefcase aside and leaned forward in the armchair to get a better look. Fog engulfed his ankles and the cuffs of his jeans, as if Wade had wandered into a music video. Dense, silver fog.

Here's the thing about the fog: only I could see it—and it's a sure sign of deception. People lie, soul gardens don't. Wade had something to hide.

"The bank told us," Ellie said worriedly, "that there's nothing they can do. Whoever's impersonating Wade is very good at covering their tracks and it's up to us to—"

"Crooks," Wade interrupted. "Rodrick—can we call you Rod?—that's what they are, Rod, crooks, every last one of them at the bank. No one checks anything, and because the bank's not on our side, the police are about as useful as ice fishing in July."

"I don't know what we're going to do."

"Catch them, that's what, El."

Ellie sat with a Log of Worry weighing down her shoulders, one she'd walked in with. She worked on a catering crew at Fireside Resort, the place that had put Two Lakes, Minnesota on the map and provided most of the town's jobs, and Wade was a landscaper. Ever so determinedly, the fog rose up his leg. *Let's see what you're hiding, Wade.* "Do either of you have any bad habits?" I asked.

"I used to smoke right after high school, but not anymore. And we have wine with dinner on Friday nights, but only half a bottle. Also—" Ellie glanced at her husband, "when we first met, Wade used to bet on sports. But he hasn't done that in a long time."

"Yeah?" I turned to him. "What kind of sports, Wade?"

Resting an elbow on the back of the couch, he casually hooked an ankle over his knee under the roiling fog, which had enveloped him up to his waist. "Football. Hockey. Bit of baseball."

"When was the last time you talked to a bookie?"

"Don't remember. Couple of years."

Hoping Ellie wouldn't feel bad about missing the signs— more often than not, people tended to trust their spouses and Ellie was that kind, trusting—I pressed on, trying to see if Wade would trip over his own story. "Have either of you noticed anything unusual—missing mail, packages, strange calls?"

"Not really," Ellie hurried to answer, "but to be honest, I've been distracted. Mom wants to come for a visit—for a whole month!—she lives in Madison—and won't let it go. She's been harping on the subject of grandchildren. I *told* her Wade and I aren't ready but she seems to think she can change our minds." The log put on pounds and her shoulders drooped. "And things are no better at work. Our old boss, Adam Lindstrom—he just died. You must have heard about it, in that big storm a couple of weeks back."

I had heard. The news had been splashed across the front page of *The Bee,* the owner of Fireside Resort freezing to death in the February blizzard. Ellie had come in right after her shift and the orange shirt she wore bore the familiar logo, a campfire paired with a canoe paddle. She went on. "*Everything's* changed. The new boss, it's all been people walking on eggshells, worried about their paycheck. Dropped trays and short tempers. I'm debating whether to quit my job."

"You can't quit, El, we need the money. So Rod, do you think you can find him, the guy? We don't want to pay a lot, though. Don't spend weeks on this and then hit us with a big bill and claim you tried your best, all right?"

I heard the phone ring on the other side of the wall and Shane pick up—I'd sprung for two lines, one for my desk and the other, listed in the phonebook, for the reception area. No point in wasting any more of everyone's time. I shot the taller of my clients a direct look. "Wade, my man."

"Yes?"

"Tell the truth."

"I—what?"

"Time to come clean, Wade."

It took another ten minutes, but he eventually did. The person behind the missing money and the suspect credit card charges was Wade himself. As the extent of her husband's lying slowly dawned on Ellie, Wade took off.

Ellie rose to her feet, thanked me, and asked what she owed for the consultation. The Log of Worry was gone, replaced by— nothing. She wasn't sure yet how to feel about what had transpired. Though the agency bank account ran light at the moment and could have used an infusion, I told her no payment was needed.

Shane, the only other employee of Soul Garden Investigations, showed Ellie out, then leaned against the doorframe between my office and the reception area. "What happened, boss?"

"The usual. A couple where one side trusted, the other hid."

"Like in my romcom?"

"But with no guaranteed happy ending."

"I broke through the writer's block, by the way." Shane adjusted the pencil behind his ear. He'd been working on the screenplay as long as I'd known him. A few months after I'd opened the agency, a young, scrawny person knocked on the door looking for a job. His parents had cast him out for what they called "his lifestyle" and he'd already tried other establishments along Main Street. "I don't have a résumé," he told me, "but I'm loyal and I'll try my best." I was not that much older and reasoned that having an assistant would give the appearance of a thriving business. What I found instead was a friend. This was eight years ago.

"Figured out how to do the meet cute," Shane said now, arms crossed over his suit, a lagoon-blue one with a dark T-shirt underneath. "Hank's on his bicycle in Central Park—all romcoms must take place in Manhattan, of course. He's eating a hotdog, mustard drips, he takes his hands off the handlebars, swerves, knocks down Mindy—who's all dressed up and on her way to an engagement party—and we're off... Boss, new client phoned."

"Good, we need a case."

"Her name's Clementine something—didn't catch the last name, sorry, boss." Green hedges sprouted around Shane. The Maze of Daydreaming was in full bloom today, its leafy walls meandering around the reception area behind my assistant. He added helpfully, "She says she knows you—oh, and she's a baker."

"Don't recall ever meeting a bakery owner—or bakery employee—named Clementine." I glanced at the wall clock. Nearing seven. "Why is she looking to hire a PI?"

"Wouldn't say over the phone. She made an appointment for tomorrow morning. Ten o'clock—I wrote it down."

Shane returned to his desk, the maze drifting along with him, and I reached into the left pocket of my cardigan. Grooves familiar under my fingers guided me to the stone I wanted. Emotion receptacles is what I call them, the seven stones. Each is about the size of a pencil-case eraser, but heavier and translucent with parallel black lines, like prison bars, instead of the rubber pink. Inside the one perched on my palm, behind the bars, sat a tiny tree.

The clock hands ticked the hour. *It's time.* I double-tapped the stone and the miniature oak uncoiled and surged out. The liberated tree planted itself in front of me, roots tangled around my feet, the crown hemming in my view. The Oak Tree of Pain. I reached out a hand to touch the rough bark. Taller today, the tree. I'd find out why soon enough—it always took a few moments for my body to reacquaint itself with a feeling.

Shane poked his head back in. "One more thing—you have to go see her, the new client."

Two Lakes is a small town. Not the first time a client preferred to avoid the very public display of walking through the doors of Soul Garden Investigations. "What's the— *Ow.*"

"Something the matter, boss?"

"I seem to have a sore tooth." My hand had flown to my cheek.

"Tree large today?" Shane knew my secret. I'm not sure when it was exactly that my assistant picked up on the fact that I'd acquired a strange ability one July Fourth not quite five years ago. In typical Shane fashion, he'd taken the development in stride. He had advice to give on the tooth. "Boss, my roommate's cousin is a dentist over in Ostford. Best not to leave it too long. I did once and the next thing you know, wham, root canal."

I no longer ground my teeth at night, but sometimes brushed too hard without noticing, then ended up with sore gums. The problem would likely clear up on its own. "What's the address, Shane?"

"Of my roommate's cousin's dental practice?"

The tooth chose that instant to deliver a decidedly not-simple-gum-irritation stab. The oak broadened, the branches all but blocking my view of my assistant. "Where this Clementine lives," I said, trying not to move my jaw too much.

"At the moment, a jail cell," Shane said. "In Chief Gustafson's police station."

"Well, let's hope whoever this Clementine is, I won't find any fog by *her* feet."

CHAPTER TWO

Clementine, a baker. Did I meet her in college, during the two semesters I was there before I dropped out? *No...*

I stood at the larger of the two windows of my office, the one that overlooks Main Street. Frost patterns traced the edge of the glass; the Oak of Pain lacked a reflection. Down one floor on street level, Shane waited on a bench, a Walkman on one hip and headphones over his hat, a bright pink bunny-eared beanie. The maze had followed him out and I thought he might miss the public shuttle but the driver honked companionably and Shane made it on. The shuttle chugged away, leaving behind a mostly deserted street. Wrought iron streetlamps illuminated late-winter mounds of snow in front of shops locked up for the night. Behind me, the office heater sent warmth along the tan carpet to coil around my ankles.

Perhaps because of the stick I'd poked in searching for the baker, I thought of it then, what happened only a few feet away on July 4th, 1980. The incident had left a permanent carpet stain, splotchy and now aged to a faded brown. On a heavy, airless evening, I had a run-in with a killer—and a meteorite I'd found as a child and kept for years, not knowing that it held a special power, saved me. But that's a story for later.

What matters is, I changed. When the cosmic rock revived me after I'd been left for dead—it carried some kind of life energy—it awakened something deep inside, as if a sleeve had been wiped across the misty window of my existence. Since that day, inner worlds present themselves as fully-fledged gardens to my senses. Around here, people get called stoic and reserved, but I could suddenly see all of it. I walk past others and their private lots unfurl a few feet in every direction. Some soul gardens are wild and overgrown, others neat and tidy. In all of them, feelings seep out as flowers, vines, creatures. Like the stereotype of the mad scientist, I observe. I catalog. I tinker, not with chemicals or electricity but feelings.

Including my own.

If I had to compare the meteorite to an everyday object, it would be a battery. It jump-started me—but, I soon discovered, it could also store. That July Fourth, I stuffed the strongest of my emotions into its fragments like packing away winter clothes. I let both laughter and tears go, the good along with the bad. I could tell you that the meteorite, having crossed lightyears of space, drove a hard bargain in exchange for saving my life. It didn't. The cosmic first aid kit landed in my backyard when I was a child and stayed by my side until I did need it.

The truth is, sometimes we hit a wall in life. I wanted peace—or close to it. And so I let it all go. The garden of my soul is sparse and orderly, and I prefer it that way.

Since then, I've been coasting along, unperturbed by life's ups and downs. I rebranded from Gray Investigations—my name is Rodrick Gray—to Soul Garden Investigations, figuring that if I called myself the Emotion Detective it might scare clients away. Other PIs rely on stakeouts and a camera. Me, I have a cheat. There's the Fog of Deception, for one. Another is the Heavy Mud of Guilt. If I spot sludge weighing down the soles of someone's sneakers—the kind that'd smear my palm if I reached down to touch it—only my palm—well, I know they're dragging around remorse about *something*. My sketchbook is a catalogue of everything I've observed around clients, witnesses, and suspects. Number of specimens in its pages: two hundred and six.

I checked the clock. *Fourteen minutes passed, sixteen to go.* Along the way I'd learned that the emotions in the stones had to be aired out now and then. Tuesdays, that was Pain's slot in the schedule.

Looking for something to do to take my mind off the throbbing tooth, I took my briefcase, a slightly beat-up leather one, to my desk and got the colored pencils and sketchbook out, then flipped to the P section and the oak. The tree bore a resemblance to the real-life one in the backyard of 12 Nestling Lane, my house, over on the west side of town by Loon Lake. It's not a coincidence. When I was eight, mere days after moving to Two Lakes with my father, I took a tumble out of the oak and broke my arm. As my mother's death in a boating accident off the coast of California took place before I could even walk, the branch cracking under my weight and the hardness of the ground meeting bone represented my first encounter with real pain. The sketchbook version lacked what's there in real life, the treehouse built by my father so I'd be safe up in the branches from that day on. I remembered Dustin Gray as a happy-go-lucky person—always cracking jokes, chatting with strangers like old friends, never too serious for his own good. The year I turned twelve, he took off with a duffel bag full of stolen bills. I hadn't seen him since and no one else had either.

I took the opportunity to deepen the grooves in the scaly bark with a brown pencil. In the before days, I would have considered pain to be purely a sensation, physical and of the body, not an emotion or a feeling. But it's right there, the word: I *feel* the toothache. The raw signal—*Damage here!*—bolts into the brain and turns into a full-blown crisis. I felt *some* way about that tooth, you can be sure, a combo of *make it stop* and *why is this happening to me*. And I'd continue to feel the same way for—I checked the digital display on my wristwatch—the next nine minutes.

At least the tooth kept away the moody questions that usually dug at me during the practice slot, the *other* kind of pain, the mental sort, mostly about my father. Remember, I told myself, that time you asked Aunt Holly whether she'd choose physical or emotional pain if given a choice? She's not my real aunt, by the way. Her husband had been one of my father's coworkers at Town Hall. That's how it is in a small town. If you're alone (and I was), someone steps up; at times, it felt like the whole of Two Lakes had adopted me. My years with my father were happy—he'd been there the day I found the meteorite, a month before he ran off with the money—and the same was true of my time at the Lund farmhouse. I'd since moved back into the house my father and I had shared, but Holly and Chad still had me over for dinner every Sunday.

I'd asked the question a few months after I moved out of the farmhouse. Aunt Holly, unaware of the stones stretching out my pocket, had taken the topic as casual conversation. "Which pain would I choose? The kind that can be treated with aspirin, Roddy."

Two minutes... One... Thirty seconds... I poked around with my tongue, searching for the tender spot. *There you are. I'll check on you in a week.* With that, I shook Pain off like a dog drying its fur. The oak shrank and melted into the stone in my hand. After a heartbeat or two, the toothache blinked away, as did minor assorted discomforts I hadn't even noticed.

The stone back in my pocket, I locked up and, whistling, drove home through hushed streets. Clementine, a baker... Could I have met her when I worked with an agency in St. Paul for the three years needed for my PI license? No cases involved a bakery, though there was a restaurant fire that turned out to be insurance fraud... Remembering is a common problem for me. The line that cuts my life in two had done the same with my memories. Whoever she was, I'd find out tomorrow.

Having warmed up a microwave dinner, I settled myself in front of the TV in time for an episode of *Moonlighting,* a brand new show about a crime fighting duo. As Hunger sits in a stone of its own, my taste buds stay at zero most of the time and food tends to bore me. Watching TV helps, plus soul gardens do not show through screens, which makes for a nice change. I turned up the sound. My fork found a carrot and I bit into it with far more enthusiasm than the soggy vegetable called for.

Pain, gone. Now *there*'s a feeling.

CHAPTER THREE

Morning arrived overcast and chilly. When food tastes like nothing, it helps to vary cereal shape and crunchiness level. The day's choice was Mr. T Cereal. Munching away at the beige letters —all of them T's—I perused the weather page of *The Bee*. Six to eight inches of snow expected starting at dusk. I'd have to pick up driveway salt. Below the forecast was an article titled *Ice Out Around the Corner!* with a picture of the mayor cross-country skiing and a warning:

> Mayor Cooper and Town Hall want to remind folks that the ice on Cooper Lake and Loon Lake is starting to thaw. The lakes are no longer safe to be out on, so please stay off and keep your feet on dry land. Broomball, ice fishing and hockey season is officially over. Time to hang up the skates and pack away the gear.

I never did any of those things—fish in holes drilled into ice, push a puck around, or wield a broomball stick—but it was nice to know that the view of Loon Lake through my kitchen window would soon include more blue. Brown mud alternated with stale snow in the backyard; beyond the oak tree, a weather-worn stair-case disappeared out of view on its way down to the ice-encrusted lake. Twelve Nestling Lane is a single-story house. Dusty-blue siding, a slate roof, cream-colored trim and front door; no porch; the garage is detached, to the left as you look toward the lake. The one peculiarity is its flag-shaped lot, the original lot having been split in half to accommodate a newer two-story closer to the street, number 12b, where my neighbors Sven and Deborah Norby live. My driveway is the handle of the flag and its length means copious amounts of snow maintenance from late November to early April.

I grabbed my coat, backed the Ford Falcon down to the street and twenty minutes later, the road-salt bags in my trunk, pulled into the police station. Sandwiched between Town Hall's taller building and the general post office, the station shares the parking lot with a fourth building, the main library branch. I left the car in a visitor spot, next to a black pickup with yellow racing stripes and a bumper sticker that said *I Don't Brake For Tree Huggers*. Briefcase in hand, I hopped over puddles to the front doors of the station, mulling over what Shane had relayed about the new client. It wasn't much, only that she'd been arrested for disorderly conduct. She probably wanted me to dig up dirt on the other parties involved, in case she ended up before a judge. Unlike Maddie and David in that new show, a real-life PI (even one that can see living gardens around people) has to make do with routine cases. I had bills to pay.

If I'd bothered to look behind me... Yeah. The Lawn Ostrich of Complacency might have been there, trotting in the puddles, eyeballing me with beaky judgment. Probably was, a lone creature in my deserted soul garden.

My boots squeaking on the just-cleaned tile of the lobby, I passed a trio of locked doors—Records, Evidence, Armory—and entered the main area of the station. At my approach, Sergeant Mendez put down the paper she'd been reading and stuck a thumb toward Booking, on the other side of the staff kitchenette.

"Gray, your client's in Cell Three. The chief wants to see you first... But you'll have to wait. He's busy."

I could see this for myself, as Chief Gustafson's office had glass walls. On the other side of them, an argument unfolded: clouds of fury dueled it out above the heads of the chief and his visitor as they faced each other across the desk, both on their feet. I only had a back view of the visitor, who was doing most of the bellowing, but it was enough, even if I hadn't already recognized the black pickup with its racing stripes. Cowboy hat, white. Suit, navy blue. Striped tie slung over one shoulder. Arms chopping air as he made his point. When Troy Cooper, the mayor of Two Lakes, planted his snakeskin boots, people listened. A word seeped out from under the door now and then: *Guests, champagne*...and a phrase I surely must have misheard above the thunder-and-lightning: *Heart's desire*.

The chief responded too quietly for me to hear but the words had the effect of calming the mayor somewhat. "*Who* did you say, Gustafson? Oh, I see..."

"Want a chair, Gray?"

"I'm good, thanks."

The sergeant flipped a page. "The hardware store's having a sale this weekend... Gray, ever think about trying for the police academy? We could assign you a desk next to Officer Lewis over there. What's the age limit for the academy, Officer Lewis, remind me?"

"Forty-five." DeForest Lewis, a recent transplant from Chicago, looked about half that, with dark freckles dotting his brown complexion above the crisply ironed uniform. Entering a stack of forms into the station's personal computer, he hadn't looked up at my entrance. An object loomed over his shoulder—the Mirror of Perfectionism, bronze and arched at the top, sported blots and blemishes. The officer applied white-out to one of the forms, blew on it, and tapped the stack and stapled it. The mirror cleared.

"Forty-five," Sergeant Mendez repeated and flipped over another page. "Gray, you're what, thirty-something?"

"Thirty-two this July fourth. But the academy's not for me. Never was," I said, then, to forestall the herd of elephants that thundered through when people took offense, added, "No offense."

Sergeant Mendez's sharp eye meant a high likelihood of her getting to the bottom of my special skill one of these days, so I moved away to where posters lined the station's walls. I passed on the typed-up list of rules and regulations, and lingered by the hand-drawn notice regarding Officer Anderson's baby shower. The truth was, I chose the private investigator route thinking it would be the fastest way to hunt down Dusty Gray and make him pay back the money he had stolen. Optimistic reasoning by a young person fully controlled by his squishier side. Still, studying a couple of missing persons posters without really taking them in, I experienced a doubt, as I did every so often. Given my gift of plainly seeing what drove people to act, I'd be an asset in a police station, on a judicial bench, in a prosecutor's office.

But that—unavoidably—meant seeing *it*. Murder. For all its heftiness, the sketchbook in my briefcase was missing a page. I didn't want to come face to face with the emotion that drives the taking of another's life. The mark it leaves behind on the soul. If you've been stabbed in the back and left for dead, you might understand. The meteorite brought me back to life, for which I was thankful, but that was enough murder for me. I hung a sign outside the agency that read *No murder cases*, not that there are many of those in sleepy Two Lakes, and that was that.

Over at the dispatcher's corner, Aunt Holly had seen me enter and waved a warm hello, rolling out a carpet of earth. The brown patch on the station's tile floor didn't look out of place in the least, and I stepped onto it, my feet sinking in.

"Hello, Roddy dear," Aunt Holly said over her shoulder, then spoke into the radio set. "Missing, you said? Gone?"

This sounded concerning. Aunt Holly wheeled her office

chair around, leaving tracks in the earth—both tracks and earth visible only to me—and relayed to the sergeant, "It's Mrs. Nelson's puppy. It got out of her house again."

Gabriella Mendez sighed and set the paper down. "This is the third time now. Officer Lewis, why don't you put those reports aside and go help Mrs. Nelson. Make sure to chat with her about a backyard fence, will you?"

Officer Lewis bundled up and left, after which the door to Chief Gustafson's office opened. The mayor strode out, wispy clouds lingering above his cowboy hat. He tipped it at us—"Folks, be careful out there, snow's on the way"—and continued on out into the cold without a jacket. Through the front windows of the station I saw him head not toward Town Hall, but the library building across the parking lot. Odd, it struck me, given that Troy Cooper preferred the gun range to gazing at books. The sergeant had the same reaction—I saw her do a double take.

I found the chief putting a ball. He missed the cup and grumbled. "For the love of Pete."

"Problems?"

He set the golf club back in its corner, not gently. "The mayor, he did not leave his comfy office to tell me how to do my job, no sir, but can't the investigation wait until after his daughter's wedding? An extra week won't matter, will it? I mean, I get it—I have four daughters of my own. Paid for four weddings." A fond glance at the family photo on his desk helped shoo away the stormy skies. He sat down and continued more calmly. "I better be sure, the mayor says. Headlines of that sort drive visitors away and the town's luck with it. Can't argue with that, I told him, but police business is police business and my investigation will damn well proceed as I see fit. If I still thought it was a prank gone wrong... But I don't, not anymore."

I took a chair, setting the briefcase on the floor next to me. "You realize I haven't the slightest idea what you're talking about, Chief."

"No?" He studied me for the briefest of seconds. "Thirsty, Rod?"

Unrolling the window open, he brought two Coke cans inside from the ledge along with a dollop of chilly air. He passed a can over. A chunk of windowsill snow landed on the pile of papers in front of him and he shook it off onto the floor, then cracked open his Coke. "I'll tell you, Rod, enjoy your youth while you can."

Before his doctor had put a stop to it, the window ledge had held something stronger than soda. The last couple of years, the patches of white in the chief's close trim had grown more prominent. He felt it, the approach of old age, a hint of autumn color bathing his soulscape. Owen Gustafson had been a mentor figure to me when I first started out. If he thought a matter was best handled outside the police station, he'd send the case my way. I remembered feeling grateful. His office door was always open and we still played basketball together on Saturday afternoons.

Sergeant Mendez had made the point that if I wanted a change, which I didn't, no time like the present. To the chief, I was still in diapers sucking on my thumb, and had plenty of years ahead of me; a view closer to the truth than he knew, given that the meteorite fragments had retained their life-saving power— seven shields, in my pocket.

He asked, "Rod, how do you know Clementine Baker?"

Not a baker, but Baker. A last name. I shook my head. "Fairly certain I don't."

"Says she knows *you*." He consulted the paperwork. "Clementine Baker, thirty, moved to Two Lakes last summer. Employed at Sol Nail and Hair Salon."

"Doesn't ring a bell. Shane said she's in for disorderly conduct?"

With a grunt, Chief Gustafson rested crossed arms over a stomach that had acquired more heft lately. "Officer Lewis and I stopped by her house yesterday to ask a couple of questions— about a case. It didn't go well. Loud and uncooperative is how I'd describe it. She tried to throw us out. Disturbed the neighbors."

The woman sounded as if she needed anger management therapy and a lawyer, not a private investigator. "Drunk?"

"No. Apparently we were bothering her dog."

"Were you bothering her dog?"

"Well, the dog sure didn't like it when we knocked and interrupted their dinner, but evening is when folks tend to be home. I'd say the lady of the house, already in her pajamas though it was not even six-thirty—long day at work, she said—was the one madder about it. Officer Lewis and I ended up taking the animal to a neighbor and Ms. Baker here to the station, where she demanded a call to your agency and I told her fine, but she was staying till dawn. A night in a cell made her more cooperative and we had a nice chat this morning... Sure you've never met her, Rod? Can't imagine why she'd lie about that."

I sipped the Coke and thought about Hunger, due to be aired out later at dinner, which I was looking forward to. Hunger is a monster, a slow-moving, multi-limbed *thing*, with appendages for Appetite, Relish, Sweet Tooth, Zest, Gusto—and more, for hunger beyond the belly kind. Though I enjoyed the bubbliness, I didn't mind not being able to taste the Coke. With the monster trapped in its stone, flavor was irrelevant and I'd have been perfectly satisfied with tap water.

This is true of a whole lot of things. Now that I had the last name, I made a real effort to dig deep into my memories. *There you are, Clementine Baker.* A childhood friend. During the school year she lived in Texas, but spent her summers visiting her grandmother, the elderly woman who used to live next door, in 10 Nestling Lane. We played together, until she stopped coming when her grandmother passed away and the house sold.

I set the soda can down. "Childhood friend. What's the case you think she has information on?"

Chief Gustafson rubbed his jaw. "You know, I think I'll let her do the talking. If you do end up helping her, Rod... Well, you saw the mayor, and Sheriff Doubek's breathing down my neck. No mistakes, he says. A bit of a minefield, this case."

We found Officer Anderson dozing at his station. Boots hit the floor at the sight of the chief. The officer stood to attention and blinked a couple of times. A thin thread stretched between an ear, pink and prominent, and the ceiling. The Spider Silk of Barely Hanging On. Andy Anderson helped with a second job at home, the caretaking of a newborn, and dark circles ringed his eyes.

"Andy. How are your charges?"

"Cell One's sleeping it off, sir. Cell Three complained about breakfast."

Chief Gustafson raised an eyebrow. "Something wrong with her meal?"

"She said she wouldn't serve it to a back-alley rat, sir."

"Well, we're not running a four-star hotel here. All right, let's get her processed out."

In the short corridor in Officer Anderson's charge, the first cell held a recuperating drunken bender on a bench along with a stain on the floor; the person snored openmouthed, a dreamless sleep with few emotions seeping out. The next cell yawned empty. The chief stopped at Cell Three, where a woman waited on the bench, arms crossed over light-blue flannel pajamas dotted with overly fluffy sheep. Fuzzy slippers kept her feet warm. A down jacket lay rolled up on the bench next to her, as if she'd used it as a pillow. A squirrel dashed up and down the bench. Real-life squirrels don't run around in a rhythmic pattern, or jump over people's laps. Soul-garden ones do—impatience.

She greeted me through the bars without getting up. "Gray, took you long enough."

"I'm here now."

"I can see that."

The chief instructed Officer Anderson to unlock the holding cell. "Ms. Baker, you're free to go. Don't leave town. I mean it. Don't slap on a wig, pack up, and drive off. It never works. We always find runners."

"I'm not gonna run." Donning the jacket, she trudged out of

the cell, head held high. "Besides, the only wig I own came with a Wonder Woman costume for Halloween and my hair's already black."

The fuzzy slippers silent on the tile floor, she trailed Officer Anderson over to his desk, where he had her sign a form. The flourish of the pen sent the squirrel away. The back of Clementine Baker's jacket disappeared out the side door. Briefcase by my side, I followed my new client out, where a choice met me, stairs or ramp. Opting for the ramp, I immediately stepped onto a patch of black ice and slid down the neck-breaking-hard cement, my free hand trained to go to my left pocket.

CHAPTER FOUR

I managed to stay upright, barely. A peal of laughter greeted me at the bottom of the ramp—and an arm.

"Joy, right?" Having missed seeing the actual garden element, I took a guess once I'd regained my balance.

"No, Clementine. If you can't even remember my name, Gray, we're not off to a great start... Boy, you must have a death wish. The stairs and a death grip on the railing was the safer choice." She noticed a piece of jailhouse gum stuck to her jacket, said, "Ew," and peeled it off and chucked it into a bin, then looked around. "Where to?"

"My car's over there."

I'd bought the used Ford Falcon when I opened the agency, a 1967 model with two doors, manual transmission, a bench seat both in front and back, and a black exterior useful for night stake-outs. The mayor's pickup was still parked next to it. I offered to swing over so Baker could keep the fuzzy slippers dry, but she shook her head. She pulled on a striped woolen hat as we started across the parking lot. "So how have you been, Gray?"

"Well enough."

"I bet you're wondering what I've gotten myself into."

"Whatever it is, it can wait. Why don't I drive you home first, so you can change?" I offered.

She stepped over a slushy pothole. "I don't care that I'm in my pajamas. Lead on to your office."

Click. "Hello, Miss Baker, *Miss Baker*, do you have a minute?" A man in a windbreaker too thin for the weather, hood drawn around his ears, popped up from around the building's corner, as if he'd been lying in wait. There was a camera hanging around his neck and I assumed he'd just taken our picture with it. I was familiar with the man. "Name's Jasper Jones," he said to Baker. "Call me Jay-Jay. Reporter for *The Bee*. Just a question or two."

Baker kept walking. "Go away."

"The readers of *The Bee* want to hear your side of the story, Miss Baker."

"What story?" Baker called over her shoulder as if she weren't slogging through police-station-lot puddles in her pajamas and slippers.

"About your relationship with Adam Lindstrom."

Baker picked up the pace and so did I. Adam Lindstrom? Ellie Gackle's old boss, whose replacement, according to her, was difficult to work with and made her want to quit. If the police were looking into it, if *The Bee*'s star reporter had sharpened his pencil... Well, it added up to only one conclusion. A suspicious death. Homicide. Maybe even murder. The very thing I was determined to avoid.

Jasper persevered, hovering by Baker's side and matching her stride. "Chief Gus arresting you like that. Doesn't look good. Lindstrom dead and here *you* are, Miss Baker, spending a night in jail."

Baker turned hotly on the reporter. A storm darkened above the striped hat as she jabbed a finger an inch from the reporter's nose. "That's not fair. Adam's death was not my fault. Not my fault, do you understand?"

"Miss Baker, what can you tell me..."—a notepad and pen

appeared in Jasper Jones's hands as I opened the passenger door for Baker; I slid the briefcase onto the back seat and nodded at her to get in—"...about that night? The night Lindstrom froze to death."

She didn't get into the car. "There's nothing to tell."

"Nothing to tell, or nothing you care to admit?"

A funnel cloud began to spin up. "Now wait a minute!"

I elbowed in between Baker and the reporter before she hit the F5 of Rage. "You've been asked to leave, Jasper."

The reporter theatrically flipped the notepad shut and produced a business card between two fingers. "Miss Baker, give me a call anytime, day or night. Twenty-four-seven. January to December, rain, shine, snow, fog. You get the idea. Call and I'll come running."

He moseyed on into the police station and Baker stomped off to toss the card into the trash bin, then joined me inside the Ford Falcon. I started the car, then cranked up the heat for her benefit. "This isn't going to work."

"You don't want to get involved?" She clicked her seatbelt in with some force. "Why, because of that pushy reporter?"

"I don't take on homicide cases."

"You haven't even heard me out."

"I don't need to, Baker. I can't help you." I backed out of the spot and idled the engine. "Where can I drop you off?"

Seeming to take my refusal in stride, she instructed, "Take a right out of the parking lot towards Main. What are these butter packets? Do a lot of takeout?"

"Emergency snack," I explained of the sandwich bag she'd found on the seat. "Concentrated calories, for when I forget to eat. A tablespoon of butter, the size of one of those squares, is a nice round hundred calories." When taste buds are at zero, efficiency, not flavor, is what matters.

"What do you do in the summer? Don't they melt?"

"I switch to crackers."

"Can I have one? A butter packet. My feet are wet and I'm

starving." She licked one off its wrapper. "Sort of like a super-rich ice cream, isn't it?"

We were at the stop sign onto Main. "Which way from here, Baker?"

"Go north."

Main Street, still known to older residents as Interlachen Drive, from before the name got changed to the more tourist-friendly version, runs north to south between two of Minnesota's ten thousand. The larger Cooper Lake, to the west, hosts Fireside Resort on its far shore. The smaller, tear-shaped Loon Lake nestles in the middle of my neighborhood. In between lies the heart of the town. Cozy restaurants and shops that spell their names as *shoppe* line the two sides of the street, with the area blossoming with tourists in high season, from May to September. What car and foot traffic shuffled by at this time of year belonged mostly to locals.

My passenger found something to complain about. "Gray, why do you keep calling me Baker? You used to call me Clem."

"You just called me by my last name."

When I drive, I keep my eyes on the road so as not to catch an accidental glance of private worlds of passersby, like the harried mom pushing a stroller down Main Street's sidewalk or the bare-headed teenager jaywalking a block ahead. When I'm working a case, I can't look away. I figure I owe it to my clients to use all the tools at my disposal, even at the price of their own privacy. I glanced over. Baker's slippers were clean—no guilt or remorse about getting in the reporter's face. No fig leaf—of embarrassment—either. Plenty of other, everyday things. She was chilly, hungry, and tired, but also curious and hopeful.

"Yeah, but you told me to, remember?" she said. "To call you Gray."

And so I had. As a child, I'd hated *Rodrick*, a combination of my father's choice, Rodger, and my mother's choice, Patrick. Other boys had normal names like Jimmy or Jack or Steve. Later I got more at ease with my given name, but back then, I would have offered up *Gray* instead.

At the next red light, Baker bounced the bag with the butters on one knee. "I have money saved up—not a lot, but some. I'm not going to try and cash in on our old friendship is what I'm saying, especially since you apparently barely remember me."

The light turned green and I pressed the pedal and told her it wasn't about money. "It's a firm rule—there's even a sign on the agency door. *No Murder Cases.* As to why, well, it's a long story."

She plunked the butter bag back onto the dashboard. "Gray, don't you remember the Crime Knights?"

At that, a vivid scrap unrolled into my mind and I found myself operating the Ford Falcon with my hands, right foot, and my brain's auto-pilot, transported back to the year my father and I settled in Two Lakes. He found a job in Town Hall, having talked them into turning their volunteer-run program into a formal Parks and Recreation Department—with Dusty in charge. Meanwhile, I had trouble making friends in our new town. My father, as most social people do, believed that I just needed to come out of my shell, best achieved by leaving me to it. The result was that I was a generally lonely kid. (It's still an effort to befriend people. But young Roddy felt the loneliness and I don't.) Things got worse when my father fled with the Town Hall money and other kids took it upon themselves to mock and tease mercilessly. But in those early years I did have one companion, from June to August each summer.

I met Clementine the day my father built the treehouse, after I broke my arm tumbling out of the oak. Besides being a conman, he had a talent for tools. We spent the morning in the emergency room. As the sun dipped toward the horizon, Clem came outside from 10 Nestling Lane to watch the build with me. I'd later learn that she lived in Houston and had four siblings. That she'd been sent north to the house of her grandmother—Helen Baker, our neighbor one front door over—while her brothers went camping with their father.

I drove up Main Street, the summers replaying in my mind. A hot and humid day would dawn and I'd fill the time by watching cartoons while next door Helen Baker made Clem do chores and practice the violin. Mid-morning, Clem would run out, ripping off the hair bow Helen thought suited her. We'd scramble down to the lake and wade into the reeds to try to catch fathead minnows with our hands, then climb back on dry land and follow the curve of the water, trespassing in backyards and keeping an ear out for the peculiar yodel of the bird the lake's named after. On rainy days, we'd sit in the treehouse with binoculars and look out onto the neighborhood.

The last of the summers belonged to Lady Clementine and Sir Gray. We were the Crime Knights, wielding swords made from cardboard, our base of operations the treehouse. It was Clem's idea—she said we had to do our part, make the world more just, more fair, by catching bad guys. She wrote up an ad on 3x5 index cards and we left them in mailboxes. Mrs. Larson, across the street, was the only one to hire us, to look for a yard intruder; we caught the culprit, a rabbit which Mrs. Larson took to the Aurboda County petting zoo.

We investigated some things of our own accord. Why did elderly Mr. Berg shuffle down to his mailbox at the same time each morning? One day an airmail letter arrived and Mr. Berg's step seemed lighter after that. Who pilfered the Johnsons' newspaper, at the corner house, before dawn now and then? That one turned out to be the retired schoolteacher at number 15, information we did nothing with, despite having gotten up before breakfast on a misty morning to spy on that end of the street.

That last year, as the summer drew to a close, Clem went home to Texas as usual. Her grandmother passed away a month later and 10 Nestling Lane went on the market. My reaction to it had been what you might expect of a twelve-year-old—anger, my ire focused on the fact that people shouldn't die. I missed Clem. On November second, my father took off for good and I moved in with Aunt Holly and Uncle Chad. They readied the spare room for me and never said a bad word about my father, nor would they allow me to.

Main Street's traffic lights are timed poorly on purpose to keep speeding down and we'd stopped again. "Why didn't you write back?" I asked Baker. I'd written a few letters to her Texas address and walked them to the post office, but never heard back.

"I did, for a while. I found out later that my mother threw away your letters, and the ones I wrote and gave her to mail. She thought it best for me to move on. But here I am... I managed to find my way back to Two Lakes."

The light changed and I switched on the wipers to get rid of a spray of road slush as we passed the corner where Soul Garden Investigation occupies the upper floor. "That was twenty years ago, the Crime Knights. A childish pastime."

"Well, yeah, we *were* children... Do you still live there, in Nestling Lane?"

"I didn't, for a while. A few years after I opened the agency, a case of theft and a grateful client brought in some extra cash and I purchased the house. The family that owned it in the meantime had split the lot and sold the lower half. The house and backyard are the same, but the front yard is tiny."

"And your father? I remember him. He made us ham sandwiches for lunch and ran Parks and Recreation, which at that age I assumed meant that he was in charge of both Yellowstone Park *and* the Grand Canyon."

I relayed the story. There was no reason not to—everyone knew it and she'd hear about it one way or another. "My father had a bright idea, to raise funds for a new park—this would have been October of 1965. He organized a raffle—one dollar, one ticket, simple enough. Half of the proceeds to Town Hall to build the park, the other half to the raffle winner. The pot grew, people kept buying tickets, which made the pot grow even more, until virtually every single person in Two Lakes had joined in, some buying dozens or a hundred tickets. And then my father looks at all this cash—over twenty-five thousand dollars, something like that, no one knew for sure—and decides why not keep it? He was supposed to take the lockbox to the bank. He never did. I returned home from school and he was gone. I was twelve."

"How terrible for you."

"It came out later that my father had fallen behind on the mortgage payments." I told her how Holly and Chad Lund took me in. "After I opened the agency, I spent every free hour trying to follow his trail for three years. All I found was proof that he'd been a conman even before we moved to Two Lakes. Guess he decided the honest life wasn't right for him—and that he didn't want a kid hanging on... At least the park did eventually get built, paid for by donations. It's Cooper Lake Park now."

"Make a right at the Dairy Queen, then another onto Second Street... And our treehouse?"

"A little bit beat up, but still there." I followed that up with a mild, "Gosh darn it, you should take more care."

The mayor's pickup had whizzed by. Easygoing, sedate, those did not describe Troy Cooper's style of driving, but the police station turned a blind eye. Chief Gustafson knows when to pick his battles. It had nothing to do with the mayor feeling that Two Lakes was *his* town and he was going to drive up and down its streets in whatever manner he saw fit, and everything to do with how his wife had died. At the steering wheel, Troy fought an unseen foe.

Baker coughed. "*Gosh darn it?* No need to watch your language in my presence, Gray."

"It's not that. I don't get angry, not really."

"Prefer to keep your feelings bottled up?"

"You could say that." In front of us, the mayor blew through a stop sign. I pressed the brake. "I had a close call a while back. It affected me... My memory, I mean. There are things I remember only with effort and others not at all. I've kind of been calm since then."

She did an odd thing. She lightly punched me in the shoulder. The polite sympathy I expected to encounter—a pair of steaming mugs of cocoa—didn't construct itself between us on the bench seat. She grimaced, as if she herself had been hurt. "I'll accept that as your excuse for barely remembering me. What happened?"

I'd long ago rearranged the tale into a few sentences easily told but not exactly truthful. "An intruder climbed up the fire escape behind the agency. I didn't have time to grab the gun I kept taped to the underside of my desk. He had a knife. We fought for it"—this was where the mix of truth and fiction began—"and I managed a stab. The intruder pushed me down, I hit my head on the corner of the desk, blacked out. He fled back down the fire escape. My assistant, Shane, found me in the morning."

"You didn't see who it was?"

I shook my head. "Only a glimpse of a figure slipping out into the July night."

"Is that when you stopped taking on homicide cases, after the brush with death? Hits too close to home?"

"Something like that." I frowned. "Baker, did you forget where you live or what?"

We'd made a loop and were back on Main Street, nearing the intersection with Carriage Way, the corner where the agency stands, for a second time.

"Your agency is where we're going, Gray."

I pulled into an empty parking spot and left the engine running. I considered kicking Baker out in the fuzzy slippers and making her walk home, wherever that was.

"Listen," she said, "I don't care that your head's not quite right. And that rule about no murder cases, that's for strangers, right? I need a friend, someone who believes me when I say that I had nothing to do with Adam's death."

"Chief Gustafson's a fair man."

Even as I said it, I recalled the chief's words. *You saw the mayor, and Sheriff Doubek's breathing down my neck... A bit of a minefield, this case.*

Baker stacked the squares of butter into an unstable tower on the dashboard top. "How about this? You take me on as a client and as for my side of it, I hereby absolve you in advance, in perpe-tuity, till death do us part, from any blame whatsoever if I do end up rotting in prison for the rest of my life. Also, wasn't I a good friend, back then? I don't want to say that you owe me, but you do. Remember our pact?" She searched the pockets of her jacket. "Here. I grabbed it before they hustled me into the police car."

The twenty-year-old piece of paper felt fragile and brittle under my fingers as I unfolded it. The Crime Knights pact, yellowed by the passage of time, signed by both of us.

> *The Crime Knights Pact*
>
> *We, Clementine Baker and Rodrick Gray, swear to be true Crime Knights.*
> *We will stick together no matter what and fight bad guys. If one of us gets in trouble, the other will show up in shining armor. (Okay, maybe not REAL armor.)*
> *No villain is strong enough to defeat us.*
> *Signed this date, June 18, 1965*
> *Clem B. and R. Gray*

Baker, sounding wiser than her then eleven years, had composed the text and had insisted we add our fingerprints in blood to the signature line. In the end we settled on red paint from the art set she'd been gifted for the summer by Helen Baker and which sat ignored.

You owe me. It could have been said many ways. Angrily. Coyly. A reminder of a past favor she'd come to collect on. Baker had said it as if explaining to a teenager that when you shared a house with other people, chores had to be done and that was all there was to it. She and I had struck a childhood bargain once upon a time. It clearly meant something to her.

The question was, did it mean something to me? I tapped the

steering wheel and considered the matter. Long ago, the smaller version of the woman on the other end of the bench seat had befriended a lonely boy. I owed her because I owed Gray the First, the person I used to be. He gave me his body and soul, after all.

Obligated to Return the Favor is a peach carnation. It had sprouted in my soul garden and poked out from the car's cigarette lighter. Tap, tap, my thumb went on the steering wheel. Outside the car, a tennis ball bounced back and forth between invisible walls, a manifestation of my indecisiveness; the rhythm matched my tapping.

My choices:

Say no to Baker. Risk a childhood friend going to jail for a crime she claimed she didn't commit.

Or say yes.

I glanced in the direction of my passenger and her inner world, a riot of color and chaos. The first rule of private investigation is that the story you get from the client isn't the whole story. People forget to mention things, or deem them irrelevant, or omit them on purpose. And so I asked myself, then and there, the question: The emotional scar of having taken a life—I Did It, Now I Feel Some Way About It—what might that look like? I'd be lying if I said I'd never wondered, despite my past. But that didn't mean I wanted to get cozy with it. Whether Baker was innocent or not, taking on the case would mean exactly that.

I killed the engine. "I'll leave the decision to Ike."

"Who's Ike?"

"Just a sec." I passed the Crime Knights pact back to her and took the dollar out of the right pocket of my cardigan, under my jacket.

"You're going to decide whether to help me," Baker raised an eyebrow, "with a coin toss?"

"If a client is ambivalent about a decision, I have them toss this coin. Maybe they like the outcome, maybe not. Either way, it reveals how they really feel."

The trick worked well because I could see the reaction in real time, and tailor my next steps based on that. It didn't work the same way for me—tossing the coin revealed nothing—but that was the point. I could simply let Ike decide.

The 1971 dollar I'd picked up at the curiosity shop under the agency premises had Eisenhower on the front and an eagle landing on a cratered surface, a nod to the Moon landing, on the reverse. I spun up the coin—*heads and the No Murder Cases rule holds firm; tails, I'll hear Baker out*—and caught it in my other palm.

Eagle.

"Lucky for you," I said. "My office is up there. Soul Garden Investigations."

Baker lightly punched my arm again. "I knew you wouldn't let me down."

CHAPTER FIVE

The agency occupies the corner of the upper level of a courtyard. Further in there's a used bookstore and a real estate firm. On ground level, the curiosity shop sits right below, there's a travel agency in the back, and fronting the street is the Home Plate Diner. Ingrid Dahl, who owns the diner, is Aunt Holly's older sister. In the summer, Ingrid sets up tables in the open space in the middle of the courtyard; as Baker and I made our way across it, we passed only a couple of bags of road salt and a stained snow shovel. We took the stairs up past the windows of Karl's Kuriosities, closed for the season. A heavy layer of dust covered everything inside—Karl always had to take a day or two to freshen up the space when he reopened in May. Baker gave a small shudder. "That's one realistic looking skeleton in the window."

"Karl keeps some odd things in there."

"You don't find it creepy?"

"Like I said, I tend to be unflappable these days."

And kept some odd things myself. Like the meteorite fragments in my pocket. And the notebook of feelings in my briefcase. Also inside the briefcase was a library copy of *Hamlet*. Same as with television, soul gardens do not show through the written word; I do a lot of both, TV watching and reading. Movie theaters are generally out because I'm overwhelmed by the sights, sounds, and smells from the soulscapes of everyone in the audience. A Rubik's Cube, sure. Bars, arcades, the mall, no.

At our entrance, Shane kicked into high gear. After he'd fussed over Baker and got her settled on the couch, sprinted down to the diner for coffee after she declined tea, and offered to scrub away the sticky spot the jail gum had left on Baker's jacket, I waved him to the chair he'd wheeled in without being asked. Shane does that once in a while, when he senses I need reinforcements.

Baker downed a good amount of the coffee, made short work of the glazed donut that Ingrid had sent up with Shane, and wiped her fingers off on a paper napkin. "Sorry. I skipped both dinner and breakfast."

"So, Adam Lindstrom," I prompted her.

Shane's mouth fell open. "This is about Lindstrom? The most handsome man in Two Lakes..." My assistant could be relied on to give a knowledgeable assessment of both men and women. "...or at least, he *was*. He froze to death in that storm a couple of weeks ago, didn't he?"

Baker cradled the paper cup in her palm. "Look, my gut's been telling me something's off. I've been calling the police station non-emergency number every day asking if there's news and what does Chief Gustafson do? Knock on my door and haul me in to give a statement."

"Individuals have been known to draw attention to their own crimes," I pointed out mildly. "Wouldn't be the first time. By the way, the chief said you were belligerent, Baker."

"Wouldn't you be, under the circumstances?"

"Certainly not."

"Why does the chief suspect you were involved, Clem? Can I call you Clem?" Shane made friends as easily as he breathed air, an ability I envied sometimes (on Saturdays, to be specific, the day I allowed Envy & Embarrassment out of their stone). "If you ask me—"

"Don't say it." Baker banged down the paper cup, sending a couple of brown drops onto the table. "That a sweet little thing like me could never hurt anyone."

"Lord, no, I would never," Shane assured her, throwing an extra napkin onto the spill. "Especially since you're on the tall side, Clem—taller than me, in any case. We haven't been formally introduced. I'm Shane Landon Hasenkamp—the third, technically, but I'm estranged from my family. We move in different social circles so there's no chance of mix-ups except maybe with parking tickets, but, luckily, I don't drive." Shane hastened to add, "What I was going to say is that you wouldn't hurt a fly."

"I wouldn't. I'd shoo it out a window."

Unless the fly made you mad, I found myself thinking. Whoa, where had that come from? Did I really think she could harm another person? All right, so she'd argued with Chief Gustafson, and the reporter. And banged her coffee cup just now. But that was hardly evidence of anything.

Pajama-ed legs tucked under her, Baker sat in the same spot as Ellie Gackle had the day before. Though both she and Ellie were about the same age, Baker's slumber-party outfit made her look much younger. I'd bought the burgundy velvet two-seater at a yard sale and it sagged in places; Shane had added a couple of pillows at some point. Leaning on one of them, fingers wrapped around the cup, Baker began her story. Or rather, Adam's story. "That evening—February twenty-second, a Friday—twelve days ago, it seems much longer than that—Adam celebrated at the resort restaurant. He'd won Business Person of the Year for the sixth time in a row."

I took her word for it. As I stuck mostly to the weather page and the day's crossword, I hadn't bothered to send in a vote to the editors of *The Bee* for my favorite takeout restaurant or the person whose superior business skills most benefited the economic well-being of Two Lakes in the previous year.

"His fortieth birthday was in a couple of days and he was on top of the world. He'd been running the resort his father built with great success. Had plans to expand, open a sister location in Duluth." Baker paused for a sip. "The mayor presented the award at the party, guests came to toast Adam, to drink his champagne and eat his food. At the end of the night Adam got into his car, a red BMW. The storm must have just started... He never made it home. The police searched in the morning. They found the BMW abandoned in a snowbank by the side of County 9, where it cuts through Lost Wolf Woods. And Adam... They looked and looked. Hours later they came upon him, sitting with his back against a tree. He was gone."

"He left his car and walked into the woods in a blizzard?" I said. "Suicide? Though it sounds like he had plenty to live for."

Baker had brought in a winter wind with her. The emotion is one of rawness, a gut punch by life. Wind that gets into your bones, as if it's never going to be warm again. But the possibility that Adam walked into the woods of his own accord, the place where my mind had instantly jumped, didn't weigh on her. "Not Adam."

Noting that Baker had yet to explain how she knew the owner of Fireside—and so much about him—I moved on to the next likely explanation. "Car trouble? Perhaps he decided to take his chances on foot in the storm and lost his bearings... Does Chief Gustafson have reason to think you did something? Tampered with the car's engine? Or that you know who did?"

"We're looking for a vandal handy with a wrench." Shane made the statement sound as if talking about defusing a nuclear bomb.

"Not a wrench." Baker set the cup down, this time gently. The winter wind stilled. "Chief Gustafson told me how it was done. Asked if *I* did it."

Shane drew his chair closer. "We know you didn't, Clem."

I didn't know anything of the sort. My job was to be objective. Tends to be easy enough with a soul garden cleared of inconvenient feelings.

"During the party, Adam left his car unlocked in the parking lot outside the resort restaurant."

Two Lakes is that kind of town, where people don't lock their cars, certainly not outside their own place of business.

Baker shifted forward on the couch until her knees brushed the coffee table, and without thinking, Shane and I mirrored the movement, drawn in by the unspoken pull of the moment. "As Adam gave his speech and accepted his award, someone popped open the gas tank of his car. Poured water in. It was enough to stop the engine—in the middle of the night in the woods, with the storm whipping up and a sub-zero windchill." Baker's voice sank to a whisper. "Enough for him to die."

CHAPTER SIX

"Baker... I thought you lived in Texas," I said.

"What, you want my life story?" She leaned back and took a sip of the coffee. "I spent my childhood in a suburb outside Houston. Every summer, my brothers—Jerry, Jeremy, Jeremiah, and Jem—would go off camping with our dad. Because I'm a girl and clearly wouldn't enjoy the outdoors, and my mom was too busy running her dance academy to watch me—I have no talent for ballet, I mean *none*, plus there's my height—off to my grandmother's in Two Lakes I went for the summer. At least for a while... After high school, the script everyone wanted me to follow didn't make sense to me. Go to college, acquire husband, mortgage, a household of kids. I stared ahead and saw nothing but...ordinary." She held up a hand. "I know, that sounds snooty, but what do you expect from an eighteen-year-old? And no one asked me what *I* wanted to do."

I glanced at my briefcase. The sketchbook in it lacked a page for Feeling Like Life's Too Ordinary. A cousin of the Steady Drizzle of Gloom & Boredom, perhaps? The drizzle made an appearance in Shane's vicinity every fall, as the days got darker. As to Baker, I read between the lines. "After four children—all of them boys, you said—why did your parents decide on a fifth child?"

The question drew out an oak from her, an aged one. Its hefty trunk pushed through the coffee table, dark green moss carpeting the base where the roots disappeared into the floor. The pain was an old one. My client answered nonchalantly enough. "I asked my parents that once. They said they wanted to see if their run of good luck would continue... Well, it didn't."

"I see. Go on."

"I worked at McDonald's to save enough for a used car—*very* used—then drove to Los Angeles. Lived there for a while out of the car, waitressing and working as a set extra. When the car died for good, I caught a bus up to San Francisco. Lived there for eight months, working at the Ghirardelli Chocolate shop and renting a basement room. Then I took another bus to Seattle. No long-term relationships, or steady jobs... What can I say, everything felt like a trap. Eventually I took the train to Chicago, where I shared a rental with two roommates and worked at a travel agency. Which led to me meeting Ester."

"I want to hear all about Ester," Shane said. "Girlfriend?"

"Employer. So this sixty-something woman comes into the agency and sits down and says she's newly widowed and has just sold her property management company. She's got money and time and a wish to see the world, only she has no children and needs help with luggage—she had a bad back—so could we arrange for a dependable travel companion? I volunteered on the spot. I got to see London, Paris, Rome... Egypt... China and Japan... Rio de Janeiro... And then one morning—after four years of sightseeing—Ester told me she'd had enough and I realized the same was true for me. I'd had my fill of ruins and the heat and big cities and endless days on ocean cruises."

"Sounds like heaven to me." Shane smacked his lips.

"Don't get me wrong, it did feel like that for a long while... Ester's decision may have had something to do with what happened in Miami."

Shane got there first. "What happened in Miami, Clem?"

"We'd deboarded the cruise ship and stepped out into air so humid my sunglasses steamed up. I took them off and spotted a man across the street. He had a leash with a panting dog on the other end of it. I marched over and told him to get the dog off the hot pavement and to give it some water. He didn't take kindly to the advice. He said he'd only bought the dog to impress his girl-friend but she'd left him and if I wanted it so much, I could have it. He kind of threw the leash at me and shoved me at the same time. Well. I grew up with four brothers, I know how to fight back. I shoved him right back. He wasn't expecting it and landed on a set of concrete stairs. Broke his wrist. Ester wrote him a check, then looked over at Hutch—the dog—and told me I now had someone new to take care of...

"So there I stood, sweating in the heat, with this dog looking up at me. My thirtieth birthday had come and gone and the last thing I wanted was to move back in with my parents. I thought of good old Two Lakes and wondered if it had changed at all. Turns out it had somewhat—Fireside Resort has stretched and the tourists tripled—but its heart still beat the same. Hutch and I found a cheap place to live and I scoured job postings on the community-center board down at the library. Most of the ads were for the resort, room cleaners and pool safety officers, things like that, but one caught my eye, for an event coordinator. I wasn't sure what that even meant, but I figured, why not go for it. This was in August of last year."

I flipped open my notepad to jot this down. August, and she hadn't looked me up until trouble knocked on her door. It occurred to me that if I were the type to get offended, I might have taken that personally and a herd of elephants would have thundered through. Luckily the whole branch—Annoyance, Af-front, Indignation, Irritation, Resentment, Umbrage, Wounded Pride—lives in Anger's stone. Just an observation on my part, that's all.

Another sip of coffee. "I walked into my interview and said

all the faraway places I'd been to, the interesting people I met, and the exotic meals I ate counted far more in terms of experience than had I spent that time sitting in an office pecking away at a typewriter. Adam saw right through me but liked what he called 'my spunk' and gave me a shot at the job. I made some whoppers but learned quick enough. I met with brides to plan weddings in the resort ballroom or on the lake beach, provided cake samples, talked through the options for the number of guests. We catered corporate events, graduation parties, funerals, birthdays. I earned enough to buy a couch, a TV, and a fancy hairbrush for Hutch. When Chief Gustafson knocked on my door last night, I'd put peanut butter treats into the oven—I had to turn off the oven, but Hutch won't mind if the treats are dry and stale. He's with my landlady, Mrs. Gibson."

Another sip, a long one. She felt reluctant to relay the rest. (The proof? The sandstone sundial resting against the leg of the couch, inches from her foot, its shadow stuck in place. The Sundial of Foot-Dragging.) I made an attempt to move things along. "All right, Adam Lindstrom hired you. Go on."

"By the time December rolled around, I'd settled in. It was a busy month of catering Christmas parties. After New Year's, I dived into planning the February dinner celebrating Adam's award and birthday. We were going all out—we gave the event a name, Toast to Adam. There were invitations to send out, phone calls to confirm. I hired a deejay, ordered centerpieces—dried flowers, the economical option for the winter—for the tables at The Cork. That's the upscale restaurant at the resort." She added an irrelevant aside: "There is also a more affordable daily buffet, The Lakeside Grill."

"The Cork—I've dined there a few times," Shane cut in. "When, ah, someone else picked up the check. It's spendy. But the *cake*... 'The best chocolate cake in the world.' They're *not* kidding. Velvety layers of pure chocolate bliss. What's it called again?"

The sundial stayed frozen. "Erin's Cake. It's Chef Urban's

signature bake. We charged an arm and a leg for it, especially in a four-tier format for weddings. Rumor has it...”

Shane leaned in. “I love rumors. What does rumor have?”

“That the cake is named after Adam’s mother, Erin Lindstrom. Conrad Urban and Fred Lindstrom—that’s Adam’s father—were war buddies before they started the business together. The chef met Erin once he came back to the States and fell in love with her, the story goes, only she was already Fred’s wife.... Then, after Fred died, everyone kept expecting the chef to make his move. But he never did.”

“But he still bakes the cake. Aww, that’s kind of sweet.”

I tugged the conversation back on track—again. “Walk us through the evening.”

Our client set the cup down on the napkin provided by Shane, unfurled herself, and went over to my desk to poke around. The sundial followed her, shuffling silently along the carpet like a chunky pet, its shadow still pointing to IV on the arc of Roman numerals. “Chef Urban made it that night, the cake. A bunch of them actually, in the shape of the award. They’re cubes, the awards, made of heavy glass—Adam used to crack pistachios at his desk with them. Conrad said it wasn’t much of a challenge to make the cubes, other than having to fit in ‘Biz Person of the Year’ on half of them. The other half said ‘Happy 40th’.”

I keep my desk neat. My briefcase lay on top of it, closed. Baker’s fingers brushed the briefcase and moved on to the Rolodex; she leafed through it without paying attention to any of the names. “Everything was perfect for Adam’s big night.”

“Obviously not, though,” I said, making an attempt to dislodge the sundial, “in the end. Anything unusual happen at the dinner?”

The sundial advanced a blink. “No idea. I didn’t attend... As a matter of fact, I quit that very day.”

CHAPTER SEVEN

Baker set the Rolodex back and picked up another item, tilting it to and fro against the daylight streaming in through the open blinds. "Gray, why is there a kitchen knife on your desk?"

'Cause it had been used to kill me. A month or so after the attack, when I repositioned the filing cabinet, there it was, kicked out of the way by the killer as they fled. A kitchen utility knife, six inches of steel, olive-wood handle. I'd thought about giving it to the police but the stain on it was *my* dried blood, not the killer's. This would have come as a surprise to Chief Gustafson. I washed the blood off in the agency sink and stuck the knife into the mail caddy on my desk. It comes in handy for slicing envelopes open.

"It's a letter opener," I said. "You quit your job the very day Adam Lindstrom died?"

"I smell a juicy tale." This from Shane.

"It's one that doesn't reflect well on me, that's for sure." Baker gave up on further exploring my office and sat back down. We were getting to it now. The sundial shadow sped up faster and faster, flying around the Roman numerals until the sundial vanished, leaving only dust particles in its wake. "Adam and I were having an affair. Before either of you say anything, no, I'm not proud of it. I knew he was married. He said that he and Tiffany were separated, living together as roommates while the details of the divorce were being worked out. I believed him. Stupid, I know, you don't have to tell me."

Shane reached over to pat her shoulder. "We've all done things we're not proud of."

Baker recounted how she'd driven to the resort that morning as usual. "Around ten, when I went to look for Adam in his office, his secretary—her name is Rosemary Moore—told me Adam hadn't showed up for work yet."

I interrupted. "Was it unusual for Adam to be late?"

She nodded. "He mostly came in on the early side, we both did. I wanted to—that is, I had a question for him. About the seating chart for the Toast to Adam dinner. It had the mayor and a couple of politicians at the head table, plus Adam's mother. That left a chair. Paul—that's Adam's younger brother—had gone up to Duluth and was staying overnight, so the extra seat wasn't for him. I convinced myself that since Adam and Tiffany were separated, she wasn't coming." Baker shifted on the couch. The Fig Leaf of Shame had made an appearance. To anyone watching—well, just me, since as far as I know, I'm the only one in the world who can see emotions—it's a basic, hand-shaped green leaf draped over the torso. But to the wearer, embarrassment is a sensory experience, as if their clothes have vanished everywhere except for the leafy spot, leaving them exposed.

"I looked for Adam again around eleven thirty. This time I found him in his office. He greeted me and shut the door, though I have no doubt his secretary had her ear against it." Baker angled up her jaw. "Like an idiot, I asked him if I could take the last seat at Table 1 and he said never mind that. He told me he'd broken the news to Tiffany over breakfast, that he wanted a divorce. She didn't take it well. To keep up appearances, she'd come to the dinner anyway. He owed her that much, he said. Starting tomorrow, we could be together the way we were meant to be. Well. I felt this wave of shame and anger rise in me from the toes up."

"Did that matter, that he fudged the truth? He did ask for a divorce in the end."

"Oh, it matters," Shane threw in.

"Shane's right, it did. Adam lied to me for months, then expected me to jump with joy at the news. I kinda lost it. I told Adam what I thought of him—I *may* have thrown a potted plant in his direction—and then quit my job on the spot."

Shane gave her shoulder another pat. "I'd have thrown a plant at him, too."

"What kind of plant?"

"Does it matter, Gray? Violets, I think. In my defense, I aimed the clay pot at the wall. It broke in half. What?"

I'd looked over at her words, startled. Sometimes this kind of thing happens. The broken earthenware matched betrayal's entry in my sketchbook. "Never mind. Then what?"

"Well, the whole office saw and heard. Rosemary came out and so did Todd West and Linda Bolander. Todd's the book-keeper and Linda's in charge of the day-to-day running of the resort. I may have also yelled things."

I was jotting down names. "*Things*? Be specific."

"You mean the exact words?"

"It would be helpful."

Shane threw in an explanatory, "It's all part of his process—of getting to know the garden of your soul, Clem, as our client."

I hoped that Baker wouldn't pick up on the fact that when *soul gardens* made it into the conversation, it was because Shane and I were discussing an actual phenomenon I could see, hear, smell, and touch. Some clients assumed that I was claiming some kind of psychic ability, others that I was religious. I never bothered denying it, as they tended not to care as long as I got results.

Baker got to her feet to pace again and proceeded to relay a string of juicy curses, concluding with an, "And that's all, I think," as she wiped her sweaty brow. I diligently scribbled the gist of it down into my case notes. Plenty of agency cases involved romantic entanglements. But Baker's had ended with a death.

After asking her to sit back down, I released a barrage of questions. "When did the affair start?"

"In early November. I was buried deep in Thanksgiving prep —it's one of our busiest weeks—extended families book group stays to celebrate together without having to cook turkey. I was by the copy machine and Adam came over and lingered a tick too long over the event schedule on my clipboard."

From my objective viewpoint, I was more interested in her side of things. Heat-of-the-moment connection during a high-stress week or something more? "What attracted you to him?"

"Other than that he was the handsomest man for miles?" Shane wiggled an eyebrow.

"It wasn't that. Well, not *only* that," Baker admitted. "Adam —he was so much further ahead in life. Older, self-confident, owned a thriving business, kept a lawn mower in his garage, paid taxes. And yeah, maybe I wanted someone good-looking and successful on my arm around town... Only it never happened. Adam always insisted we stay in. He didn't want to share me with anyone, he said. I should have figured it out right then and there, but I didn't. I could kick myself."

"We see only what we want to see... Where did you and he spend time together?"

"My house, or a resort room."

"If you'd known about him and Tiffany not being separated, you wouldn't have gotten involved."

A soul scientist, floating a theory. The wrong one, apparently. She tossed her head back. "I might have! He never gave me the chance to choose for myself."

"I get it, Baker. If you're going to do a bad thing, you prefer to do it with your eyes open, not be led to it."

"Wanna hear something even sillier? I miss him."

Sunbeams filtered through the half-closed blinds of the window overlooking Main Street, casting stripes of light and dark across the room. A new arrival interrupted the pattern: a weeping willow took up residence behind the couch, its droopy branches throwing a circular shadow onto Baker. Shane slid the box of tissues toward her. She plucked one out and blew her nose loudly. "The time we had wasn't long enough for me to get to know him, not really. I wasn't in love. An infatuation, that's all it was. But it still mattered."

The phone rang in the reception area and Shane went to answer it. I gave my attention to the names in my notes, Adam and his inner circle:

Adam Lindstrom. *Handsome. Lied to Baker.*
Tiffany Lindstrom. *Wife. Just learned husband wanted a divorce.*
Fred Lindstrom. *Father. Deceased.*
Erin Lindstrom. *Mother. Cake named after her.*
Chef Urban. *Creator of the cake.*
Rosemary Moore. *Adam's secretary.*
Todd West. *Bookkeeper.*
Linda Bolander. *Resort Manager.*

And a last one:

Clementine Baker. *Adam's mistress. Ex-employee of Fireside.*

Baker gave a final blow into the tissue. "Don't forget to add... Hutch. *Dog.*"

Privately pleased that I'd figured out that she was making a joke as soon as I heard it and not with a delay (Friday is reserved for Joy & Humor on my schedule), I played along. "Is Hutch part of the case?"

"He and I are a package deal."

I caught myself tapping the pen against the notepad. When it came to people's appearances, often a single detail caught my eye. Shane's hair, which streamed freely down his back, a match to his outgoing personality. Sergeant Mendez's scar on her hand, from when she stood up to a bank robber while off duty. Officer Anderson's ears—of a memorable size and prone to going pink when he felt self-conscious. As to Baker—eyebrows. Dark and expressive, they had strength to them, a solid frame to her eyes. When she looked at you, she looked at you. Black hair pushed its way out from underneath the woolen hat she'd left on.

The hat—a hat, of all things!—brought on another unasked-for recollection and really, the pop-up memories needed to stop. A sunny day played out in my mind: Clem and me on our Schwinns, mine a blue that matched the sky and hers the pattern of the hat, pink with forest-green stripes she'd taped on herself. A neighborhood bully, Bruce, had pelted eggs at our treehouse and Clem had stomped off into her grandmother's kitchen, chosen three large, juicy tomatoes, then hopped on her bike, with me racing to catch up. The bully received the tomatoes straight in the face and Helen Baker had grounded her granddaughter for a week. I remembered teetering between admiration and another feeling—embarrassment at not standing up to the bully myself. Later on, my adult point of view reframed the incident. Bruce had wanted to be invited into our club of two.

Shane poked his head back in. "Amy wants to know what time you're bringing the stuff?"

"Tell her I'll stop by this afternoon." Amy Lightfoot is the superintendent of the Aurboda County school system, one of my steadier gigs being background checks for new teachers, a task that didn't involve my special skill. "And that all her candidates passed."

Shane went back to the reception area and I stated the obvi-ous. "The affair started three months into your job. The newness had worn off and your life started to feel ordinary again."

Baker crumpled up the used tissue and nodded thoughtfully. "You might have a point there. Things can only stay shiny for so long, right? Careful what you wish for, as they say. Getting hauled off to jail—nothing ordinary about that."

The flaw in my *seeing* is that I can only observe what's around a client in the exact moment—11:43 a.m., according to my watch. I had no idea what emotions Baker might have felt at 7:43 a.m. or 8:43 a.m., or what she might feel once the agency doors closed behind her and she was out of my sight. Her emotional landscape teemed and fluxed with life, a creature or plant liable to pop up from every nook and corner at any given minute. I'd noted a storm, winter wind, a sundial, a fig leaf, a willow. Step one was to make sure my client hadn't done what the police suspected her of. She and I could sit here all day talking about murder, me hoping to draw out the garden element so I could say *gotcha*—but what chance did I have of recognizing murder's mark if I had no idea what it looked like?

Practically speaking, there were only three possibilities.

Scenario A: I'd know it when I saw it. The mark would turn out to be a visual detail, a sound, *something* that stayed with me from before the No Murder Cases sign went up on the agency door. Gray the First had worked on a handful of homicides—well, only two. One was a baseball coach whose hit-and-run death led his family to hire me (turned out there were some ugly rivalries simmering between amateur teams and the hit-and-run was no accident.) The other was an elderly woman who died in a burglary; the police got the culprit and I was the one who tracked down the missing family heirlooms.

Scenario B: I'd know it when I saw it because *I* had been the victim of murder. A remnant of that July night, then? Perhaps I should be on the lookout for a knife buried in soul-garden soil, a knife that resembled the letter opener on my desk.

The final scenario, C? That I wouldn't find out what murder's mark looked like until I caught Adam Lindstrom's killer.

I had yet to spot the Fog of Deception near my childhood friend. I said, "Baker, sounds like you had plenty of reason to want Adam Lindstrom gone."

"Chief Gustafson certainly seems to think so."

"Take your mind back to the day he died. Tell me about your state of mind, both emotions and feelings."

"Is there a difference?"

Shane came back in. "You better settle in for a lecture, Clem."

"It's simple enough," I began. "Emotions are of the body, observable. Feelings are of the mind, private." *Except to me.* "Confusingly, the terms are often used interchangeably. Take infatuation. There it is in body language: a flush in the cheeks, dilated pupils, a goofy smile... But it's a feeling, too. Daydreaming about the individual, working up your courage to ask them out, counting the seconds until you see them again." Both the emotion and the feeling generate a swarm of fireflies, reflected in the blushing cheek.

"I'd settle for the feeling of *not in prison.*"

"I need you to be serious, Baker."

"Fine. How did I feel? Well, I was angry about how Adam had treated me. Ashamed of my part in his cheating on Tiffany. The next day, after they found him, I was sad. Then after a couple of days, I became determined to find out what really happened... And now? Hopeful. That I'll be able to clear my name—with your help, Gray."

"Did you murder Adam Lindstrom? By dumping water into the gas tank of his car?"

"No."

From the armchair, I had a view of her slippers behind the coffee table. No silver mist, nothing but clear air.

She'd started to gather her things. I stopped her. "One last thing. The mayor all but told the chief to back off. Something about a wedding."

Shane knew all about it. "The mayor's daughter, Nicole Cooper, is marrying Paul Lindstrom. Adam's younger brother. Alas," Shane threw in sadly, "*not* as handsome. The wedding's next week, on Tuesday."

"That explains Mayor Cooper's mood," I said. "No father

wants sordid news stories stealing the spotlight away from the radiant bride in white."

"In black, actually," Shane corrected me. "I heard from my friend Sue—she works at the resort spa—that Nicole and Paul planned a Goth wedding. An evening banquet at the resort ballroom, followed by a midnight ceremony complete with black candles and creepy organ music at the Oldehouse."

The Victorian Gothic, the first house built between the lakes in the 1870s, is a local landmark. The mansion served as the Aurboda County Historical Center before the museum moved to a modern glass building in Ostford, leaving behind peeling paint and leaky windows.

"I like to see people unabashedly express their personalities," I said, "but why is this Goth wedding being held on a Tuesday in winter, in a mansion that's been condemned? They didn't postpone after Adam died?"

"There's some urgency." Shane relayed a final piece of gossip. "Nicole's expecting. September, they say."

He wanted to know if he should bike over to the library to photocopy news stories on Adam Lindstrom's death, but Baker shook her head. "No need, Shane. I saved it all."

I noticed her studying me as we got back in the car. She gave me directions—real ones this time, for 23B Sycamore Drive, on the west side of town—and then said, "You seem different, Gray."

"How so?"

"You've acquired a sort of buttoned-up manner... Listen. It *was* my fault that Adam died."

CHAPTER EIGHT

The fact that I was driving meant I could only spare a glance at the passenger seat. "If those are the circumstances, you need a good lawyer who can argue that you acted impulsively. Water in the gas tank—you probably expected the car wouldn't start at all, or if it did, that it wouldn't get very far. You couldn't have anticipated that it would break down in the worst possible location, Lost Wolf Woods."

"What are you talking about, Gray? Also, that's very understanding of you, had I actually done it... Here's the thing. Adam asked Tiffany for a divorce."

"That very morning, you said."

"Because of *me*."

"Oh, you suspect Tiffany. Well, the spouse is the first place to look. And I'm sure Chief Gustafson will do just that." The problem was, the police chief must have started with Tiffany...and yet had shown up on Baker's doorstep.

"The chief knew about me and Adam," Baker said. "How I quit... It all adds up to trouble for me, doesn't it?"

"I'd say so."

"You don't have much of a bedside manner, Gray, do you? You believe me, don't you? That I didn't kill Adam."

If only it were that easy. Same as a polygraph, I can be beat. As a shortcut, the Fog of Deception works only if it makes an appearance. Clouds of silver vapor rise if the person *feels* dishonest: *I'm such a liar.* Or feels the *need* to be dishonest, like Wade Gackle. But there's nothing to see if someone acts on instinct, or bases the decision to lie on rational thought. Or maybe they are a habitual liar, any associated emotions long forgotten. A stronger feeling might dominate and disguise the fog.

Truth can be a matter of point of view. Baker might have convinced herself into a different reality, maybe something like this: *she* didn't kill Adam, the place where the car happened to break down did. She'd merely spun the wheel of fortune and the rest had been up to fate, Lady Luck, the hand of God, merely what her lying lover deserved.

I hadn't seen Baker in twenty years. I had no idea what kind of person she'd become. She could very well be sad even if she'd been the one to kill Adam. The shame could be not at coming between husband and wife, but at vandalizing Lindstrom's car in a mad moment. *Hoping to clear my name* said nothing about whether that name was mud with just cause. Even "determined to find out what really happened" had an alternate explanation. She might be curious about Adam's last hours, in a ghoulish way.

"I really am glad to see you, Gray," Baker went on, seeming to interpret my silence as a yes, unaware of the dark thoughts swirling around in my mind. "I always wondered what happened to the boy next door. I meant to look you up after I moved back to Two Lakes but then I thought, what if you grew up into the kind of man who never showers, or smokes too much, or whatever? I saw you across the street one day—I have a new job at Sol Nail and Hair Salon, answering phones and sweeping floors—and almost called over a hello. Then I heard my mother's voice telling me there's no going back. So, are you married with three kids?"

Gray the First had wondered about her, too. "None of those."

"Steady girlfriend?"

"Not that either."

"Well, I'm done with men for a good long while. In case you get any ideas."

"My policy is to never date clients."

"No need to be snooty about it, Gray."

"And I'm too busy to date." I slowed down to let a bundled-up pedestrian cross the street. "After the knife incident, I put aside the goal that had driven me for three years—finding my father—and came up with a new one. To help everyone in Two Lakes."

"What do you mean, *everyone*? Is there that much criminal activity in Two Lakes?"

"Not really, but ripples can spread far. One time, I helped a choir group where someone kept damaging music stands and other equipment—I discovered that the custodian didn't like their choice of songs. So that was twenty-four people helped right there."

"How many have you checked off so far?"

"Six hundred thirty-six." The list included the whole eight years of my PI career and a new name, Ellie Gackle, as well as Wade. He'd probably disagree, but it was better for him in the long run to have come clean.

"And the population of Two Lakes is what?"

"Thirteen thousand and eighty-six..." I made a slow turn onto Sycamore Drive. "...so you can see why I can't afford distractions.."

"This is me, that house right there... What about after?"

I pulled to a stop at the curb of a duplex. "What do you mean, after?"

"After you've helped all of Two Lakes."

I'd never considered the question before. "Maybe I'll shut down Soul Garden Investigations and grow sunflowers."

"Why sunflowers?"

"Why not? Shane will have sold his screenplay by then, but if he hasn't, he can chip in with the selling and shipping of the flowers."

"Wait here, I'll be right back."

She went into the door on the right side and after a couple of minutes, reemerged with a thin manila folder. I leaned over to unroll the window and she passed it over. "Everything I have on Adam. I was worried the police took it away, but I found it right where I left it, on the kitchen table."

I opened my mouth to explain that the police would need a warrant to search and remove items, but the front door of the residence connected to Baker's burst open and a large golden retriever bounded down the path, tail wagging, to jump a hello at my client. An elderly woman in a big overcoat followed the dog out, fussing in one long sentence. "Clementine dear, you're going to catch a cold that way, how about you take a bath and I'll warm up some chicken soup, maybe open a bag of oyster crackers, unless something else works better after a police station visit, well, not *visit* perhaps... Hutch, no, you can't run out onto the street, come back in..."

"Be right up, Mrs. Gibson."

Hutch ran back up the path and Baker gave a shiver. Her cheeks had lost their color, and not due to the chilly air. "When you asked how I was feeling earlier, Gray, I left one off the list. I'm —well, I'm afraid."

"Afraid of what?"

"Of whoever did this. That I might go to prison in their place. That they'll remain free to harm others."

I saw it then, all around her. The contours of a dark, over-grown forest, a very old one. The eerie thing about the Forest of Fear is that it creeps closer with each heartbeat, a sinister, silent EKG closing in on the person. It was then that I made the deci-sion to believe my childhood friend—without reaching for Ike.

"Baker." I stopped her as she turned to go. "You did find what you were looking for, here in Two Lakes."

She leaned back into the window. "Did I? I returned to a place where I spent a handful of summers and managed to fall flat on my face in both my job and my relationship."

"Are you're planning on moving away after all this is over?"

"No—I suppose not."

"Somewhere along the line, you must have felt it." A feeling it took me a long time to recognize and sketch into the H section. "Homeful."

She gave a thoughtful nod. "Maybe. Could be I wasn't looking so much for my passion as for a place and I ended up finding it in little old Two Lakes... Thanks for the pep talk."

I glanced at the folder next to me on the bench seat and raised my arm in a short wave. "All right, I'll be in touch."

"That's all you have to say after I bared my soul, I'll be in touch?"

"You're right, I should tell you my daily rate." The Crime Knights pact promised we'd stick together, not that either of us was obligated to do it for free.

"Can I come along as you investigate? After all, it's my hide that's on the line."

"I work alone... One more thing. Before, you said you had a gut feeling. What made you keep pestering Chief Gustafson?"

"Look, it was a brand new car. Adam had owned it only for a few months, called it the Beamer. Not necessarily the vehicle you want to be driving as a blizzard's starting to whip up, but I couldn't see any reason why it would sputter to a stop smack in the middle of the woods."

"Your gut didn't think much of plain old-fashioned bad luck?"

Something in the question set her off. "You don't understand," she said sharply. "Adam and bad luck—they didn't go together in the same sentence."

CHAPTER NINE

Baker's folder waited on the passenger seat while I drove over to the school district offices to drop off the new hire paperwork. I ended up chatting with Amy for a while about her problems with her mother-in-law, then went to the bank to deposit the check she signed and afterwards wrote some checks of my own to pay bills and dropped them in the mail at the post office. By the time I returned to the corner of Main Street and Carriage Way, it neared five and approaching clouds had muscled out the sun. I'd forgotten to eat lunch, beyond a couple of butter packets.

Ingrid looked up from the register as I walked into the Home Plate Diner. While Aunt Holly got their mother's brown hair and smaller frame, her sister inherited their father's broad-shouldered build and blondness. Ingrid kept bees in her backyard and had an intense way of staring that always made me nervous as a kid. Later on I'd figured out that it was simple curiosity. Like Holly, she had no children of her own and here I was, an abrupt addition to her sister's household.

"Rod, booth or counter today?" A thistle crown (Life Likes to Lob a Challenge, Whatcha Gonna Do) rested on blond hair streaked with soft gray.

"Booth," I said, glancing toward the back. "Shane's joining me."

She nodded, already turning to prepare the spot. Crowded as usual at this time of day, the Home Plate Diner was where you ate if you were too tired, too busy, or too lonely to cook. The kitchen served hamburgers and such, nothing fancy. Shane once called it greasy fast-food heaven. The booths alternated between families with rowdy kids and groups of international students stealing an hour away from their jobs at the resort, chattering away in foreign languages. Sated Monsters of Hunger lounged around and the yet-to-be-fed ones stretched gnarled tentacles toward plates. The row of eat-alone customers at the counter may have been acoustically quieter, the conversation limited to an occasional word or grunt with a neighbor, but their soul gardens were just as vivid.

Reminding myself to chew on the right side for the sake of my sore gums, I set my own monster in its rocky jail cell on the table. Shane, having greeted a couple of resort kids he knew, slid in across from me and Ingrid took our order. She didn't make her waitstaff wear uniforms beyond a name tag, but Ingrid herself always donned an ankle-length skirt and what Shane had once told me was a peasant blouse. The reason for the thistle crown revealed itself. "Meal's gonna be slow coming out today, you two. Gayle had to stay home—her boys have the flu—and Regan *has* the flu." She shook her head. "Just happy the cook's here."

Our drinks arrived, hot tea for Shane and a strawberry milkshake for me—on Wednesday evenings I got to enjoy something other than plain water. Officer Anderson had needed a key to let Clementine Baker out of her jail cell but all I had to do was double-tap the stone: the restless monster, a restaurant customer only I could see, unwrapped itself, grew, and oozed over to my side of the booth. I took a long, delicious slurp through the straw, hoping we'd not have to wait long for the meal. In the meantime, Shane and I got to work, emptying the manila folder of its contents. Three articles from *The Bee*. A single Polaroid. A pencil sketch. And a short stack of cards and notes. Baker had kept it all, a memento of her brief time with Lindstrom.

Shane dunked the Lipton into his mug and pronounced the cards wanting. "*Counting the minutes until tonight*, unsigned... And this one? *Happy Halloween to my Favorite Ghoul*. That one is before they started the affair, a bit of flirting—and also a terrible pun. And what do we have here? *Thankful for you*, also unsigned. Bet that came attached to a Thanksgiving pumpkin pie... And a Christmas card, a cutesy pop-up holiday scene."

The Polaroid showed Baker and Lindstrom at a BBQ on the resort grounds along with other members of the staff. Labor Day perhaps, judging by the pockets of fall colors in the nearby trees. Lindstrom stood a foot taller than Baker, with perfect hair, teeth white in a grin, and an expensive-looking suit even for the outdoor occasion. The pair were helping grill burgers.

Soul gardens don't show in photos, but Shane had an opinion. My assistant bent his nose over the photo. "He has that air, as if everything in his whole life worked out perfectly up to that point and would continue that way forever. He'd regale you with lively conversation all evening and afterwards you'd realize that all the stories had been about him and he'd not once asked a single thing about you. Yet here you are, thoroughly informed about how many miles he runs before breakfast and his financial portfolio... Water in the gas tank—whoever did it must have hated his guts." Shane shook his head at the Polaroid. "But look at those cheekbones."

To my eye the cheekbones did their job, provide solid support to facial muscles. Maybe Shane was right and Lindstrom's soul did sprout artificial flowers. Illusion elements show up in my office now and then. Joy's sunflowers, which upon closer look turn out to be plastic, their owner trying to convince themselves or others that they're perfectly happy, nothing to see here, thank you very much, they just happened to stroll into a PI agency.

Now and then the plastic's not an illusion. Not everyone has feelings that breathe and live. Usually it works out well enough for the garden's owner. They lean on superficial smiles and small talk to keep others from noticing there's nothing underneath—a trick that, disturbingly often, works for the kind of people who end up on magazine covers or behind executive desks. Or, at least, that's what I'd observed the couple of times I'd found myself in the vicinity of a high-profile person at an airport lounge or in the public gallery at a court case.

We turned to the earliest of the articles, dated mid-December. A list of the best-of winners in Two Lakes' end of the year contest, front-page stuff for a small-town paper. Baker had probably kept the clipping because of the accompanying photo of Lindstrom. It showed the resort's owner in his office, again in an expensive suit and tie, and wearing the same flashy grin. The article informed the paper's readers that awards other than Business Person of the Year would be given out at Town Hall at ten in the morning on Friday, February 22. Public welcome. Business Person of the Year to be presented the same day at The Cork at 7:00 p.m., featuring an introduction by Mayor Troy Cooper and an open bar. Invitation only.

"Only the best for Two Lakes' best," Shane commented.

The next article was dated two months later, February the twenty-fourth.

Fireside Owner Perishes in Storm

Tragedy struck Two Lakes sometime between midnight on Friday, February 22 and early yesterday morning. At 6:30 a.m. on Saturday, Officer Anderson responded to a call from Erin Lindstrom of 8 Hillview Drive when her son, Adam Lindstrom, failed to return home from the celebration held the previous evening for the accolade awarded to him by Town Hall and the readers of this very paper. The search instigated by the police, hampered by the fresh snow, commenced at sunrise and led to the discovery of Lindstrom's BMW by the side of County

Road 9 inside Lost Wolf Woods. The officers located Lindstrom's body near marker 12 in the woods, about half a mile from the car.

It's unclear if alcohol played a part but Lindstrom is thought to have consumed several glasses of champagne during the dinner celebration honoring him.

Tiffany, Adam Lindstrom's wife of seven years, is reported to be devastated. Rosemary Moore, Lindstrom's secretary, said that he will be sorely missed. A second resort employee echoed the sentiment...

The accompanying photo must have been the last one taken of the man himself: Lindstrom mid-speech at the dinner, microphone in hand. In the final paragraph, the reporter—Jasper Jones, I noted—posed the question of whether alcohol should be served at events sponsored by Town Hall and invited readers to chime in on the issue. Big city papers have separate departments for news and editorial; in Two Lakes, they overlap.

"Bet they got a lot of letters, prim types railing against a glass of champagne or two," Shane commented. "At least there's no mention of Lindstrom's midlife crisis."

"Midlife—oh, Baker, you mean." I took another long, glorious slurp of the strawberry shake. "We ran into Jasper Jones at the police station. He's got the story. Let's hope the mayor leans on the paper to keep things quiet until after his daughter's wedding—that'll give us a week, at least."

The third and final article was an obituary.

Adam Thomas Lindstrom, born February 24, 1945, died February 23, 1985. Preceded in death by father, Fred. Survived by wife, Tiffany; mother, Erin; brother, Paul; and Aunt Donna Nelson of Las Vegas. A funeral service will be held on Wednesday, February 27th at St. George's at noon. In lieu of flowers, donations are accepted at...

The rest gave the timeline of Lindstrom's life. College. A stint on Wall Street. Once he returned to his hometown, he'd won the community award every year except for the first one, right after he took over his father's business. The citizens of Two Lakes had waited to see how Fred's son would do before warming up to him. Sounded about right.

"Totally interesting, boss—the mother reported him missing." Shane tapped the article. "Not the wife."

"Yeah, I noticed that. Suspicious, so why is Chief Gustafson looking at Baker?" I said, but our meals had arrived and I promptly forgot all about my client. I dove in, as the allotted half hour was ticking away fast. I chewed the first mouthful with enthusiasm, my taste buds as sharp as a chef's knife. Ingrid had adjusted the recipe of the veggie burger and I kept on chomping, determined to get to the bottom of it. Black beans, prebaked; bell pepper, red, not grown locally in a greenhouse but an arrival on a truck from California... no, Mexico; onion, yellow; breadcrumbs, whole wheat; olive oil, extra virgin, imported from Italy; garlic, cumin, and a new spice, which one? *Smoked paprika, that's it...*

I always ordered vegetarian on Wednesdays. Eating beef, which I did now and then on other days, is one thing; tasting *cow* on the tongue and deconstructing particulars—the age of the animal, which field it grazed in—well, that's quite another matter altogether.

I chewed some more and mused on the greatness of pickles, glugged the shake, sank into the subtleties of the melted slice of provolone, soared on the tanginess of BBQ sauce, and quietly appreciated the envelope that tied it all together, the toasted sesame-seed bun... *Maybe I should hang out with Hunger more often.* One of its tentacles lay wrapped around my shoulder, another circled the plate. I dabbed the last of the ketchup off with a finger and licked it clean...

"Boss?"

I realized Shane had been trying to get my attention for a while. I moved the plate to the side, causing a disappointed monster limb to drop limply under the booth, and wiped my fingers on the napkin. I'd forgotten to chew only on one side. "Right, the case."

A final item rested in the folder, a sketch. Fireside Resort, with its extensive parking lot and squiggles representing Cooper Lake. A square labeled The Cork stuck out to one side of the lodge. Baker had drawn in a narrow utility road leading to the restaurant, probably a loading and unloading area for supplies and catering. She'd penciled in an X marked *Adam's BMW* in the main lot—the owner's dedicated spot, presumably.

I stared at the X. My job was to tease out the unknown in the equation of Lindstrom's life and death, unearth who in his circle hated him to the extent of dumping water into his gas tank on a frigid winter evening. "Shane, when I used to take on homicide cases—before—where did I start?"

Shane stirred a second sugar packet into his tea. "The victim. Always there, boss. You'd make an effort to learn as much as possible about the victim."

Translated to my current skill set, *learn as much as possible* equated to taking notes on what grew in someone's vicinity. Little hard to do when the person at the center of it all is six feet under. I reminded Shane of this and he came back with, "Boss, the dead do speak, in what—and who—they leave behind." He skimmed the obituary. "We can probably rule Aunt Donna out...though if you need anyone to hop on a plane to ask her a few questions, I volunteer. Never been to Vegas."

Empathy is an unusual feeling in that when it's in play, you see it in the proximity of the *other* person, the one being empathized with. At Shane's words, I found myself staring at my own likeness across the booth, always a startling experience. I had sent a clone over by his side. His problems belonged to me as well. Outside the diner windows, the snow had started and I suddenly wished quite strongly that I could afford to send Shane to Las Vegas for a weekend of sun and slot machines. He was a stellar assistant. He deserved a break.

Hunger's stone peeked out from under a paper napkin and Shane wordlessly pushed it back out of sight. Worriedly, he blew his nose on a tissue—winter's hard on his sinuses—and drank more tea, Ingrid having brought him a refill of hot water. "I like Clem, boss, but what do we do if she is guilty? Whether she meant to kill Lindstrom or not, well, it happened. I mean, murder's murder... Was it Ike's decision, taking the case?"

"At first," I admitted. "But I believe Baker."

"No fog?" Shane had more than once leafed through my sketchbook and was by now familiar with the gardenly elements that surfaced over and over during investigations.

"None. Plus there's her personality. If Baker had caused Lindstrom's death—accidentally or on purpose—she'd have owned up to it, I think. Also, I can't have been childhood friends with a murderer." I added, "That last one's not based on logic. Obviously it happens to people."

"For what it's worth, I believe her too, boss."

"Well, let's hope we're not both wrong." Learn all you can about the victim, Shane had said. I found a lost crumb and transferred it to my mouth with a fingertip. "The widow's the place to start. First thing tomorrow, I'm going to pay a visit to Tiffany."

Ingrid chose that moment to come by to clear our empty plates. "It's Wednesday and I know that means dessert, you two. We got carrot cake, blueberry cheesecake, pecan pie... The day's special is cookie cake. It's not really cake, to be quite honest with ya, pretty much just a giant cookie cut into quarters, stacked up, and served warm with a scoop of vanilla ice cream."

I glanced at my watch. With the slower than usual service, it was ten minutes past the allotted half hour for hunger. *Just this once.* "That last one. Definitely that one."

CHAPTER TEN

I rolled out of bed with a groan, my insides heavy with last night's dinner. The bedroom window overlooked the backyard, where the branches of the oak creaked under a fresh layer of snow. Morning rays reflected brightly all around. I checked on the tooth in the bathroom mirror and noted some minor swelling. Not a good sign. I skipped the usual bowl of cereal and bundled up. Out front, the driveway rolled downhill in a carpet of white. I opened the garage and grabbed a candle, already worn down to a nub, and the toboggan leaning against one wall. Having waxed its underside, I emerged with the toboggan under one arm. Striking a standing pose, I surfed down the long driveway, arms spread like wings for balance.

Walked up and did it again, this time with my eyes closed. Then in reverse, with my back to the street.

It's the kind of thing you can do when there's no pain to be afraid of. I didn't do it for fun, exactly. For one thing, it wasn't Joy's day. More of a reminder to myself of how free I now was, an activity I'd never have considered in the old days.

Seven runs later, the toboggan back in its place up against the wall of the garage, I embarked on the more mundane task of clearing the driveway. The snowblower vibrated loudly under my hands. It wasn't long before an idea struck. I pressed the off switch, then dug around in the garage until I found an old watering can. Having filled it in the mud room sink, I went back out. The cap of the snowblower's gas tank hanging by its cord, I tipped the spout in. To Sven Norby, who was finishing up his own much shorter driveway in 12b, it must have appeared as if I was merely topping up the gas.

The snowblower started up again promptly. I soon forgot about the experiment, clearing the snow in neat columns, down to the street, then back, up and down.

Suddenly—a rattle, and the machine sputtered to a halt.

A few things were immediately clear.

One, that water and gasoline are not a good combo. That much I knew already.

Two, if I ran the experiment a thousand times, the exact breakdown spot would meander all over the driveway. Whoever decided to ruin Lindstrom's special night must not have cared where the BMW would stop, or whether it would start up at all. Which pointed to a spur-of-the-moment act, not a calculated desire to kill.

And three, the snowblower would have to go back into the garage until I could figure out how to get the water/gas mixture out of it.

I got to work with a shovel. Without the noise of the blower, the snow squeaked under the soles of my boots as I worked bare-handed. With the Oak of Pain packed away, the cold could creep unnoticed into my fingers and toes, frostbite a possibility, but not on a day like this, with the morning sun out in full force and the temperature mild, in the high twenties. A trickle of melt-off made its way down the part I'd already cleared. Pain-free meant that I couldn't feel my arms ache, but by the time I wrapped up, my sweaty undershirt stuck to me as I bent down to dig up *The Bee* from the bottom of the driveway, where the teenager who delivered to Nestling Lane had tossed it in its protective plastic, after which it had been covered by the city snowplow.

The front page caught my eye. *Drat.* An article by Jasper Jones. I quickly skimmed the two columns.

Local Woman Questioned

In a bombshell development, this paper has learned that Adam Lindstrom's death is no longer considered an accident by the Two Lakes police department. As we all know, the owner of Fireside Resort experienced car trouble on the night of February 22, an incident that led to his death. Mike Nowak, of Mike's Motors, has told this reporter that he found a good quantity of plain water inside the gas tank of Adam Lindstrom's BMW, a 1984 model, and reported the fact to the police. With the low temperatures on the night in question, it's likely the water froze up inside the car's fuel line, he said.

A prank turned deadly—or an action meant to cause bodily harm? That's the question on everyone's lips. While a businessman as successful as Adam Lindstrom no doubt made many enemies along the way, the police are focusing their effort on the personal angle—namely one Clementine Baker, age thirty, currently employed at Sol Nail and Hair Salon. Originally from Houston, Texas, the recent transplant is an ex-employee of Fireside Resort and is rumored to have been Lindstrom's mistress.

When the police attempted to question Clementine Baker at her residence, 23B Sycamore Drive, the commotion ended with Miss Baker's arrest.

Asked to respond to the allegations about her involvement with Lindstrom, the woman who spent a night in jail and sat through a police interview had little to say beyond spewing venom in this reporter's direction. Last seen in the company of Rodrick Gray of Soul Garden Investigations, a childhood friend, it appears Miss Baker is determined to prove her innocence.

We can quote—

Spewing venom? An unfamiliar growl escaped my pocket. Sven, who'd re-emerged to pick up his mail, didn't react. It hadn't been a growl audible to the ordinary ear. How had Jones managed to dig up the fact that Baker and I were childhood friends? Pondering which of the creatures in the pocketed meteorite fragments had emitted the sound, I read on.

We can quote Mayor Cooper, who's on the cusp of tying his family's fortunes to that of the Lindstrom family: "If the police have their woman, I tip my hat at them and we can put all this behind us. I'd like to remind folks of the happy event to look forward to—my daughter's wedding this upcoming week."

The Cooper/Lindstrom wedding will kick off with a rehearsal dinner at The Cork on Monday, followed by a feast on the following evening in the resort ballroom for a hundred guests, culminating with the marriage ceremony at midnight in the former home of the Aurboda County Historical Center.

When asked why he was recently spotted in the Two Lakes Library, Mayor Cooper gave us an exclusive. He's been researching the history of both families in dusty tomes, in preparation for his speech as the father of the bride.

The concluding paragraph amounted to the final nail in the coffin, cementing the impression that the police had indeed found their woman, if only *The Bee* could say so without the risk of being sued.

This reporter reached out to the police department and was told that Clementine Baker is not officially a person of interest. The police are merely seeking information at this stage. Chief Owen Gustafson has asked for patience.

So much for the story staying out of the paper until the Goth wedding. Perhaps the mayor had realized it was a futile effort.

With a slow step, I headed back up the driveway, studying the accompanying photo of Baker and myself exiting the police station. If my client subscribed to *The Bee*—and almost everyone in Two Lakes did—this was not a great start to her morning. I hoped she'd get any excess anger out with a long, brisk walk with Hutch.

CHAPTER ELEVEN

The two-lane road curved back and forth as it ascended through the upmarket neighborhood. Near the top of Goat Hill, the only hill in Two Lakes of any size, I made a right onto a private drive. No gate, only a mailbox. A driveway cleared by a professional crew led between rows of dignified elms, bare in the season, to a sizeable house. I pulled to a stop and stared above the steering wheel. One half of the lopsided residence exuded a stately presence, though weathered: the ochre color of the front door had faded, windows frames were eaten into by water and age, and mismatched tiles dotted the roof. The mirror wing had been built to match but with its bright colors and new construction only managed to advertise itself as a cheap copy, down to the gaudy yellow door. A four-car garage separated the two sides.

I rang the doorbell on the newer side. No answer. Shane had phoned earlier and the message he left on Tiffany's answering machine had yet to be returned. I shuffled over to the other wing, where a brass knocker and a doorbell forced the visitor to make a choice. I used the knocker. Adam Lindstrom's mother lived here. A difficult place to start, were it not for my underplanted soul garden. The PEGS quartet would do its thing—pity, empathy, guilt and sympathy were all bonded to me, their stone gone, which is another story for later—but I wouldn't drive away from the interview feeling sad. Sadness, well, that has a stone of its own.

A woman of late middle age in a linen dress opened the door. Smudges of paint marked the white apron she wore over the dress, the hues moody, charcoal, indigo, violet; drops in the same color family dotted her bare feet. She eyed me up and down before I could introduce myself. "You're the PI?"

"I don't look like one?" I asked, momentarily thrown.

"I've never met a PI, so I wouldn't know. I'm Erin. Come in. What do I call you?"

"Gray is fine."

I followed Adam's mother down a tight hallway with walls covered in unframed paintings, their subject still life, which always struck me as a somewhat contradictory term. A tidy living room led into an all-season porch. "Let me put my brushes away and then we can talk. Perhaps you can help me with a dilemma," Erin said.

The porch doubled as her studio, with floor-to-ceiling windows facing Cooper Lake, where the mid-morning sun played with the cracks in the ice. I poked around while Erin rinsed brushes in a small corner sink. The scent of oil paint dominated. Canvases leaned against the walls, three and four deep. More still lifes—baskets of apples, a plateful of oranges, a loaf of bread. I gave my attention to her current project. The canvas on the easel in the center of the space was heavier in mood. Autumn on Cooper Lake, with shapeless clouds reflected in the water, the trees mere dark silhouettes; off-center, a lone boat gave the impression that its single fisherman had yet to catch anything.

"I don't sell my art. Mostly they go on the resort walls," Erin explained, scrubbing paint off her hands with a rough-textured soap. "But that one's just for me."

"You're depicting a feeling."

She dried her hands on a clean spot on the apron, and waved me to a wicker two-seater. "Sit, please, Detective Gray. I suppose I am. I'm painting my grief *out*, giving it a place to go."

I'd long ago given up on reminding people that my business card was that of a private investigator, not a detective, and that in any case, it wasn't a formal title. I nodded at the painting. "Is it working?"

"Not really." She spun around the chair facing the easel, one at odds with the rest of the space—an office chair, brown and wheeled. "That's my fifth attempt. I tossed out the first four. It's the up and down of it all... I'm grieving for Adam but happy for Paul, my younger son. A funeral behind us and a wedding and a baby on the way."

Grieving and *happy* were just words; with a visitor present, she kept a firm check on her emotions. She offered me a cigarette—I passed—and lit one herself, a subtle tremor evident in her fingers. "I gave up smoking fifteen years ago but I've gone back to it. After what happened to Adam, I found I couldn't paint. The nicotine steadies my hands. I try to only smoke half." She added a wry, "Not of the packet, half of each cigarette. It sounds like the same thing, but it's not. You tell yourself I need just one more the same number of times."

"I'm sorry. Sorrow's a tough one."

A puff. "Detective Gray, I'd ask who hired you, but I read the paper. Clementine Baker, that's why you're here."

"Is it all right if I ask a few questions? You won't find it too upsetting?"

Clear eyes met mine over the cigarette. Upright and straight-backed in the office chair, every line in her features suggesting a story Erin would never want to tell, she said, "Don't be ridiculous. In my day, we took whatever came and faced it with our chin up and our shoulders squared."

"It's still your day, isn't it?"

"You mean, I'm not dead yet?" A brief moment: a polka dot balloon rose up and disappeared into the ceiling. She was mildly amused at my comment. "I'll be sixty this September but yes, I've still got some things I crave out of life... But you asked about Adam. He was my pride and joy." Her voice shook, as if that's where the tremor of her fingers had gone, and she covered it up with another drag of the cigarette. She left the room and returned with a photo album. Inside it, a chubby infant dressed in pale blue stretched to a gap-toothed kid in a mud-stained soccer T-shirt and shorts, and then to a high-school graduate in a cap and gown. The pictures stopped there, when Adam stepped onto his own path and became a man.

"Adam took after his father, had that ambitious streak. With his good looks, he did TV commercials while still in high school, for a sporting goods store up in the Twin Cities. That helped pay for college, the University of Wisconsin in Madison. He sailed through his degree in economics and landed a job on Wall Street. Worked long hours, made money, dated Tiffany... And then Fred died. My husband. Adam and Paul's father. Heart attack. We had thirty-four good years of marriage and it ended, just like that." She left the room again and came back with a framed picture. "Our wedding day, Fred and I."

In the photo, the lines texturing her face were gone, replaced by a youthful roundness of the cheek. Equally young, Fred stood a bit taller.

Erin dunked her cigarette—glasses of water dotted the room, on tables, the windowsill, the floor—and lit a fresh one. "I grew up in an upper-middle class family in Ostford"—a twenty-minute drive to the northeast, the sister town to Two Lakes is industry-heavy, with a string of factories, a mall, and the highway and rail-road passing through—"and Fred was my high school sweetheart. My parents were dead set against us marrying. Fred came from the wrong side of the tracks, his folks barely scraping by. He said no to working in my father's construction company. My parents called him lazy but I knew the truth. Fred wanted to make it on his own, without a leg up. When he came back from the war—Sicily is where he and Connie had been sent..."

I interrupted. "Connie?"

"Conrad Urban. Fred's buddy from the army. Fred got out first. He was shot in the left shoulder—he could never move it at all after that. When he came back with his arm in a cast in the fall of 1943, we jumped in a car and I drove us to Nevada through the night and we got married. I was all of eighteen… Have you ever been in love, Detective?"

"I'm not sure, to be honest." *No fog by my feet.*

"Then you haven't. Fred and I stayed in Nevada for a while, worked retail jobs, ate peanut butter sandwiches for dinner, and had a blast. Eventually we wound our way back north to Minnesota, but my parents were still not talking to me. They changed their minds later, when Adam came along and then Paul—and when they saw Fred's entrepreneurial side. But in the beginning we were on our own. We settled in quiet Two Lakes. Connie had finished cooking school and didn't have family of his own. When he came to visit, the two of them—Fred and Connie—sat down one evening and hatched a plan to open a restaurant. Fred would run the books and Connie would be in charge of the kitchen. The three of us scraped together every last penny we had and opened a bar and grill. The location was on the wrong side of Cooper Lake, across from the downtown, in the marshy area where residents dumped yard waste. The restaurant failed."

The Table & Cocoa Mugs of Sympathy assembled itself between us, an offering from my side. The universe had wanted the young trio to work harder.

Cigarette in hand, Erin thumbed the edge of the photo. "Fred and Connie persisted and got Town Hall to drain the marshy land around the restaurant and sell it to us for cheap. By this time my parents had thawed—Adam had just turned two—a sunny toddler, everyone loved him—and were willing to lend us money. Fireside Camp started out with a few wooden cabins by Cooper Lake, but the real golden idea that Fred and Connie came up with? To take the restaurant from burgers and soda to upscale, gourmet, extraordinary. Against all odds, it worked… Families returned year after year and word of mouth grew—and so did the business. Suddenly everyone wanted their special event held at

Fireside and its star restaurant, The Cork. Fred and Connie built the lodge, renamed the camp to *resort...*"

I cut in with a housekeeping question. "Conrad Urban is a co-owner of the resort?"

"Connie devotes all his time to running The Cork, but yes."

"Go on, please."

"After Fred died, Adam stepped up and quit his Wall Street job. Married Tiffany and brought her back to his birth town. He felt the family should stick together and built the new wing."

Shane had found all four listed at the same address—Adam and Tiffany, Erin, and her other son, Paul. This year's phonebook, without Adam's name, would arrive in mailboxes in a month or two.

At my question about the difficulty of four adults sharing a space, Erin released a dry chuckle. No balloon this time. "Sometimes I wondered if both sons still living at home pointed to bad parenting. We were under one roof, but we occupied ourselves with our own routine."

"You painted, Adam ran Fireside. What about Tiffany? And Adam's brother?"

"Paul did odd jobs at the resort." Erin tapped ash into the glass. A she-lynx had joined us in the room, curling up by her feet; muscle, sinew and bone woven from sentiment—even with her offspring gone, Erin felt protective. "As to Tiffany... Adam never asked my opinion but I have one. I'm not one of those mothers who think their sons walk on water. Tiffany was Adam's one mistake. They were never well matched. Tiffany always puts Tiffany first." Another drag. "You know, I can't say that that's wrong as a life philosophy. I wasn't that kind of wife and mother, but who's to say what's best in the end? Have you talked to her yet?"

"She wasn't at home."

"She's gone shopping for shoes."

The she-lynx uneasily roaming the enclosed porch, Erin drifted off into memories. I took a stab that there hadn't been a trio after all. "Did you mind not being included in their venture, Fred's and Conrad's?"

"I had my hands full with the kids." Erin dunked the second cigarette into the glass and this time didn't reach for another. "When Fred and Connie started the company, they agreed to split everything—profit and loss—fifty-fifty. They played cards one night to decide whose initial would go first. FC Enterprises. Fireside Camp, before we expanded. Fred got to keep the F in Fireside Resort and Connie got The Cork... After Adam and Paul grew up, I turned to painting." The she-lynx padded away softly. Erin touched the seat of the office chair. "This is Fred's, from work. When he died I brought it here, to remind me of all the late nights he spent at the resort, working. I thought it might make the loss more bearable. It didn't. He wasn't perfect, but when you come down to it, is anyone, really? I don't know why I'm even telling you all this."

I knew why. Everyone tells me more than they mean to. People pick up on the fact that there's something different about me. I'm a safe ear. I never judge, mock, pass gossip on. I didn't judge Baker for her affair, or Wade Gackle for his gambling problem. More than the seeing, this is my daily superpower.

"The truth is that I can see Tiffany's side of it," Erin continued. "When she agreed to move here, she probably wasn't expecting Two Lakes to be so small, or to be living elbow to elbow with her mother-in-law while her husband spent most of the day at work. I saw the way she looked at Adam, as if she held a scale. One side, Adam's failings. The other, the bank account."

"They didn't have children?" The obituary had not mentioned any.

"Adam would have liked it, I think, but Tiffany didn't want his children, only his money. Maybe that's too harsh, I don't know."

I had yet to meet Tiffany, but she didn't sound like a person who'd take the news of a divorce well. When I asked if Tiffany had a job, Erin answered, "She's involved with a non-profit, World

Connect—they are the ones who bring seasonal workers over for the resort. And she teaches ESL—English as a Second Language—twice a week. Tiffany's students are in their mid-twenties. Not too young for her, if you know what I mean. Better than staying home alone, I guess."

"Is that what drove your son to seek comfort outside his marriage? Tiffany's affairs?"

"Comfort? That's a prudish way of putting it. It was none of my business." Adam's mother got up to crack open a window and cold air wafted in. "My younger son disapproves of my smoking. The smell of paint bothers him too, but paint I cannot do without... Would you care to see Adam's room?"

Upstairs, Adam's childhood space had been left unchanged from his teenage days. Music posters, track-and-field awards, textbooks, comic books. I ran my finger along a bookshelf. No dust. Across the hall stood a slightly smaller bedroom, its open door allowing a glimpse inside. This was a messier, lived-in space with a laid-back feel to it. Unlike his brother, Paul had never left home and the room had morphed with him as he grew into adulthood. Unmade bed, TV set and boombox, empty pizza boxes and soda cans. Socks and sports magazines littered the floor below a dartboard. Incongruously, a black tuxedo hung on a hook on the closet door.

An obvious question struck me. "Why did Adam come back from Wall Street to take over running Fireside? Your other son"—Paul's office was my next stop—"was right here in Two Lakes."

"Fred named Adam as his successor. But in the end it went to Paul after all, the responsibility." Erin shut the door to Adam's room. "Here's my dilemma, Detective Gray. Paul and Nicole are putting in a bid on the Oldehouse—that's where they're having the wedding ceremony—Nicole's family used to own it back in the day. The place needs a ton of work, so Paul and Nicole want to move into Adam's wing after the honeymoon. It would mean kicking Tiffany out. I do own the house outright, both halves, but Tiffany probably has some legal standing. The new wing has been her home for seven years, after all, and Adam did pay for it. So what do I do?" She added as we took the stairs back down, "Or are you going to hint that Tiffany will be arrested any day now and that'll solve my problem? Isn't that why you're here? To prove my daughter-in-law took revenge on Adam after he asked for a divorce?"

"You tell me. How did she take the news?"

"Not well—I could hear the argument all the way here on my side. Not what they were saying, but raised voices. Later, at the Toast to Adam celebration, Tiffany was awfully fond of her champagne. She and I were at Table 1 with Mayor Cooper and a handful of bigwigs whose names I can't remember. She didn't eat much, just left the food there and drank glass after glass. I kept an eye on her, worried she'd cause a scene—and she did, right after Adam's speech. She stood up to corner him and got loud, so I enlisted Todd West—he's the resort bookkeeper—to help her into my car. She silently cried all the way back home."

We were back downstairs, in the narrow hallway. "And Adam? What was his mood like?"

"His speech stunned us all."

This remark surprised me. What had Adam said, other than *Thank you for the award—yet again*? "How so?"

"He told the room he was planning on a change, a big one. Stepping away from the business, finding a place by the ocean somewhere, moving away." A willow tree joined us; under its branches, Erin permitted herself a sigh for the future denied her son. "I should have known. He'd been distracted for weeks."

Maybe Shane's theory about a midlife crisis was correct. "When people turn forty, they often reevaluate their life... Or did something happen?"

"He met Clementine Baker," she said simply.

"I see."

"It must have seemed like a grand adventure, to pack a suitcase and start life from scratch with her in San Diego or Key West or Maui, he hadn't decided where yet, he said... It was one of his strengths, that singlemindedness. Adam would charge ahead with an idea and assume everyone would fall in line. He'd forget that other people might have an opinion of their own. Now I don't know Clementine very well, but it seems to me that she came to Two Lakes looking for a home. It probably never occurred to Adam that she might prefer to stay here."

"You've met her? Clementine."

"Briefly, at the resort Christmas party. Fred always said we needed good-looking employees interacting with customers. We're not supposed to say things like that anymore, but it doesn't make it less true."

I offered the advice she'd asked for. "This is what you should do. Tiffany stays until she's ready to move on. Paul and Nicole live in Paul's room upstairs, and you can refashion Adam's old room into a space for the baby. When the Oldehouse is ready, Paul and Nicole move out and the crib stays for when you babysit."

Willow branches never go away, not really, but their shadow can lessen with time. She considered my words. "Adam would have liked that, I think, his room going to the next generation."

"I'll do my best to find out who was behind what happened to him," I promised.

Erin picked up a glass from next to a bowl of keys, opened the front door, and dumped water and stale ash onto the snow in the yard. "Listen, Detective Gray... Do you have any children? No? Perhaps you don't understand, then. I'm not sure I care who did this. Nothing you can do—or the police or a jury—will have Adam striding back into this house."

I got the hint and the door closed behind me.

Tap. Tap. I'd been about to pull out of the driveway when a knock on the car's side window made me stop. Erin had thrown on boots and a coat, and followed me out. I rolled the window down. She wasn't a tall woman, and didn't need to bend her head much as she leaned in. "Look, I know I said some harsh things about Tiffany but fair's fair. I'll tell you what I told Police Chief Gustafson. That morning, after Tiffany and Adam had their argument, he left for work. I was dropping off a new painting at the resort, so I offered Tiffany a ride—she had an appointment at the Fireside spa, an all-day one. Massage, lunch, hair and nails done for the Toast to Adam celebration. We walked in together at eleven thirty. I carried three small paintings and she had her evening wear in a bag—she brought her dress along so she could get changed there."

"Are you saying Tiffany stayed on the resort premises all day?" With Adam's BMW parked right outside. This was promising.

"Yes, but it won't help you. When you're at the spa, you're at the spa. I watched her go in and returned at six to wait for her—I didn't want her to have to walk into the restaurant alone. She came out looking as if she stepped off a page of a fashion magazine. We chatted awkwardly as the other guests trickled in, then sat down together at the head table."

"No bathroom break during the dinner for Tiffany?"

"I'd have noticed. Like I said, I stuck by her side. I took her home after Adam's speech and helped her to her side of the house. I kept an ear out for Adam, so I'd have heard if the garage door opened again... What I'm saying is that Tiffany wasn't the one who did the horrible thing to my son, pour water into the gas tank. She couldn't have been."

I drove off with cargo on the bench seat next to me. Cocoa mugs, sympathy distilled into a steaming liquid neither of us could drink.

CHAPTER TWELVE

I passed tree-nestled cabins, a nine-hole golf course, and a lake beach with a rack of canoes waiting for summer before pulling into the parking lot of Fireside Lodge. The lodge, with its three stories of red cedar below a shingled roof, makes its appearance in every postcard of Two Lakes. Adam Lindstrom gave seven years to this place—more, if you counted his childhood—and now it all belonged to his brother. Or, at least, half of it did, the other half to Chef Conrad Urban of the famous cake.

I'd never had a reason to go inside the lodge before. A life-size wooden moose guarded the entrance. A wood collage in the shape of Minnesota, each puzzle piece a county, decorated the wall behind the reception desk. Logs crackled in a huge brick fireplace and the walls, above a carpet of a gently worn brown, exhibited Erin's paintings. Both receptionists were busy with guests, so I checked out the indoor pool—noisy and crowded with kids, with parents reclining in chairs and keeping an eye out on their offspring—then followed the corridor in the other direction, to where it ended at a set of glass doors. These opened into a short passageway which led to a brick building, the resort's star restaurant, The Cork. I peeked inside—lunchtime traffic had started trickling in—then returned to the front desk.

"You mean Ms. Bolander?" the young staff member wanted to know when I asked to speak to the boss.

Baker had mentioned that Linda Bolander ran the day-to-day side of things. I shook my head. "Her boss. Paul Lindstrom."

"We don't see him much," she whispered in a confidential tone. "That way."

"Wait, Jen," the other receptionist interrupted, "you'd better check with Rosemary first."

"My assistant called ahead to make an appointment," I assured them.

They directed me to a door marked *Employees Only*. It opened into a corridor perpendicular to the main one, lined with photos of the resort in various stages of growth. I passed a couple of open doors belonging to housekeeping and maintenance, then a closed one whose nameplate caught my eye and made me stop. *Nicole Cooper, Event Coordinator*. Totally interesting, as Shane would say. Paul's fiancée had been given Baker's old job.

Across the hall stood an open door. *Linda Bolander, Resort Manager.* I poked my nose in. A secretary's desk, its chair empty, and behind it an inner office where a fifty-something woman in a broad-shouldered suit chatted on the phone, the Windmill of Efficiency spinning on her back as if she were a wind-up toy. She saw me and sent a friendly wave my way.

That left the two offices at the end. A cracked door—*Todd West, Bookkeeping*—and, across from it, an open door with a nameplate twice as big: **PAUL LINDSTROM, RESORT DIRECTOR**. The short segment of wall in between held a single black-and-white photo, the trio in front of the original Fireside Camp sign. A young Erin, flanked by Fred and a second man, in a chef's apron and hat. Conrad Urban, presumably. A blemish marred the plaster under the photo. A new flower pot, the plant care instructions tab still sticking out of its plastic container, perched on the table set against the wall.

I went into Paul's office. Though the carpeted floor muffled my step, the individual seated at the desk just inside, as if on guard duty, had already put down the magazine she was perusing. The nameplate on the desk read *Rosemary L. Moore, Personal Assistant*. Glasses perched halfway down her nose, she greeted me less than hospitably over a December issue of *TIME*. "Can I help you?"

"Rodrick Gray, PI."

The door to the inner office was shut. She made a show of checking the time on her wristwatch. "You're early."

"I don't like to keep people waiting."

Adam's assistant—now Paul's—reached for the phone. "It's the investigator... He's here already."

Having informed me that Mr. Lindstrom would be out shortly, she went back to reading the magazine. I strolled over to the window, with its view of the lake, and took the sole visitor chair. With her solid frame and woolen, coffee-colored clothing, Rosemary seemed one with the worn carpet, as if she too had been there forever. A murky pond—of grievances and grudges—seeped beyond the desk, carrying with it an acrid odor. I'd stepped over it on my way to the visitor chair. The desk lacked personal photos, with everything tidily organized—typewriter, Rolodex, cup with pens and scissors, stapler. A bottle of glue perched near the desk edge. Rosemary saw me looking and moved the glue into a drawer. I picked up a magazine from a stack of them—the selection was evenly split between bridal magazines and outdoorsy ones—and settled in to read.

A good twenty minutes past the agreed-on appointment time, after I'd had my fill of the latest in wedding-dress fashion and floral arrangements and had drifted to backpacking gear ads and fishing knot tutorials, the inner office opened.

I got up and stuck my hand out. Paul shook it, his fingers barely meeting mine. "Roderick, you said?"

"Rod-rick. Rod-rick Gray."

"I'm going to need a few more minutes here. Why don't you head over to The Cork and have something to eat while you wait? On the house."

On the surface a nice offer, underneath a power play and not a particularly strong one either. More waiting on my part and there'd be a treat in it for my troubles, lunch.

I noted the waves of the Sea of Adrift sloshing against Paul's loafers below a shiny polyester suit, said sure, and left. Linda Bolander's office now gaped empty but her secretary had returned, so I left a message, then shuffled one door over to knock on the door of the woman who'd taken over Baker's job. Receiving no answer, I doubled back and tried the office of Todd West, bookkeeper. A man in a tan suit and a dark blue tie, with thinning hair above, peeked out. Vines of anxiety, sickly green, twisted tightly around his arms; knots pressed against bare skin below his sleeve, like shackles around his wrists. "Yes?"

"Can I come in? I have a couple of questions about your late boss."

"Adam? Uh, yes, of course." He moved back to let me in. "There's a mark on the floor—there—can you leave the door in that position?"

I left the door a quarter of the way open, as instructed. Back at his desk, fingers speedily moving over calculator keys, Todd resumed working through a stack of credit card slips, the personal computer in front of him awaiting the total. "I, uh, already spoke with the police. Chief Owen Gustafson. He came along with Officer DeForest Lewis."

I took the chair across from him and explained, "I'm not with the police. I've been hired by Clementine Baker."

The calculator hand ceased its movement. Worried eyes met mine over the computer. "I liked Clem. I was sorry to see her go. She was nice to me."

"Were you here the day she quit?"

Todd's gaze settled back on the receipts, as if they threatened to fly away. "Yes," he admitted. "Heard it all, right outside my door. When I came in that Friday—five minutes to nine is my usual time—Clementine was my co-worker. By twelve-oh-seven she no longer was. She, uh, threw a plant. Left a dent on the wall.

The next morning, we found out that Adam had died. Everything changed in twenty-four hours."

"Just like that, you had a new boss. And one of the first things Paul did was to hire his fiancée as Clementine's replacement."

"That's, uh, not correct," Todd responded politely. "Linda Bolander slotted Nicole into the job. That same afternoon, right after Clem quit. Friday. We needed someone to step in... Paul Lindstrom moved into the big office the day *after* the funeral. Thursday."

"Once again, you needed someone to step in."

He answered as if I'd merely made a practical point. "Yes, but I expected it to be Linda. So soon after the funeral and Paul had never shown an interest before..."

He tapered off. Todd's office had no windows. A large cabinet overflowed with memorabilia: photos taken at company events, framed versions of past menus, and a line of Two Lakes' business awards starting with 1957, the early ones Fred's, the later ones belonging to Adam. It struck me as mildly odd that the awards were in this office and not the main one across the hall. "How long have you worked here, Todd?"

He glanced at the cabinet and the awards stretching back as if they were a measure of his own efforts. Perhaps they were. "Seventeen years and four months."

Seventeen years. A long time. Maybe Todd had felt unappreciated. "When did you last get a raise?"

"Three years, two months ago. But I don't need more. I have all my expenses worked out to the penny. Fifteen percent of my paycheck goes into a savings account every month."

"Were you at the Toast to Adam party?"

A creak across the hall, as if Rosemary had shifted her chair closer.

"Yes, I was."

"Did you go outside during the dinner—or before it—and tip water into your boss's car?

"No, sir... What are you doing?"

"I thought I dropped my glove. Ah, there it is." I bent down for the nonexistent glove. No fog. This man was not the sort capable of easily or habitually lying. No fog meant he was telling the truth. I straightened back up and asked him if he'd been surprised to learn Adam was leaving.

This elicited a nod. "It shook me. I had trouble finishing my meal after the speech. I don't like change—and he was a good boss."

"Anything else out of the ordinary happen during the evening?"

I'd assumed that Todd West had spent the dinner preoccupied with his own anxieties, but he'd witnessed the scene between Adam and Tiffany. He confirmed what Erin had said. "Right after his big speech, Adam and Tiffany argued by the buffet table before taking it out into the corridor. Couldn't hear why, I was seated near the kitchen."

A minor point caught my attention. "If you couldn't hear, how could you tell they were arguing?"

He shrank, as if I'd accused him of making things up. "Body language. Then Mrs. Lindstrom—Mrs. Lindstrom senior, that is —Erin—tapped me on the shoulder and asked if I could help get Tiffany into her car—Erin's car, I mean. I did so and afterwards headed home. I live over on Shepard Grove."

"What time was that?"

"The police asked me. I told them that it must have been about"—he winced at the imprecision—"a quarter past nine, because I got home halfway through *Miami Vice*."

"Todd, is there anything you're holding back?"

This question went a long way in my experience. Todd gulped, anxiety's vines tightening around his wrists. They were a fact of life for him. "No."

Even if it weren't for a lack of the Fog of Deception, I wouldn't have really suspected this mild-mannered man. "I know it's barely been a week, but how has Paul Lindstrom been as a boss?"

Todd straightened his receipts. He looked up to speak but a sharp knock sounded at the door. Rosemary pushed it open way past Todd West's preferred line. "Your table is ready," she informed me. "Mr. Lindstrom will be along shortly."

It being clear that she'd stand there until I left, I dropped a business card on Todd's desk. "Give me a ring if you remember anything more."

Todd met my eye with effort. "Clem. I hope you clear her name."

CHAPTER THIRTEEN

The restaurant hummed with lunchtime chatter and the din of
forks hitting plates. Poultry turned on a woodfire spit, fine glass-
ware hung upside down behind the bar, and a waiter with a
loaded tray burst through the swinging doors of a bustling
kitchen. Plentiful windows offered views of Cooper Lake, its
broken-ice surface gleaming in the sun. It was all very nice and a
slurping sound escaped my pocket: Hunger, threatening jailbreak.
They didn't happen often, these jailbreak attempts. Since I mostly
stuck to eating at home or at the Home Plate Diner, the monster
and I had reached a sort of a stalemate, but a new and inviting
place was catnip for the monster. Not wanting my focus to be on
the meal instead of the case, I leaned on Disgust (a cousin of
Hunger, it lives in the same stone and acts as a counterweight). I
eyed the spinning poultry and pictured a hair, long and black,
draped over one of the warm, spinning chickens. *Ugh*. The fabric
of my cardigan twitched as the Rodent of Disgust stirred in its
stone. Driven back by the much smaller creature, the Monster of
Hunger quieted down.

I gave my name to the hostess who greeted me with a jaunty,
"Just one?" and followed her to a table by the window. The prices
on the menu were double those at Ingrid's. Paul came in about

halfway through my meal and I complimented him on the food, as I imagined the steak tasted perfectly fine, even if my zero-taste buds could not confirm. He nodded as if he'd prepared the meal himself and slid into the seat across from me. "I can only give you a few minutes, Gray, the phone's been ringing off the hook. It's this damn story in *The Bee*. Guests are worried about leaving their cars overnight in the lot after what happened to Adam. I've been doing a lot of reassuring over the phone and we've had some outright cancelations... No one's said it straight out yet."

I speared a roasted Brussels sprout. "Said what?"

"The reason you're here. Why Chief Gustafson's been asking questions."

"And what reason might that be?"

"Adam's death"—he didn't bother lowering his voice—"was murder, plain and simple."

"Murder?" I put the knife and fork down. "Who killed him?"

Paul settled back in the chair and swapped the positions of the salt and pepper shakers in the middle of the table. "I didn't say *I* thought it was murder. As a matter of fact, I'm not sure I believe anyone poured water into his gas tank at all. I have experience with cars and an ordinary winter problem is condensation. It can be enough to freeze up a fuel line."

"Is that so?"

The waiter interrupted to ask Paul if he wanted anything. He responded with a brusque negative and pointed to me. "But he'll have a slice of Erin's Cake." Once the waiter left, he told me, "You need to try the cake."

I resumed eating, remarking between bites, "Chief Gustafson is confident water was poured in on purpose."

Paul scoffed. His teeth were less perfect than his brother's had been, as if he'd gotten the shorter end of the stick there too, on top of the whole ambition thing. The polyester suit hung weirdly on his frame, its back riding up as he leaned forward. "Gustafson likes to feel important. He's not considering how these rumors reflect on *us*—the resort. The town."

"Your future father-in-law agrees with you." During the argument I'd witnessed at the police station, the mayor had told Chief Gustafson pretty much the same thing.

"It makes Mayor Cooper look bad if the crime rate's up," Paul said sourly.

Clang. Bells, cast-iron and loud, made an appearance on either side of him, hanging in the air as if mounted on an invisible chain in front of an invisible schoolhouse. *How can no one else hear that?* I almost covered my ears.

Bells equaled stress. The new job and the big shoes Paul needed to fill? His intimidating soon-to-be father-in-law? Wedding jitters? I'd never been married and wasn't planning to be anytime soon. Perhaps a constant state of stress went with the territory. I wondered why Paul had bothered with speaking to me at all. I wasn't the police. Simplest explanation, he had nothing to hide. *Or wants me to think that.*

Rosemary appeared with a stack of papers for Paul to sign, a task I suspected could have waited. This gave me a chance to excuse myself briefly and make my way over to the parking lot payphone.

"Soul Garden Investigations."

"Shane, there's a dictionary on the shelf in my office, dark blue cover. Can you look up something for me?"

"Sure thing, boss. Give me half a sec." I heard creaking, a door open and close, and Shane got back on. "What are we looking up?"

"Murderous."

"Murderous... We want to know what it looks like, right, boss? Let's see... We've got ourselves two—no, three definitions. One: capable of, guilty of, or bent on murder. Two: deadly, brutal. And three, the everyday meaning, 'a murderous deadline.'"

"Hmm. Only one of those has to do with a past action and it doesn't help. *Guilty of murder* is a fact, not a feeling, which means I can't see it... Shane, let's say Paul Lindstrom—I'm having lunch with him here at The Cork, by the way."

"Order the cake," Shane said at once. "I know it's not Wednesday, boss, but it might be worth breaking out Hunger."

"Already ordered, by Paul. But I don't need the distraction—I'll get it to go. Where was I? All right, so let's say Paul schemes to ruin his older brother's big night and ends up accidentally killing him. Or not so accidentally. Though," I was forced to admit, "if he is carrying the Heavy Mud of Guilt on his loafers—guilt, unlike guilty, *is* a feeling of course—I haven't spotted any yet."

"He might not feel guilty, boss. He could be triumphant, or scared, or pleased."

"True, but I have to believe that there's something *more*, that a killer is forever haunted. That the unforgivable deed leaves a scar in a soul garden. A mark of murder." I added, "No idea what it might look like, though."

Shane rose to the occasion. "Bloody gardening gloves only you can see? A stained shovel carelessly left leaning against a soul-garden fence? Or how about a plant? Seven hundred plant species are toxic to humans and their pets, and that's just in North America—I found that out doing research for the screenplay. Hank was going to be a botanist before he became a woodcarver. Then there's the Venus Fly Trap, lethal if you're an insect... Or an ungodly shriek in the distance?"

"I'll keep an ear out. Whatever it looks like—or smells or sounds like—and assuming we're not dealing with a psychopath, which I don't think we are," I said into the phone, "it came into being on February twenty-second." *Frame it correctly. You're looking for a feeling.* I worked it out as I spoke. "If Paul did do it, afterwards he'd have felt...differently about himself, that's what. The blood will be on his hands forever. Same way that winning an Olympic medal or a Nobel prize alters how a person sees themselves, but...evil. Whatever it ends up being"—in a hurry to get back to the lunch table where Paul waited, I spoke fast—"I can't imagine that it likes sunlight. It'll be hard to draw out."

I found Paul where I left him, along with the stress bells. My meal had been cleared away. I sat back down and, making an effort not to raise my voice above the clamor audible only to my ears, poked at Paul. "Some people might say that your older brother achieved more in life than you did."

Paul gave a weird sort of laugh—an overdone, donkey-ish *ha ha*. "If money and a cushy office is your yardstick, then yes." He flecked a nonexistent speck off the sleeve of his polyester suit. "Before you get any ideas, you should know that I was away that day. Up in Duluth. Adam sent me to take photos of potential locations for a sister resort."

I found this hard to believe. "In February?"

"It's important to visit the sites in all seasons. And...I might have offered. If you must know, I wanted to avoid having to watch him receive yet another award. He already had a shelfful. I had them moved to Todd's office afterwards." Paul volunteered further information. "Two rolls of film—gave them to the police —prove I was in Duluth. After I finished with the last of the locations—the radio kept going on about the storm—I checked into Bear Lodge for the night and ordered pizza."

"Duluth's, what, a four-hour drive? Maybe you risked it, driving back down in the dark and the storm instead of waiting for sunrise. Maybe you intended to strand Adam, a little payback for all his success, but it all went wrong. Well, for Adam. It went right for you. Better than you could have ever dreamed of, in fact...if money and a cushy office is the yardstick, that is. Because here you are, in charge of the place, with a fiancée who works across the hall from you. Did you kill him?"

I dropped my napkin as I spoke, planning to reach down for it while on the lookout for fog, or mud, or the mark of murder (whatever it might be), but he grabbed my arm across the table. Unlike his handshake, a strong grip. "I did no such thing. I know what you're thinking. It's exactly like my brother and *his* event coordinator. Well, it's not. That was sordid and this isn't. Nicole and I are getting married."

I backpedaled. "What kinds of jobs did you do before, other than take photos?"

He'd let go of my arm, the bells quieting. "It varied. I drove the catering van, subbed as a waiter if we were short, cleaned the pool, took an occasional shift at the front desk. That's how I met Nicole."

"You must have been angry when your father's will named your brother as his successor."

"And, what, waited seven years to do something about it?"

He had a point. I made one in return. "It's different now. You have a fiancée, a child on the way, a demanding father-in-law."

"Look, you can insinuate whatever you like but Adam *offered* it to me."

"Offered what?" I said, confused.

"His cushy office, his half of the FC Enterprises, all of it." Paul made it sound as if his brother had tossed him a hand-me-down sweater. "Said it was mine if I wanted it."

"When did he tell you this?"

"That afternoon. I called to give him an update on the sites we were considering for the sister location. He barely listened, said he'd had an epiphany."

"Yeah? What kind of epiphany?"

"That all his life he'd only thought about money and how to make it. The next forty years would be different. He'd slow the clock, enjoy every minute. He'd live on the beach and open up a boat-rental shop. He planned on leaving at the end of March, as soon as I was settled in."

"Was Adam fond of boating?" I asked.

"We kayaked on Cooper Lake as children. I imagine he felt that made him an expert on boats... He was in a good mood, despite Tiffany not handling the news of the divorce well—and Clementine rejecting his proposal."

Proposal? *Baker forgot to relay that minor detail.*

"One slice of Erin's Cake, here we are."

Uh-oh. A tall slice: three levels of chocolate sponge, sandwiched with rich, velvety chocolate cream, coated in in shiny chocolate frosting and crowned with a delicate whipped-cream rose. A lean tentacle crept out of my pocket, up my cardigan, and sidled toward the dessert plate. Hair on the plate! Ants! A fingernail! The tentacle retracted.

"That he'd chosen to turn his back on his wife and the family business—" Paul crossed his arms, sending the suit bunching up higher. "—didn't bother Adam in the least. He was sure that he'd get Clementine back, that it'd all work out."

I remembered the napkin and bent down to pick it up. *Gotcha.* A trace of silver fog, by the chair leg.

Much to unpack here. In the hour or so I'd known Paul Lindstrom, I'd witnessed the Sea of Adrift, heard the Garden Bells of Stress, and just now encountered the Fog of Deception. He'd lied to me. About what, exactly? That Adam offered to put him in charge? That he spent the night in Duluth? Adam's boating experience? I was digging around a stranger's soul garden uninvited, uncertain what I was looking for.

"Paul, you don't really believe that it was condensation, do you?"

He leaned in and this time did lower his voice. "I have a theory. Wanna hear it?"

"Certainly."

I expected him to say that it was a prank by a resort employee who had too much beer on a winter's night. But what he said was, "I think he did it himself."

"Suicide?"

His words echoed Baker's. "Not Adam."

"Then why?"

The garden bells faded away for good. Now more at ease, as if some danger point had passed, Paul reached over and plucked the whipped-cream rose off the cake with two fingers and popped it into his mouth. "Sorry, I hope you didn't want that... Adam liked grandiose plans. He dreams big, my mother used to say. He left Two Lakes determined to conquer Wall Street. Returned with his new wife and hired a construction crew to double the size of the house. Talked about opening not a single sister location but two or more. And the final plan—to leave it all behind and move to the beach with Clementine by his side. I think he *pretended* his car broke down. Intended to call Clementine from a payphone— there's one by the clubhouse in the woods—so she could come and rescue him. Nothing like saving someone's life to convince you to give that person a second chance. Only he lost his bearings in the storm and never made it to the phone."

I took a beat to consider this sliver of amateur psychology. Private investigation had taught me that people often behave impulsively, especially where love is concerned. "If that's the case, quite a risky gamble. And the water Mike Nowak found in the gas tank?"

"Adam stuffed snow in there himself, to make it more convincing."

"What does your mother think of the possibility that Adam did this to himself?"

"I haven't brought it up—and don't go mentioning it to her. She's elderly and fragile."

Nothing about the woman sitting straight-backed in her studio struck me as either elderly or fragile. "Is she? I wouldn't have said so."

I'd overstayed my welcome. Paul rose to his feet. "What did you say your name was, Rodrick Gray? Well, Rodrick Gray, it's time for you to leave."

I signaled the waiter for a to-go box for the cake. I'd leave— but not in Paul's debt. "I'll pay for my meal."

"Suit yourself."

"Let me handle this for you, Mr. Lindstrom." As if summoned by Paul's change in mood, Rosemary had reappeared.

Paul left and I put a couple of bills down, added an extra one for the wait staff, and donned my jacket from the back of the chair. Rosemary stuck by as if I might have trouble finding the exit.

She led the way, a mistake on her part.

CHAPTER FOURTEEN

"Chef Urban!" I called over the swinging kitchen doors. On the other side of them, pans sizzled, cookware clanged, hastily shouted orders rang out. Amidst the chaos, an aproned man calmly worked on a row of gingerbread shapes, meticulously dotting on decoration. Rosemary, realizing I'd stopped, stomped back to pull at my elbow. The hostess stared uncertainly, as if gauging whether it was part of her job description to pull on my other arm. "You were asked to leave," Rosemary said through gritted teeth. "Hildy, get security."

Resisting Rosemary's pull—I'd probably have welts on my arm later—I planted my feet firmly on the tiled floor and bellowed. The man working on the gingerbread figurines looked up. Wiping his fingers on the apron, he approached the swinging doors. "Is there a problem with your meal, sir?"

"Rodrick Gray, private investigator. May I speak to you?"

"It's all right, Rosemary. Give me a second to wash off and I'll come out."

The hostess went back to her station and so did the elderly security guard who'd huffed in through the door at the ready.

"You forgot this, sir." The waiter who served me lunch materialized by my side. Rosemary shot me a stare, snatched the small box from the waiter's hands in a minor victory—I'd trampled on her turf—and marched through the passageway into the lodge. She halted briefly by a trashcan to dump the cake.

Its creator emerged, drying wet hands on a clean spot on his apron, reminding me of Erin Lindstrom doing the same. "Rosemary tends to forget she's not in charge. Follow me."

Stairs hidden behind a door led a level down to a heated basement that served as an extension to the kitchen above. Whenever I walk into an unfamiliar space, I try to get my bearings quickly, so I clocked the immense glass-fronted refrigerator, the walk-in freezer, a row of lockers. Shelving held linens and a digital clock, plus a small lockbox with a triple-digit combination lock, for receipts or petty cash maybe. Two doors, one by a wall phone and the other propped open into the garage, where a crew was in the middle of loading a catering van. I'd seen the vans around town, with their resort logo. I recognized Ellie Gackle in her orange uniform; she'd called yesterday to let me know that Wade had taken out a second mortgage on their house without her knowledge and that they were talking about divorce. My policy being to protect client privacy, I didn't greet her, but Ellie half-whispered in my ear as she passed by carrying a stack of covered trays. "New boss still terrible. Thinking of opening a bed-and-breakfast."

She and the rest of the crew left. Chef Urban had exchanged the apron for a fresh one from the linens shelf. Tying it in the back, he joined me at the glass refrigerator, where I stood staring at the row of cakes and the gingerbread couples on top of them. "I never use plastic toppers," he explained. "The newlyweds get a kick out of it—some keep their gingerbread twins in the freezer forever, others eat them up at the reception. Paul and Nicole's Goth wedding is a nice change—I'll be doing a black dress and red cowboy boots for Nicole's stand-in. Paul gets the usual black tuxedo..." He added a dry, "but I'm making the groom's head a smidge larger than I usually do."

I liked him at once. Operating under the assumption that Shane's sources were correct (and they usually are) about Conrad

Urban being in love with Erin Lindstrom but not making a move after Fred's death, I'd expected to encounter a diffident personality similar to Todd's. I recalibrated. No vines of anxiety here, but the man had a moat.

Now, there's plenty of reasons to have a moat. Unease in social situations. A fondness for one's own company. Feeling undeserving of the attention of others. A toxic experience leading to a hermit's desire to be left alone. The deep, dark water sloshing around Conrad Urban's moat hinted at either the slow accumulation of years or sudden trauma, and lacked a drawbridge.

He pivoted away from the fridge. "You're not here to chat about cake, are you?"

"No."

He shook his head. "Terrible thing. For Erin especially."

"Any chance it was a prank that went wrong? Or a member of staff acting out?"

Another shake of the head. "Nobody who works here would have done such a thing. If they have a grievance they go to Linda Bolander and she's damned good at settling them fairly."

"In other words, everyone gets along wonderfully?"

"For the most part, yes. It is Two Lakes, after all."

I brought up Clementine.

"It traveled around the resort, the gossip about her and Adam. For what it's worth, I can't picture her taking revenge—not like that. She'd have run him over with her own car, not poured water into his on the sly. I don't mean she *did* do it, just that I'd have an easier time believing it."

I brought up Paul's theory next, about his brother putting himself in jeopardy. "The goal, apparently, would have been to win Clementine Baker back. Adam stages his car breaking down, heroically makes it to a phone on foot, and his brush with death makes Clementine realize how much she loves him after all."

"Nonsense," the chef scoffed. "Clementine wouldn't have fallen for it."

"But you can see him coming up with such a scenario and going through with it?"

"Adam was in a strange mood that day, that much is true. Almost euphoric. He stood right about where you're standing and talked about his fortieth birthday and how he planned on changes. I told him he was far too young to retire. This led to, well, let's call it a disagreement."

"A disagreement? About what?"

"We like to say that FC Enterprises is a family business, but it's not—there's no relation between me and the Lindstroms. I hold fifty percent of the company and Fred held the other fifty, which went to his older son. I said to Adam, if you really want to step down, transfer your half of the company to your mother and let's have Linda Bolander take over the daily management, with Erin as a silent partner. Have you met Linda? She's a dynamo. But Adam felt he owed his brother a shot. I tried to talk him out of it."

"The terms of the partnership agreement didn't dictate your input with regards to Adam's successor?"

"The contract Fred and I drafted was not much more than a page... Don't get me wrong, I like Paul. He was dependable enough in his various jobs around the resort. But a business like this always needs to be moving forward. Adam had vision, same as his father. He added the indoor pool, fixed up the lake beach, expanded the golf course. Started the ball rolling for sister resorts. I reminded Adam of all that, asked him to really be sure of what he wanted to do."

"You didn't offer to take charge yourself?"

"My tools are a mixer and a spatula, not a Rolodex and a balance sheet."

"How did Adam respond to your concerns about Paul?"

The chef glanced at the clock on the shelf. "He didn't listen to me much, not like his father did. We were a different generation. I suspect he thought I was too set in my ways, and that's probably true enough. Still, I hoped he'd reconsider his choice."

"He said nothing one way or the other during his big speech?"

"Only that the details would be settled soon. I assumed he was still thinking about it."

"Maybe Adam had decided to follow your advice after all."

"If so..." Conrad said the next bit reluctantly. A sundial joined him on the other side of the moat, only for a beat. "What you should know is that Adam's will and legal documents named Paul as his successor. Seven years ago, when Adam took over after his father's death, he had to put *someone*'s name down in the paperwork. I got the sense he did it as a placeholder, until the day came when he'd actually have to decide."

"And that day had come. If he *did* change his mind and Paul found out..."

The side door opened and a blast of cold air and two people entered. "Well, we've brought it, folks," one of them said. "Who're you?"

CHAPTER FIFTEEN

Mayor Cooper and his cowboy hat had sauntered in, along with a young woman with similar features above a cream woolen coat and cowgirl boots. His "Who're you?" had been addressed in my direction. He jabbed a finger. "There's something familiar about you, can't place it."

I doubted he remembered me from the police station. I introduced myself and Troy slapped himself on the forehead. "Of course. Look just like your father. Hopefully more law-abiding though, right?"

I didn't need to reach for the Humor stone to understand that the remark was meant more as a dig than a joke. Similar comments had been made often enough over the years; the town had taken me in as one of their own, but no one had forgotten. I pasted the obligatory smile on my face. "You knew my father? Good old Dad, with his fake raffle."

"Ten dollars from my wallet."

"Ten dollars from your wallet, Mr. Mayor, ten dollars from your neighbor's." And so on, all the way down the Two Lakes phonebook; whatever the final sum had been, it was enough to propel my father and the money out the door of 12 Nestling Lane for good.

Oblivious to my discomfort—that is, the discomfort that would have been gripping me if Embarrassment had not been packed away—Troy Cooper reminisced briefly. "We had offices side by side, Dusty and me. He headed up Parks and Recreation and I was the deputy mayor back then. Did they ever find him or the money, son?"

"No, sir."

"Thought he might have gone back to California, that's where he said he was from—but who knows, eh? Well, glad you're here in any case, we might need help carrying."

"The question is, will it *fit?*" Nicole shook blond curls out of a hat the same color as her gloves and coat, cream. Based on what Shane had said, I'd expected to see Goth clothing and makeup, but perhaps the resort had rules about avoiding the look at work.

"Now Nikki, let us do the heavy lifting," her father reminded her, making the assumption that the chef and I would jump in to help without being asked. He backed his pickup into the spot vacated by Ellie's crew. We propped open the connecting door to the garage, where folded umbrellas and other patio furniture crowded the perimeter. A hefty object covered with a blanket sat on the truck bed. Nicole gave the blanket a tug. I gaped at the immense ice sculpture. A beaky bird whose wingspan rivaled that of the folded umbrellas, every edge and curve of its chiseled form catching the sunlight streaming in like glass, its talons grazing its icy perch as if the creature were about to take flight.

With Nicole chiming in with suggestions, the rest us wrestled the sculpture down and onto a dolly, then wheeled it through the door, careful not to break off a wingtip. It just fit, sideways. More maneuvering and the sculpture was settled into the center of the walk-in freezer, sandwiched between oversized tubs of ice cream and plastic-wrapped meat and fish. After the mayor gunned the pickup out of the garage, the newlywed-to-be put her finger to her lips, the nail polish a bright red. "No one spill the beans to Paul, he thinks I'm at a doctor's appointment. I want the raven to be a surprise."

"It will be," Chef Urban said. "Paul no longer comes down here."

I was curious about the woman who'd moved into Baker's old office upstairs—and her choice of theme for the big event. "A raven, because no Goth wedding is complete without one?"

This was met with a pert, "It really isn't."

"Why Goth? Went through a phase when you were fifteen and it lingered?"

She stuck her nose in the air. "I'm gonna let you work on figuring that out."

I gave it a try. "It's a family thing, isn't it? Your wedding venue—the Oldehouse."

I'd passed the Gooseberry Lane mansion on the way over. Everyone in Two Lakes knew the story of the Cooper family, as it featured large in the mayor's election speeches. So much, in fact, that I more or less could recite it word for word: "My grandpa— also a Troy, I'm named after him, folks. A founding father of our great lil' town here. Started as a poor rancher. Pulled himself up to prosperity with calloused hands, the sweat on his brow, and back-breaking labor from dawn to dusk. Grandpa cleared off the wetlands, sold off some of the land and kept the rest. Built himself a big house between a pair of lakes. Other folks moved in to be his neighbors, opened businesses. Built themselves a village, then a town..."

That's where the mayor usually stopped, as that's where the good fortune ended. At some point, the money had been lost and the mansion sold out of the Cooper family. More recently, the historical society had stuck a For Sale sign in the window. Another story that came up often was the mayor losing his wife tragically young, in a multivehicle pileup. Nicole's mother. I said, "Your mother, she passed away when you were small, didn't she? I know something about that. A nod to your roots, choosing the Oldehouse as the venue. Paul putting in an offer to buy it. A way to reassure your father that you aren't leaving him behind all alone, perhaps?"

I guessed Nicole's age to be in her late twenties but she came across as if she still had one foot in her teenage years. She gave a little shriek. "It's just been Daddy and me as far back as I can remember, but I'm not wearing black at the wedding because Momma's gone. I barely remember Momma and yeah, that part of it is sad but, like, I don't know what I'm missing, you know? Daddy does and it makes him sad sometimes. I've told him it's fine to remarry but he says there can be no replacement, not ever. The Oldehouse is *neat*, that's all. It's got a creepy tower and every-thing." She tossed her blond hair back. "And I didn't want a carbon copy of everyone else's wedding. White gowns and lace and, like, layers of frilly white cake. So I said to myself, what's the opposite of that? And we're doing it the wrong way around—banquet first, *then* the I do's."

"Some might say you two have done other things wrong way around too."

Chef Urban held the conventional belief that marriage came first, then babies.

Nicole let the comment pass by. "At first the historical society said no to us having the ceremony at the mansion, which was *annoying*, it's not like they're using it anymore. Daddy changed their mind. The caretaker will sweep the floors but leave the cobwebs in place. We promised to stay off the upper floors because the stairs aren't safe. Daddy doesn't mind the Goth part —he said whatever makes me happy as long as there's a priest and it gets done. The *I do*'s, I mean."

Chef Urban contributed another comment, a less pointed one. "I'm making black buttercream frosting. The cake will go into the fridge on Sunday."

"Right on the center shelf for all to see?"

"Center shelf."

Nicole gave a little squeal of delight and that's when I saw it. A fence. As with moats, there are many reasons for a fence—and a variety of construction materials. Chalkboard segments, matte black and scribbled with graffiti, made up Nicole's. Chalkboard is common in soul gardens of teens unready to accept the challenges and rewards of adult life. Nicole was about a decade too old for it. The question was, what hid behind the fence?

I broached the subject of Nicole's whereabouts on the night in question.

"I was home," she said briefly. "Why do you want to know?"

"Just trying to get a clear picture of everyone's whereabouts... Your father was at Table 1 at The Cork. Can anyone confirm that you were at home?"

"Sure. I called friends—to tell them that Paul had asked me to marry him and that I said yes. He proposed over the phone, can you believe it? I told him it only counted if he did it properly when he got back from Duluth. Like, one knee and a ring. He'd just talked to his brother. Adam offered him—well, everything," she said brightly. "And he wanted my hand."

Ah. I'd assumed the wedding had been in the works for months, but the Lindstrom brothers had made their marriage proposals the same day. Unlike Adam's to Clementine mere hours before he died, Paul's had been accepted—and the wedding date set for barely ten days later. "The funeral baked meats did coldly furnish forth the marriage tables," I quoted.

Nicole stared blankly at me but Conrad Urban nodded approvingly. "Didn't think anyone read the classics anymore. *Hamlet*, right?"

"Hamlet makes the remark in response to his mother's wedding to his uncle," I explained for Nicole's benefit, "taking place so soon after the funeral for Hamlet's father. Leftovers and cold cuts to be served."

"Well, we're not having leftovers and cold cuts. Paul said whatever I want, as long as we don't serve fish at the reception. We're having rare steak. Get it, blood red?... Daddy insisted we get married soon, before I started showing. He's old-fashioned that way. Good thing I'm an event planner, right? I can get it done in ten days, no problem. I phoned a stationery store up in Minneapolis —Saturday morning, before we knew about Adam —and put in a rush order for the invitations. Daddy, Paul, and I have been calling everyone to tell them to be on the lookout for the invitations in the mail and to circle the date on their calendar."

No way to tell if the Fog of Deception hid behind the fence, it was so tall and sturdy; teens can be quite strategic about lying and though Nicole was well past the age, the fence proved she'd retained some of the mindset. "These friends of yours, would they be able to corroborate your story?"

"You mean would they, like, remember?" Nicole said from behind the fence. "Why would they forget talking to me? I dialed my maid of honor first, then my four bridesmaids—well, there'll be five, counting Tiffany. I surprised them with my Goth idea and we talked dresses and shoes and makeup and hair."

"So did he?" Chef Urban asked.

Nicole tilted her head. "Did who what?"

"Did Paul propose properly?"

"Sure did. A couple of days later, after he shopped for a ring. This one." Having showed it to us—Paul had leaned into the Goth theme and the ring featured a pair of skulls propping up a hefty diamond—she proceeded to pat her belly. "Now if you'll excuse me, I need the bathroom."

The whirlwind that was Nicole took the stairs up. Chef Urban shook his head at her back. "You're lucky the mayor wasn't around for the prying you just did. If you ask me, Cooper never remarried because he has his hands full with Nicole. I wonder how he felt about having to pay for *that*." He gave a nod toward the ice sculpture in the freezer. "Between you and me, I'd have gone for a swan."

I asked him straight out why he'd named his signature cake after his managing partner's wife. The response was a curt, "None of your business."

"Fair enough. What's in it that makes it so special?"

"Well, a whole lot of chocolate. I start by melting the chocolate over the stove on low heat—you can't have even a drop of water in the pan or it ruins the process—and hand stir it. The rest of the ingredients, I never tell." He jerked a thumb back. "I keep the recipe in the lockbox over there."

His eyes went to the row of wedding cakes in the glass fridge and he suddenly got chatty, the way people often do with me, the way Erin had. The moat narrowed to a ribbon. "I've been here for as long as this brick building has. Took it from a single cook—myself—to a staff of twenty-five. These days I manage the kitchen, refresh the menu with the seasons, bake Erin's Cake and the odd dessert. The rest I leave in the hands of the younger and the more energetic." He pressed a fist against his chest, as if a burden hid inside. "I set out to create something for customers to enjoy. I had no idea the cake would be so popular. I've lost count of how many times I've made it over the years, gingerbread pairs for the happy occasions of others... Ever since that talk with Adam, I've been thinking that maybe it's time to retire. I might ask Paul to buy me out. It would suit us both."

I brought up a passing remark he'd made. "Why did Paul stop coming down here, to the restaurant basement?"

"He's the boss now. This area is for more lowly employees. He's stopped eating upstairs too—blames his fish allergy, says we're careless. In my kitchen! The allergy didn't used to be a big deal—he'd lend a hand with catering, dine with his brother, though not on fish, obviously. In my opinion, he thinks a boss shouldn't be seen eating, that it'd diminish his stature or something."

"Chef Urban... Did you sabotage your late partner's car?"

"No."

Perhaps he considered it none of my business and the "no" was a non-answer, a brush-off, not a denial. Whatever the case, not a wisp of fog hovered above the water inside the moat.

He donned a fresh chef's hat. "I spent that day in the kitchen. Came out to greet Adam and his family and afterwards did my job, cut up cake. That's the last time I saw him. Now, is that all? Erin's about to call. Since Fred left us, we talk every day."

The phone rang and he forgot all about my presence.

CHAPTER SIXTEEN

I checked the trashcan where Rosemary had dumped the cake slice. No luck. The cleaning crew had made its mid-day rounds and a fresh plastic bag gaped empty.

Outside, I consulted Baker's hand-drawn map. The spot with the X, the one that equaled Adam's red BMW, lay about as far from any of the resort's entrances as you could get. An odd choice for the owner, who also happened to be the guest of honor that night. Late to work, Lindstrom had parked, after which the BMW sat unattended. He'd walked from his office down the corridor to the party in his honor, and at the end of the night, got back into his vehicle.

I set about counting exits. Ignoring fire doors, The Cork had three: the enclosed passageway through which Rosemary Moore had marched off with my cake; the main doors to the parking lot; and a patio door not in use for the season. If a guest slipped out unnoticed during the celebration, the air temperature would have required coat, hat and gloves—or a very speedy exit and return, with telltale red cheeks and nose. Far easier to pour water into the gas tank on the way into the restaurant when already bundled up, or on the way out. An event of that sort, it'd be difficult to pin down who left when.

And of course, easiest of all: for someone *not* attending Toast to Adam. Paul, say. It would have been the work of five minutes to pull in next to Lindstrom's vehicle—after sunset had sent shadows settling onto the resort property—pour water in, and leave.

The lodge stays busy even in the off-season. Bundled-up kids ran around as harried parents dealt with luggage and delivery trucks rumbled in and out. This time of year, the sun set around six. If the opportunity window started then, its end was when Adam drove off the premises for the last time, award in his pocket and public cheers ringing in his ears.

There was not much to be gleaned from an empty parking spot to help Baker. I headed to my own car. I'd crossed back to the pedestrian path along the length of the lodge when a shout rang out in my direction. "Watch out!"

CHAPTER SEVENTEEN

Linda Bolander strode purposefully in my direction, the sails of the Windmill of Efficiency spinning fast on the back of the coat she'd thrown over the pantsuit.

I thanked her for the warning. A largish icicle had come crashing down from the lodge roof and missed me by inches. Good thing I always carry chunks of space rock in my pocket— you never know when you might need your life saved.

She shook my hand in a firm grip. "My assistant said you wanted to talk to me, thought I'd try to catch you before you left. I read in *The Bee* that you're helping Clementine Baker out. The way I figure it, the sooner this is put to bed, the better for the resort, so go ahead and ask your questions. But I don't know what I can tell you—I was in Iowa, attending the birth of my niece. My sister's fourth, a girl. Just over eight pounds."

She stopped here for breath and I congratulated her on the new family member. "You missed Adam's big speech, then, Ms. Bolander. Were you aware he intended to step down?"

"Call me Linda. I heard the next day. Conrad phoned me. I couldn't believe it. Adam, gone."

"And did you hear, Linda, that there'd been talk of putting you in charge of FC Enterprises?"

A thistle crown (Life Likes to Lob a Challenge, Whatcha Gonna Do) settled on her no-nonsense haircut. But only briefly. Linda Bolander met the world as it was. "Not until Chief Gustafson told me the other day. Adam never said a word, nor did Conrad. Not one word."

I showed her the map Baker had drawn and asked of the X, "Adam didn't have a reserved spot by the front doors?"

Her tone told me she'd been fond of Adam, though it didn't rise to the level of earth under her soles. "He had a policy. Parking spots nearest to doors should be for lodge guests, not employees— not even upper management." Then, less fondly, "Paul parks by the main entrance. We're having a *Reserved* sign made."

"I'm a little unclear on the organizational chart. Who did Clementine report to, you or Adam?"

"She worked with all three of us, Adam, Chef Urban, my office, pulling together special events. But really, though, she did her job well and didn't need much oversight. We hired her after Mary Sue Bachman, who'd held the position for years, retired. I had my doubts about Clementine's level of experience but Adam suggested we give her a chance. She turned out to be a quick learner, so it ended up being a good call on his part."

"Were you aware of the affair?"

A forthright nod. "I suspected. Let's just say they weren't particularly discreet. It didn't violate company rules, and he was the boss, of course. I did wonder if Clementine had the full picture but it wasn't my place to tell."

"Who else knew?"

"Rosemary, I'm sure." Linda Bolander stopped, then reconsidered. The blades of the windmill stilled. "Ordinarily I wouldn't say more, but under the circumstances..."

"Go on."

"Rosemary Moore made devotion to Adam her reason for being, her whole life. Sometimes she struck me as—well, I don't like to use the word—but unhinged, really. She's been here as long as the resort has. Adam's father hired her when they first opened.

I got the sense she expected Adam to compensate her for years of loyalty by moving her up in the company. But that's not how it works, not with some jobs. I saw how upset she was when we hired Clementine Baker for the event-coordinator position and she got passed over. It wasn't the kind of thing Adam would notice in a million years. I'd asked him more than once to refer to Rosemary as his assistant, not his secretary, a small thing she'd have appreciated, I'm sure. He never remembered to do so. When Clementine quit, Rosemary must have gotten her hopes up again... But it wasn't my business to reassign his staff."

"Walk me through that day."

The windmill started up again, steadily. "Let's see. Around noon—I'd been about to start on the salad I'd brought in for lunch—I got the call that my sister had gone into labor. I'd made it to my car when Rosemary hobbled out—on crutches because of a twisted ankle—and informed me that Clementine had quit. That threw a wrench into things. I found Clementine in her office, tossing personal items into a copier-paper box. I made an effort to get her to stay, but she wouldn't hear of it. She apologized for leaving me shorthanded." A bullet point in a hectic day, the incident, one Linda had dealt with promptly. "Nicole Cooper from the front desk had been putting in some hours helping with the bigger events and learning that side of the business—plus she and Paul were dating and rumors were she'd be marrying into the family soon. I poked my head into Adam's office and offered to stay and help—everything was set for the Toast to Adam dinner, but we were hosting a two-day weekend seminar for real estate brokers—but he said let's just toss Nicole into deep water, she can handle it. We agreed she'd start at once... Nicole's been focused on her own wedding, but she'll do all right. She's got a bubbly personality and the brides like her well enough. The parents paying for the weddings, perhaps not so much." A chuckle, deep-throated, and a polka dot balloon floated up into the sky. "Let's just say she's enthusiastic when it comes to spending other people's money.

Weddings aren't exactly a repeat kind of business, so it's all right in that sense."

"To confirm, having agreed on Nicole's new assignment, you left for Iowa without seeing Adam again."

"I did see him one more time."

"When?"

"In the parking lot, when I did finally head out. It would have been just past one o'clock by then."

"Did he say where he going?"

"I didn't ask. He rolled down his car window and said congrats on being a fourth-time aunt. I congratulated him back on the award and wished him many happy returns—his birthday was on Sunday. That's the last time I saw him."

All of this would have been confirmed by Chief Gustafson, presumably. If so, Linda Bolander stood in the clear. Literally—no fog.

I brought up the person topping my suspect list. "I expect that before, Paul had plenty to stew over. How unfair for Adam to lounge around in his cushy office with his fifty percent while he, Paul, sat behind a steering wheel or carted trays around and saved up pennies... Nowadays, the buck stops with him and Rosemary Moore tracks his every move. Paul wouldn't be the first to go after something, then realize it wasn't at all what he imagined."

A nod. "Sure, sure. But you're wrong about one thing."

"Which part?"

"Paul didn't stew or complain. If you ask me, he seemed happy enough where he was."

CHAPTER EIGHTEEN

Back at the office, I tried Tiffany's number again with no luck. I put in a call to the police station and left a message with Sergeant Mendez asking the chief to call me back at his convenience, then stepped out of my office past Shane's desk. He didn't look up, his pencil moving swiftly across a page of the screenplay, the faint leak of a mixtape—"Purple Rain"—seeping out from under the headphones of his Walkman. I went into the small agency bathroom. Today was Thursday and that meant Anger. I have set times of day for two of the stones (Pain at seven p.m. on Tuesdays and Joy at noon on Fridays), but for the others, I fit them in as best I can.

I set the stone, which held everything from the Thunder-in-the-Distance of Irritation to the F5 of Rage, on the corner of the sink and double-tapped it. A chat with the chief usually guaranteed mild irritation and nothing more. The bad weather moved over. No reflection of it in the mirror but, looking up, I caught a glimpse of a gathering storm above my scalp. What the mirror did show was the puffiness in my cheek. *This pesky tooth.* I needed to concentrate on helping Baker, not troublesome bits of fake bone sticking out of my gums. The solution was obvious: call the dentist. For some reason this irritated me even more. *Really, do teeth have to be so delicate?* Fussy prima donnas, demanding cleaning twice a day and frequent visits to strangers who wield sharp tools. *What's all that about?*

The ominously churning storm and I returned to my desk, where I slumped in the chair, staring at nothing. I didn't have to do it long. The phone rang.

"Well, I haven't ruled her out, if that's what you mean."

Baker's name was high on the chief's suspect list, that much was obvious, but I wanted to hear him say it.

The chief is a man who can't be hurried into an answer. "To begin with," he said, and I thought I heard the creak of his office window being unrolled, then rolled back, "we assumed Lindstrom's BMW ran out of gas. That, or—to be frank with you—that he was drunk and swerved the vehicle into a snowbank. His wife said he was planning to get a fancy car phone later in the year—some new network's going up across the Twin Cities, *cellular*, she thought it was called—but he didn't have the phone yet and it wouldn't have worked this far south anyways. He got out, and, we think, tried to reach The Clubhouse Grill on foot. The restaurant closed early due to the weather but there's a payphone right outside." I heard the *pop-tsss* of the aluminum seal breaking on a soda can. "He must have gotten lost in the woods, possibly walked in circles. At some point he ditched his outer clothing. It happens when people get that cold—their body thinks they're burning up and so they shed clothing. Officer Lewis found a hat and gloves not too far from where Adam ended up, sitting with his back against a fallen maple tree. Officer Anderson dug out the overcoat about ten feet from the maple—cashmere, knee-length and expensive looking."

"Did he have too much to drink, what did Dr. Wu"—Greta Wu's our county medical examiner—"have to say?"

An aggravated grunt carried down the line. "The family initially said no to bloodwork and an autopsy. By the time we figured out something was very wrong—on Monday, when Mike Nowak called to say he'd found water in the gas tank—more than forty-eight hours had passed and the alcohol-level results were inconclusive. Dr. Wu gave an estimated time of death between two and four a.m. on the twenty-third, the cause of death exposure."

"Back up. The Lindstroms refused an autopsy?"

Another grunt. "Bad publicity. If alcohol contributed to Lindstrom's death, they didn't want it getting out. It's a family resort. But what Mike Nowak found was enough for Dr. Wu to overrule the family—though at the time it still smelled of a prank and nothing more. Someone emptied a water bottle into Lindstrom's BMW on a dare, or a bet. Witnesses reported a group of high school seniors on a joyride near the resort. I figured they saw a fancy car and maybe one of them wanted to prove himself. Have you ever tried getting a straight story out of two hundred high schoolers?"

"Can't say that I have."

"Well, there we were, Officer Anderson and I, in the principal's office and an announcement is made for anyone with information to come forward. Jennifer somebody gets a pass from her Spanish class teacher and tells us that *she* heard from her friend Petra, who's in algebra at the moment, that Steve from the wrestling team borrowed his parents' car without permission that night. Steve is called to the principal's office and shows up in gym shorts and says he most certainly did not borrow his parents' car, but his twin sister Clara, *she* went to a party thrown by Greg, another senior, and a car *might* have been taken out for a joyride. We track Greg down in the cafeteria and he tells us the car keys never left the bowl in the hallway of the party house... None of it panned out." On the other end of the line, his tone grew serious. "The more I poked into things, the more concerned I became. Adam Lindstrom talked to a lot of people that day. He told Tiffany—the wife—that he wanted a divorce, over breakfast. Then he went to work, where he had his second shouting match of the day, with the mistress—your Clementine Baker. In the afternoon, he spoke with his brother up in Duluth. Discussed matters with Conrad Urban sometime during the day. And in the evening, gave his big speech and told everyone he was stepping down."

"What do you make of him deciding to leave it all behind?"

The phone crackled. "He was about to turn forty. Often reason enough."

I thought back to my morning experiment with the snow-blower. "Did Mike Nowak say how long the water sat in the gas tank?"

"I asked him the same thing. You know Mike, he scratched the top of his head with a wrench and said the only thing he knew for sure is that he found an iced-up fuel line after his truck towed the car in. He thinks the tank read about a third full before two cups or so of water got in there."

I put forward a name, a person I had yet to talk to, and the chief said, "Tiffany, sure. She spent most of that Friday at the resort spa—an all-day special that included lunch and whatnot. She got ready there, dress and everything." Gustafson said it as if talking about going to the moon. He confirmed what I'd already heard from Erin Lindstrom. "Erin dropped her daughter-in-law off mid-morning and saw her into the spa, then came back at six to wait for her in the corridor."

I raised an objection. "Doesn't mean Tiffany stayed inside the spa that whole time."

"According to the spa staff, she did. But you're right, people had to have taken bathroom or lunch breaks. If Tiffany timed it perfectly, maybe. Near the dinner's end, she and Erin left the restaurant together. Once they got home, they split up to their sides of the house. Tiffany says she poured herself a glass of wine, on top of the champagne she'd already consumed, drank it, and went to bed. Erin put in some time in her art studio. Kept an ear out for Adam but the garage door stayed shut." I heard him shuffle papers around. "Erin went to bed around eleven, figuring that Adam had decided to stay in one of the lodge rooms, given the storm and the argument with Tiffany. He'd done it before. She woke up in the morning uneasy and dialed the resort to check, and he wasn't there, of course, so she called us next... Point is, unless Tiffany managed to waltz out of the spa and over to the BMW in broad daylight—or during the dinner, unnoticed by her mother-in-law or the parking lot attendants and without getting her fine shoes soggy—she's out."

Humidity rose in the room—frustration on my part. I switched ears to jot things down and managed to tangle up the phone's cord. "Did you say parking lot attendants?"

More shuffling of papers. "World Connect kids, here to work for half a year, one from Turkey, the other from Argentina. Helped park cars for the VIPs. Once the event began, they got inside quick and kept an eye out while perusing magazines to improve their English. I didn't ask what kind of magazines. Can't blame them—no one was going to steal a car, not on a night like that. Only a notch above zero, and the windchill pushing it below."

I floated the idea of Tiffany messing with her husband's car in the privacy of their garage before Adam left for work, minutes after he asked for a divorce.

The chief wasn't buying it. "Mike doesn't think the car would have started up more than once and certainly not four times."

"Did you say four?" The holes he kept poking in my theories had created a steady rumble of thunder, low in my ears, and I found myself speaking loudly.

"Four, ayup. Adam drove in to work. As Clementine packed up her things, Adam ate lunch at his desk—rather cold-hearted, that strikes me—and around one, left to pick up his favorite tie from the dry cleaners, to wear it that evening. Suits-n-Suds, over on Third Street. Tiffany says the tie had a mustard stain on it. Rosemary Moore, his secretary, usually ran errands for him but she had a taped-up ankle, apparently. He also got a shave and haircut at the barbershop next door to Suits-n-Suds. Adam returned to his desk at a quarter past three—late for a staff meeting, according to Rosemary... And the fourth time, when he pulled out of the parking lot at the end of the dinner."

Phone sandwiched between one ear and shoulder, I looked at the timeline in my notes. "Back up. Two hours to pick up a tie and get a shave and haircut?"

"I had the same thought and asked around. Renner says his barbershop wasn't busy—Adam didn't have to wait. That's thirty to forty minutes of Lindstrom's day, unaccounted for." The chief paused for what I guessed was a sip, then went on. "His brother phoned him at four, after which Adam worked in his office until it was time to go over to The Cork just before seven. Guests started drifting out around nine, but Lindstrom himself stayed until the restaurant locked the doors for the night at eleven."

I brought up Paul Lindstrom, which resulted in more shuffling of papers. "Paul left for Duluth before dawn. Once he got up there, he drove around snapping photos of sites and talking to contractors, only taking a break for lunch. He's given us the photo rolls and sure enough, there's pictures of empty lots... He checked into Bear Lodge in the afternoon and dialed his older brother to give him an update, and they had their big talk. Paul called his girlfriend next, after which he ordered a pizza and beer and crashed in front of the TV for the rest of the evening."

"So he says."

"Well, you're not wrong there, Rod. He paid upfront, so nothing to prevent him from driving off at any time. Can't find anyone who can confirm either way. Have you talked to Conrad Urban? He tell you Adam was torn between his brother and a non-family member, Linda Bolander? Paul, he says his brother had settled on him."

Here I had more information than the chief: the fog around Paul's loafers that I'd seen. "Let's say he's lying. Paul learns he's being passed over. Adam's fifty percent of FC Enterprises will be transferred to their mother, with Linda managing the business. Paul's about to be shut out—but knows he's named as the successor if Adam dies. No time to lose. He hops into the car and drives back down, in the storm and the dark."

"Sure, except water in the tank's a poor way of going about

killing. How do you guarantee the car breaks down in a bad spot?"

The bad weather above my scalp intensified. The tangled cord wasn't helping. The way the call was going, my options were narrowing—so much that I might have to reach for Paul's theory that Adam staged everything. The chief was right, though. The location where the BMW sputtered to a stop really couldn't have been any worse. "How did Adam end up all the way on County 9 anyway? The direct route home from the resort would have taken him through well-lit neighborhoods, yards from someone's front door and a phone."

"Tiffany says he'd taken to driving around after dark, doing his thinking. The mistress—Clementine—said the same."

"Still, in a blizzard?"

"You'd be surprised. Some people are convinced they're inde-structible." Being a person with extra lives in my pocket, I stayed silent. The chief continued. "Look, about Clementine Baker. I know firsthand that she has a temper. Arrested her for it."

I felt the push of air on my skin and a crack of thunder rever-berated around my office. Gustafson had an answer for every-thing. Tiffany's fine shoes would have gotten soggy. Water in a gas tank was a poor way for Paul to try to get rid of his brother. Baker has a temper.

"Clementine wears her heart on her sleeve. No sneaking around for her." *Crack.* "So you gotta make up your mind, Chief. A crime of passion or a strike from the shadows?"

"If you ask me, I say both. Your client saw opportunity for revenge, then and there, and seized it."

"What do you mean, then and there?"

"Clementine came to Fireside that night, she tell you that?"

CHAPTER NINETEEN

A matter took away the chief's attention in the background and I had to wait a couple of minutes until he came back on. The facts were damning. "Rosemary Moore stepped out to fetch her purse —she'd forgotten it in her car—and saw Clementine's blue Honda hatchback idling in the parking lot."

I countered with, "If Rosemary could hobble to her car for her purse—or drive herself in, for that matter—she could have hobbled some more, all the way over to her employer's car to empty a water bottle into it. She'd been passed over for the promotion—again—that day."

"I don't know, Rod. Everyone I spoke to mentioned Rosemary's devotion to Lindstrom. It was a bit of a running joke in the office, apparently... Now do I think Clementine meant to kill Lindstrom? I do not. More likely the goal was to ruin his big night, make it so the car wouldn't start. But it did and he died. Rod, I've got five witnesses—Rosemary Moore, Todd West, and three other resort employees—who all swear that Clementine wished death and destruction on Lindstrom the day she quit. Frankly, when we knocked on her door to ask a few questions, I thought she might throw a flowerpot at *us*, only there were none in her house."

"You accused her of causing the death of her employer—her lover." A new sound entered the room. A growl escaped my pocket, the same one as before, echoed by an outright snarl on my part. "Of course she got angry."

"Easy, Rod. I'm only telling you the facts as I see them. What is it, Officer Mendez?... Hold on, Rod." He covered the receiver with his hand and I heard another muffled conversation.

I realized I was on my feet and that I'd sent the desk chair toppling back. I righted the chair, sat down, unwound the phone cord, and took a few deep breaths. *Clementine Baker's just another client with feelings that got her in trouble.* The creature growling in my pocket—from which stone? the question would have to wait till later—quieted.

The chief came back on, sounding more resigned than exasperated. "I gotta get off, Rod, Sheriff Doubek is on the other line. He's asking for an update."

Sheriff Doubek of Aurboda County considered his job to be more political than investigative, never straying far from his Ostford office. It usually fell to the chief and his officers to put in the legwork—roll up their sleeves, knock on doors, pound the pavement.

I made a final attempt to salvage something positive from the call. "Anything else you can tell me, Chief?"

There was a beat. "The car keys. Lindstrom left them behind, on the driver's seat. For the tow truck, probably, that he would have had to call. Still, most people stick to the habitual thing in situations of that sort, lock up the car or house behind themselves and take the keys along."

"The car keys. What else?"

"Nothing." He added, "Rod, cases like this, well, be careful, that's all. People—even people we've known a long time—can change. Sometimes in a moment, if it's that kind of a moment."

For a second I wondered if he was talking about me—or Baker. After hanging up, I immediately dialed her number. She didn't answer and I left a message. The phone rang after thirty seconds and I snatched it off the hook.

"I'm screening calls, Gray. That reporter—Jasper Jones—keeps bugging me. Hutch, keep it down, it's just melting ice sliding off the roof!... I don't know what he thinks I can tell him."

"Who, the dog?"

"No, Jasper Jones."

I got right into it. "Why the lie?"

Even through the line, I could sense the switch flipping on, the spinning up of storm clouds. Her tone sharpened. "What lie?"

"Rosemary saw you. In the resort parking lot."

"So I was there."

"You admit it?"

"You never asked me what I did that evening. I gave you the parking lot sketch—which I did from memory. How else would I've known where Adam parked?"

"Oh. Well, you could have said so."

"Try spending a night in jail and see how clearheaded you are the next day."

More barking. "Can't you get the dog to stop already?" I sniped. "It's distracting."

"Deal with it."

"Fine. Are you clearheaded now?"

"Do you really want to know why I drove to Fireside?" Hutch took a break from the barking and Baker lowered her voice to a normal level, though I had to strain to hear her through the curtain of thunder rumbling inches from my ears. Anger is quite distracting. "When I got there, I pulled into a—"

I interrupted. "What time was this?"

"It's not like I looked at my watch but it must have been about a quarter past eight. Adam had started his speech—he had a microphone in one hand—which I know because I pulled into a space where I could see into the restaurant. Near his BMW, yes, but that's because I'd driven over planning to leave a note on his car. To tell him I changed my mind about breaking it off."

"And then what?"

"And then nothing. I stayed maybe fifteen minutes, long enough to realize I was being a fool. I watched Adam enjoying himself as if he didn't have a care in the world. As if Tiffany and I didn't matter. And I realized I hadn't changed my mind after all."

The Crime Knights pact she'd left behind lay on my desk, folded into quarters. My storm quieted. "You wanted closure."

"Something like that. When I looked over just before driving off, Adam had wrapped up his speech. People were giving him hearty pats on the shoulder as he made the rounds of the room. You said Rosemary came out? I never saw her." The Storm of Anger had passed on her side as well. "It's a terrible thing to say, but Rosemary tends to blend into her surroundings. Everyone's used to seeing her around the resort, doing this or that for Adam."

"Why did she have the crutches?"

"I did wonder about that." She paused and I heard a bag crinkle. "Here you go, Hutch, what a good boy."

"Wondered about what? Did Rosemary fake the injury for some reason?"

"She said she slipped in her driveway over the holidays, but whether she sprained or strained the ankle, I have no idea, if that's what you're asking. But she enjoys being fussed over—it did cross my mind that she might have kept the crutches longer than she needed to."

"When I stopped by the resort, she no longer had them," I said. "Anything else?"

"Such as?"

Should have waited to have the conversation face to face so I could keep an eye out for ground fog, but here we were. "Such as...that Adam proposed."

Stunned silence, as if I had sprung a surprise *marry me* on her myself. When she found her voice, it brimmed with indignation. "What are you talking about, Gray? I mean, Adam did say let's spend the rest of our lives together now that Tiffany will be out of the picture, but if that counts as a marriage proposal, well, I missed it completely!"

"Would it have made a difference?"

The reply was a firm no.

I brought up the late-night drives and she told me that Adam had been having trouble sleeping. "He'd loop around rural roads and dictate memos to Rosemary. He must have been working it all out, whether to leave Tiffany and quit his job, move to the beach... and ask me to marry him apparently. I did pester Chief Gustafson about Adam's voice recorder—the one he carried around to dictate the memos—whether anything had been found on it. I thought maybe if Adam realized he wasn't going to make it, he might have left a message. The chief wouldn't say."

"Why take a drive that last day, if he'd made his decision?"

"No idea. Maybe he was wound up from the dinner in his honor, all the people."

I relayed Paul's theory, the staging of everything by a man sure he could win his mistress back if she saved him from a close brush with death. "Would it have worked?"

Another no. "What a way that would have been to start a marriage, with more lies—especially given his pledge."

"What pledge?"

"After he told me about the divorce and the rest of it, he promised he was done with secrets. He'd lied to Tiffany. To me. From then on, he'd live an honest life." Hutch gave another short bark and I heard the bag crinkle again. "If only Hutch could talk. He was in the passenger seat—he'd confirm I never got out of the car. After we got home, Hutch dozed and I ate ice cream in front of the TV."

"Your alibi is that you stayed in your car and then drove home for ice cream?"

"Haven't you ever eaten a tub of Rocky Road to make yourself feel better?"

"Not lately."

"Have some now, Gray. You seem crabby."

CHAPTER TWENTY

Anger stowed away in its stone until Thursday rolled around again, I was back on Goat Hill, in Tiffany's side of the house. She'd finally returned the call and invited me right over.

A woman in a pink pantsuit with padded shoulders and hair blow-dried into an airy puff answered the door. I followed her into the living room, best described as opulent, at least by Midwestern standards. Shiny gold-tinted lamps sat on tables; sparkling threads drew attention to sofa pillows; the chandelier above the grand table in the adjoining dining room consisted of a thousand glittering baubles. It gave the impression that Adam and Tiffany had been a couple who'd never wanted for anything... except, perhaps, a happy marriage.

She led me to a spotless white sofa. The coffee table was piled high with shopping bags. "Here, sit."

She dropped onto the sofa and I sank into a cushion. Tiffany perched stockinged feet up on the coffee table between two of the shopping bags and gave a nail-polish bottle a twist. "Detective Rodrick... Don't mind if I get ready for a board meeting while we gab, do you?"

East Coast accent, New Jersey maybe. "Not at all. And Rodrick is my first name."

"I like first names. Boy, do my feet *hurt*. I've been shopping all day—for shoes! I'm one of Nicole's bridesmaids, which means matching dresses in—wait for it—wait—*emerald green*. Apparently that's what you want when the bride's wearing black. Terrible color on me, green. The bridesmaids—five of us and a maid of honor—we're going to look like a flock of tropical birds."

She wasn't a quiet speaker and her voice, if it accompanied a harsher personality, would have come across as grating. Instead, it conveyed a cheerful energy at odds with a grieving widow. Not a willow tree in sight. She brushed a bright red streak along one nail. "At least Nicole isn't insisting we *all* wear cowboy boots, just her and Daddy when he walks her down the aisle. But I ask you, *what color shoes with an emerald green dress*? I thought about black but it's not my color, not even for footwear. When Adam died I considered wearing it but then thought, who am I kidding? We were about to divorce."

I stepped into the opening. "My condolences. If you don't mind my saying, you don't appear to be sad about your husband's passing."

"Congratulations, Einstein, you've discovered the obvious."

A candid answer, not a nasty one. In the middle of the living room, on the far side of the coffee table, a statue reigned—one of Tiffany herself. The Statue of Me, a toga-clad, marble version of its owner on a pedestal, facing said owner. It can be a healthy thing, a belief in one's own worth. But on occasion that belief can spin out of control and cause drama...and maybe, this time, a death.

When I asked Tiffany what went wrong between her and Adam, she had a ready answer. "You mean his mistress? No, that's not fair, we were both to blame and that's the truth. We had different lives." She expertly flew down the line of nails as she spoke. "Back in New York, he was busy with his job on Wall Street and I with mine. I worked for *Vogue* as an intern, dreamed of my own fashion line, but it wasn't meant to be. Then his father died and Adam says let's move to his hometown in the Midwest. Asks me to marry him. I thought about it and said yes to the marriage and Two Lakes. And do you know why?"

"Lindstrom's charms? The rustic beauty of Two Lakes?"

"The choices were be a big fish in a small town, or a small fish in the Big Apple. And so we moved and Adam got busy with the resort and I took charge of our social life." She blew on the nails. "I organized, volunteered, hosted dinner parties. I'm on the board of World Connect—they run a work-travel program, college students from abroad to fill jobs at the resort, housekeeping, waiters, things like that. I teach ESL for free. But they don't give awards to the volunteer of the year, only to businessmen. Adam stuck me in the same house as his mother and brother, and spent all of his time at his desk."

"You didn't want kids, you and Adam?"

"Neither of us ever said a word about it. I think we both felt it was the wrong road. And it would've been."

"When he asked for a divorce... Did it surprise you?"

She gave the bottle a shake and got started on the other hand. "I knew he had *someone*. It wasn't the first time. In public, Adam and I were the perfect couple. Privately, he had his affairs and I had mine. The word, though, it never came up before. Just like that, over toast and eggs, he says across the table, 'I'm done. I'm filing for a divorce.' Well. I told him he was throwing our marriage away. Our life wasn't perfect, far from it, but regardless of what his mother likes to go around saying, I had his back. I looked out for him." The hand slipped and the varnish smudged. She made a *tsk* sound. Not in anger; she felt betrayed by Adam—broken earthenware had popped up all over the cream carpet. "It wasn't for him to decide he was done with me. We'd spent more time discussing what kind of wallpaper to put on the walls, for God's sake."

The choice they'd made hovered on the knife's edge between tasteful and tacky, substantial vertical gold stripes in an ivory background.

Tiffany fixed the nail and set the bottle down with a tiny thud.

"Adam had big plans—to step down and move to the beach with his mistress—and I said, excuse me? I came to Two Lakes because of *you*. Did he expect me to fly back east and start from scratch? You're a fool, I said—and I was right. I got the whole story from Rosemary, his secretary. She's always been a snooper. She called the spa—I'd gone there to get ready for the dinner—Toast to Adam, he didn't mind one bit about that name. Rosemary got me on the phone to fill me in. Guess she was on my side of it. She told me that Clementine had it out with Adam. Threw a potted plant. You know, I kind of like her for that, despite things. It's strange..."

Suddenly a weeping willow shot up, overshadowing Tiffany's world. A tear rolled down one cheek, followed by another, seeming to surprise their maker. She didn't bother wiping them away and they left a streak in her makeup. "Adam and I, we spent most of our days in silence or fighting. And yet I still miss him."

There's only so much you can tell from a willow tree, but one thing I'd learned along the way is that people are complex.

"The grief is not only for Adam. It's also for the chapter of your life now in the past."

She tilted her head. "Yes, I think that's right. A new chapter... which means I better act like it."

The willow sent away, she got up and went into the hallway, the Statue of Me coasting along. I followed. The builders of the newer wing had kept the narrowness of the hallway but countered it with multiple mirrors on either side, and she stopped at one of them to fix her makeup.

A glossy card rested in a corner of the framed mirror, a wedding invitation. Tiffany dabbed at her face with a tissue, careful of her still-drying nails. "Only about thirty guests got *that* invite, for both the reception *and* the evening ceremony. It's a tight squeeze inside the Oldehouse."

I plucked out the card. Luxury cardstock, with elegant white lettering on a black background.

You're Invited to Celebrate
the Wedding of
NICOLE VANESSA COOPER
and
PAUL GERALD LINDSTROM
Tuesday the Twelfth of March, Nineteen Eighty Five
Banquet at Eight O'clock in the Evening
Fireside Resort Ballroom
Followed by
The Ceremony at Midnight
at the Oldehouse

I set the invitation back in its place and, keeping an eye out for fog, asked Tiffany straight out if she'd poured water into her husband's BMW.

"Did I go outside into the grimy parking lot, you mean? In my heels and *very* expensive red silk, side slit, plunge-back evening dress? Fat chance. I stayed on dry land until Erin pulled her car to the door to drive me home."

Not a wisp of fog. "You don't drive?"

"Not when I'm dressed like that I don't."

"And dinner was the last time you saw Adam?"

She carefully crumpled up the tissue. "It was. If you ask me, he must have had more to drink than anyone realized. I'd have stayed in the car waiting to be rescued, wouldn't you have? Not wandered off into the woods." She flip-flopped immediately. "Then again, Adam being Adam, he'd have been sure it'd all work out just fine."

I brought up Adam's money. "If the divorce had gone through, you'd have gotten only half—"

"Of the joint bank account, sure," she cut in. "Can you open that box for me?"

A velvet box sat on the side table under the mirror. Jewelry, a lot of it.

"Hand me those gold hoops, please?" Still careful of the nails, she swept her hair back and held a hoop against one ear. "Too much for a stuffy board meeting?"

"It depends on the message you're trying to convey."

"Everyone knows I'm not exactly the grieving widow, so the message is that life goes on, perhaps? New chapter, like you said."

"As to the money—"

"I get all of what's in the bank, sure. But the bulk is tied up in the resort—and that's only for pure Lindstroms. Spouses don't count. The prenup I signed made that much clear." She reached to touch her reflection, leaving a smudge. "I'm going to miss this house. Paul wants me out—well, Nicole probably, and she's prodded Paul into demanding it. A baby on the way. That's nice and all, but doesn't mean I have to pack up and leave, as if there's no room in Erin's wing. I have no close family back in New Jersey anymore and I've put roots down here."

I floated the possibility of Paul having been the one to harm his older brother, expecting her to take the bait, but she shook her head. "Doubt it. Paul has never been much of a self-starter. If his fiancée pushed for it, maybe, but even Nicole has her limits. Besides, Rosemary whispered in my ear the other day that she saw Clementine in the parking lot. Count on Rosemary to notice. She went out for her purse or something—on crutches!"

"About Rosemary…"

"Yes, exactly." The smile vanished. "Come this way."

She led me into the study. Paneled walls, mahogany desk and bookcases, velvet curtains drawn against the evening. The muted tones contrasted with Tiffany's personality; this had not been her space. She flipped on the desk lamp and started opening drawers haphazardly. "You gotta understand, Rosemary's never happier than when she's got a gripe. Last summer, a week or two after Adam hired Clementine Baker…" She rooted around and pulled out a white envelope. "…this arrived."

Typewritten address, to Mr. Adam Lindstrom. A postage stamp showed the letter had passed through the Two Lakes general post office. No return address. Inside, the sender had folded the single page into thirds. The message, delivered in text cut out from magazines and glued on with a careful hand, equated to a warning and hinted at an unstable personality.

> YOU Should HAVE TREATED ME Better
> I KNOW all Your SECRETS
> You Might WANT TO Remember THAT

Tiffany wrinkled her nose. "Nasty. And a threat with no teeth—as I said, I knew about Adam's affairs and he knew about mine. Clementine was his latest, Kostas is mine. Adam and I didn't keep anything from each other. There was no reason to."

The letter lacked a signature but a dried-out, brittle sprig of rosemary slipped out of the envelope and fell onto the carpet. I picked it up. The bottle of glue on Rosemary's desk at the resort office. Doubtful that Adam had been the only one who'd incurred her wrath over the years. Had she been working on another anonymous letter right before I came into the room? And for whom?

Tiffany snorted at the herbal signature. "Not too subtle, right? We consulted the police and a lawyer but were told Rosemary stayed just shy of the line of what might be considered an actual threat. When it came down to it, we had no proof she sent it. Adam wanted to fire her, but I was worried it might push her over the edge."

Devotion, if it flips, can lead to trouble. Maybe it had. "At the party, how did Rosemary react to her employer's big speech?"

A shrug, one that people who *have* give about the have-nots. "I didn't notice particularly. I think she was at a table by the kitchen. To be honest, I passed the time downing champagne and glaring at Adam. And before you ask why I went at all, what was I supposed to do, sit at home and watch TV? Not the dutiful wife standing by her man—I wasn't doing it for him! I'd bought the dress, made the spa appointment, told everyone I'd be there. I made sure the photographer from *The Bee* snapped a few of me—

without Adam." She made a whiplash change of subject. "Detective Rodrick, why do you wear that?"

I was taken aback. "I beg your pardon?"

"That beige, buttoned-up vest is as dull as dishwater. It makes you seem like you're playing it safe. Also, that mustache should go and a haircut wouldn't hurt."

My argyle vest, today paired with corduroys and a turtleneck, sported diamond shapes in two shades of brown on a background of the aforementioned beige. I got mildly defensive. "I'm not playing it safe. If there is a message to my clothes, it's that I'm perfectly satisfied with the present state of affairs in my life."

"Satisfied with your life calls for more pizzazz. Let me know if you want tips."

I asked if I could borrow the anonymous letter and drove to the drugstore to make a photocopy. By the time I made it back up Goat Hill, a motorcycle had pulled into the driveway. The man who hopped off had not bothered with a helmet. Leather pants, jacket, boots. He said hello with an accent.

"You must be Tiffany's friend," I said.

"Could be I am, yes. Who asks?"

"My name is Rod Gray, private investigator. I'm looking into Adam Lindstrom's death."

"Gray, like color? Very good. I'm Kostas—from Greece. Lifeguard at resort."

"So, you and Tiffany are an item. A couple, that is."

Either Kostas didn't mind answering questions or he'd misinterpreted my status, assumed a connection to the police. "Item, yes, I know what it mean. Meet at English class. Tiffany teacher. See... Tiffany not happy despite..." He gestured toward the immense house as we headed toward the shinier of its front doors. "I help. Buy flowers, take to movie, spend night together. Tonight, I chauffeur Tiffany to meeting of board. That make her happy."

"With Adam gone, Tiffany is yours forever."

"No, no." He held up a finger. "One more month. Improve

English and earn dollars. Then go home, buy minibus and drive tourists around. I already told all this to Chief Gus. I'm legal alien. I have paperwork. He say don't leave town and *I* say five months over, one left. After that, I go. I don't want to be *illegal* alien."

I blocked the doorbell with my back. "You work as a lifeguard at the resort, you said? Did you have a shift the day Adam Lindstrom died?"

"Had morning shift. Tiffany call the pool office, got me on phone. Tell me about divorce. Want me to go to Adam's big night with her. I say no. Invitation only and not right. I say I'll come after but she say not to bother. I come anyway, on my motorcycle. But too late, Tiffany gone home already. Only Adam."

"You went to the resort? And saw Adam?"

"Sure, sure. He help a woman into her car first. She had, what do you call..." Kostas, taller by about a foot, scratched a stubbled chin. "Critches?"

"Crutches. All right, so you saw Adam assist his secretary into her car. Then what?"

"Adam drive off in Bem-Veh. Ah, that is nice car. Two-door, henna red—very sharp. Those round headlights, classic style, very German precision. And the black leather seats, quality, look very comfortable... She purr along happy."

"You mean the engine sounded just fine?"

"Yes. I know engines. As I said, plan is to chauffeur tourists."

"Being an expert on vehicles, you didn't mess with the gas tank yourself?"

"Why do that? Adam was Adam and Kostas is Kostas."

A tropical breeze emanated from his person—someone at ease in their skin. Not a breath of fog.

He entered the house without ringing the doorbell. We found Tiffany in the living room, sipping a glass of wine. "Kostas, darling, there you are." She took care of what remained in the glass, tossed her car keys to Kostas, and settled a cashmere wrap on her shoulders. "Gold, if you're wondering," she told me.

I set Rosemary's letter down by all the shopping bags and asked, confused, "Gold what?"

"The shoes I bought for Nicole's wedding." She held up a foot for us to admire. "I'm breaking them in."

"Look very nice, darling Tiffanee."

CHAPTER TWENTY-ONE

I spent the morning of the following day, Friday, on the phone doing background checks for new tenants for an apartment complex in Ostford. At eleven thirty, I strolled the couple of blocks to Cooper Park and found a free bench. Anticipating the wood might be wet, I'd brought along my copy of *The Bee*—the Friday edition had weekend ads and coupons, making it more hefty—and spread it open before sitting down, the stones in my pocket clicking with the motion.

I came to the park midday every Friday with clockwork regularity. Not always the same bench, as the park and its playground could get busy, especially on a day like today, when the weather cooperated. But the bench I perched on currently happened to be the one where I'd made THE DECISION.

Haven't thought about that day in a long time.

Or what preceded it.

A different season, summer, early July. That morning I'd stumbled on a lead in a cold case—my father's case. An article in the science section of *The Star Tribune*, the Minneapolis-St. Paul paper, had caught my eye. It included a quote about nuclear reactor safety following Three Mile Island by a physics professor at St. Sunniva University—about a two-hour drive to the north—

his name given as Durston Grey. A one-letter change in the last name, two letters in the first, and a fake degree being likely the level of effort my father would have put in, I'd swapped my usual suit and tie for a more casual outfit from my closet, an argyle cardigan and brown corduroys, and driven up to campus. I tracked the professor down at his house, where he was hosting a July Fourth barbeque, only to discover that it was a dead end. Durston had a Boston accent and bore no resemblance to my father.

Back in Two Lakes, the air-conditioner unit on the fire-escape window of my office had given up. As early fireworks rumbled in the distance, I opened both windows, hoping to stir up a breeze. Shane had the day off. Mulling over whether the cardigan vest made me sweat more or did the opposite, keep the heat out, I opened the filing cabinet to put away the file on my father.

Maybe it was the oppressive humidity. Or the fact that I'd hit one dead end too many. Or maybe it was the fact that it happened to be my birthday. Whatever the reason, I faced the truth in my office that evening. I'd wasted three years looking for my father. Spent them chasing Dustin "Dusty" Gray. Tried my best to track him down, make him pay back the money he'd stolen all those years ago. Failed.

The folder brimmed with yellowed news articles, faded witness statements, reports of sightings that turned to be nothing. I dumped it all into the trashcan. Took the battery out of the ceiling smoke detector. Lit a match. My back to the open fire-escape window, watching the paper burn, I picked up the last item in the room that reminded me of my father, the paperweight from my desk. He'd been there the day I found the meteorite.

I came back to the present to check my wristwatch. *Sixteen minutes to go.* The seconds on the display crawled. Joy and Humor awaited me.

I let my memory drift back again. As the fireworks continued to boom in the distance, the meteorite-turned-paperweight in my hands, I pondered whether to toss it into the trashcan fire, knowing, of course, that it wouldn't burn. It had survived atmospheric entry, after all. But I was going to try.

Oddest thing, though—it began to warm in my palm, as if the fire had already reached it somehow. A warning.

It came too late.

The intruder's step was light and quick on the carpet. I didn't even register the cold, sharp steel of the knife slip between my shoulder blades.

Then—a gap where memory should be. Seconds? Minutes? Time stood still.

A slight movement transpired next. My eyes snapped open. I lay on the floor by the filing cabinet. The meteorite had cracked open: a single fragment lay in my palm; the remainder, I was dimly aware, lay scattered around me. Growing smaller and smaller, the fragment I clutched sent a fine salt-and-pepper powder raining onto the carpet. Nerves inside my body mended, fibers knit together, blood vessels reopened. I hung in some undefined space halfway between life and death and just...let everything go.

Pain, burning in my chest.

Anger at the person who stabbed me.

Embarrassment—I had failed to react fast enough. Failed to defend myself.

Envy of everyone in the whole world who still breathed.

Hunger—I tasted blood, intrusive and metallic, and a fierce desire to live past this day gripped me—but I released that desire too.

Joy and humor. Despite it all, I wanted to laugh at the banality of dying from a stab in the back.

Sorrow for the future I'd lose.

Guilt and sympathy—I wouldn't get to say goodbye to Aunt Holly and Uncle Chad. Shane would lose his job, he was a good assistant...

And, finally, pity for the stabber, whose face I never saw. For being desperate enough to take a human life.

The maelstrom poured into the remaining fragments, a migration of color, creature and everything else from deep within me. Boom, boom, boom. There may not really have been a thunderous sound as my emotions settled into their new home. That part could be a trick of memory, just more July Fourth fireworks. What's sure is that at the end, my chest rose and fell, and I gathered seven fragments to my chest, newly minted containers for the feelings I'd abandoned, plus a final fragment that, as I would later discover, stayed dark.

All other emotional bits and bobs—surprise, hope, confidence, confusion, doubt and more—stayed inside me. Even an extraterrestrial rock can only soak up so much. Along with the smell of burnt paper, the air carried a hint of petrichor.

Reborn, my load lightened, I gathered everything into the pocket of the cardigan. Clawed past the trashcan—it still emitted a thin wisp of smoke—and over to the desk. I pulled myself up by the chair and reached for the phone. I never got to make the call and instead collapsed into unconsciousness, the desk edge meeting my skull before the floor did.

In the morning, Shane showed up at the same time as Arlo from the appliance repair shop, there to fix the air conditioning. They found me semi-conscious behind the desk and *holy cow*-ed at the amount of blood as they helped me up. I got a single word out, "Intruder," and Shane and Arlo together filled in the rest. The intruder attacked me from behind, we'd tussled for the knife, and I managed a slash up, accounting for all the blood on the back of my cardigan. The injured assailant then pushed me down— causing me to hit my head on the edge of the desk—and made a run for it. That's the story that made its way to the police.

I spent a day at the hospital so the doctors could keep an eye on my head injury, then exited into a sunny afternoon with the discharge instructions recommending rest tucked under my arm, and strolled over to the park. A pair of doors awaited and I had to choose. No Ike to toss, not back then. Just the facts.

Such as that I'd always felt too deeply—all the way down to

the very center of Earth, it seemed at times—and it's not the easiest way to go about living. I'd been called sensitive, not as a compliment. Told by my father that boys don't cry. By girlfriends that I was too needy. By my PI mentor that I got over-invested in cases. Told myself that puppies in TV commercials shouldn't bring tears to my eyes.

That day, I considered all this as I took out the stones and set them on the bench next to me, puzzling out the contours of objects inside them, a tree in one, a gnome in another, figuring out which feeling had landed where behind the black veins tracing a pattern across the surface of each stone.

Thought to myself, *You have to let them back in.*

Argued back: *Feelings got me killed. Don't remember why exactly, but they did.*

I brought the first of the stones up to my chest, and...stopped. Of the Earth's five billion inhabitants, I alone had a cheat. Muscles I didn't know I possessed loosened. Nerve endings unclenched. Never would I grind my teeth at night again, or sweat on a Ferris Wheel. The burden of existence—the human cargo— rolled off my shoulders.

I was free.

I threw out the ruined cardigan, with its slash in the back, and bought a dozen in the same style and color. Made it my uniform. I sported a turtleneck underneath in the winter; in the summer, a T-shirt. Now and then I tried to leave the stones behind and go out on my own, but I'd end up feeling drained, as if the meteorite's fragments kept me tethered to life. As if I really was hooked up to a battery. Beyond that, I didn't spend much time analyzing what happened that evening. No sleepless nights speculating who might have attacked me, or grateful visits to church to thank the gods above for sending me the meteorite. I just...moved on, and that was that.

Ten minutes to go. *Distract yourself. You didn't just move on, did you?*

No. Later, I found out the hard way that it wasn't that easy.

That isolating the feelings had the effect of rendering them pure and strong—and eager for a jailbreak. Driving one night along a rural road, I passed a dark shape by the side of the road, a deer. I pulled off to check if I could help but it was too late. As I stood gazing upon the animal's still form, I sensed movement in my cardigan pocket. I reached in to take a large lens out. Pity's lens. It generated a light of its own and distorted the air. Through it, the deer looked small and fragile—too fragile for this world.

Distracted, consumed by pity, I managed to get hit by a passing motorist. The car's twenty miles per hour over the speed limit broke my neck instantly. By the time the shaken driver got out of his car—he'd stopped about a quarter mile ahead—and hurried over to where I lay, shoeless in a ditch, what had been the Pity, Empathy, Guilt & Sympathy fragment—PEGS—had used itself up to bring me back to life. Only a pile of salt-and-pepper powder remained in my palm. The motorist helped me up, dusted me off, made sure I was okay and left, relieved to be driving away with no one's death on their conscience, and I slipped my shoes back on and climbed behind the steering wheel of the Ford Falcon.

That's how I learned that the stones are more than storage containers. That the life-saving power of the meteorite is there in its remnants too. When the intruder stabbed me, I came back to life as Rodrick Gray the Second. It had happened again, the rebirth, and I was now Gray the Third.

With the stone used up, pity and the other three inhabitants —empathy, guilt, sympathy—had nowhere to go. I'd seen the objects inside the stone: a lens, a miniature of myself, a glop of brown, and a matching pair of mugs—and now they had moved back into my soul garden like unwanted guests. It took me weeks to adjust to having PEGS back. I carried a distorting lens in front of me like a torch, and pitied everything in sight: bookends for their inability to read the fairy tales they propped up, and cross-walk lights for missing out on colors beyond red and green. I saw a reflection of myself in the night sky, in empathy with stars that never touched the coolness of rain. My shoes heavy with a strange mud, I felt guilty for killing germs when I cleaned the sink. I drove around with a passenger—mugs of hot cocoa, in sympathy with potholes for being hated by everyone.

Lens, my own likeness, mud, cocoa. For *weeks*.

Once things calmed down, I drew the obvious conclusion. I'd have to air out the remaining seven stones so I'd be better prepared in case I had to sacrifice another one to save my life. After some trial and error, I figured out that double-tapping a stone had the effect of emptying it. Seven stones fit neatly into the week. One a day, for no less than thirty minutes and at most an hour. The schedule had served me well.

One minute. Watching children run around the park, I pondered why I'd revisited the past after all this time. *This case*. *Baker*. Quite likely I'd already spoken face to face with Adam Lindstrom's killer. But which one of them?

"Ready or not, here I come!" came the shout from the playground.

A kid crouched behind the bench, not a very effective hiding place, and whispered, "Can I have that rock? It's funny looking, like a square marble with black stripes. I like the black stripes."

"Sorry, no."

Unbothered by my refusal—children are very honest about the concept of It's Mine, And I'm Keeping It—the boy tip-toed off to hide behind the big pile of parking-lot snow, and I did what I'd came to the park to do, double-tapped the stone.

CHAPTER TWENTY-TWO

Joy's bright yellow sunflowers caught a ride on a bouquet of Humor's balloons and floated over. As simple as that, the wood of the bench softened. The playground now rang not with clamor but with laughter. I breathed in air that carried on the promise of spring and counted the cottony clouds floating above. The sunflowers multiplied, their yellow heads poking high out of the playground snow all around me. I sprang to my feet, lightly. What a glorious day, absolutely glorious. I half-danced, half-jogged along the pedestrian path that follows the curve of Cooper Lake at that end of the park, humming a melody. I heard a honk and sprang aside in a merry—or dare I say joyful?—fashion to let a bicycle splash by. *How good it feels to be alive.* So I had a swollen cheek, a murder to deal with, and a mysterious growl in my cardigan. *Everyone has problems!* With a sudden clarity I saw my way out. Tiffany Lindstrom did it. Adam dead equaled revenge, sympathy, and the whole of the personal bank account. Murder's mark—*gosh, when will I find out what it looks like?*—probably hid behind that Statue of Me, along with any fog of the silver, soul-garden kind. I simply had to break Tiffany's alibi—easy-peasy; I had a plan—and the creature responsible for that growl? It'd reveal itself eventually. As for my swollen cheek and what was clearly escalating beyond sore gums into actual dental trouble, all I had to do was pick up the phone and make an appointment. The path twisted away from the lake and I pirouetted across a pedestrian bridge. Dentists were great. I should leave all my worldly goods to dentists.

I watched a squirrel, white and agile, scamper up a tree. Back at the bench, I set about building a ball with the heavy, wet snow, then a smaller one. People were beginning to stare but I didn't care and oh, that rhymed!

"Gray? What on earth?"

"I'm making a snowman, Baker." I grabbed her by both hands and spun her around. "Lovely day for it, isn't it?"

She let go and dropped down onto the bench. "Not so lovely for me."

I balanced the smaller of the balls on top of the bigger one and tucked in a pinecone to serve as a nose. "Trouble?"

"You could say that. The police confiscated my passport. Apparently, they're worried I'll make a run for it over the border to Canada." She leaned back, closing her eyes against the sun's rays, letting them warm her face. "Oh, and I just got fired. My manager read this morning's story in *The Bee*. Did you see it?"

"I saw it. It's a lot of bad news, Baker, but things'll be all right."

"At least I can do Hutch's morning walk at a more reasonable hour, I've had to get up at five... Gray, what are you doing?"

Eager to share my mood, I'd sat down on the bench next to her to pat her hand.

She's a client, I reminded myself, and you have a job to do. Time to fall back down to Earth. *But I don't want to give up joy,* my insides bawled. *I want the full hour, we're not even halfway there. I'm owed it, the time!* I willed my tongue to form the words. "Give me a sec." I turned aside, frowned at Baker's decidedly unhappy situation, and shook off Joy & Humor, disguising the motion as a shiver against the cold. The sunflowers and balloon floated back down into their stone. The colors of the world dimmed, as if the sun had disappeared behind a cloud. I slipped the stone back into my pocket, moved away from Baker, and asked how she'd known I was at the park.

"Shane said this is where to find you on Fridays at noon." She caught sight of the edition of *The Bee*, looking slightly worse for wear. I'd read the article, byline Jasper Jones, over breakfast, and it had elicited the mysterious growl for a third time. Leaving the soggy part of the paper on the bench, I tore off the front page. "I wanted to ask you about this story of Jasper's."

"Read it to me."

"The article? Why?"

"To remind me never to make such a mistake again."

This didn't strike me as particularly logical, but I went along with it and proceeded to read the whole thing out loud to her.

Questions Grow in Lindstrom Death

Readers of this paper will recall that Rodrick Gray, private detective, has been hired by Clementine Baker in a desperate bid to prove her innocence after her recent night in jail. Rodrick Gray is reported to have caused a lunchtime scene at The Cork yesterday in his efforts to offload the blame for Mr. Lindstrom's death away from Miss Baker. He is said to have demanded time in the busy schedules of Paul Lindstrom and Chef Conrad Urban— along with a slice of the chef's famous cake (and what good cake it is!)

Further, this reporter has learned that the late Adam Lindstrom and a member of his staff—who happens to be the very same Clementine Baker—frequently stayed late at their jobs at Fireside Resort, ostensibly to work. In actuality they met up in a resort room after hours— Room 312, privately referred to by other members of the staff as Lindstrom's Love Nest. Mr. Lindstrom is rumored to have bestowed an expensive gift on Miss Baker for

Christmas, a pearl necklace with an 18-karat white gold clasp.

But this romance was about to end badly.

A lovers' quarrel midday on February 22th sent Clementine Baker storming away. It's fair to ask what that storm might have led to.

Chief Gustafson has requested that the public be reminded that all persons are presumed innocent until proven otherwise.

Baker was silent when I finished, her attention on the ground, where she was digging a hole into the snow with one booted toe.

"What I wanted to ask you is how Jasper Jones got access to all the—"

"Salacious details?" Baker cut in. "Rosemary talked, probably. No reason why she shouldn't have, it's all true. But the article makes it sound as if I spent all my time gazing dreamy-eyed at Adam instead of doing my job—and then *killed him*. The salon manager told me they insist on *standards* for their employees." Baker kicked a clump of ice, almost hitting an elderly man with a cane. "Sorry, sir."

We vacated the bench and I said, with less certainty than I'd felt ten minutes ago when I was enjoying the effects of Joy's stone, "Leave it to me. I'm going to make an attempt to break Tiffany's alibi."

I relayed the details of Tiffany's schedule on the day. "We know Adam's car was still running normally when he returned from his errands at a quarter past three. Erin showed up at the resort at six and kept Tiffany in her sight from then on. That leaves just under a three-hour window for Tiffany to have acted. I'm going to see how easy it would have been for her to pop out and back into the spa. Shane called in a favor and got me a last-minute appointment. I think he had an ulterior motive—he wants me to bring back a slice of Erin's Cake."

"When's your appointment?"

"At one thirty."

"I'll drive you and wait."

"Won't you be bored?"

"My Honda will play the part of Adam's car. See if you can sneak out to it."

As we got into the Honda in the park's lot, she tilted her eyebrows in my direction. "You know, I can't seem to get a handle on you, Gray. At first, I thought you'd changed. You were distant, as if life's been tough. But just now in the park you seemed like the old Gray I remember."

"The old Gray is gone."

"New one's not so bad."

Lakeside Drive took us to the resort. Baker pulled into the lot and stared at the lodge above the steering wheel. "Haven't been back since I stopped by to pick up my last paycheck, the week after Adam died." She checked her watch. "You still have a few minutes before your appointment. Let's get that cake that Shane wants."

"I was going to pick it up on the way out," I informed her.

"We can do it now. It won't spoil in the car."

"You don't have to go in, you know."

"Gray, I'm not gonna hide and hope this blows over."

We entered the restaurant's foyer only to encounter the resort's co-owners, Chef Urban and Paul Lindstrom. Their voices low, the pair were engaged in a heated conversation, storms of matching strengths clashing above their scalps.

"...Nuances? *What* nuances?" This, from Paul.

"I'd rather not get into that now."

"You're bluffing, Conrad," Paul retorted and turned in his loafers to push through the corridor doors. We watched him stomp off in the direction of his office. Chef Urban sent an exasperated look after his business partner, then caught sight of Baker. The moat slimmed to a thread and a broad smile planted itself on his face. "Clementine, how have you been?"

Having heard why we were there, the chef instructed us to

wait and returned after five minutes with a large box. "Three slices, on the house. Enjoy it—I'm retiring the recipe. I've asked Paul to buy me out."

"Conrad, you're leaving?"

"It's time, Clementine. I've been ready for a while. Paul's perfectly happy to buy me out—on one condition. That I leave the recipe for Erin's Cake behind. I said no, so it's a stalemate."

"Won't whoever he hires to replace you want a menu of their own anyway?"

"I told him that, but he wants the new menu built around Erin's Cake..."

I only half paid attention to the conversation. Baker's presence had attracted attention. The law might presume everyone innocent until proven guilty, but the citizens of Two Lakes had cast their judgment. Granite figures had sprung up all over the dining room: gargoyles, cold and hostile condemnation in their eyes. All in all, it was a good thing Baker couldn't see them.

CHAPTER TWENTY-THREE

"Having trouble with soul gardens, boss?" Shane asked between forkfuls of cake. "This case... At its center, Adam Lindstrom, a man who had it all—a successful company, a big house, a gorgeous wife *and* a gorgeous mistress."

"Thank you...I think." This from Baker, who had a plate on her lap. We were back at the agency, with my assistant and client side by side on the burgundy couch and me in my armchair.

Shane added, "All of which Lindstrom intended to leave behind for some reason."

"All except Baker," I said. Shane wasn't wrong—I was having trouble with soul gardens. So far, my hunt for *I Did It* in the vicinity of suspects had yielded zilch.

"Then there's this water business," Shane said.

I flipped my case notes to the suspect list. "Let's decide once and for all. Was the intent to kill Adam? Not vandalism. Not a prank. Not to inconvenience him."

"I knew something was wrong...but murder?" Baker shook her head, but not in a no. "I must have been thinking it all along, that gut feeling I had, but I never let myself say it out loud."

"My gut...." Shane scraped the last crumb off his plate. "...agrees."

I stayed silent. Gut feeling—I used to rely on it a lot. Not so anymore. I figure it's a cocktail, a spoonful of this, a pinch of that from the meteorite fragments. Or it's a thing of its own and hides in the seventh stone, the cloudy one.

Baker picked up the sketchbook, which I'd carelessly left on the coffee table, and began leafing through it. "What are these soul gardens of yours anyway, Gray? At first I took it to be a marketing gimmick, but you really seem to believe in them."

"I sketch feelings, emotions, and moods the way I imagine they might look if we could see them." I hoped she'd buy the explanation.

"Like doodles to help visualize motives and whatnot?"

"Something like that." I pushed the third slice across the table; with Hunger packed away, it was wasted on me. "You two split it."

This had the intended effect of making her forget about the sketchbook. After a delay while the slice was divided equitably, Shane asked how it went at the spa. "Manage to poke a hole in Tiffany's alibi, boss?"

I'd waited to recap things until we were back in the office so Shane could listen in.

"He never came out. Not for almost two hours." Baker had waited in her Honda during my spa appointment, and had informed me after I came out that it took a superhuman effort on her part to not tuck into the cake right then and there.

"The spa session wasn't cheap, by the way," I began.

"Add it to my bill," Baker said promptly.

"You lost your job," I pointed out.

"I'll pay you back in installments. Or maybe I'll agree to an interview with Jasper Jones and ask him for money."

"I don't think that's how it works... Sticker shock aside, the pampering started as soon as I walked in. They gave me a robe, slippers, and a foot soak in cucumber water. Guess they don't want customers with smelly feet. Etienne—my masseur—chatted about his home city of Paris while I lay on the table pondering if, when it comes to feelings, murder counts as one."

Shane chimed in with a suggestion. "How about an aura that lingers, boss? We could call it a murderglow... Or murdermoss, quietly creeping along, spreading its secrets and paranoia over everything?"

"What's this?" Baker glanced from Shane to me.

I'd have to remind my assistant to be more careful. "For the sketchbook," I said. "The way I see it, the act of killing changes the person. They feel differently about themselves from then on, forever. It's not necessarily guilt. More of a darkness, a residue, a sense of power... It's not *murderous*, which is more about the exact moment the crime is committed, the now of it."

"Murderglow? Murdermoss? We're making up words now? How about murdery...for when you've been planning it for ages and are just waiting for the right time? *I feel murdery*. Murdery leads to murderous, which leads to murderglow, a chain of criminality." Having made that lighthearted statement, she remembered that her freedom was at stake. "Are you trying to picture what it might look like from the outside, having blood on your hands? Like an eye tic or something?"

"I wish I knew." My client resumed eating cake and I returned to the tale of my attempt to break Tiffany's alibi. "The massage took forty-five minutes, followed by an aromatherapy session. Etienne darkened the room, lit scented candles, put on soothing music, and left. This gave me my chance. Not counting the emergency exit with an alarm, there's only one way in or out for customers, past the spa welcome desk—staffed by Shane's friend Sue. Glass doors sit between the welcome desk and the resort corridor. There are maybe four or five massage rooms, plus two small locker rooms with showers. I slipped out of the massage room I was in, number three, with a story at the ready, that I needed the restroom. Luckily Sue had stepped away to show a new customer in. My next stop was the locker room where I'd left my things—Tiffany could have hardly gone into the parking lot in a robe—but before I could get to it, Sue came back to fetch a towel from a closet. I crouched behind a large potted palm and waited. The manager came out of the break room, saw me, and threatened to call the police."

Baker almost choked on a bite. She put her hands up to her mouth in laughter, sending polka dot balloons bobbing up against the ceiling. "Oh, no."

"Picture me in the robe," I continued grimly, lacking the help of the Joy & Humor stone to provide insight into what was so funny, "without a business card to show the manager. Her name is Mrs. Malquist, by the way. With Sue's help, I managed to convince Mrs. Malquist that I was merely conducting an experiment. She told me in no uncertain terms that her customers don't wander in and out of rooms, and certainly not into the corridor or the parking lot."

"Tiffany's out, then, boss."

I nodded. "Seems so. During the daylight hours she was in Mrs. Malquist's domain and later in her mother-in-law's, until she and Erin went their separate ways in the house. Erin kept an ear out for Adam—she'd have heard if Tiffany got into her own car and doubled back to the restaurant."

"Good." Baker took a largish bite of the cake and said the rest through a full mouth. "I don't want it to be her, because then it'd be my fault."

"Tiffany is responsible for her own actions." I added a blunt, "Besides, according to Tiffany, Adam had other affairs over the years. You weren't the first."

A lingering polka dot balloon popped and vanished. Baker pulled in her shoulders. "Ouch. But I don't care—I still don't want it to be Tiffany."

"How do you feel about Paul?" I tapped the notepad. "Not as successful as his brother, never left home. Claims he stayed overnight in Duluth. When I talked to him, he fidgeted, avoided eye contact...." And had fog around his loafers. "How well do you know him, Baker?"

"Paul? He helped out with catered events once in a while, sometimes as a driver, sometimes as a waiter. He was friendly but did the bare minimum, you know? He'd never show up early or offer to stay late." She held up a hand. "But I don't want it to be Paul, either—he's about to be married and a father. If you try hard enough, Gray, you can come up with a motive for anyone, even"—she glanced across the coffee table at my list and plucked out a name at random—"Todd West, who's the most mild-mannered person I've ever met, and that includes you, Gray. You're a pendulum that never moves, as far as I can tell, and Todd is as jittery as a drop of water on a hot stove."

"For all we know, Todd's been stealing from the resort for years and Adam found out."

"Todd would never cause trouble by stealing—or by sabotaging Adam's Beamer."

"As it happens, I agree with you there. Paul's a different story. The younger brother, always second. He probably imagined everything going perfectly once Adam was out of the picture. Doubtful he anticipated that the police would look so closely into his brother's death, and that there'd be trouble at the resort too—Conrad Urban announcing he was retiring, along with his famous cake."

"Not the cake!" Shane exclaimed at this, and then did an immediate one-eighty. "But it makes sense and is kind of romantic. He named it for Erin. He doesn't want it in another chef's hands."

Baker set her empty paper plate down and wiped her fingers on a paper napkin. "I'm not surprised Paul's demanding it stays. 'The best chocolate cake in the world.' It's good advertising and one of the pillars of the catering menu, weddings in particular."

"Baker, I'll give you another possibility. Rosemary Moore." I passed over the photocopy of the letter sent anonymously to the Lindstrom household. Baker read it and tossed it to Shane, who wrinkled his nose. "Gross."

Baker's chin shot up. "I received one back in the fall. Words cut out of magazines, same as this, anonymous. I tossed it in the trash."

She stopped there and Shane prompted her, "What did it say, Clem, the letter?"

"*Your luck will run out one day.* I knew who it was. Rosemary made it her business to point out that other people were born lucky. Not her. Everything was hard for her. Honestly, I wanted to slam the letter on her desk and tell her to get moving and find a different job instead of waiting for one to be handed to her. I didn't do it. I tried to keep the peace." Baker ran a slow thumb along the nook between her shoulder and neck. Frustration. The feeling manifested as a sudden rise in humidity, a garden element I'd had difficulty drawing into the sketchbook in the F section.

"Even if I hadn't come along, " she went on, "Adam wouldn't have given event coordinator to her. Rosemary just isn't the right fit for the job. She dresses frumpily, but that's fixable." Baker waved that particular problem away. "Part of the role is to charm the happy couple and the parents paying for the wedding, assure them they're in good hands and that everything will be as promised on the big day, from the mini-quiche appetizers to the four-tier version of Erin's Cake. Rosemary, she has these beady eyes that stare at you disconcertingly. I always felt as if she was watching me... She'd have sent clients scattering away. And the job isn't glamorous at all, not really. It's mostly demanding brides-maids and last-minute cancelations and rain showers interrupting events. The odd thing is that Rosemary is great at what she does, being an assistant. She's the first to come in, the last to leave, never a day of vacation... There's something else."

"Another reason she wanted a promotion?"

Baker nodded. "Technology. Adam used to rely on her for practically everything. Then one morning she walked in and there it was, on Adam's desk. An Apple computer. I imagine she worries about becoming superfluous."

The Log of Worry made an appearance across Shane's shoulders. "Are we thinking of getting a computer, boss?"

"Seems to me like we're doing just fine with a typewriter and notepads." Which we were.

"Next," I said, "Kostas, Tiffany's boyfriend, the lifeguard. He admits to being at the resort that night. He might have been hoping to marry Tiffany for a green card, but why go to the trouble of killing Adam with the divorce about to happen? Unless he wanted to speed things up so he could avoid overstaying his visa."

"I asked around about him, boss. His full name is Kostas Vasilakis. He has a ticket booked for a return to Athens in April." Shane added as an aside, "That's how it works with World Connect. They bring people over for six months. Sue—from the spa—says a few bad apples do sneak off to Chicago or Los Angeles and disappear, but according to her Kostas talks a lot about how he misses home and how much he hates snow."

I stared at the remaining name on my list. "Baker, were you aware that Nicole has your old job now, a promotion for her?"

"I heard. Not a surprise. She helped out with events now and then, and is about to marry into the family."

"What's your opinion of her?"

"She didn't have much time for me. Mostly she wanted to impress the top bosses, Adam and Chef Urban."

Shane had data of his own. "I knew Nicole in high school— we're the same age, twenty-nine. Homecoming queen. I, on the other hand, was a spectacularly awkward teenager. I don't think Nicole spoke a single word to me for the whole of the four years."

I thought back to the chalkboard fence Nicole had constructed around herself—and that persistent fog by her fiancé's loafers. "Say Paul is lying."

And he was, about something.

"Adam had settled on Linda Bolander after all." I worked it out as I spoke. "Paul is stuck in a low-paying job for the foreseeable future, his mother is controlling the family fortune, and there's a wedding and baby on the way. What does he do, up in Duluth? Relay his disappointment to his girlfriend over the phone. And what does Nicole, freshly engaged, do? Spring into action. And our everyman's-friend the mayor knows what his daughter's done and that's why he's been insisting that Chief Gustafson stop looking into things."

Shane floated a suggestion. "Could it have been the mayor himself, boss? He attended the Toast to Adam party."

I shook my head. "The method doesn't fit the personality. Had Adam been shot, maybe. But water in a gas tank barely counts as violence. It's hesitant, squeamish. It might not have harmed Adam at all."

"Not manly, you mean?" Baker interrupted a touch sarcastically.

"The mayor's anything but subtle... I've ruled you out as the murderer for the same reason, Baker."

"Gee, thanks."

I reached for the photocopy of Rosemary's letter. Surely her Pond of Grievances would have shrunk away if Adam's assistant had succeeded in taking revenge on her boss. The thought made me conclude that it likely wasn't her hand that poured water in. I wondered about something else. "You said it yourself, Baker. Rosemary was watching you all the time—and not only you. Look what she says: *I know all your secrets.* When Adam told you he wanted to live an honest life, you assumed he meant his love life, but what if there was more to it? A professional secret tied to the resort. And Rosemary knows what it is."

"Like what? And will she be willing to tell?"

"Good point, she didn't seem inclined to do you any favors, Baker."

"Money." Shane accompanied the words with a shrug. "Usually works."

"I got fired, remember? I drained my bank account to pay the rent and utilities this month—and a vet bill. Hutch had a limp that thankfully turned out to be nothing. The vet says it might have been a sympathy limp. Hutch can sense something's wrong."

I made a mental note to check for the canine equivalent of

table-and-cocoa in Hutch's vicinity the next time I saw him, and admitted, "I don't have a ton of money either. I like to keep my rates low."

"Don't look at me," Shane said. "I don't get paid enough to have a stash under the bed."

"Well, we're a group." Baker's eyes suddenly lit up. "Wait, I got it. My pearl necklace. The one mentioned in today's article in *The Bee*."

"Will Rosemary accept jewelry?" I recalled my visit to the resort's offices. "She wasn't wearing any, only a watch and even that was a basic, faux-leather strap."

"Oh, she'll want the pearls. It'll feel like a win over me. Jasper Jones the reporter had it right—Adam gave them to me for Christmas. I got him one of those astronaut space pens. He liked gadgets and new technology and things like that."

"Do you mind, Clem?" Shane asked. "Giving up the pearls?"

"Let Rosemary have them. With Adam gone, I'd never be able to wear them anyway."

"I'll approach her," I said. "Meanwhile, there's something I want us to do, Baker."

CHAPTER TWENTY-FOUR

The plans for the night requiring caffeine, I was at the Home Plate Diner. Baker had left to walk Hutch and drop off Shane on the way, saving him a trip on the tourist shuttle. I'd taken a single sip when a body thudded into the booth across from me.

"Jasper. Feel free to sit down, why don't you?"

The reporter already had a notepad in hand. "Heard Miss Baker came to the resort earlier today. Would you know anything about that?

"We were getting cake."

"Cake again?" Jasper Jones jotted this down. "Whose birthday?"

"No one's."

"Just felt like having a couple of slices, I see. Learn anything while eating cake?"

"Nothing I'd care to share."

"Rodrick Gray, PI, declined to comment. Is it possible that what his inquiries have uncovered thus far casts a grim light on his client?"

Amazing, I thought, that the growl emanating from my pocket turned no heads in my direction. "Nothing of the sort."

"When pressed, he got defensive."

You had to hand it to Jasper, he was persistent. I made a calculation, in case Rosemary proved to be difficult to entice, even with pearls. "Fine, print this. Adam Lindstrom had a secret...and I don't mean Clementine."

This got the reporter's attention. "Business or personal?"

"That's all you're getting from me."

"Secret, unspecified. I can work with that." Jasper reached for a packet of sugar, tilted it into his mouth, and left.

"Let's see," I said to no one in particular, "what *that* shakes loose."

CHAPTER TWENTY-FIVE

It neared midnight when Baker and I swung into the pull-off alongside County 9. No streetlamps. There was a deer crossing sign. Ahead of us, the road disappeared into an army of trees, tall and dark; behind us, it made a turn as it left the woods in a gentle downward slope toward a sleepy neighborhood a couple of miles to the south. Above the treetops were the usual things, stars and a plump setting moon.

The circles from our flashlights bobbed on tire tracks and bootprints as we got out of the car. A path led between dogwood shrubs, red and bare for the winter, onto a dual-use trail. One side of the trail had parallel grooves from skis; the snow on the other side had been beaten down by hiker bootprints. I consulted the map Shane had obtained from Sergeant Mendez, which had another X on it: the location of the body. I pointed the flashlight. "That way."

Encountering a marker now and then, Baker and I forged ahead under trees laden with snow. Shane had jotted down the specifics of the February storm, from library copies of *The Bee*. Fifty-mile-per-hour gusts and a windchill of minus nine. The cashmere coat Lindstrom wore to dinner, while adequate for the short distance from car to indoor environment, would have provided little protection. Stranded, Lindstrom must have sat in his car waiting for another vehicle to pass by. None had rumbled by in the few minutes Baker and I stood looking around, and the chances were even smaller under the conditions that night. At some point—probably when the car's temperature plunged to match the outdoor one—Lindstrom had set out on foot, following the trail as best he could. Without a flashlight, his night would have been darker, the whiteout conditions rendering all directions the same. Little difference between path and forest floor and the trail markers all but invisible.

Baker broke the silence. "Something's been worrying me."

"We'll get you out of this jam, Baker."

"It's not that—well, not only that... What if the fact that I told Adam we were done affected his mood that night? Made him think less clearly than he would have otherwise."

"According to Paul, his brother sounded upbeat on the phone."

"Still." She sent a glance back to where we had left the car on the other side of the trees. "I'd have stuck to the road, followed it back to that neighborhood we passed on the way in, wouldn't you have?"

"It's a solid couple of miles that way. Whatever drove Adam—alcohol, panic, hubris—he must have weighed his options and opted for the closest phone, the clubhouse one." A marker arrow directed us towards the clubhouse. "And he really should've had a winter kit in his car, or an extra blanket at least."

"That was for other people. Those with bad luck."

The trail curved. Baker and I kept on, aided by the map and the numbered posts alongside the trail. She shone her light ahead, illuminating pockets of hushed winter forest. "Do you think whoever did it feels freed?"

I glanced over. "The killer, you mean? Freed from what?"

She pulled her hood snug around her face with one hand. "The weight that pressed on them until they had to act. What I called the murdery feeling. But maybe afterwards they found out it hadn't made a difference after all and they still carried the weight, just a changed one."

"Murder's soul mark."

"I didn't really understand what you meant before, but now I think I do."

We came to a fork in the trail. The wider path led to the Lost Wolf Woods clubhouse, visible up ahead through the trees. The clubhouse was where you rented cross-country equipment during the day; on weekends its fine-dining restaurant, The Clubhouse Grill, offered what Shane had once described as a cozy and romantic vibe. The building's lights were off, though a handful of streetlights illuminated the parking lot.

A narrower trail scooted off to our right. Lindstrom had gotten turned around, perhaps zigzagged, and ended up on the side path, and then off it. I swept the beam across a clearing, the most direct route to the X. "That way."

We navigated the knee-deep snow, moving slower now. Footprints left by creatures of the forest crisscrossed the flat expanse; after the spring melt-off, green grass and flowers would populate the meadow. Soon we were back under the trees and on the lookout for a fallen sugar maple. Sergeant Mendez had told Shane that's where we'd find the X.

"There." Baker pointed to a mighty tree downed by nature's fury in a past storm.

"It probably progressed something like this, the sequence of states," I said to Baker as she wordlessly pondered the horizontal tree. "First came the pain in his extremities. Fingers, toes, ears, nose. Next, the trembling of the whole body. It ceased as Adam's body temperature sank to a dangerous level and confusion set in. Feeling as if he was burning up, he shed his outerwear and sat down against the tree trunk. Suddenly, the pain's gone. In its place, a peacefulness... Baker, I have tissues back in the car, if you need them."

Baker aimed the flashlight beam into my face, blinding me briefly. "It's allowed, Gray. Tears, pulling at your hair, stomping your feet, sorrow, rage, all of it. But none of that is left, not anymore. That day in your office is the one and only time I shed a tear for Adam. It was the first time I felt unjudged, in the presence of friends. Here, hold this." She pushed her flashlight into my free hand, fished out a small ceramic jar from her down jacket, and set it against the base of the maple. She applied a lighter to the candle inside.

"What's that for?" I asked. The flame burst forth inside the jar, flickering with the light wind. "He's not buried here."

This merited a glance in my direction. Although I merely pointed out a fact, I had come across as insensitive.

"Listen, Gray, I'm not particularly religious but I thought it important to pay my respects at the spot where his soul left his body. Do you believe in souls, or was I right and Soul Garden Investigations, the name, is just a marketing gimmick after all? Do me a favor, turn off the flashlights for a minute."

I did as instructed. Other than the candle's flame braving the cold, it got very dark. As to her question, I did believe in souls—I could see pieces of them, after all. My father had not been one for church. For a while, I went to Good Shepherd with its pointy spire on Sundays with Aunt Holly and Uncle Chad, but no longer, even though I had much to be thankful for. Perhaps I stopped because my own soul wasn't whole. I carried bits of it in my cardigan, like pocket litter.

Baker crouched to move the candle into a small hollow in the tree, a spot better protected from the wind. "I'm glad we came. I thought it would be horrible but it's actually kind of peaceful. Is that why you brought me here?"

"I wanted to see the scene of the crime."

And your reaction to it. This was a case without a body to view, nor was there a murder weapon to examine, as Paul had already sold his brother's car. I had to be certain. If anything were to draw murder's mark out—the soul stain we were just discussing—if it did live in the vicinity of my friend—surely it would be the corner of the woods where Adam drew his last breath. The beam of my flashlight swept over a landscape that was there in reality and one that wasn't, the trees of Lone Wolf Woods and the greenery of Baker's soul. A sound had broken through the winter hush—a fountain gurgled tranquilly next to her. When she said it felt peaceful, she meant it.

We made our way back to the Ford Falcon and I moved the flashlight in a slow circle. The location where Lindstrom's car broke down really couldn't have been much worse. "Baker, how long were these drives of Lindstrom's?"

"I don't know, an hour or two? I was never invited along."

Take luck out of it.

"What if—yes—what if someone followed Adam that night?"

She understood at once. "Followed him—and forced him off the road."

I took another look around, this time with fresh eyes. "The snow would've covered a second set of car tracks by morning."

"If that's what happened, they made him get out and sent him off into the woods and the storm to his death. How awful."

I kept the focus on the practical. "The killer must have stuck around to ensure Adam didn't come back—and to stage the scene. Pour water in, run the engine awhile, make it seem like the BMW broke down. According to Chef Gustafson, Adam left his car keys behind."

"Or was made to leave them." Baker stared at me. "The voice recorder, the one Adam carried around to dictate memos to Rosemary."

I'd called in an inquiry to the police station about the voice recorder but hadn't heard back yet. "You think Adam had it in his pocket and left a message behind? Named who followed him that night?— No, can't be that easy, the police would have made an arrest."

We got back into the car, Baker shivering as the engine rumbled to life. I cranked the heat all the way up, but that wasn't it.

"I got scared there for a second," she said, her eyes big. "That the engine would be dead. That we'd be stuck here, same as Adam that night."

The dark forest cramming the inside of my car mirrored the real-life one outside, closing in on my client heartbeat by heartbeat. I rarely bothered with the radio in the car, as it was permanently stuck on a Top 40 station, but I switched it on then. "Material Girl" and Madonna's voice flooded the car. I saw Baker's shoulders relax. The shadowy trees climbing the upholstery hung on for a while as we drove and then vanished.

CHAPTER TWENTY-SIX

Saturday dawned with a cool, dull sky. My watch read a quarter to nine as I pulled up at the address listed under *Moore, Rosemary L.* in the phonebook, 19 Duckwood Drive. I parked on the street and climbed the steep driveway on foot. The property had seen better days. Uneven pavers wobbled under my boots and I almost slipped a couple of times. The driveway ended at a detached garage in need of a good coat of paint. On the single-story house, shutters hung crooked, roof shingles looked worn, and gutters sagged with leaves and debris. I imagined a pair of eyes peering out from behind the closed curtains, spying on neighbors, the occupant reluctant to answer a knock.

The opposite happened. The side door between the house and garage opened and Rosemary stepped out, locking up behind her. She saw me. "What do *you* want?"

I jumped right into flattery, Jasper Jones style. I didn't like having to do it. Something for the Fig Leaf of Shame, due to be aired out at some point in the day according to the schedule. "I think we might have gotten off on the wrong foot. I've heard that you're the best person to talk to. That you're the lifeblood of Fireside Resort."

Rosemary patted a hair into place. "I'm on my way to work, but I can spare a minute."

"You're going in on a Saturday?" I asked, though I too was obviously working.

"There's a lot to do," Rosemary informed me, "before Mr. Lindstrom leaves for his honeymoon. He and Nicole are driving to Chicago."

"Right, the wedding. Are you invited?"

She gave a small sniff. "My invitation got lost in the mail, but I asked Mr. Lindstrom for another. It's the proper one, for the banquet in the resort ballroom *and* the ceremony later at the Oldehouse."

What choice did Paul have? He'd probably read the anonymous letter to his brother, perhaps even received one himself. Figuring she'd relish the chance to badmouth Baker, I hung out bait. "Were you there when Clementine and your boss—your former boss—had their big fight?"

She snapped to the lure. "Heard every word. Clementine stormed out of Mr. Lindstrom's office and slammed a plant against the wall. Dirt all over the corridor carpet. Called him names, then strode into her own office, found a cardboard box, and started packing. Ms. Bolander tried to stop her, but it was no use." Rosemary added in a confidential tone, "I heard that Clementine wrote a *card* later."

"A card? To who?"

"The janitor. To apologize for making the mess with the plant. She sent him a *box of chocolates*."

Rosemary made it sound indecent. I was a safe ear, but I had my likes and dislikes, and Rosemary was difficult to like. "Given that Clementine quit so thoughtlessly, it's a good thing you were there to help out. Especially since you had a leg injury at the time."

She didn't ask how I knew. "These things constantly happen to me. Bad luck—I'm a magnet for it. Twisted my ankle on New Year's Day, right there." She gestured to where standing water had done its damage between the house and the garage. The brick pavers were worn and sunken in, their edges sticking up at odd angles, the injury less the result of the claimed bad luck and more of an accident waiting to happen. "I'm getting to the age where it takes a while for things to heal. At least it was my left ankle and I could still drive in to work—and attend Mr. Lindstrom's party. I spent the evening in my seat, watching others enjoy themselves. I had to appeal to Todd to bring me a plate from the buffet."

"Not the whole evening," I reminded her. "You went back out to your car."

"Well, yes," she admitted. "As it happens, I forgot my purse on the passenger seat when I moved the car closer to the restaurant after finishing up work for the day. I had my pain medication in there and I needed it. I wasn't about to interrupt anyone else's enjoyment, so I hobbled out to get the purse after Mr. Lindstrom's speech. You want me to say that I made it up, seeing Clementine Baker's car. Well, I didn't. It's very recognizable. A Honda Civic hatchback, blue, with a rusted undercarriage and taillight that hadn't been working for about a week. She pulled into a dark corner of the parking lot, right near Mr. Lindstrom's car, then waited in the shadows." An acrid odor rose from the pond that accompanied Rosemary wherever she went, tickling my nostrils unpleasantly. The Snake of Spite, with its narrowed eyes and forked tongue, had slithered out of the murky liquid.

"You saw her in the parking lot. And then?"

"Nothing. I got my purse and returned to the event. I had responsibilities—to make sure the evening ran smoothly for Mr. Lindstrom."

"I thought that was Nicole Cooper's new job. Coordinating events."

"She went home at five as usual. Imagine!"

Unasked, Rosemary launched into an accounting of every single task on her to-do list. I started to feel sympathy for her for being so overworked, the table-and-cocoa assembling themselves between us above the pond, when she added, "Clementine... I knew from day one that she didn't belong at Fireside. Everyone saw what went on between her and Mr. Lindstrom. Very unprofessional of her."

"And him, surely?"

Rosemary took a step back. The pond's cloudy water seeped into the cracks between the patio pavers, the snake gliding in a tight circle under the surface. "I don't speak ill of the dead."

I offered faux commiseration on her favorite grievance. "Adam should never have hired Clementine. The position of event coordinator should have gone to you."

Beady eyes, rather like the snake's, met mine. "I deserved it."

"You were passed over once. Then it happened again—that very day, in fact. Clementine quit and Nicole was asked to step in. That must have been a gut punch. Did you blame your boss?"

I'd pushed too far. "It was Linda Bolander's call... Now if that's all, I really must go."

As she opened the garage door, I stuck the copy of the anonymous letter under her nose. "Did you write this?"

She glanced at it—too briefly. "Never seen it before. Looks like a vulgar note."

"According to this, Adam had secrets. His mistress, or something more?"

"I wouldn't know anything about that."

The air above the pond stayed clear, but penners of anonymous letters tended to be practiced, habitual liars. "Let me ask you this, then. Adam talked to his brother up in Duluth. Did you happen to overhear their conversation?"

"I did not."

"Did he record a memo to you that night as he drove around?"

"No idea. You'll have to ask the police."

I was pretty sure she'd just lied to me three times in a row, but none of my questions had elicited fog. My superpower of people confiding in me had met its match in Rosemary. I made a final try.

"Adam helped you to your car at the end of the night, didn't he? Happen to see anyone trail his car out of the parking lot?"

She considered her response. "And if I did? What's it worth to you?"

"You don't believe in justice?"

"Justice? I think that's a made-up word, paper thin. Nothing's fair in this life and if you think it is, you're a fool."

"Since you asked what the information is worth, how about a set of pearls, a memento of your old boss? He chose them for Clementine as a Christmas present. You may have read about it in *The Bee*."

She laughed. It wasn't a pleasant laugh. "He didn't choose them, *I* did. It was my job to buy gifts for the staff. For *her*, Mr. Lindstrom said money's no object."

"I'll bring them to the resort," I offered.

Would she take the victory over Baker? Apparently yes, but there was a condition.

"Not the resort. Dinner—somewhere else."

I suggested the Home Plate Diner. Too cheap. We settled on The Clubhouse Grill and she climbed into the garaged car, dragging the stagnant pond in with her like a soggy security blanket. I headed back down the wobbly pavers.

CHAPTER TWENTY-SEVEN

Chief Gustafson owed me an explanation, I felt.

We'd met up on the YMCA basketball court, same as every Saturday afternoon. No running involved; we took turns from the free throw line on one end of the court. Chief Gustafson, in shorts and T-shirt, was warming up and, as he'd arrived first, got to take the first shot. He made three in a row before I sent a mild rebuke his way. "You let me waste time on Lindstrom's parking spot at the resort and the window of opportunity. Neither matters, as it turns out, right? Someone followed him that night, didn't they?"

The chief twitched and the ball bounced off the backboard. He glanced at the dad and three kids tossing the ball around at the other end of the court. "For the love of Pete, lower your voice, Rod... And let me remind you that I don't work for you."

That second part may have been said gruffly, and also not for the first time, but there was no anger behind it. Once, back when I was still a rookie PI, after I'd barged into the police station yet again, I'd asked the chief why he didn't just toss me out on my ear instead of doing what he usually did: drop a quiet tip here, run a name plate there, or leave a file open on his desk and step out for coffee. Crossing his arms, the chief had taken his time answering. "I'll tell you why, Rod. One, living in a small town means we look out for each other. If a neighbor is elderly, you shovel their driveway. If a house a block over gets damaged in a storm, you pitch in to clean up the mess. It's what I like about Two Lakes and I want to do my part to keep it that way... And two, I knew your father. I was a deputy back then. We used to shoot baskets behind Town Hall during our lunch hour."

He'd invited me to continue that tradition at the YMCA that had been built in the meantime, but made sure to say, "You're not him, Rod." He was not talking about basketball, but embezzlement.

The hand is steady when a stone heart guides it. I took my shot, then another, and kept going. I missed the sixth on purpose and tossed Chief Gustafson the ball, along with a quieter, "The killer forced Lindstrom off the road—or pretended they had a flat tire and he stopped to help. Either way, they probably pointed a gun at him and sent him into the woods."

"I wondered when you'd get there." The chief missed, grumbled, and bounced the ball back to me.

I readied the ball and then it all went wrong.

Saturday meant another kind of practice. Given that Envy & Embarrassment—I like to call it E&E—is a stone best taken out under controlled conditions, not at a dinner date with a potential source of important information, I'd emptied it on my way into the gym, by eyeing the muscular physique of the front-desk attendant, knowing I'd never be *that* fit, even if I had an interest in exercising three hours each day, which I don't. With the double strand back in my soul, I had no idea which *E* the rest of the practice session would swing toward, the fig leaf or the Gnome of Envy.

The fig leaf is probably obvious, but as to why it's not Shakespeare's green-eyed monster that resides in Envy's stone... Shane asked me about it once, when he saw the sketch of the gnome in my notebook. "It's from the yard of my next-door neighbors,

Sven and Debbie. One of their decorative ceramics," I'd explained. "A rosy-cheeked gnome about a foot high."

"You covet a garden gnome, boss?"

"There's something about it, not sure what... Did I mention that their wedding date is painted in chunky red letters on the gnome's shoe? Debbie's been refreshing the paint for forty years."

"I get it, boss. The date represents a history, two people who've seen each other at their best and worst and still chose to stay."

He wasn't wrong. For someone used to chasing lies and secrets (and who has quite of a few of his own) that kind of real, lasting connection feels out of reach, almost a fairytale. Well, if the small, pointy-hatted creature was anything to judge by, exactly like a fairytale.

Wink. The gnome perched under the backboard. I was envious of the chief's ability to take a shortcut—by relying on gut feeling. I missed and told him, "You had a hunch about there being another car."

"What I had was Lindstrom, dead. Now, I believe in fortune, good and bad, but the BMW sputtering to a halt right by a convenient pull-off far from civilization? No, siree."

He made a couple of baskets and then it was my turn again. E&E wasn't done with me yet. A group of teen girls in leotards, legwarmers and headbands had noticed me and the cardigan I'd kept on over the T-shirt and shorts (in accordance with my motto: *You never know when you might need your life saved.*) Loud giggles floated over. The fig leaf did its thing, I looked down to check how much of me had been rendered naked even though I knew the effect was for my eyes only, and—*thwack*. I missed so badly that the ball hit the gym wall behind the backboard.

My cheeks flamed. Cheered up by my spectacular miss, the chief willingly answered when I brought up the voice recorder. "Lindstrom left it in the glove compartment. Panasonic, micro-cassette."

"Anything on it?"

He made a clean basket. "The cassette was new, blank. No memos, nothing."

"Someone exchanged the tape?"

"Could be—or Lindstrom didn't record anything that night."

After the game, we went to the juice bar, a new feature at the Y that had the locals raising their eyebrows. With the Rodent of Disgust, with its short tail, perching on one shoulder, the chief sipped a bright green smoothie. "When Erin Lindstrom rang the station that morning, Sergeant Mendez responded by calling in the cavalry—the right call, but it meant that by the time I made it over—I'd gone to check on a fallen power line and we had a barn roof collapse too—well, there were vehicles all over the place. Police cars, an ambulance, Mike Nowak's tow truck, Erin's car— she'd driven herself and Tiffany over. A reporter from *The Bee* had parked behind the ambulance. I sent him packing. Tire tracks everywhere in the snow, road and shoulder. No way to be sure if there had been a second car. I'll say this, though, Rod. A detail bothered me the moment I got there: the car keys."

"Right. You said Lindstrom left them behind for Mike Nowak."

"Maybe, maybe not. They had an attachment, one of those mini-flashlights." The chief held invisible keys in the air, as if seeing them with me. "Not a strong light, but better than nothing if you're gonna be messing about in the woods."

"The killer needed the keys to run the engine, having added water to the gas." About to take a sip of my bottled water, I didn't. "They must have stuck around for a while to make sure Lindstrom didn't return, then took off in their own car. Even if Lindstrom managed to get back to the BMW, it was unlikely to start up."

"If that's what happened, well, there's killing and then there's killing—and this was the heartless kind." We were no longer dealing with a murder committed in a wishy-washy manner. The chief took another unhappy sip of the smoothie. "Rod, I gotta ask. Does Clementine Baker own a weapon?"

"I have no idea."

"Might be worth finding out. She may be guilty, you know."

I had been about to shake E&E off, its hour being up, when an impulse stayed my hand. It's my belief that the desire to chase the odds, to flirt with chance, has Envy at its root and that the gnome was restless and eager to find a target. It's the only way I can explain why I responded with, "Care to bet on it?"

"Rod, we've never bet on a case."

"I'm willing to wager on this one…if you tell me one thing. When you said you found nothing in Lindstrom's BMW, you didn't mean just the blank tape, did you? *Something* went missing, something that should have been there."

"Thought you'd have noticed by now."

I defended myself for being a step behind. "It's not as if I have access to an itemized list of contents of the victim's vehicle like you do."

Chief Gustafson pushed the remainder of his smoothie away, sending the rodent scurrying away, and ran a hand through his graying hair. I pictured my father doing the same somewhere out there, the years having caught up with him, too. "Rod… Cases where you know the client personally, it messes with your objectivity. Still interested in that bet?"

"Yes—but not for money." I thought back to the onslaught of gargoyles in the dining room of The Cork. "When I prove Baker's innocence, Chief, you make sure *The Bee* runs a front-page article about it."

"And if I have to arrest her and send the case over to the district attorney?"

"Not gonna happen."

"That certain, huh? How about if your Clementine did do it, you go back to calling me Gus. To show there are no hard feelings."

"Because you'll have sent my childhood friend to prison?"

"That…and for being unable to find out who attacked you, Rod, back then."

I twisted and untwisted the water bottle. I wasn't sure what to say. The truth was that I'd moved on years ago—with Hunger and Anger dormant in my pocket, I wasn't driven to either revenge or justice, though I could hardly explain that to the chief. Owen Gustafson is a man of rules. I'd admit to being stabbed in the back, dying, being brought back to life by a meteorite I found as a child. Oh, and I now had the ability to see, touch, hear, and smell other people's emotions. And the chief—if he believed me, that is —would reach for the nearest phone and a black van would whisk me away to a windowless room somewhere to be poked and studied. *Rather not be poked and studied.*

The fig leaf on my person covered not much at all. I'd spent five years lying to this good man and felt no small amount of shame.

"Deal," I said. "This goes south, I'll go back to calling you Chief Gus."

"By the way, your face looks a little odd."

"Tooth trouble. I'll deal with it when this case is over."

I checked my watch, finished off the water in one go, and rose to my feet, prompting the chief to ask, "Got a hot date to get to, Rod?"

"Just a business transaction to take care of."

CHAPTER TWENTY-EIGHT

I followed County Road 9 into Lost Wolf Woods, past the pull-off that Baker and I had investigated not twenty hours earlier, and made a right onto a side road that dead-ended at a wide parking lot. Enclosed in a compact weather shelter, a few steps away from the spot I pulled into, stood a payphone—the one Lindstrom had likely been trying to reach. A somber thought.

Jewelry box in hand, I got out of the Ford Falcon.

The half of the clubhouse that served as a rental place for sporting equipment was dark; soft lighting illuminated the restaurant, an inviting hum of laughter and clinking glasses greeting me. I'd been concerned that it would be difficult to get a last-minute reservation, but Shane had come through via his friend Barb, the hostess at The Clubhouse Grill.

He'd also told me firmly, "Boss? For Rosemary, no cardigan and jeans. Or corduroy pants. Suit and tie is what you want. Oh, and boss? Order wine for the table. Water won't do."

Since all it did was impair my coordination and judgment without giving me a buzz, I usually tended not to bother with alcohol.

And so I shook off E&E and transferred the pile of stones into one of the suits from the back of my closet—the stones were a little cramped in its pocket—and stopped by Baker's house on the way to take custody of the pearls.

Barb led me to a table for two by the restaurant's kitchen, whispering, "Best I could do on short notice."

I thanked her and, while I waited for Rosemary like a hopeful suitor, peeked into the box. Shiny pearls, linked by a nylon cord, sat on soft black velvet. They reminded me of the row of awards in Todd West's office, the ones carrying Adam Lindstrom's name. Maybe Lindstrom's awards had slid onto their shelf, one after another, due to long hours at his desk combined with the good fortune of being born into a prominent family in a small town and inheriting a successful business. Or did, as I suspected, a secret hide behind the row of awards, something that led to Lindstrom's car being tailed on a frigid February night?

Rosemary had the goods, I was sure of it. If a secret existed, she knew what it was. And she had seen—I was pretty certain of this as well—the face of the person who followed her boss as the winter storm descended on Two Lakes.

Moreover, I'd arrived at the conclusion without Gut Feeling or any of the messy, chaotic flora, fauna, and weather in my pocket. Had it been Joy's day, I'd probably have pumped up a triumphant fist in celebration, there at the table for two by the busy kitchen. As it was, I tossed Ike to decide on a bottle of white or red for the table and sipped the tasteless liquid, waiting for the empty chair across from me to welcome my dining companion for the evening.

CHAPTER TWENTY-NINE

The insistent ringing of the phone woke me out of a dreamless sleep. My bedside clock said seven-oh-five. On a Sunday. Something was wrong. I didn't need a gut feeling to tell me that.

Last night, I'd waited for Rosemary. And waited. When it neared nine, I stepped out of the restaurant—having consumed two glasses of wine on an empty stomach—to the payphone and called her house, then, with the aid of directory assistance, tried Paul Lindstrom's office. No answer at either place. Figuring the lure of the pearls had not proven to be enough, I paid the bill for the wine and drove home without incident.

Shane sounded rattled over the phone. "Another death, boss. It's bad."

What he told me—few details, only rumors traveling through the town grapevine—sent me tumbling out of bed. I threw on clothes and rushed out past the jewelry box on my kitchen table, where I'd left it last night.

A single thought gripped me as I drove now, my vision blurry from the early wake-up call, the morning sun too bright in a cloudless sky. When the secretary privy to the private affairs of the Lindstrom brothers failed to appear for her dinner date with me I should've done more than shrug and go home. Should have informed the police. Should have gone to her house.

Vehicles with flashing lights lined the driveway and spilled onto Duckwood Drive. I parked just past number nineteen and walked back, my step heavy. Officer Lewis lifted up yellow tape to let me through and nodded up. Keeping to the snow-covered lawn, I followed the slope up to the patio between the garage and the house. A crumpled form covered with a blanket lay on the paver bricks. Next to the body, a velvet purse with beadwork around its edges had spilled open, sending its contents—stamped utility bills, hairpins, loose change—across the pavers.

Dr. Wu stood by supervising the transfer of what was under the blanket onto a gurney. She shook her head at no one in partic-ular. "Sad business." As the emergency responders lifted the body, a thin hand slipped out from under the blanket, exposing the faux-leather band of Rosemary's wristwatch. The procession care-fully navigated the driveway downhill toward the back end of an ambulance.

Chief Gustafson met me on the front steps of the house. "Rod."

"How did it happen?"

"Well, now. Looks like she slipped and hit her head. Bled out. We got a call from Josh Kalinsky, the teenager who delivers the newspapers for this block. Apparently Rosemary complained if her paper was left at the bottom of the driveway, so Josh got off his bike and climbed the driveway, same as he does every morning. Otherwise it might have been hours before anyone spotted her. She lived alone, and see there?"—the chief pointed—"those bushes. She wasn't visible from the street."

"What time?"

"What time what?"

I made the wrong decision. "When did she slip and fall?"

"Dr. Wu thinks she lay there all night... Rod, what's the matter?" He listened to what I had to say and rightfully demanded, his words accompanied by the rumble of thunder only I could hear, "For the love of Pete, you didn't bother checking on her when she failed to show up at the restaurant?"

My response sounded weak even to my own ears. "I concluded that she changed her mind about meeting up with me. That she was screening calls, wanted to be left alone."

That pond. I'd tossed Ike to decide on red wine or white at The Clubhouse Grill, but not for what to do when an hour passed and Rosemary's chair stayed empty. She's playing games, I'd deduced. In the morning I'd get a call asking for money in addition to the pearls, because she felt the world owed her that.

"Judging by the heeled boots, nice dress, and her best coat," the chief said evenly, "she was on her way out. To dinner with you, apparently."

"Chief... Rosemary died before she could tell me what she knew."

Gustafson scratched the back of his neck. "Yup. I don't like it, Rod."

The ambulance left and Dr. Wu came back up, slipping latex gloves off, the Windmill of Efficiency spinning silently as she squatted to peer at a paver that stuck up at an angle. A thin, darkish stain had spread across it, like crimson paint diluted by winter slush. Only it wasn't paint. "Most likely Ms. Moore got a heel caught, or stepped on a slick spot," Dr. Wu said. "Probably the second, as I would think a caught heel would send you pitching forward. She fell backwards and hit her head, hard. See the edge of that paver, how sharp it is? Just bad luck."

"What if it wasn't?" There it was again, the word. "Bad luck."

"You want an alternative scenario?" Dr. Wu considered this. "I suppose it's possible Ms. Moore argued with another individual, got shoved, and the individual panicked when they saw all the blood and took off, leaving her there."

The chief clarified. "Could she have been hit on purpose? And the scene staged?"

It wasn't the kind of question that got asked in Aurboda

County often and Dr. Wu frowned at us. "I did note some movement—you can see how the blood is smudged—right there—though the coat of ice softening with the sunrise this morning didn't help matters. My assumption was that Rosemary made an effort to reach the door, dragged herself along the ground before succumbing. But," she gave us another frank glance, "if that's where we are, yes, someone could have staged things, certainly. I'll know more in a day or two."

After Dr. Wu left, Gustafson nodded at me. "Come inside, Rod, something you need to see."

"Give me a second, Chief."

I hurried down in a half-slide after the coroner. Once I caught my breath, I asked, "If she had been found immediately—if she hadn't lain there all night—could her life have been saved?"

Dr. Wu dropped her bag on the driver seat of the white station wagon and studied me, arm draped over the car door. Sunlight reflected blindingly from the side mirror, its cheeriness at odds with the situation. "Head trauma and blood loss are tricky. If help had gotten to her in minutes—perhaps. Anything longer than that..." She shook her head.

Dr. Wu's words didn't let me off the hook, nor did the fact that the wine might have dulled my thinking. Maybe I wouldn't have arrived in time to save Rosemary's life. But I could have saved her from having to lie there alone all night. "Dr. Wu, if this was no accident... What should I look for?"

"You mean behavior wise?" She shifted her bag to the passenger seat and got in. "I'm no expert, not in that side of criminology. Flesh and bone speak to me, a silent conversation. But it seems to me that it can't be easy to kill a person, can it? Because if it was, then it's evil you're looking for, Mr. Gray."

I climbed the driveway again past the yellow tape and Officer Lewis. Inside, the house overflowed with things. Wall-to-wall beige carpet. Bulky furniture. Embroidered pillows and cutesy, farm-themed decorations—a cowbell, a horseshoe, a ceramic hen nestled in straw. Few framed photos, all of them of older family members. A stack of library books, romances mostly, sat on a table by the afghan-draped rocking chair near the front windows.

I found Chief Gustafson in the kitchen, where Officer Anderson stood guard next to the table. Its wooden surface held two things: a napkin-holder shaped like a dog in overalls, and a letter. Soggy, stained pink, and opened.

"Look, but don't touch, Rod," the chief instructed me. "We rescued it from a puddle. Rosemary's purse must have come unclasped when she slipped—or when someone knocked her down. Nothing missing as far as we can tell. Wallet's there and all the other purse whatnots. A few bills had slipped out, and this letter. Rosemary hadn't sealed it yet or the puddle loosened the glue. Or the killer—if there was one—opened it and read it."

The typed-up envelope was addressed to Clementine Baker, 23B Sycamore Drive, Two Lakes, its stamp untouched by a trip through the post office. No return address. The letter that had been inside had curled up around the edges as it dried, leaving a discoloration behind. Same as the one sent to the Lindstrom house, it delivered its message in text cut out of magazines and newspapers. A slew of insults and rude names—along with an accusation leveled at my childhood friend:

ADAM LINDstrOM IS dead
BECAUSE of YOU
Burn In HELL

No herbal signature in this one. Rosemary had opted for full anonymity.

A strong gale blew toward me from the storm brewing above the chief's scalp. I knew it wasn't me he was mad at, not really. "Rod, who had the information that Rosemary was about to have a sitdown with a private investigator?"

"Shane, of course…" It couldn't be helped and I continued on reluctantly, "and Clementine. But why would Clementine have left the letter behind? It all but names her as Lindstrom's killer."

"Maybe so I'd come to the same conclusion you just did. The real killer wouldn't have left incriminating evidence behind—or so we are meant to think." As Officer Anderson stood by pretending not to listen but sporting the Monocle of Curiosity in one eye, the chief sent me a look. "I keep telling you, Rod, you're too close to this case."

CHAPTER THIRTY

A road cleared and seasoned with de-icing salt curved past headstones peeking out from under a field of white. There was a service taking place in the tiny chapel and the lot was full, so I parked along the shoulder and made my way over to the cemetery office on foot. Inside, an elderly gentleman sat behind an ornate desk. The thick carpet, dark furniture, and framed watercolors gave the impression of a luxury hotel. "Hello there," he greeted me. "I'm Caleb. Here for the service for Mr. Oldman? Interested in buying a plot for yourself? Or come to visit one of our residents?"

"Adam Lindstrom."

"Oh ya, Lindstrom, the son? Sure thing. Take that path there —" A bony finger angled toward a broad window overlooking the expanse holding Caleb's charges. "—over to row eighteen. First four plots, those're the Lindstroms. Flowers? We got full bouquets, but single yellow roses, they're real popular too."

Behind him, vases lined the shoulder-height shelf. I'd taken them to be office decoration. No matter. None of the flowers matched what resided in the Sorrow stone. I thanked Caleb and, as attendees of the service for Mr. Oldman spilled out of the chapel, followed the footpath to row eighteen, where I found a wooden cross, a more durable headstone awaiting the spring melt-off. *Adam Thomas Lindstrom, February 24, 1945 — February 23, 1985*. Next to it, a headstone read *Frederick Matthew Lindstrom, January 2, 1922 — November 21, 1977*. Father and son, both taken before their time, one by a heart attack, the other by a blizzard a single day before his fortieth birthday. Snow had been cleared off the graves by bootprints smaller than mine; the visitor had left hand-painted ceramic tiles against the grave markers, their explosion of color suggesting a celebration of life rather than the burden of grief.

As if I'd planned it that way, for Rosemary to die on schedule, Sunday was my usual day for sitting with Sorrow for thirty to sixty minutes. Well, rarely more than thirty—plus I tended to cheat. Aimed for places where there's not much to be sad about: The grocery store. An early morning showing of a comedy at the movie theater at the Ostford mall. During a bracing morning walk to Loon Lake beach and its dock.

A willow tree drooped its branches over the Lindstrom graves. I took out Sorrow and balanced the stone in my palm. The miniature willow inside it matched the real-life ones dotting the cemetery. I'd driven past the cemetery often enough and had seen the somber ceremonies from afar—but that wasn't why. Since my mother was lost at sea, my father hadn't arranged for a formal memorial, but there *was* a funeral I attended as a child. Clem's grandmother.

An autumn day. On the drive over from Nestling Lane, the wind had scattered yellow leaves along the side of the road. Clem and her family had packed up their station wagon and driven up from Houston, a twenty-some hour endeavor. Afterwards, at the wake at Mrs. Baker's house, it had been decided that Clem's noisy brothers should play outside while she stayed in to keep her dress clean of mud and pitch in with food serving; it was the last time young Roddy saw her, holding a lemonade tray. Later the moodiness started. I moped at breakfast. Sulked around at school. Came home to mope around the house some more. My father tried to cheer me up, but I knew Clem was never coming back.

And then, one morning a couple of weeks later: a glint of something against the sun, under the top step of the creaky wood staircase that's still there, winding its way down to the reeds of Loon Lake. Embedded in the grass lay an object unlike anything else on our lawn, one of many similar lawns in Two Lakes. Elated, I'd run to my father, cradling the rock in the crook of my arm. He had professed his amazement from the stove, where he was making Sunday pancakes. "What a find! Can you picture the rock traveling millions of miles, Rod? Passing stars, planets, moons. What it saw in all that time, what it knows?"

I rinsed my find in the kitchen sink. Translucent except for thin black lines crisscrossing it, the rock glistened against the white of the kitchen counter. It was about the size of the porcelain sugar bowl, this rock that *knew* things. I asked my father if I could keep it.

He'd nodded. "But you must promise to take good care of it."

He was gone four weeks later.

The meteorite stuck around, at first on my bedstand at 12 Nestling Lane, than at the Lund farmhouse, followed by a brief stint in my college hamper. Then on a shelf in the room I rented in St. Paul while I worked at a PI firm for the three years needed for my license. And on my desk after I returned to Two Lakes in 1977 and opened the agency.

All that time, I never wondered how it got under the backyard staircase. Had my father hidden the meteorite for me to find, an effort to cheer me up? He probably mail-ordered it. *If so, the joke's on him.* It had proved to be worth far more than the town money he'd disappeared with. *A carrier of life energy*, of all things. Bet you didn't know that, Dad.

This led to a morbid, self-centered thought as I stood in the row of graves, my fingers wrapped around the Sorrow stone. Had I not been using the cosmic rock as a paperweight—maybe it landed in our backyard of its own accord, maybe my father planted it for me to find—Gray the First and Only would have a grave of his own nearby. He'd be dead. *I'd be dead.* In a coffin, under dirt and snow. I'd never grieved for Gray the First. I'd pushed away the weight of his memories and the messiness of his emotions, only half-heartedly cooperating with Chief Gustafson's investigation and not bothering with one of my own. So I didn't have Anger or Hunger. Gray the First still deserved justice.

As did Adam and Rosemary. A malicious act on a stormy night had deprived Adam of his life—and now Rosemary had lost hers. All along, I'd been keeping my fingers crossed that the incident would turn out to be a prank. I didn't want it to be the other thing, and not only for Baker's sake.

I'd come here to remind myself to whom I owed the truth.

A dusting of snow slid down a branch. I double-tapped Sorrow. An extra willow now stood in the cemetery, sunlight vanishing in a neat circle around me. The cross with Adam's name stood before me. I hadn't known him personally but I could picture the telephone wires that had extended from his soul garden, toward Erin, Paul, Clementine Baker. Tiffany. And in his work circle: Conrad Urban, Linda Bolander, others.

Rosemary's garden had lacked telephone poles. The Pond of Grievances didn't allow for ground stable enough.

Should have said no to taking the case.

My hands hadn't been the ones that pushed her down, but they might as well have been.

Fighting the impulse to drop on my knees, crushed by the burden of it all, the passing of things, I stood at the silent grave and let the tears fall for Rosemary.

CHAPTER THIRTY-ONE

Shivering, I checked my watch. Almost an hour had gone by. With some effort on my part, the willow returned to its stone, leaving me puffy-eyed—but with a new growth by my side. The Redwood of Determination, a huge tree that dwarfed the few occupants of my soul garden. I would see this case through no matter what. Find Adam and Rosemary's killer.

Back at the main office, Caleb took one look at me and set about making Hershey's cocoa. While he poured steaming water from an electric kettle into a pair of paper cups, I explained that I was an old friend of Lindstrom's. Said we'd fallen out of touch. That by the time I heard about his death, the funeral had come and gone. Silver vapor swirled around my boots. In reality, Adam would have been well ahead of me in Two Lakes' school system, not to mention that given the teasing about my father, I mostly kept to myself.

Hands veined with age stirred powdered cocoa in. A faded garden, crisscrossed by well-worn paths, filled the office. Caleb passed a cup over to me, then got started on the second one. "That's how it goes sometimes. I hear it a lot. Folks lose touch, and it's nobody's fault. They show up at the funeral feeling bad about it and all."

I did feel bad, and partially responsible for Rosemary's fate. *But no longer sad*. I'd neatly packed that away. I warmed my fingers on the cup and asked Caleb if he'd worked the Lindstrom funeral.

"Haven't taken a day off in years—work, it keeps me topside." Caleb returned to his magnificent desk. A quiet creak of his own joints and a groan from the chair as he sat down. "The Lindstrom funeral, won't be forgetting *that* one anytime soon. Our winter services, they usually take place in the memorial chapel with the remains in an urn, waiting for spring interment. But the Lindstroms, they wanted a proper burial, oh ya. We brought in heaters to warm the ground, and a backhoe with frost teeth to dig it up. Catering by the folks over at Fireside Resort—hothouse flowers, candles in the chapel, quite a turnout. Outside, the wind'd give you frostbite in the blink of an eye. Everyone huddled around the heaters, watching the coffin go down."

Remembering the petite bootprints, I asked if they belonged to Erin Lindstrom.

"She's here every morning, unless the weather's real bad. Tough lady, that one. Been coming since Fred passed—must be seven years now. Brings a snow shovel in winter, or garden gloves for weeding in the warmer months. Let the crew take care of it, it's not that spendy, I've told her again and again. But she says it's her duty now and cheaper than a gym membership."

"What about the younger Mrs. Lindstrom? How often does she stop by?"

"The wife?" Caleb gave a slow shake of the head. "Hasn't been by since the funeral."

"Unusual—for a widow."

Caleb jabbed the bony finger. "Hold on now. Who'd you say you were again? You're not a journalist, are ya? Our family members don't much care for us talking to *The Bee*."

Fog swirled higher up my pants leg. "As I said, a school buddy. We did have a mutual friend—Clementine Baker."

"Baker? Oh, that's the gal they're saying did it. I remember her from the funeral—stood back there by that tree, shivering." The finger angled toward an old willow, its branches heavy with snow from the recent storm. "The other woman, folks are saying. Stayed outta sight of the family—respectful, I guess. If you ask me, she seemed sadder about the whole thing than the wife. Wouldn't have pegged her for violence, though. But if it's true what they say, well, emptying a water bottle, it's not exactly violence, is it?"

Maybe—but forcing another car off the road was. Chief Gustafson had voiced the opinion that I was too close to this case. The Redwood of Determination stood by my side like a second backbone. Being objective meant looking at Baker as a suspect first, childhood friend second. "Has she been by? Clementine."

Caleb took a sip of his cocoa. "Don't think so. The brother— Paul—he stops by on Sunday mornings to visit his father, and now Adam. Complained more than once about the shoveling and his mother having to do it. I told him about the extra fee for the crew, but he didn't wanna hear it. We got a hundred-eighty beds here. It'd take me weeks to do 'em all myself, and by then, I'd have to start over... He stopped by that day, he did. Adam."

I thought maybe old Caleb believed that Adam's ghost had attended his own funeral, looked on from the next world, but this wasn't the case. "The day he died—in the afternoon, to visit his dad. Gave my window a friendly knock, then headed down to the resting spot. Stayed for about a quarter hour. In the summer, folks tend to linger, but in winter, just making the trip is a sign of respect."

The missing forty-five minutes of Adam's day, accounted for. I finished off the lukewarm cocoa and came clean. "Listen, I lied before. I never met Adam. I'm a private investigator hired by Clementine Baker."

He nodded. "Thought it might be something like that."

"So you'll understand when I ask this. At the funeral, did anybody seem to be faking it?"

Caleb scratched his nose. "It?"

"Sorrow at Lindstrom's death."

"Ah, can't rightly say. We get folks who are dry-eyed but grieving real deep. Others empty a box of Kleenex but are already thinking about hitting the town later for a party. Snowflakes, they say no two are the same. Grief, same thing."

"And Clementine?"

"Your gal, no tears on her, oh ya, not a one."

CHAPTER THIRTY-TWO

"Is it true about Rosemary?" Baker sounded rattled, the ghostly contour of the Dark Forest of Fear surrounding her. She was on her feet, an empty to-go coffee cup on the table. Shane must have phoned her after unlocking the agency doors.

"I'm afraid so." I relayed the scant details.

No Maze of Daydreaming for Shane, not today. "An accident, boss?"

"Dr. Wu still has to give an opinion on that," I said grimly, taking off my jacket and tossing it on top of my desk before settling into my armchair, "but I consider it improbable."

Baker drove away the fear by giving into anger. She whopped the wall with an open palm. "Damn it."

"Don't damage my wall," I said mildly.

"Gray, how can you be so calm at a time like this? We schemed to get Rosemary to talk to you...and now this. I'm not going to lie, I didn't get along with Rosemary or think much of her methods, but I never wished anything of this sort on her."

"I'm mad too, Clem." Unusually for Shane, he had spun up charcoal clouds. He made the remark softly.

I took out my case notes with their list of suspects. It felt wrong to cross Rosemary's name out. In the end, I left it unmarked. "It's small comfort but this settles it once and for all—Adam Lindstrom's death was no drunken prank gone wrong."

Baker started pacing. "When you made the dinner date, what did Rosemary say to you?"

"Not much. I spoke to her for ten minutes, if that. She was on her way to work. She was evasive when I raised the question of a secret Adam may have had. Denied overhearing the conversation between Paul and his brother. I got her attention when I brought up the possibility of someone trailing Adam's BMW out of the resort's parking lot. She left me with the distinct impression that she saw who sat behind the steering wheel."

"Could she have meant Kostas, on his motorcycle?" Shane suggested.

I shook my head. "Doubt it. Kostas readily admits to being there."

"She gave no hint as to who could it have been, Gray? Not a word?"

"No. Sit down, would you?... The better question to ask is, how did the killer find out Rosemary was about to meet a PI? She and I spoke in her driveway. Not a soul within earshot."

"I didn't tell anyone, boss."

"Me neither." My client settled distractedly onto the couch, sending a pillow onto the floor.

"It's possible she mentioned this dinner of ours to a neighbor or at work, but to be honest I don't see why she would have."

Baker snorted. "Give yourself some credit, Gray. You made for an interesting gossip cookie."

"I beg your pardon? Gossip cookie?"

"Rosemary bragged in the office, to Linda Bolander or Nicole Cooper or whoever. About the fancy dinner date. And the other person laughed about it behind her back—well, not Linda. But Nicole would have, and then spread the story. The resort's a big place, but not *that* big. Things have a way of making the rounds. If Rosemary whispered into one ear, she might as well have used a bullhorn."

"And trouble followed her home... If we're right and Rosemary saw the killer's face, she kept quiet about it. Not a word to the police."

Shane supplied the word. "Blackmail?"

"If so, a dangerous game." Blackmail and extortion cases knock on the agency doors now and then, and I had formed an opinion on the matter: knowledge plus greed equals trouble. "Some people don't see it as dishonorable. The blackmailer reasons that having to pay up for years *is* a kind of punishment and if they benefit, all the better. And Rosemary, she felt the world owed her."

Baker asked, "If Rosemary got paid for her silence by the killer, why agree to meet with you?"

"Let's rewind. Rosemary sees a car following Adam's, hears the news next day, and puts two and two together. She'd witnessed a murder in progress. Then what? She makes a phone call, gives instructions in a voice disguised by a scarf? Leave a wad of cash inside a tree hollow somewhere?"

Shane blew his nose. "Letter."

Baker nodded. "I think Shane's right, a letter."

"Right, her preferred tool. She writes: I know who you are and what you did. Money to be left somewhere or other, or I'll talk. It works and she gets a nice chunk of cash. Maybe that would have been the end of it, but Chief Gustafson starts asking questions and I show up on the scene. She gets greedy—greedier. The plan is to lob a misleading morsel or two in my direction, and get a nice meal and a set of pearls for her troubles."

"Playing both sides. Tracks so far, boss."

"But—unbeknownst to Rosemary—the killer is aware of her identity. He learns about her planned rendezvous with a PI, decides Rosemary's becoming too much of a risk. She has to die. They sneak up on her, then shove or strike her down and leave her to bleed out."

A brief silence met my words. I shifted in the armchair so that I faced Baker directly. This kind of thing—knowing you're about to deliver bad news—always made Gray the First uncomfortable, but I came straight out with it. "Speaking of letters, the police found one next to the body. Rosemary's purse had come unclasped when she fell and it slipped out. It was addressed to you."

She gaped at me. "What did it say?"

"A lot of insults which I won't repeat. And also..." I didn't have a photocopy but I didn't need it. I'd never forget the final lines. I quoted them:

ADAM LINDstrOM IS dead
BECAUSE of YOU
Burn In HELL

A new visitor entered the soul garden of my childhood friend —an overflowing bucket swung into view and splashed water into Baker's face. Shock.

Shane made an attempt to reassure her. "Rosemary blamed you for capturing the attention of her employer, Clem. If that led to Adam wanting to make a big change in his life and *that* led to his death for whatever reason, well, it's not your fault."

I got up out of the armchair to look out the street-facing window. On Sundays in the off-season, the doors of the businesses along Main stayed shut and little traffic trickled by; there was, however, a police car parked right across the street. I thought I caught sight of one of Officer Anderson's ears against the glass, as if he'd succumbed to a midday nap, overtaken by the fatigue of being a new parent. "Chief Gustafson will want to verify your whereabouts yesterday evening, Baker."

She still had bucket water dripping down her face. "I had no idea I'd need an alibi, if that's what you mean. Hutch and I drove over to Ostford for our after-dinner walk."

Twenty minutes there, twenty minutes back. "Long way to go for a walk."

"If you must know, I'm starting to get looks from neighbors.

It's all those damn stories in *The Bee*. *I* don't care, but Hutch is starting to pick up on it—the stares, neighbors crossing the street when they see us. It's making him uneasy. I'm worried he'll start limping again."

"Did anyone see you in Ostford, Clem?" Shane asked.

"Doesn't matter," I interrupted before she could answer. "Even if they did, we have no way of proving you didn't make a quick stop on the way there or back—to attack Rosemary."

Baker winced. "Well, I didn't. Hutch and I parked at the mall, walked around for thirty, maybe forty minutes, then got back into the car and drove straight home. After which we crashed in front of the fireplace, Hutch with a bone—a deer antler, to be specific —and me with a book. Agatha Christie, *Death on the Nile*. Picked it up from the library the other day. I have all this free time now that I'm out of a job so I thought, why not immerse myself in mysteries? Might pick up some pointers from Poirot and Miss Marple... That's not very helpful for proving my innocence, is it? You said the letter fell out of Rosemary's purse? Too bad there wasn't a second letter—addressed to the *real* murderer—for the police to find."

I sat back down. "By the way, I still have your pearls, Baker. They're back at the house. I can drop them off later."

She shook her head. "No, I don't want them... You know what? I'll give them to Adam's mother. Maybe he and I didn't work out, but he did choose the gift."

Shane shook his head at me, but I'd had seen enough fog lately. "He didn't. According to Rosemary, it was the assistant's job to buy gifts."

Baker recovered quickly. "Erin might want them anyway. The pearls are proof that her son lived and loved and did foolish things once in a while."

"Don't we all," Shane said.

And then it materialized, simple as that. A creature swung into view, its long arms wrapped around my client's neck. A ring-tailed lemur. Perky-eared, it's not a monkey or an ape but something *before* on the evolutionary tree. I'd seen one in a zoo once and it struck me as being smart without the baggage. Less thinking, more instinct. The one in my office was small, wiry, with big, orange-tinted eyes.

Gut feeling—Baker's.

She had sat up. "Just now when I said if only there was a second letter.... *What if there was?*"

Shane and I gawked at her and she got animated at our slowness to catch on. "Having announced that yes, she would like the pearls, thank you very much, Rosemary readies two letters to drop off at the post office. One is to taunt me, hurl insults in my direction for whatever faults she imagined I had. In the second letter, the one to the target of her blackmail, she assures them their secret is still safe. Don't worry about this meeting with Rodrick Gray, PI, but I'll need more money. Meanwhile—as you said, Gray—the killer has decided that Rosemary's become too much of a risk. They intercept her on her way out to the spendy dinner with you. There's an argument and the killer pushes Rosemary down. Her purse unsnaps and the pair of letters slide out. The killer reads them and understands their mistake—Rosemary wasn't going to talk. But it's too late. They pocket the letter and disappear into the evening, leaving Rosemary to bleed out and the letter addressed to me behind."

I held up a hand. "Hang on. There's no evidence of a second letter. We don't even have proof of blackmail. I can loop in Chief Gustafson, but it'll take time for the police to check Rosemary's bank account for any unusual deposits. Not to mention that Dr. Wu hasn't even ruled the death a homicide yet."

The lemur bounced onto the filing cabinet and commenced sunbathing in a sitting yoga pose, arms stretched out to the side, face turned upwards, knees bent outward. "Look, I was right about Adam, wasn't I? This feels similar—call it a strong hunch, if you like."

"Kinda makes sense, boss." Shane gave a slow nod. "That

Rosemary would ask for more money for having to lie to you, as well as the police."

"We should go to Rosemary's house." Baker got up, energized, an adrenaline push. A windmill spun on her back. "Rummage through her recycling for the newspapers and magazines she used to make the letters. Are the police still at her house, do you think?"

"The house," I said, "is not where we need to go."

The envelopes of the two letters I'd seen—the herbal-signature one sent to Lindstrom and the one in Rosemary's purse—had been typed up. I didn't remember seeing a typewriter at Rosemary's residence, only on her work desk...along with a bottle of glue. I relayed all that and Baker responded with, "Office trash gets emptied at the end of each workday, then goes into the bins by the back parking lot. One of them's for paper. They get picked up on Monday mornings—tomorrow. If we're gonna do this, we gotta act fast. Not *we*. I'll go alone. I'm already in trouble. What's a little more?"

My hand went to the pocket with the Ike coin. If one considered the facts, nothing—zilch, nada, not a gosh-darned thing— pointed to the existence of a second letter. *It's how gut feeling works.* Without warning, without fanfare, there it suddenly is, the lemur. The bug-eyed creature had leaped from the filing cabinet to the open door, where it hung one-handed from the top, its legs swinging back and forth. The idea was to follow it.

If a chance existed that Rosemary could speak from beyond the grave, I owed it to her to listen.

I slid the dollar back into my pocket and took out my car keys. "We'll both go. Oh, and Baker? You have a tail." (And I didn't mean the question-marked-shaped appendage that belonged to the lemur dangling on my door.) "Take the fire escape, I'll meet you in the back alley. Shane, once we're gone, why don't you go down and offer Officer Anderson a nice cup of tea?"

CHAPTER THIRTY-THREE

Shane breathed a sigh of relief when Baker and I trudged back into the agency, dragging a large trash bag filled with printed matter. "Boss, glad you and Clem weren't arrested for trespassing."

"Me too," Baker said. "That jail cell was nasty."

Despite the broad daylight, nobody took much notice when Baker and I rummaged through the recycling bins behind the lodge, picking through flattened cardboard boxes and used-up paper towel rolls. The adjoining waste container caused Baker to complain of nausea and me to be quietly thankful that Disgust lives in my pocket next to Hunger. We didn't linger.

Officer Anderson had gone when we pulled back in underneath Soul Garden Investigations.

Having pushed the coffee table aside, we dumped the contents of the trash bags onto the floor and spread out in a circle around them, our backs against the seating elements. Brochures, irrelevant paper scraps, and intact magazines and newspapers made a growing pile to the side. Shane hummed as we worked. I'd lost track of time when Baker let out a triumphant, "Here."

She held up a magazine. The December 24 issue of *TIME* that I saw Rosemary perusing in the office. The cover touted the new gadget, the VCR (*Santa's Hottest Gift: The Magic Box That Is Creating A Video Revolution*). Inside, scissors had produced neat little windows of missing text. I laid out the options. "We could try deducing the words based on context, or make a trip to the library to photocopy the original pages. Accuracy suggests the second."

"To the library we go. If this weren't sad because of Adam and Rosemary—and carried the threat of prison time for me—it would all be very adventurous."

Shane reminded us that it being Sunday, the library was closed, then proposed a solution.

"One of the librarians—Zachary—is a friend of mine."

"Shane, you do seem to have a lot of friends," Baker commented, with a brief flare of wonder rather than envy.

"I'll give him a call and beg him to come over and unlock the door for us."

Before he could do so, the phone on my desk rang. Sergeant Mendez, looking for my client—the chief had some more questions for her. I put my hand across the receiver and lifted an eyebrow at Baker.

"I'm not hiding. I'll go in and speak to them... But perhaps I won't mention our little project here."

Shane made his call and we all bundled into the car. At the public services parking lot, Shane crossed over to the library to wait for his friend, and Baker and I entered the police station. With me hanging in the background like a fake attorney with little knowledge of the law, she gave a statement about her whereabouts the previous evening. I took the opportunity to beg the sergeant for a copy of the letter from Rosemary's purse, the anonymous one addressed to Baker.

By late afternoon, the three of us were back at work, having moved the evidence that we'd obtained in a legally dubious manner over to my kitchen table. Shane had used up a handful of coins to photocopy the relevant pages from the library's edition of the *TIME* issue. Each page in Rosemary's defaced copy was a building; when overlaid onto the photocopied original, the missing words popped up in the windows. Her weapons ordinary, printed matter and sharp scissors, Rosemary Moore had found a way to invoke emotion in the recipient—unease—despite the letter writer's departure to other shores.

Or at least, that's what I heard and saw all around Shane and Baker. Not full-blown fear—what was there to be afraid of, in my kitchen with its sunny view of Loon Lake? Just the rustling of leaves and faint silhouettes of trees at the far edges of the room.

In a mirroring of Rosemary's own actions, my own scissors led to an increasing pile of cut-out words in the middle of the table. Baker shuffled them around. "The letter she mailed to me back in the fall... What a horrible thought, that she sat an office away from me and obsessively searched for the exact phrase to let me know how much she hated me... And now this new one. She hated me even after I quit my job, even after Adam died." Baker used a finger to push aside the snippets used in the rude letter addressed to her, one by one, going off the photocopy Sergeant Mendez had provided.

This left a smaller, second pile.

Lemur for the win. The letter to Baker was likely crafted by Rosemary the day I spotted the magazine in her hands and the glue on her desk, but she must have had another go at the edition of *TIME* right after speaking to me, prompted by the offer of pearls.

Her scissors had defaced various headlines and ads. *The Postman Rings Twice*, on the price of a stamp going up to 22 cents, had yielded the word *Twice*. Adam's name had been constructed out of an *A* from a business-section headline and a *dam* from the longish article on VCRs ("Network schedules be damned...") The cigarette ads all had the Surgeon General's warning but Rosemary had chosen a bigger font, from a Chevrolet ad (*Warning: This Car Could Change Your Lifestyle.*)

Shuffling it all around led to a four-line arrangement.

Adam'S CAR
Warning: REMEMBER SAW YOU
WON'T Tell but NEED
Twice what YOU paid LAST TIME
leave in same PLACE

I leaned back in the kitchen chair. "Well, we guessed right. Rosemary saw who followed Adam that night and upped her price."

"Wait," Shane tapped a scrap, "there's a word left over."

He was right. The orphan word was *in*.

"In," I repeated. "Did we miss a page? Perhaps she added Adam's last name. *Adam Lindstrom's car.*"

Baker moved things around. "How about this?"

Warning: REMEMBER SAW YOU in Adam'S CAR
WON'T Tell but NEED
Twice what YOU paid LAST TIME
leave in same PLACE

We studied this for a beat. I spoke first. "The killer hitched a ride. There was no second car but there *was* a passenger—either by invitation or hiding in the back."

"Adam's driving along without a care in the world," Shane cut in, "and suddenly—*wham*—he feels the cold barrel of a gun against the back of his neck."

"Whoever is holding the gun instructs Lindstrom to pull to the side of the road. Sends him into the woods to his death. The killer drives off, doubles back after a good long while, dumps water in... and what, takes off on foot themselves and manages to avoid freezing to death in a blizzard?"

"A partner," Shane suggested. "Someone to pick them up."

"Right. We're looking for two people."

I saw Shane raise a fist in celebration. Rosemary had readied one letter for Baker to provoke and rattle her, the other for her blackmail target, the actual killer. If it weren't for the bottled-up feelings, I'd probably have had a similar reaction to Shane's. *Baker and the killer are not the same person.* I did catch myself exhaling deeply—and noting the data point. Baker appeared to have a dependable enough gut.

For her part, my client had gone silent. She was methodically taping the reconstructed letter onto the back of one of the photo-copied pages. "They killed her needlessly. She wasn't going to tattle."

"Blackmail—I said it before—is dangerous." I didn't add, *as Rosemary found out.*

I took out Ike and spun the dollar on the table's surface, not in decision-making but thought. The first X—on Baker's sketch, marking the spot where Adam parked his BMW that fateful night —had proved irrelevant. Sergeant Mendez had drawn another X on a map, where the police had found the body. Now we were looking for X and Y: *killer and accomplice.*

The phone rang and answered it, then held out the receiver. "It's for you, Baker. Your landlady."

"She's watching Hutch, I hope he's not being too much trou-ble..." Baker got on and listened for a minute or two. "Yes, I see. It's fine, don't worry about it, Mrs. Gibson..."

She hung up and informed us, "The police are at my house."

"Really?" I said. "They got a search warrant that fast—and on a Sunday?"

"I gave them permission. While you were chatting with Sergeant Mendez."

Shane and I exchanged a silent conversation, in that he glanced at me and I shook my head. Inviting the police in without a warrant tends to be an unwise step. I had faith in Gustafson but the legal system is far from perfect.

Baker had something to say about our attitude. "You're not getting it, you two. I have nothing to hide. I don't want to put up roadblocks. What I do want is to find out who killed Adam and

Rosemary...and my name cleared fair and square, *with* a headline in *The Bee* and all."

This echoed what I'd requested of Chief Gustafson, but I'd been the one to see the gargoyles, not Baker. "What is it, Baker? Something's happened."

Fear's forest inched closer as she gave in to the feeling. "This morning—when the news about Rosemary started circulating—a brick came flying through the living room window. Woke me up. I ran out onto the front porch and saw a car speed off."

Shane gaped at her. "Did you call the police, Clem?"

"No point. Anyway, they'll see the sheet I taped over the window. Hutch and I weren't hurt and I cleaned up the glass... But I got the message."

"From the killer?" Shane asked.

She shook her head. "That the neighbors want me gone. I recognized the car—it was a beige Buick, Lorna's—she lives across the street. She quietly came back later with groceries and pretended she didn't see me sweeping glass."

CHAPTER THIRTY-FOUR

Baker drove off to wait with her landlady while the police searched her residence and I pulled up in front of the Lund farmhouse. It was still light but I dropped Shane off at the Uff Da dance club on the way, one frequented by the resort's seasonal workers. He was going to hang around and chat about Rosemary, or as he put it, "Let's see who the gossip cookie—you inviting Paul's assistant out for dinner—might have reached, boss."

Sundays meant dinner with Aunt Holly and Uncle Chad.

The Lund farmhouse sits on a rising slope; my adoptive aunt and uncle don't do any farming but there are chickens, a couple of dogs, and apple trees. The kitchen faces west. During the second serving—I always made sure I piled my plate up, even though Hunger stayed put in its stone so I could give the people of the house my full attention—I asked Aunt Holly and Uncle Chad if they remembered Clementine Baker. "She used to spend her summers with old Mrs. Baker, next door to the Nestling Lane house."

"Of course I remember her, Roddy. Pretty girl. Somewhat of a handful for her grandmother. More mashed potatoes?" Aunt Holly nudged a bowl my way. The news of Rosemary's death had added fuel to the rumors flying around, but my adoptive aunt's opinion on Baker had been formed years ago. "This murder business, I don't believe it of her but then again, you never know, do you? I always believed she'd become a writer. Not a journalist—a novelist, I mean. She liked to spin stories, even as a child. There was this one time, Roddy, when your father hosted a barbeque—Dusty had plenty of friends—my sister, Ingrid, was there and a whole lot of others. It was late August, the first nice day after a string of them so humid you could hardly breathe. Old Mrs. Baker, even though she rarely left her house, came out to sit with us in the backyard. You and Clementine were expected to be on your best behavior while we adults attended to the grill and chatted."

"Never worked," Uncle Chad, who kept his commentary short during meals, broke in. "You kids found grownup conversation boring."

"You'd turned ten a few days earlier, Roddy, or was it eleven, do you remember, Chad?" Aunt Holly went on without waiting for a response. "There we were cutting up watermelon and suddenly you and Clementine were nowhere to be found. We checked inside and started to get worried, when up the lake stairs you came, soaked and muddy to the bone, your clothes a mess. Can you pass the peas, Chad?... Clementine burst into tears and relayed a tale that almost had us calling the police. A long-haired man had pulled the pair of you kids into a canoe and you managed to free yourselves and dive into the lake and swim back to shore. A kidnapper! You only just made it out alive, she wailed. It really was very convincing."

"How did you figure out she wasn't telling the truth?" I asked.

Aunt Holly gave a deep-throated laugh, sending balloons to the ceiling. "You were staring at her as wide-eyed as we adults were, except for old Mrs. Baker, who was unbothered. I had an inkling that Clementine wasn't protecting herself, she didn't want you getting in trouble."

Uncle Chad splashed a second serving of gravy onto his mashed potatoes. "I always liked her for that."

"Well, your father thought some kind of punishment should be involved and so, once you dried off, you and Clem had to do the dishes. Afterwards you played the piano for us, Roddy."

I'd forgotten that day. Clem had declared that we were treasure hunters. We poked around the lake beach and accumulated pennies, a rusted-out fish bucket, a discarded toy shovel. Clem announced whoever dove in the water first got to keep the treasures. I won. It wasn't a trick—she jumped in, too.

I'd also forgotten the piano playing—and the associated emotion. "I never liked the performing part, everyone staring at me."

"Is that why you gave it up after your father left? I've been hoping we'd get to hear you play again, Roddy, now that you're back at Nestling Lane."

The piano had come with the Nestling Lane house when my father purchased it and survived the intervening years in the same corner during house ownership by another family. Nowadays its lid stayed shut and dusty.

I'd never posed the question to my adoptive aunt and uncle: *Did they suspect my father of being a conman?* There was no need. No one had suspected.

After Uncle Chad left the dining table to get the fireplace going and turn on the TV, Aunt Holly scooted a plate of brownies closer to me. "What's she like nowadays?"

"Clementine? A bit lost, I think. Looking for purpose."

"I won't be nosy, Roddy, other than to ask what made you change your mind and take a murder case."

"She said I owed her."

Aunt Holly tsk-ed. "For being your childhood friend? That's a little manipulative."

"Not like that," I defended Baker. "She and I, we made a pact twenty years ago—that we'd be knights, side by side, watching each other's back forever. We signed a piece of paper and everything. She meant that I owed her not to forget that pact. That it represented a life contract of sorts."

"If you ask me, it still seems presumptuous of her to cannon-ball into your life like that. But maybe she was desperate, with the police knocking on her door."

Had the police had finished searching Baker's house? *What are they looking for?* Gray the First would have probably had it all figured out by now.

"Aunt Holly, remember that intruder in my office five years ago? Was I different before?"

Aunt Holly rarely minced words. "Sure were. You're calmer nowadays. I'm not saying you used to have a temper or nursed grudges, Roddy. But sometimes a thing grabbed hold of you and you pursued it, whatever it took, to the end. Not that you give up more easily these days. You're just less intense about it. What's wrong with your face, Roddy? Your cheek looks puffy."

"Tooth." I'd made an effort to chew on the other side. "I'm hoping it clears up on its own."

"You should get it looked at. No sense putting it off."

"I will," I promised. "Once this case is over."

"Show's starting," Uncle Chad called over from the living room.

Aunt Holly settled onto the couch next to Uncle Chad and I took the rocking chair, what was left of the brownies on the coffee table between us. As *Murder, She Wrote* got going, it struck me that it really was too bad that soul gardens don't show through TV screens, as one of the actors might have successfully channeled murder's mark and I'd know what it looked like. As to the other thing, about me having changed, Aunt Holly didn't have it quite right. Maybe my goal of helping all of Two Lakes wasn't the burning kind but it still framed my life, this purpose of the mind rather than the heart. *Sweat only, no blood or tears.*

After the show ended, I rolled up my sleeves to do the dishes, same as I'd done two decades ago as punishment. Usually my socked feet sank into pillow-like earth when I visited this kitchen

—this was a place where people loved me—but today I encountered pebbles, ones of my own making. Rosemary's death had left me unsure, full of doubt. I shifted my weight from one foot to the other as I scrubbed dishes with more force than necessary. Clementine liked to spin stories, Aunt Holly had said.

What if she's still doing it, spinning stories?

CHAPTER THIRTY-FIVE

I read Monday's *Bee* over breakfast. Baker was still asleep.

A couple of minutes before eleven, an hour after I got back from the Sunday farmhouse dinner, she'd knocked on my front door, Hutch tagging along. She carried a dog bed under one arm. "Gray, I feel strange about spending the night at a house that's been searched by strangers—and had a brick thrown at it. Plus it's chilly because of the broken window. I've already imposed on Mrs. Gibson enough. Do you mind if Hutch and I crash on your couch? If it'd be awkward, you can say no."

The awkwardness was on her side—literally. A tightly pruned topiary creature accompanied her like a second pet. Unlike Hutch, who fidgeted on his leash, the Snail of Awkwardness stood rigid, its leafy antennae sticking up above its perfectly manicured coiled shell. It sat by an oddly tilted path—the *feeling strange* Baker had mentioned.

"Why would it be awkward? You and Hutch can have the bedroom," I offered. "I'll take the couch."

As Hutch sniffed around my place, Baker did the same, treading the thirty-year-old floorboards with socked feet. She walked into the bedroom, where I'd begun exchanging the bed linens for fresh ones, and stopped at a framed photo of my father and me, but didn't comment on it. After I gave her a spare set of pajamas and she helped Hutch onto his bed in a corner and hit the shower, I settled onto the living-room couch for the night. The Underfoot Pebbles of Doubt had followed me over from the Lund farmhouse and morphed into pebbles inside the couch cushions. I found it hard to get comfortable and ended up lying awake, staring at the ceiling and replaying recent events.

Baker's gut feeling, specifically. The Bucket of Cold Water that preceded the lemur had been real enough—and had two competing explanations. If she wasn't guilty, the malice Rosemary had felt toward her had shocked her. If she *was* guilty, she didn't anticipate that the police would find a letter blaming her for Adam's death.

I let the second scenario play out in my mind. Rosemary Moore gets one payment out of Baker—who tells Shane and me that she's low on funds. Rosemary plans to ask for another payment maybe in a month or two, and in a meantime readies a rude letter, a reminder of the goods she holds over my client. But the situation changes. The police are involved, and so am I. Rosemary pens a demand for another payment and readies to mail it.

Except, one way or another, Baker has discovered her blackmailer's identity. She attacks Rosemary, either pushes her down or strikes her on the back of the head with a rock or something similarly heavy. The purse falls open, a stack of envelopes slips out, all bills at first glance except what's on top. Baker wets the envelope in snow and opens it, careful not to tear it. Reads it with the flashlight she must have brought along and concludes that getting rid of Adam's secretary had been the right thing. The blackmail was never going to end. It's dark and she's in a hurry to leave. She misses the other letter addressed to her, one that Rosemary had prepared before things changed.

The police find it and I tell my client about it. And so the shock. *She'd pocketed one letter*, not realizing there were two. Bucket water dripping down her features, she decides to act fast. The police are likely to poke around and she knows Rosemary discards magazines in the resort recycling. Better for me—a friend —to find the evidence. And so the lemur, impatient to get going. A hunch that *pretending to have a hunch* about a second letter she knows for sure exists is the way to go. I'd see it as proof of her innocence.

And it had worked.

I flopped the other way on the couch. *Or everything's as it seems.* My childhood friend had committed no crimes and if I didn't manage to prove it, she'd be going to prison for a long time, perhaps the rest of her life.

Guilty or innocent. I gave up on trying to sleep, turned on a side lamp, and spun Ike. Heads, innocent; tails, guilty.

Heads.

A coin's opinion meant nothing, except that it meant something. I had an irrational trust in Ike.

I moved to the window. A police car lurked up the street, its lights off. It hit me then, as I stared out at the slumbering houses, that someone else out there might be awake. The person who had, with the aid of an accomplice, taken two lives. Eyes kept open by fear of being found out.

Worse: if the killer slumbered peacefully, having gotten what they wanted—two people out of the way and a scapegoat in the form of one Clementine Baker.

It wasn't a restful night. Dark shadows morphed the familiar furniture of my living room into a sinister lair, as if murder's mark had followed me home. I finally managed to drift off for a couple of hours.

I got up before Baker and Hutch, and fetched *The Bee* from the bottom of the driveway. I crunched cereal and read the front-page story on Rosemary Moore's death, referred to as an unfortunate accident. Few details were provided, though the paper made sure to remind residents to employ road salt on their property.

A second article, byline Jasper Jones, lay below the fold. Breaking news he must have managed to get in right under the go-to-press deadline.

POLICE FIND EVIDENCE

Investigators from the Two Lakes police department were spotted yesterday afternoon searching one side of a duplex on Sycamore Drive, the space currently rented by Clementine Baker, the main person of interest in the untimely death of Adam Lindstrom.

Neighbors report that the police carried out a paper bag and took it away with them. Chief Owen Gustafson and his officers refused to comment on what evidence the bag held.

A suggestion has been made that Adam Lindstrom hid more than a mistress. This reporter has found no confirmation of this as of yet. When asked about the possibility, Paul Lindstrom responded with outrage at what he described as an attempt to smear the name of his older brother, who can no longer defend himself...

So. Jones had downplayed the possibility of a second secret in Adam's life. As Shane would say, totally interesting... The police took something from Baker's residence. An item that fit in a paper bag. Documents? Photos? *A gun?*

I pushed aside the empty cereal bowl and popped my briefcase open. I leafed through the sketchbook until I found what I was looking for. I'd penciled in the rough-hewn planks of the tree-house, with its sloped roof, uneven walls, and rickety ladder early on. Written *Friendship* in the margin. Five summers. Bikes, the treehouse in the rain, Loon Lake on sunny days... and I'd forgotten all about Clementine until she called from jail.

I flipped to a blank page and wrote Murder's Mark at the top with a business-like flourish. Had I already spotted it in the soul garden of one of the people I'd interviewed but failed to recognize it? If so, it meant that my mental image of the mark had not been set by past cases or the murder of Gray the First, but had yet to come into focus. The weapon used against Adam Lindstrom had been a blizzard. Rosemary had landed on a paver or been hit on the back of the head... Was my thinking too pedestrian and I needed to look at motive, not physical objects? Not the how, but the *why*...

The ringing of the phone interrupted my chain of thought—and what I heard on the other end sent me out the door.

CHAPTER THIRTY-SIX

Shane looked up when I hurried into the agency. An early riser, he usually arrived first and perused *The Bee* with a cup of tea. Based on the road splatter on the sleeve of the jacket he still had on—the building is slow to warm up during the colder months—he'd biked in on this particular Monday.

I hung up my coat. "Is he still here?"

"In your office, boss. By the way, no luck at the Uff Da." Shane showed no signs of having stayed up into the early hours of the morning, although he must have. "Everyone I ran into the club who works at the resort knew who Rosemary was, but it sounds like they all went out of their way to avoid interactions with her. Nothing to report on the gossip cookie front, other than a lot of rumors flying."

Maybe our luck was about to change. Todd West, the Fireside Resort bookkeeper, perched on the edge of the burgundy couch inside my office, accompanied by his Vines of Anxiety. It looked as if he straightened up somewhat. That was all right. I didn't mind people touching my stuff and if it helped set his mind at ease, all the better. I settled into my armchair and readied my notepad and pen. I didn't think he'd come to confess, though you never know. "Todd, what brings you here?"

"I need to tell *someone*."

"And I'm it. Just so you understand, it doesn't work like with a lawyer or a doctor. There's no expectation of confidentiality between a private investigator and a client. That aside, it's *my* rule that unless there are safety concerns for you or another person, I can be trusted to keep silent."

"No—you can tell others." The vines that twisted up and down Todd's arms coiled tightly, almost obscuring the white of his shirt. "I don't want to be next."

I stared at him. "Next?"

"Rosemary. I read about it this morning in *The Bee*. Slipped, they said... Did she?"

"The police aren't sure what happened. Did Rosemary relay something to you in confidence, Todd? Is that why you're here?"

"I saw it with my own eyes."

He stopped there, words seeming to fail him. I made a suggestion. "Grin, Todd."

"Grin?"

"Even a forced smile sends a signal to the body to relax."

He did as instructed and the vines eased their death grip on him. The uncomfortable, lopsided grin sent staccato sentences pouring out. "That night. Of the Toast to Adam party. I saw *his* car. Here in Two Lakes."

"Whose car?'

"Paul's."

Paul Lindstrom, in Two Lakes on the night his brother died. *I knew it.* He'd been lying about *something.* "When did you see him? At what time, I mean."

"Driving back from the restaurant, at the intersection of Main and Hickory." Grin still there, anxiety's vines tight around each finger, Todd picked at the edge of a throw pillow. He winced at the imprecision. "Must have been nine twenty-five or so."

"It would have been dark. How can you be certain it was Paul's car?"

"There are streetlamps at that intersection. We'd both stopped for a red light and I was behind him. I couldn't see much beyond the back of his head—but it was definitely his car."

I noted this down. "Main and Hickory. What model and make does Paul drive?"

"I don't know cars."

I looked up from the page. "Then how?..."

His fingers threatened to unravel the pillow stitching. "I recognized the license plate number."

"You just happened to remember Paul Lindstrom's license plate?"

"It's memorable. CPA 123. Blue letters, white background."

"CPA is memorable?"

"Certified Public Accountant. I don't think the license plate stands for that, though."

I tapped the notepad with the pen and made an assessment. Not a wisp of fog—and for a person of Todd West's temperament, there would have been plenty of it if he were lying. "Why didn't you report this to the police?"

The question rattled him further, though it wasn't meant to. "I had no idea Paul wasn't supposed to have been in Two Lakes that day. They were gossiping about Adam's death in the break room at lunch on Friday—did Clementine do it? someone else?— and Paul's name came up. Linda told everyone it couldn't have been Paul, because he was four hours away. Once I realized that only *I* knew the truth, I spent the weekend trying to decide what to do. I considered going to the police station. It's just... So many people. Phones ringing. Individuals behind bars. It's not...pleasant." He put down the pillow. "Then this morning I read about Rosemary."

I understood why it had been impossible for him to act at once. Todd had been overwhelmed by the emotional burden of having to report his boss to the police. He'd waited too long and Rosemary had paid the price. I hoped Todd wouldn't blame himself. "Let me see if I have this straight. You saw Paul's car—his personal vehicle, correct, not one of the resort vans?—on the night of February twenty-second around 9:25 at the intersection of Main and Hickory. Which direction was he headed?"

"He made a left onto Hickory. West."

Toward the resort. "Was he alone?" Todd nodded and I went on, "You're worried if Paul finds out you saw him, he might come after you. Todd, the police can protect you. I can't."

"But now we *both* know... In case something happens to me."

"The police will want to confirm this."

"Yes, all right."

Again, I understood. The police calling *him* was different. He would merely be asked to help, and he didn't mind that.

Todd checked his watch and jumped up. "I have to go. I'll be late for work."

I accompanied him to the door, where Shane helped Todd with his jacket, which the bookkeeper zipped exactly three quarters of the way up. I warned him to keep his knowledge to himself. "Let your co-workers gossip away even if their facts are wrong."

"It's all anyone's been talking about—that and Chef Urban baking his very last Erin's Cake, for the wedding. Paul's mad about it. I don't get it. If I were Paul—if it were me getting married, I'd be over the moon. I wouldn't care about a cake recipe and who gets to keep it."

"Me too, Todd," Shane said, "me too."

After Todd left, I promptly dialed the police station and asked to be put through to the chief. This didn't always work, but this time it did, surprisingly fast. Chief Gustafson greeted me with, "Rod, I was about to get you on the phone. Interested in what we uncovered at your client's place?"

Less curious about the item than I'd have been half an hour ago, I said, "According to Jasper Jones of *The Bee*, something that fit in a paper bag."

"Jasper's not wrong. You know how the Lindstroms, father and son, accrued a shelf's worth of awards over the years?"

This struck me as an odd aside. "Sure. They're in Todd West's office. He's just been here, by the way... Paul had the awards moved after he settled into Adam's chair. Can't say I blame him—his brother had won six years in a row. I'd probably have moved them over to Todd's office, too." *Especially if I'd just killed my brother.* "What about it?"

"Town Hall likes to go all out. The things are made of real glass. Hefty cubes with solid edges. Similar in shape to a patio paver. I took one to Dr. Wu. She called back ten minutes ago to tell me that the edge matches the lethal wound sustained by Rosemary Moore. She thinks it's the murder weapon—the patio pavers would have left debris in the injury and a less defined fracture line. Dr. Wu says it was a single blow with quite a lot of force."

"Chief... Are you saying one of the Business Person awards on Todd West's shelf is the murder weapon?"

The line crackled. "Not from the shelf. Multiple people saw Adam Lindstrom pocket the award at the dinner's end. When I asked around after he died, no one seemed to know where it had gone. It wasn't with his belongings in the woods near his final resting spot. Mike Nowak didn't find it in the BMW. I had no idea what to make of it."

"The killer took it?"

"Yup—and we've found it in Clementine Baker's house."

I digested this in silence for a moment, picturing Todd's desk and, in the cabinet across from it, the row of awards lining the shelf in their bases. The ones with Adam's name, 1978, 1979, the years getting closer to the present... The one voted on last December wasn't there. I'd missed it.

The chief had said "Nothing," when I asked him if anything of interest had been found in the car. This is what he meant. Business Person of the Year 1984 should've been on Adam's person or in his BMW, and it wasn't.

I commenced pacing by my desk, the back and forth limited by the phone cord. "Clementine returned to the resort to collect her last paycheck. Maybe Adam left the award in his office and she took it. A keepsake."

"Ah, Rod. Won't wash. If the circumstances were innocent, why hide it?"

"Hide it?" This stopped my pacing. "Where did you find the thing?"

"The back wall of the house. There's an opening, an old dryer vent from before Mrs. Gibson split the house into a duplex. It was never filled in. The spot's hard to find unless you know it's there. We only noticed the opening because the recent snow had weighed down the shrubs in front of it. The award just fit in. So unless you think the landlady, eighty-something Mrs. Gibson, schemed to do away with Lindstrom and steal his award, things don't look good for your Clementine... Rod, you still there?"

The chief's office door must have been open; the background sounds that seeped through the line included Aunt Holly's voice. "It's Mrs. Nelson's puppy. It's wandered away again..."

"There's only one explanation," I said. "The killer took a souvenir and put it to use, then planted it to frame Baker."

"Rod, if she weren't a friend, you'd at least consider the possibility that your client is a killer."

I have.

"As to why she took the award in the first place," the chief went on, "take your pick. Fingerprints needed to be wiped off. Or Lindstrom fought back and it had her blood on it—it was bleached clean, according to Dr. Wu. I'm not saying it's her for sure, but have you noticed that Clementine Baker has no alibi for either of the deaths?"

He put his hand across the mouthpiece and I heard a muffled exchange with Sergeant Mendez.

The chief came back on. "I gotta get off, Sheriff Doubek is on the other line. Phone's been ringing off the hook. Concerned citizens demanding Clementine Baker be jailed before she hurts another person. Two Lakes was a quiet town before she showed up, they say, and now we've had not one, but two unnatural—"

I interrupted him. "Todd West."

"What about Todd?"

"You're gonna want to talk to him. Today."

CHAPTER THIRTY-SEVEN

Her step slowed by age, Joanne Gibson led me out onto the back deck shared by the two sides of the duplex. "There, behind that boxwood shrub... Nineteen years it's been since my Lenny died, went in his sleep. I needed to supplement my pension so I divided the house to rent out half. The living room got split down the middle, the old guest room is now my kitchen, and the old laundry room became a bathroom—the washer-'n-dryer went into the basement and the crew built a cabinet over the old dryer vent. I worried we might get a creature nesting in there, but nothing ever did and to tell you the truth, I forgot all about it till the police came." Mrs. Gibson put a veined hand to her heart, the Log of Worry heavy on an already hunched-over spine. "And now look what's happened."

In the yard, the police had left bootprints in the mushy snow. They'd pruned the dwarf evergreen—the matching one on the opposite side of the deck sagged under its weight of snow. I stared at the gap in the siding, the size and shape of a saucer. The backyard lacked a fence. Easy enough to approach if you were looking for a place to hide a murder weapon. I'd have to ask Baker whether Hutch had barked recently for an unknown reason.

Mrs. Gibson had not seen what the police found. "They made

me wait in my kitchen. I did peek out the window, but their backs were to me. Lorna—she lives across the street—says it must've been a weapon and that Clementine made Adam Lindstrom go into the woods at gunpoint. But I don't believe it, Clementine's too nice to do anything of the sort." At least someone believed in my client's innocence. Barely pausing for breath, Mrs. Gibson continued to fuss. "A reporter stopped by, he's worried about her too. Jay-Jay, his name is, so curious about everything, reminds me of my son—Alex is in California, saving the whales. Jay-Jay said my coffee is the finest he's ever had. I grind the beans, with a little machine. It makes all the difference."

Back inside, she made me a cup. "Delicious," I said without knowing whether this was the case or not. "Were you here two evenings ago, Mrs. Gibson? Saturday."

"That's an easy answer, I'm here every evening."

"Clementine says she drove to Ostford to walk Hutch."

"I don't blame her, poor dear. The other day when she took Hutch out on his morning walk, I stepped out to the curb to get my mail and Lorna came out to chide her about the dog—it had, you know, gone on her lawn, as if it's anything special, you should see it in the summer, all yellow grass... And later I saw Grant from two doors down straight-out cross the street to avoid meeting Clem and Hutch. And then that brick, through her window! Lorna told me I might be harboring a *murderess* and I should kick her out before it brings down house values all along Sycamore Drive, but I enjoy having Clem as a tenant, and oh dear, I don't know what to do..."

Mrs. Gibson seemed oblivious to the fact that it was Lorna herself who threw the brick. I took another sip of the thick, tasteless liquid. "Mrs. Gibson, if I might give you some advice. Don't listen to Lorna—and be careful what you say to Jasper Jones of *The Bee*."

"Do you want to see her side of the house? Clem's?" she offered. "I have a key. I'm sure she won't mind."

I took a quick peek. A messy living room, although I couldn't tell if that was its natural state or if the police left it that way. A bookshelf held a row of paperbacks, mostly mysteries with familiar titles. I didn't linger. Rooms without people in them have little to say to me.

At the resort, I pulled in just in time to see a police car drive away. Todd West had told his story. Good. I appreciated Chief Gustafson arriving in broad daylight. He didn't take Paul Lindstrom in to question him or to charge him with obstruction of justice—there'd been no one in the back seat, only Chief Gustafson and Officer Lewis in the front. The chief had to tread carefully. The Lindstroms were a wealthy family, about to be connected by wedding bells to Mayor Cooper, who had the ear of Sheriff Doubek—and the sheriff had the Two Lakes police station on speed dial.

I'd passed the Gothic mansion nicknamed "the Olde-house," with its dusty-yellow façade and square tower, on the way over. Preparations for Paul and Nicole's ceremony were underway, with folding chairs being unloaded off a truck parked outside. Tomorrow, the chairs would be joined by the bird from The Cork's basement freezer—unless the ice raven was destined for the banquet in the resort ball-room, next to the black cake—and the happy couple would say their *I do*'s.

I got out and heard the slam of a car door and the thump of boots hitting the ground. The mayor had parked his pickup a few spots down. I rather thought that, like me, he'd been watching the police car drive away.

Nicole stepped out of the lodge to greet her father and draped herself over the side of the pickup, which was stacked with cool-ers. "We better count them, Daddy. Make sure they didn't cheat us." She circled the vehicle, counting crates. "Eight, nine... I thought they said *ten*, Daddy."

"Let me carry it all in, Nikki, and we'll count. Dusty Gray Junior, hello." The cowboy hat tipped at me. "Care to lend a hand?"

"Not today." I glanced at the coolers. "Champagne for the wedding?"

"Tulips, black," Nicole chirped.

"Must have been hard to find this time of year..." I remembered the haste that had to have gone into the planning of everything in the space of two weeks. "...and so fast."

"I found a hothouse in Wisconsin that grows them. Daddy bought everything they had on the spot. One for every guest, the rest for decorating the Oldehouse, to go with the cobwebs and creaky floors." No Log of Worry weighed down those slender shoulders in the white coat; the fuss about the number of crates was for her father's sake. A ploy for attention from a young adult who still showcased the chalkboard fence. "We won't bring in heaters, I want it creepy and chilly, just *perfect*..."

A flutter of wings overhead caught my ear. I looked up. If it had been a bird returning north after a long winter, it'd already gone. The other possibility was a feathered creature stirring in a soul garden as we all carried on with the moment: Nicole chatted about the Oldehouse, her father adjusted crates, Chef Urban passed by with grocery bags of fruit and a wave, a family of four departed in a Chevy, and I stood by taking it all in.

"Nikki, where do you want them?" The mayor tapped a crate.

"Not here, Daddy—in The Cork's basement. I'll get Paulie and we'll meet you there."

"I better drive around, then."

"Miss Cooper—" I began.

"No one calls me that! It's Nicole, or Nikki."

"Nicole, I'm here to talk to Paul. Might have a couple of questions for you as well, if you have a free minute." Whatever Paul had done, I suspected that Nicole knew.

"Can it wait? *So much to do.* The rehearsal dinner's tonight. We're not having an actual rehearsal of the ceremony—too much bother. Just a meal at The Cork with the relatives. Everyone's staying at our house. You wouldn't believe the number of *boots* in the mudroom. And I'm packing for the honeymoon. I can't travel far"—she patted her stomach—"so we're driving over to Chicago for a few days."

Her father had climbed back into the pickup; a she-lynx joined him, roaming back and forth on top of the coolers. The mayor rolled down the window. "Nikki, you don't have to answer any of his questions. He's not the police. It can wait until after the honeymoon, right Gray?"

With a look that promised trouble if I kept badgering his daughter, Mayor Cooper gunned the pickup down the side road, the muscular wildcat lounging on top of the coolers eying me as if I were its next meal.

CHAPTER THIRTY-EIGHT

I held the resort door open for Nicole and trailed her inside and into the staff corridor. She poked her head into the Resort Director's office and called past the empty secretary's desk, "Paulie, are you busy? Daddy could use a hand carrying the crates in."

"Nikki, sure thing, let me just put on boots." Nicole went into her own office and Paul stepped out after a moment. He saw me. "What do you want?"

"A few minutes of your time."

"I'm busy."

"I don't mind waiting."

"Suit yourself."

He and Nicole left. Finding myself alone, I did the obvious: snooped around the desk that had once belonged to Rosemary. I tried to do it respectfully, if such a thing is possible. I began by lifting the dust cover off the electric typewriter, hoping the ribbon might have traces on it—for example, of the name on the envelope of the second letter—but the cartridge was fresh.

I turned to the desk drawers next. Reams of paper, stapler refills, push pins, and, in the bottom drawer, a stack of old *TIME* magazines, along with glue, scissors, and a small bag of dried rosemary. If Paul was the killer, Rosemary had plotted her blackmail from ten feet away.

Inside the inner office, which Paul had left unlocked, the décor reminded me of Caleb's office back at the cemetery: thick carpet, mahogany desk, black leather chair. Erin's artwork, with its bold lines, added a splash of color. No flowers here, but a low shelf behind the door housed a row of brand-new loafers. Paul had inherited a personal computer, sleeker than the one on Todd West's desk: a Macintosh, with its apple logo and what I knew was called a mouse, though I had yet to use one. A framed photo of Paul and Nicole sat next to the computer. The happy couple in simpler times, helping clear the resort beach for the season, Paul's gaze spelling out adoration for all to see; had I witnessed the tableau in person, I'd have no doubt seen doves.

I reached for the desk phone. Baker answered after the second ring. "Gray house."

"It's me."

"Where are you? You took off early this morning."

"There's been a development." I'd penned a note for Baker instructing her to stay in. "It can wait."

"Why can't you tell me now?"

"I have reasons."

Just one. *I want to see your reaction in person.*

"Is that why you took the newspaper? You might as well tell me what it is or I'll go out and get a copy for myself. In fact, I think Officer Anderson is parked outside, reading the funny pages."

Admitting defeat, I filled her in about Adam's award going missing and where the police found it.

This was met with stunned silence. When Baker recovered her voice, she sputtered, "Well, I mean—what—I didn't put the award there. I had no clue about the old dryer vent. You can ask Mrs. Gibson, she never showed it to me. The award he received at Toast to Adam? I never even saw it. Obviously the killer took it from Adam and planted it to frame me."

I heard voices in the corridor, Paul exchanging a word with Linda Bolander. I said, "All right. I'm following a lead. In the meantime, stay put. There's cereal in the kitchen if you get hungry."

"What am I supposed to do, watch TV all day?" Barking had started up in the background. "And what about Hutch? He'll need a walk."

"I have a backyard," I reminded her. "Throw a tennis ball for him or something. There's gotta be one in the garage."

I hurried out of Paul's office and closed it just as his form rounded the doorframe. "You still here, Gray?"

He exchanged the boots for loafers and dropped into the chair behind his desk. He didn't invite me to sit. I did so anyway. A very different man than the one in the framed photo faced me. Tension in his features and the sporadic clang of the stress bells, one on either side of him. Maybe he was the killer. If he wasn't, he had other problems. His job would get easier with time, but life with Nicole? The order of importance was Nicole, "Daddy", Paul.

"I'm sorry for your loss," I said.

It took him a moment. "You mean Rosemary." He continued, as if not wanting to come across as unfeeling, "I didn't know her that well. When Adam was alive, I spoke to her only when I had to get past her—and she worked for me for not even two weeks."

"Is that why you're not postponing the wedding?"

Clang. "We can't cancel. Relatives, the cake, everything's in place. Nikki is so excited... Then there's the baby. No, we can't delay."

I imagined that Troy Cooper had a say in the matter as well. Paul and Nicole's Goth festivities would proceed at the decaying house on Gooseberry Lane as if Rosemary didn't matter at all. Though she was gone and wouldn't feel the snub, I experienced it in her place.

Paul shifted in the chair. "Why are you here?"

"You were seen in Two Lakes the night Adam died."

He slumped back, as if I'd socked him on the chin. "Says

who? Todd West? Is that why the police were in his office and why I've been asked to stop by the station at my earliest convenience? So what? Doesn't mean I did anything to Adam."

"You don't deny it?"

"What would be the point?" The bells, instead of going into overdrive, faded away. The reveal of the truth had lessened his load. "Yes, I drove back down early from Duluth. Do you want to know why? *That's* why." He jerked his head toward the hallway, where the mayor's familiar twang could be heard. The Lemon Tree of Bitterness sprouted on the desk, its branches stretching over the Macintosh. "Strutting around carrying tulips when he should be in his office in Town Hall. There'll probably be a story in *The Bee* starring Mayor Cooper, devoted dad." Paul bent forward, nose in the lemon tree branches, and lowered his voice. "The mayor is a fraud. You should look into *that*, since you're an investigator."

"A fraud? How so?"

"Nikki told me the *real* family history. There was no cattle rancher to justify the cowboy hat, not even a corn farmer. In the 1860s, something like that, the first Troy Cooper—that'd be Nikki's great-grandfather—stepped off a boat from Liverpool in New York. He took the train to Duluth, and having settled himself in the New World, spent all his time drinking and gambling until fate smiled on him." Paul glanced at the notepad sticking out of my pocket as if expecting me to be jotting this down. I obliged and he went on. "Old Troy won himself a chunk of marshy, unusable land in a card game, between what's now Cooper Lake and Loon Lake. He hired laborers to drain the wetlands—they used hand pumps, built ditches, carted in soil— and paid them off with tiny lots. Built himself a huge Gothic mansion, then sold off the rest of the land, having promised left and right that the railroad was going to come through any day now. The railroad went through Ostford instead, but he got his town."

I looked up from the notepad. "If you're thinking this is a case of fraud, then it's a very cold case."

Paul went on as if he hadn't heard me. "Old Troy kept gambling, married late in life, and had lost all his money along with the mansion by the time his son—Nicole's grandfather and Troy's father, also named Troy—came of age. This Troy worked as a shoe salesman, a decent, hardworking man by all accounts, but it's not his father's story the mayor likes to tell. He once told me: 'Son, you gotta give 'em something to look at.' That's why he wears the cowboy hat and boots, drives the pickup with the racing stripes, all of it. He learned it from Old Troy. The Gothic mansion Old Troy built, it gave 'em something to look at. Made him important, trustworthy... Nikki wants to live there. The historical society still owns it. I've put in an offer."

Give 'em something to look at. This, I did write down. "That's quite a story, Paul. If you really want the truth about your fiancée's family to get out, Jasper Jones is a better person to talk to than me. But you're not going to do that, are you?"

He crossed his arms in defeat. "No, I'm not."

"What does any of it have to do with you driving down from Duluth the night of the blizzard?"

"The mayor was going to be at the Toast to Adam party, to give away the award and get his picture in *The Bee*. Which meant that Nikki and I had the evening to ourselves. We figured Troy would stay out late and return tipsy and fall right into bed."

"You drove back early to spend the night with your girlfriend without her father's knowledge? You're adults. You can do whatever you like, surely."

"It was Nikki's idea. We both knew that Troy Cooper didn't approve of me. Now that I'm making good money and own half of this place, I get lots of father-in-law-to-be pats on the back."

"If you knew you weren't spending the night in Duluth, why bother getting a room at Bear Lodge?"

Another shrug. "Adam paid for it. Company credit card."

This is Paul's secret, the source of the fog? *It can't be.* "Where did you and Nicole meet up that night? Her house?"

"The plan was the Roadway Motel." On the outskirts of Two Lakes. "But in the end we didn't go. I called Nikki after I got off the phone with Adam. I told her that he offered me his half of the resort and she had news on her side, too. Linda had given her the event coordinator job—and she was pregnant. I asked her to marry me... Not that that's the only reason, I want to marry her."

"You both had news. Then what?"

"When I pulled up in front of the house—around a quarter past eight—I found Nikki in planning mode, making calls to girl-friends. She said she wasn't feeling well, let's skip the motel. Nikki suggested I go to a movie, so I did."

"You went to a movie instead of your brother's big night? The night he announced he was stepping down?"

"Well—yes. For one thing, Adam thought I was still up in Duluth. And he only talked about himself, anyway, and his dream of moving to the beach. That's what I heard."

I made an effort to poke a hole in his story. "What movie did you watch?"

"*Beverly Hills Cop.* By the time I got home—half past eleven —my mother had turned in and the house was dark."

That explained a detail, the she-lynx I'd seen in Erin's vicinity. Protectiveness—not for Adam, but Paul. She must have heard her younger son come in. I got up to lean against the wall, giving me a clear view of the tasseled loafers. The next question I posed had a biblical ring to it. "Paul, did you covet your brother's life?"

He swiveled the chair and met my eye. "Why would I have? I had a job I enjoyed, a girlfriend, a good life."

Direct gaze, open shoulders, clear voice—and no fog this time. I'd envisioned him confessing that his brother chose Linda Bolander instead of him, that he'd felt the betrayal keenly, and had acted on it. I made a final, feeble attempt to rattle him. "What about this past Saturday? Where were you?"

"At home."

I believed him. He wasn't the killer.

The phone rang on Rosemary's desk in the outer office and Paul waited, as if he'd forgotten again, before reaching for his own phone and pressing a button to answer impatiently. "Yes?... No, what's there to talk about? Nuances? That again?... Look, I don't care. The contract doesn't specify I have to buy you out with any speed, not until you give me what I want, got it?"

He slammed the receiver down.

I raised an eyebrow. "Everything all right?"

"Chef Urban's being stubborn. Holding on to the cake recipe with frosting-stained fingers. Says it's his to do with as he wishes. Keeps talking about the nuances in the situation that I'm apparently blind to. Well, we'll see about that."

I felt the need to offer Paul a little life advice. "If you don't mind my saying, it's never a good idea to tie yourself up into knots to fit into a job. Take what Adam left you and make it your own. Let Conrad Urban leave and bring in a new chef."

"I didn't ask for your opinion." He walked me to the door just as Nicole popped her head out. "Paulie, I've been craving banana bread *all day*. Could you ask Chef Urban to make some for the rehearsal dinner?"

"I'll go tell him at once, Nikki," Paul jumped to her aid, the bad blood with the restaurant chef forgotten. "Were all the tulips there?"

"We're missing *two dozen*." She gave an exaggerated sigh. "Daddy called them and yelled that they better drive them over in time for tomorrow."

"Don't worry about a thing, Nikki. Troy and I will handle it all. You go home and get ready for the dinner." The adoring fiancé, indulging all whims. A pair of white doves circled the cramped corridor space above the couple. Paul would no doubt have been embarrassed if he knew the birds were there for me to see.

No doves on Nicole's side. She was a taker, not a giver. She held one of the tulips, its velvet petals a deep purple that bordered on black. Queen of the Night. I was familiar with the variety from the stack of gardening books in my living room, none of which I used for actual gardening. While I believed that Paul had gone to a movie the night his brother died, I wasn't so sure that his fiancée had spent a quiet evening at home. The exotic tulip, whose color struck me as having a slightly sinister vibe, wasn't in my sketchbook. Not yet, anyway.

Nicole slipped her arm into Paul's elbow and they left before I could ask her any questions.

CHAPTER THIRTY-NINE

"If you're here to badger me about not hauling in Paul Lindstrom, you're wasting your breath, Rod. I'm not going to arrest a suspect on the eve of his wedding, and it's not because of pressure from the mayor. What if I'm wrong and I've ruined a couple's special day, with all the guests and the money spent on everything from cake to flowers to God knows what, I'd never forgive—"

"I'm not here because of that. Here."

I dropped Rosemary's carved-up *TIME* magazine on his desk, along with the letter Baker, Shane and I had cobbled together. The chief read through the letter twice, the second time more slowly. He sent me a sharp glance. "What is this?"

I explained.

He chewed me out, rightly. "For the love of Pete, you don't tamper with evidence, Rod! If there's something that might exonerate your client, you give me a call and we do it properly. You *know* that. I oughta charge you with interfering with an ongoing investigation."

"In my defense, I didn't expect that we'd find anything."

"*We?*"

"Shane and I." My client didn't need a trespassing charge

added to her woes. "Look, the important thing is we now know that we're looking for two people—the killer and an accomplice."

Arms crossed, wearing a storm like a furious hat, he watched me. "Maybe. Doesn't let your Clementine off the hook, though."

"I have a theory."

"Yeah? Have a seat."

I took a seat. "It's based on facts, four of them."

"Go on."

"I'd rather not say any more, not yet."

He stared at me. A hard stare, all traces of his usual easygoing manner gone. The storm churned ominously. "Rod, what is it that you're thinking?"

I rolled out a length of coiled barbed wire—guardedness— onto the desk between us. Jasper Jones knew that Baker and I were childhood friends, that Adam gave her an expensive necklace... "I'm thinking that stuff has a way of making it into *The Bee* lately."

It was not the nicest of things to say to an old friend and the storm clouds darkened to a tornadic, turbulent wall that made me want to seek shelter; I'd have preferred thunder and lightning. Keeping his tone even, the chief said, "Not from this office they don't. I told you about the award being found at Clementine Baker's house because I've known you a long time, since you were a kid, Rod, not because I go around blabbing—and my officers don't either."

"About that award. Who knows it was used in Rosemary's murder?"

"Other than you and me? Dr. Wu, of course. Sergeant Mendez. I'm holding off on giving an update to Sheriff Doubek until I know more." This I understood to mean that the sheriff would have demanded Baker's immediate arrest. Chief Gustafson was giving her every chance that he could—for my sake, not hers. He crossed his arms. "This is where you return the favor by answering my question. What four facts?"

I stayed silent.

"You really won't say more than that, Rod?"

The barbed wire had split us into two camps, the opposite sides in a war for Baker's freedom. My response came out flippant, though it wasn't meant that way. I quoted his own mantra back to him: "I don't work for you, Chief."

He got up to pull the door open but it stuck and he had to tug hard, rattling the glass and turning heads in the common room. "Out!" he bellowed.

CHAPTER FORTY

Back at the office, I found Shane noodling on screenplay dialogue and asked him as I hung up my jacket on the coat rack, "Shane, what makes each individual unique? Why should it matter that Clementine Baker was once a good friend?"

He was used to strange questions from me. "That's how it is. We're not sheep. One person is not as good as the next one... Unless sheep feel the same way about themselves, which they might, for all we know." He stuck the pencil behind an ear and leaned back, hands resting behind his head. "Boss, when you were kids, did you have a crush on Clem?"

A crush. Hunger held all that, and more. One time, a couple of years ago, I aired out the monster in a bar over in Ostford, which, combined with alcohol, led to a one-night stand. It'd been satisfactory enough. Shane and I had chatted a couple of days later and he'd offered the opinion that for the *real thing*, one needs Joy and all the other stuff in the meteorite fragments.

I dug into my memories and answered Shane's question. "Maybe—but that was a long time ago. She's just a client."

"If she *were* just a client, you'd not need to say so, boss."

I changed the subject. "How's the screenplay going?"

"Excellent. All this talk of secrets gave me an idea for a snippet of dialogue. One of my leads, Hank, says: 'Your philosophy of life is to start every relationship by lying?' And Mindy—she never tells anyone she's rich, not at first—responds with: 'It's the good kind of lie.'... How did it go with Paul?"

I relayed that I'd crossed Paul off the suspect list. "I'm chasing shadows, not answers... Shane, am I too close to this and is that why Rosemary is dead?"

"Boss, somebody hit Rosemary on the head and it wasn't you. I hate to say it but it sounds like she was a nosy woman, got greedy, and it cost her."

"Gustafson's not sure the blackmail letter clears Baker—but he's forgetting one thing. She'd have needed a partner, someone ready to don their coat and boots in the middle of the night to fetch her from Lost Wolf Woods, no questions asked. Baker said it herself, she only spent time with Adam. She was new in town, didn't know anyone, had no friends."

"Yeah, but you know what the chief's thinking, don't you?"

"What?"

"You, boss. She knew you."

CHAPTER FORTY-ONE

As Baker dished out pizza slices, I discreetly double-tapped Monday's stone and rolled it under the extra napkins on my kitchen table. The final meteorite fragment did not resemble the rest. Six of them were jail cells, transparent with black lines, holding gardenly prisoners inside; the seventh was more of solitary confinement—an ashy black clouded the stone's surface, like smoke frozen in place. I had no idea what, if anything, hid within. Whatever I tried, nothing ever allowed itself to be coaxed out. Still, I kept experimenting. Pizza and wine with murder as the dinner topic of conversation? *Why not.*

On her side of the table, Baker sported a steady drizzle. Gloominess.

She had not, in fact, stayed in all day as instructed. When Shane and I came through the door of 12 Nestling Lane, pizza boxes in hand, she confessed. "I took the pearls over to Adam's mother. She refused them—not angrily or anything like that. She was nice about it. I didn't want her to think I've moved on so soon after Adam's death, so I told her the truth, that I haven't and won't, not until we find out who killed him." Baker picked an olive off her slice. "Erin suggested I take the pearls over to Pass It On Closet, over on Cottonwood, so that's what I did. They give away work attire to people who need it for interviews. The jewelry they keep on hand is imitation stuff. They took the pearls and put them in a safe to auction off at the next fundraiser, and gave me a donation receipt for tax purposes. Only…" She tapered off, a growing pile of olives to one side of her plate.

I could guess where this was leading. Gargoyles. If I failed to catch the killer, they'd always be there. The good citizens of Two Lakes rarely forgot anything; I had better cause than most to know the validity of this. "It didn't go well, did it?"

"The way they looked at me, the two women inside. As if they were accepting blood money."

"This is why I said to stay in."

She gave a nonchalant shrug, but I could tell it was only skin deep—the drizzle around her was still there. "At least I had company. A police cruiser followed me there. I had a nice chat with Officer Lewis before getting back in my car. Did you know he collects comic books?"

This got Shane's attention. "Does he? A few friends and I are getting together next weekend for a charity drive—for the animal shelter—and since DeForest is new in town, I thought I'd invite him to join us. I'll bring him a comic book to help break the ice." Shane took off his pink bunny ears, then poured out glasses of wine, wasted on me as usual.

We ate with the blinds closed. Officer Lewis, parked up the street and unaware we were talking about him, would have to make do with our silhouettes.

At one point, Baker passed a bite of crust down to Hutch, who lay under my kitchen table in a lazy doze punctuated by fits of barking. Hutch lived in the Sunlit Meadow of Contentment, which he'd dragged out with him when I first saw him bound out of Mrs. Gibson's house. He sprawled in his green meadow under the table, a Scarecrow of On Alert popping up occasionally in the middle of the grass. When that happened, the dog would thunder away to the front windows to raise a ruckus at a passing car, or the back window to bark at a yard creature; then, nails clicking softly on the kitchen tiles, he'd shuffle back to curl up by a table leg in his meadow and await whatever might drop down from up above.

Once the pizza boxes were empty and the wine bottle down to an inch, I instructed Baker to think back to Saturday night. "Do you remember Hutch barking at any point? The killer—after attacking Rosemary—must have snuck into your backyard to hide Adam's award."

She slipped the dog a last bit of crust—both she and Shane had been doing it, Hutch taking his time to play with each bite before chewing it up—and wiped her fingers on a napkin. "Gray, I love Hutch but you see how it is, he barks a hundred times a day. At airplanes. Squirrels. Trucks. To join in with other dogs barking away in the neighborhood. I gave up on getting up to check if we had an intruder a week after he came into my life. What's with your face?"

"Troublesome tooth."

"Want me to make that call to the dentist, boss?"

I wished everyone would stop asking me about it. "It can wait." I was rummaging through my kitchen cupboards. I didn't have visitors often enough to justify having much in terms of dessert on hand, but I did manage to find an old box of cookies. While Baker and Shane divided them up, I sat back down and took my pencil set and case notes out of the briefcase, leaving the sketchbook inside. I proceeded to make a handful of quick sketches next to a handful of names in my notes.

Baker peered over. "What are those doodles?"

"Possibilities for murder's mark. I know that sounds odd, but you'll have to take my word that it'll help me find out who—"

"No, I get it. You're associating a unique object with each person, something that gets at their core. That black tulip for Nicole—it's because she likes things to be special, unique, different, right?... But why a yellow shoe for Tiffany?"

"It's gold, but I don't have a pencil of that color." Those gold pumps, carelessly thrown on; maybe if I looked hard enough, I'd spot gilded gardening boots in Tiffany's vicinity: opulent, gaudy, out of place in a normal soulscape. As for Nicole, I'd debated on the chalkboard fence as a candidate for murder's mark, but I'd seen the fence before in the vicinity of clients in ordinary circumstances. The Queen of the Night, with its sunlight-absorbing velvet and unnatural color, on the other hand... If I saw its double in Nicole's soul, an abnormal bloom in a sea of green, I'd know at once what it stood for.

Baker frowned. "Chef Urban is on your list? And is that a bagel?"

"It's a moat." I penciled in a water wave inside it. *Did murder build the moat?* That sounded like a title of one of the mysteries Baker was reading. Committing the worst crime of all might just leave behind a lasting barrier to human connection. As with the chalkboard fence, I'd seen the garden element before but not often and there'd always been a specific reason for it. I'd have to have another chat with Conrad Urban and dig deeper.

My client had her own take on the moat. "If you don't know him well, the chef can come across as standoffish and crotchety, sure, but I've never seen him be anything but kind to a soul. He's stern with the kitchen staff but show me a chef who isn't. I wasn't even aware he owned half the resort my first month there, it was so unusual to see him out of the kitchen. He has a good heart and people with good hearts don't commit murder ... Did you just draw a fish inside the moat?"

"Yes," I said, penciling in fins. Not that I'd spotted fish the couple of times I'd seen Conrad Urban and his moat—I hadn't. Just an idea. "Let's focus on facts, what we know for sure. Incidentally, Baker, I count anything confirmed by two witnesses as fact."

She raised an eyebrow. "Even things I say?"

"Even things you say."

"Fair enough. Wait, you're doing a sketch by my name? What is that, stairs with a stick figure tumbling back?"

"From when you pushed that man down in Florida and broke his wrist," I reminded her. Not that I was expecting to see a stick figure traipsing through her soulscape, but I could imagine a bloodstained set of steps lurking in a shadowy corner somewhere.

Baker almost choked on a cookie and had to reach for a glass of water. Hutch stirred, a little Log of Worry joining him at Baker's reaction. "Ouch. Listen, Gray, I try to keep my temper under control. I fail on occasion. I'm human—and that day in Miami poor Hutch looked like his paws were in pain from the hot pavement. And yeah, I threw a flower pot against the resort wall the day I quit, in case you want to sketch that too. Doesn't mean I followed it up by scheming to murder Adam—and then Rosemary."

Shane knew why I chose that moment to tighten my shoelace. I straightened up. "I believe you."

"Good, then." She glanced back at the list and sketches. "Why is Tiffany and her gold shoe on there? I thought we'd ruled her out."

"I know you don't want it to be her, Baker, but there *is* a scenario, now that we know it took two people. Tiffany pretends to be drunk at the Toast to Adam celebration and is brought home by Erin. On her side of the house, Tiffany ostensibly goes to bed but in reality sneaks out to meet up with Kostas, who's on his motorcycle at a prearranged spot far enough for Erin not to hear the rev of the engine. The pair return to the resort, Tiffany hides in her husband's BMW and Rosemary sees, sealing her fate. Later, Kostas picks up Tiffany at a prearranged spot in the woods." I scratched an ear. "She makes a better suspect than Nicole, who doesn't have a clear motive. I believe Paul. Adam offered him his stake in the resort. So why would Nicole have wanted Adam gone?"

"We still don't know this secret of Adam's, boss," Shane reminded me. "If there is one, maybe Nicole's motive is wrapped up in it."

"Possibly... One person has an obvious motive—Conrad Urban. Here's where the facts come in, four of them. First: Conrad wants to retire and take his famous recipe with him.

Second: Paul wants the recipe to stay and is refusing to buy out the chef until that's resolved. Third: Despite the stand-off, the chef is happy to make Paul's wedding cake. And fourth: Paul's allergic to fish." I added, "That last one I still need to confirm."

"You think Chef Urban is behind all of this?" Baker glanced at me as if I'd gone mad. "That he harmed Adam and Rosemary, and what, Paul's next?"

I made my case. "The first murder, on February twenty-second. Conrad, who's expecting to be told that he and Erin will be silent partners with Linda Bolander running things, learns otherwise. He concludes it's time for him to retire and Adam responds by demanding the recipe stays, perhaps even has some way of enforcing it, a contract from years ago." An old contract, as I had good cause to know, could reappear out of nowhere, long after you'd forgotten about it. Would Baker be sitting on my couch if we'd never signed the pact? "But the chef can't let go of Erin's Cake. He's still in love with its namesake. He waits until the end of the night and hides in Adam's BMW. Rosemary sees, engages in a spot of blackmail, and pays the price. And now it's all playing out again, with Paul."

"I don't know, boss. Couldn't a new chef reverse engineer Erin's Cake?"

"The catered food has a list of ingredients because of allergies and stuff," Baker informed us, "so I can tell you there's flour, eggs, chocolate, the usual things, in the cake. As to the quantities of things or the order they go in, no idea." Baker reached for the last of the cookies, then changed her mind. "But I'll never believe it of Chef Urban, that he's so possessive of the recipe because of unrequited love for Erin that he killed Adam rather than give it up and is about to do the same for Paul. This is all very far-fetched."

I permitted myself a sigh. "Baker, if I'd said to you beforehand, don't date a married man, would you have listened?"

"Probably not."

"If Conrad Urban loves Erin, and has poured that love over the years into batter and frosting, then his extreme attachment to the recipe makes sense. Then there's this: Whose shoulder will Erin lean on, when she has no one else left, with both Adam and Paul gone?"

Baker stuck the cork back into the empty wine bottle. "You make him sound calculating, like a villain in one of Officer Lewis's comic books. If what you're saying is true, Chef Urban made me the scapegoat. Hid the award at my house. You won't get me to believe any of this... Is that why you drew the fish in the moat, because you think he'll poison Paul that way? I don't remember anyone mentioning this alleged fish allergy. What if it's a mild one?"

"If the goal is to murder the groom on his wedding day," Shane said, scooping out the cookie crumbles left in the box, "lacing the cake with an allergy trigger is one way to go about it. Here, have a slice...and a bit of poison, too."

"Let's find out about this allergy."

Erin answered after the first ring. "I can only give you a few minutes, I'm about to head out to the rehearsal dinner."

"It's important. I won't keep you long."

She sounded troubled. "I heard about Rosemary. *The Bee* says she slipped and hit her head. Very sad. I don't believe she had any relatives, only an estranged sister in Wisconsin. We'll arrange for a memorial service and funeral costs after the wedding. She did give the best part of her life to the employ of our family." Erin was quick to add, "I know what you're thinking, but what else can we do but wait until after the wedding? And no one asked my opinion about it anyway, whether the right thing would be to postpone... What can I do for you, Detective Gray?"

"Paul has an allergy, doesn't he?"

"What does that have to do with anything?"

"Humor me."

"Well, he's had it since he was a child. Finned fish—salmon, tilapia, tuna, trout, catfish... There's a whole list, but generally if it swims, he can't eat it. His airways swell up, which we found out the bad way, on his fifth birthday when he tried fishsticks. That meal ended with a trip to the emergency room. I'll never forget it."

All of this was pure speculation, but I wondered if Paul had sensed it was no longer safe for him to eat in Chef Urban's restaurant. Nicole must have insisted on the location for the rehearsal dinner, and the choice of wedding cake. "Why has Paul started avoiding The Cork?"

"He's still adjusting to being in charge of things. He'll find his way. He needs time, that's all."

I said the next part carefully. "If Paul were to be out of the picture, what happens then?"

"You mean if he resigned or moved away, or something like that? I suppose it would be Connie and me behind the curtain, with Linda running the show. Surely you don't suspect Linda of anything, for heaven's sake. She's salt of the earth people, hardworking and honest."

"Not Linda." *You're forgetting about the nuances of the situation*, Conrad had told Paul. "Is Conrad in love with you?"

Her tone sharpened. "I'm going to assume you have a good reason for asking. Now and then I like to imagine he is."

"And yet he's never said a word."

"It's loyalty—to Fred. The same goes for me, I admit. But I've known Connie for forty years. He'd *never* have hurt Adam."

"Are you willing to bet your younger son's life on it?"

I heard it then, through the phone line. The soft rustle of leaves. Alarm. It battled trust of an old friend, one whose love Erin quite possibly returned. After a beat, she came back with, "It's not Connie. But if you really think Paul is in someone's way, what are we going to do about it?"

"Leave it to me."

I hung up and discovered that Baker had dealt with a bit of spilled wine by transferring a wad of napkins, revealing the stone underneath. "What's this? Do you collect rocks?"

"Just a few."

I slipped the stone back into my cardigan and strolled to the living room window. If anything hid inside the seventh stone, it hadn't budged. I'd hoped maybe it'd turn out to be Gut Feeling after all and a bug-eyed lemur would bound into view, bringing with it the name of the killer. Just another failed experiment.

Baker brought up a final objection and called out from the kitchen, "Who's Chef Urban's partner, then? There to pick him up on the night Adam died, a willing accomplice. Not Erin."

"I haven't figured out that part yet," I admitted. The police car was still parked down the street. I turned back. "Look, I trusted your hunch. Your turn. These are simply the facts and Chef Urban is who they point to."

"Boss, if he killed Adam and Rosemary and means to poison Paul, how do we convince the police to listen? Clem—no offense—makes a much better suspect."

"We get our hands on a sample of the wedding cake and check for fish. You don't still happen to have a work key, Baker, for The Cork?"

She shook her head. "I had one but tossed it on my desk when I quit."

"Plan B, then." Back in the kitchen, I leafed through the phonebook under the wall-mounted phone until I got to the G's, and dialed again. "Ellie, sorry to bother you, it's Rodrick Gray."

She jumped right to the news. "Wade and I decided to divorce."

"Things will get better, give it time." I believed this to be true, which is why I said it. "Listen, I called to ask for a favor. You're on the resort catering crew. Do you have a key to The Cork?"

"Is it to get proof—for a client with a problem?"

"Exactly, yes."

There was a pause and then a decision. "I'm not supposed to give out the keys, but seeing as I might not work there much longer..."

"You're leaving?"

"New boss still ugh. I've been looking around for a suitable location for a B&B. I did put in an offer on the Oldehouse, but somebody outbid me. I'll find another house, something with a nice yard. Picture it: a breakfast buffet, yoga before lunch, archery in the afternoon, tea and coffee in the evenings by the fireplace..."

"Sounds lovely," I said and Baker, who could only hear my half of the conversation, sent me an impatient glance from the table, where she'd sat back down to finish the last drops of her wine.

"When do you need the keys, Rodrick? Now? All right, come by. Just get them back to me by the morning."

After I hung up for the second time, Baker pushed her glass away. "I'm still unclear on how this'll work. Even if we manage to steal a sample of the cake, getting it tested for fish will take time and the wedding is in less than twenty-four hours."

"He doesn't need a lab," Shane said.

"That's true, I don't. I'll taste the cake and check for fish."

"No one has taste buds that fine," Baker protested.

"You'll see. The restaurant closes its doors at eleven, is that right? I'll aim for midnight."

"I'm coming along, Gray."

I shook my head. "The last thing we need is for you to be caught breaking in, key or not."

Shane also offered to join me but once again I shook my head. "I have another task for you... Baker, is there a night guard?"

"Don makes the rounds every couple of hours in a golf cart... Gray, if we really think Chef Urban is up to something nefarious —and I don't, but still—maybe it's better if you're, you know, armed? Do you own a gun?"

"It's in a safe back at the office and no, I won't need it."

We killed time by playing cards by the gas fireplace in the living room while Hutch snored in his meadow. At half past eleven, I put the cards down. "Shane, I'll need to borrow your hat and coat."

"Sure thing, boss, but why?"

"So Officer Lewis out there, who, as you mentioned, is new in town and doesn't know that you dislike being behind the steering wheel, can watch you drive yourself home. Your job, meanwhile, is to be me and pretend to go to bed and turn off the lights."

"And what should I do?" Baker asked.

"I guess you get the couch."

I went into the kitchen to rummage around for a flashlight— and to summon my appetite. It wasn't Hunger's day but taste-buds were necessary for the job I had to do. The monster oozed out of the stone and stretched a limb toward a cereal box on top of the fridge. I ignored it and stuck Shane's pink bunny ears on my head, then donned his coat, somewhat tight on me. Once in the car, I slumped in the driver's seat to match my assistant's height, and drove off, the Monster of Hunger in the seat next to me like an eager passenger. The police car remained where it was.

CHAPTER FORTY-TWO

Most of the lodge windows were already dark. The security guard came out right after I killed the headlights. By the time he finished his cigarette and set off on his rounds in the golf cart, I'd eaten all of the butter packets. The inside of the Ford Falcon must have been quite chilly, though I felt nothing, of course. Ellie's key in one hand and a flashlight in the other, I got out to take the side road on foot, the one that led down to the restaurant's basement. *The Bee* had promised a light dusting of snow and wet flakes landed on the asphalt, looking otherworldly in the flashlight's beam.

Somewhere, a car door opened and closed.

I heard footfalls behind me but didn't turn, figuring it was my own Scarecrow of On Alert tagging along. The straw-filled creature with a burlap sack for a face shows up now and then, usually not because of my personal safety—with my extra lives, what do I have to be afraid of?—but in situations where it's important not to get caught. Such as when sneaking into a restaurant at midnight.

"Gray, wait up."

The urgent whisper had come from behind me. The scarecrow had never spoken to me before.

I turned to whisper back, sharply. "Baker. What are you doing here? And where'd you come from?"

"Crime Knight, reporting for duty. I hid in the back of the car when you went into the kitchen for the flashlight. It wasn't Shane's fault. I convinced him to distract Hutch with a bone—I usually have one in my purse—or Hutch would have whined to be taken along. Anyways, here I am."

"I can see that."

"Before you say it, yes, I know it'd be bad if I were caught breaking in. Jasper Jones of *The Bee* would spin it as definitive proof of my guilt and so might Chief Gustafson. But I couldn't sit at home—or at your place—doing nothing."

Reminding myself to have a talk with my assistant later, I told her, "Since you're here, you may as well come along."

Almost slipping once or twice on the down-slope of the road and steadying each other, we used Ellie's key to unlock the basement door. There being no windows inside, it was safe to flip on the lights. I immediately gravitated to the fridge, where elaborate creations awaited. "How do we know which is Paul and Nicole's?"

Baker ran an expert eye over the selection. "There. Couples usually don't choose that color for the frosting."

Perched on the center shelf: the cake. Five levels of a shiny black, standing out in all the white. On the top, facing each other, a gingerbread couple had been given life with a design in frosting. One of the figurines sported moody Goth colors: a black dress paired with crimson high-heeled boots with jaunty spurs; the other had been given the usual black tuxedo but sprouted a subtly bigger head. I had a sudden doubt that Chef Urban would allow himself to mar his masterpiece by sneaking anchovy paste into it, but there was no turning back now. "Who eats what at these things?" I asked Baker.

"What do you mean, who eats what?"

"The ginger couple. Does the groom get his gingerbread self, or the bride's?"

"There's no hard and fast rule," she explained. "When I worked on weddings, sometimes the couple saved their ginger selves forever in their freezer at home. Mostly the groom is handed the slice of cake with the bride's stand-in and vice versa. It's more fun than getting yourself."

I passed the flashlight on to Baker, opened the fridge door, and used both arms to move the cake closer to the edge, as if giving it a big hug. Dowels and sturdy plastic-coated cardboard of increasing size supported the five levels. I reached up to pull out the bride on her plastic stake, leaving a teeny hole behind in the frosting. I aimed for a corner of the gingerbread figurine, but the monster, looming behind me, nudged my elbow and I broke off the entire toe of one of the cowgirl boots. Baker admonished me. "Gray!"

"Sorry." I placed the tidbit on my tongue and rolled it around while my client stared. "Let's see... Ground ginger, cinnamon, cloves, nutmeg... molasses, butter, brown sugar... baking soda... flour, white and unbleached... egg—from a local farm, I'm pretty sure—and lastly we have vanilla extract and a pinch of salt. Zero fish elements. Moving on to the icing, we have powdered sugar, egg whites—wait, what's this? An odd taste, almost metallic?... Never mind, it's the red food coloring for the cowboy boots. The splash of fish juice or whatever must be in the groom figurine, then." I stuck Nicole back and, moving on to mini-Paul, managed to do worse and broke off one of the hands completely. Baker rolled her eyes. I munched and shook my head. No fish.

"If we're wrong, we're going to have to leave a note," Baker grumbled as I set mini-Paul back.

"What for?"

"So the staff doesn't get blamed for the damage we've inflicted. *And* we'll owe Chef Urban a huge apology."

"Let's worry about that later." I dabbed frosting on my finger, then licked it off. Nothing out of the ordinary. "It's gotta be in the body of the cake, then," I concluded.

Baker pushed in front of me. "Let me do it. Do you have a penknife?"

"Why would I have a penknife?"

"Don't private investigators carry a toolkit?"

"I don't, unless you count my sketchbook and pencils. Which I left at home."

"Get me a cake knife from that drawer over there, then."

I did as instructed and returned with what most resembled a knife, a triangle-shaped cutter. Baker gently bent down the edge of the cardboard supporting the topmost layer, exposing the underside. She scooped out a morsel and passed the cake cutter over to me. Once again, I savored each ingredient. *It has to be here, the proof that will clear Baker.* "Chocolate, dark, sixty percent cocoa—no, sixty-five. Vanilla bean, Tahitian. Same flour as before." I kept on going, the theory I'd constructed on four facts and a moat collapsing around me with each ingredient I listed. "White sugar. Egg yolks. Butter and bacon fat in equal quantities. And a pinch of salt. Well. That settles it. Not a whiff of fish. I was wrong."

Baker, who'd been about to shut the fridge door, spun around to face me. "Back up. Did you say *bacon fat*?"

"I presume it's a good substitute for butter. Why does it matter? It doesn't swim."

The Oversized Raindrop of Incredulity appeared to Baker's left, suspended motionless in the air. She stared at me. "But... bacon? I don't believe it. Erin's Cake is listed in the catering menu as *vegetarian*."

This struck me as tangential to the reason why we'd snuck into a restaurant's basement at midnight. "So the chef made a small oversight."

"You don't understand, Gray. All these *years*, customers enjoying their slices, and none of them ever knew what was on their fork. Not only vegetarians, but customers with religious concerns or allergies, not to mention the whopping fat content... Are you sure? Gray?"

"Hmm?" I battled a major impulse to fling myself atop Chef Urban's masterpiece. "Yes, I'm sure. Besides the smoky undertone, there's a particularly rich, velvety note to bacon fat. One to be appreciated, not frowned upon, if you want my opinion." The Monster of Hunger agreed, a tentacle wrapping itself around my wrist in an attempt to guide my hand toward the cake. I was having trouble resisting its push. I reached out—but Baker scooped out a morsel for herself. Tried it. Shook her head. "Now that you've pointed it out, I can taste it. No idea how I missed it before."

A thought fought its way in between ones that mostly had to do with further munching and finger-licking. "We found it, the motive—the real reason why Chef Urban doesn't want to part with the recipe. It's not because it's his signature creation, not because he dedicated it to Erin. He wants to retire without anyone finding out the truth about the secret ingredient."

"I can't believe it. He's been lying for years."

With a gigantic effort, I pivoted away from the fridge. "I try not to judge. People do things."

"Oh, I'm definitely judging."

"This must be the nuance in the situation that Chef Urban hinted at to Paul. The chef's got the upper hand, even if Paul doesn't know it yet. Paul will have to let him retire along with the recipe, or risk the bad publicity."

"What's wrong with you? You sound odd."

For half a second, I thought the problem tooth had started affecting my speech, but that wasn't it. Maybe it was the midnight silence of the place, or the fact that we were keeping our voices low, but a different kind of hunger flamed up inside me as Baker went to the fridge past me, saying, "We better put everything back."

She moves with such grace.

How had I not noticed that before? I watched her tuck mini-Paul nearer to mini-Nicole so the groom's missing hand wasn't so obvious. She let the fridge door close, then took the cake cutter to the sink, passing me again—*her eyes, endlessly deep*—to rinse it out, the curve of her neck elegantly arched as she bent over the sink. A heady fragrance entered the room, rich and whispering with undertones: mulled wine, rain-soaked earth, a hint of sea air, a droplet of golden honey. I took a step forward, gripped with a strange desire to nibble on one of the fingers she was drying on a paper towel, the rough cellulose fibers meeting elegant digits, rose nail polish, and smooth skin...

And stopped as she spoke, her tone matter-of-fact, the words those of a Crime Knight—not a potential lover. "This was Chef Urban's secret, but it can't have been Adam's."

I cleared my throat. "Why not? It all makes sense. We know that Adam wanted a fresh start, everything out in the open. He must have insisted they come clean about the world's best cake. With his business partner ready to tell the world, Chef Urban has no choice but to act fast. His reputation is at stake—and Erin's good opinion of him."

"Adam didn't know."

Adam. Maybe she hadn't been in love with him, she'd said as much, but we'd come here for a reason. *Because he died*...and Baker phoned an old friend for help.

"What makes you so sure he didn't know?"

"He'd have put a stop to it. Too much legal risk—and it would have been the right thing to do."

"Maybe you didn't know him as well as you thought."

It was a low punch, one I regretted immediately.

She slid the cake cutter back in the drawer. "Maybe I didn't."

Coiled barbed wire now cut the room in half. Without meeting my eyes, she went to the linen shelf, where the small lockbox sat. "You don't think it's in there, do you? The recipe?"

"I can't imagine he'd have written the bacon part down."

"As you say, people do things." She started trying out combinations.

I was wrong about the fish. What else had I been wrong about? The Monster of Hunger, pushed back by the barbed wire, demanded a reason and suspicion entered the room, a thin, misty cloud. Baker had grown up on the lowest rung of the hierarchy in her family, behind her brothers. Homeful is why she returned Two Lakes. She thought she had that with Adam—a found family—but it had turned out to be a lie.

But the letter we reconstructed, it cleared her, I reminded myself. Rosemary fashioned one to taunt Baker, the other to the real killer to ask for more money.

Unless...

All the doubts I'd pushed away came back in a rush. I could only see what I was allowed to see. *I'm not a magician.* I'd had my doubts about the lemur. I studied Baker's features as she tried combinations and thought, *It's hopeless.* Every statement, every feeling and emotion I'd seen with my own eyes, it all could be explained as either innocent or as ruthless. *Sure, I threw a flower pot against the wall. Doesn't mean I followed it up by scheming to murder Adam.* Not a lie, necessarily. She hadn't meant to kill him, just teach him a lesson, but he'd died... In which case, I stood in the middle of a restaurant basement captivated by the Fragrance of Attraction—to a killer. *Nonsense,* I told myself, *all of it.* But was it?

This is what feelings do, muddy matters.

I said, "Baker, excuse me for a minute."

"Where are you going?" she said without looking up from the lockbox.

"Back in a jiffy."

I left her still trying out combinations and disappeared behind the inner door to the darkened garage. *Hair on cake! Bugs on cookies! Mold on soup!* A furry rodent emerged and chased Hunger back into its stone, following it in a shrinking jump. As the distraction vanished, so did the Mist of Suspicion, into some hidden corner of my soul garden.

I returned to find Baker standing in a cloud of stifling humidity. "How hard can it be to guess three digits? You don't happen to know Chef Urban's birthday, do you?"

I was back to thinking clearly again. Of course it wasn't Baker. The two hundred and six entries in my sketchbook, everything I'd learned about the human soul, led me to believe that Baker would never have stranded Adam, or paid Rosemary for her silence and then killed her. Maybe she had murder in her—maybe there's murder in everybody—but not like this. To defend another person, even a stranger perhaps, from immediate danger, but that was all. "Try Erin's birthday. She told me she turns sixty in September. No idea what date."

"Right, 9-0-1... 9-0-2..."

Conrad's undisclosed ingredient seemed to have done the job of convincing her of his guilt, but I had fresh doubts. "I wonder if you're right and Adam had no idea about the cake's top-secret ingredient."

"You've changed your mind?...9-0-6...9-0-7...9-0-8... Finally!" The lid opened under her hands to reveal recipes on index cards, about forty of them. She thumbed through. "It's not alphabetical. Chocolate mousse, tiramisu, rhubarb pie, potica, Bundt cake... Here we go, Erin's Cake! Yup, he wrote in *b. fat,* 1 cup along with the rest of the ingredients. Well, I'll be."

"What's that? Under the recipe cards."

She lifted it out. "A letter."

I groaned. "Not *another* one."

CHAPTER FORTY-THREE

Two pages, handwritten and folded into thirds, with Sunday's date at the top, the day Rosemary died. The chef must have taken his time composing the text. Nothing was crossed out or corrected, and the phrasing leaned toward formal. We read together, Baker gripping the letter as I hovered over her shoulder.

Dearest Erin,

A matter has been troubling me since Adam's passing and I wanted to get my thoughts down on paper. Whether I'll give you this letter remains to be seen. If, come the morning of Paul and Nicole's nuptials, the police have not arrested anyone, I'll hand-deliver this to your door and we can decide together whether Paul should be warned.

Were I in possession of undeniable evidence, it would be different. What I do know wouldn't fill a teaspoon— but it left a strange taste in my mouth and I can't seem to get it out of my mind. That terrible day, I overheard Nicole Cooper speak to Adam. Just a short exchange in the corridor in the late afternoon. It barely registered with me at the time. Nicole asked Adam if he planned to drive around at the end of the evening as usual. A natural enough question given the weather, concern for her employer—if it weren't Nicole asking it. Adam replied that he wasn't, what with the storm. Yet he ended up in Lost Wolf Woods.

So there you have it. A passing question that proves nothing. Certainly not worth going to the police with.

Still, I'll never forget the look in Nicole's eyes as she watched Adam walk away. There was a cold, cruel depth to them, unless that's my imagination talking. Rosemary happened to pass us and I wonder if she saw as well and that's why she died.

So, should Paul be warned not to marry Nicole? I'm not sure, even as I write this. I feel it's my duty to speak, at the risk of alienating him. At the risk of alienating you.

Another matter weighs heavily on me, the reason why I've never spoken about us all these years. Dearest Erin, it's not because of loyalty to Fred even in death. I didn't want to lie to you. I knew the truth would make you think less of me. The cake—

The letter stopped here, near the bottom of the second page, as if its penner had been interrupted in the task. Baker silently folded it back into its envelope.

"The Goth wedding..." I spoke slowly, still working it out. "Paul relayed a bit of inside knowledge, a mantra that Troy Cooper learned from his grandfather—and Nicole probably learned from him. *Give 'em something to look at*. And so a midnight ceremony at the Oldehouse—how unusual, how unique... All to take our eyes off of the murder?"

"Paul must have been lying about his brother choosing him over Linda Bolander."

I shook my head, though I couldn't very well explain why I believed Paul. "Whatever issue Nicole had with her future brother-in-law, it wasn't going to be solved by Adam moving to the beach. Here is what must have happened... Having said yes to Paul's proposal when he calls from Duluth, Nicole goes home at the end of the workday as usual. Spends some time calling girlfriends, asking them to be in the bridal party, so sorry for the short notice and how about emerald green dresses? Paul knocks on the door but she sends him away to a movie. Once he leaves, she gets off the phone and, having borrowed her father's gun—"

"Do we know for sure he owns one?" Baker interrupted.

"More than one, based on photos in *The Bee* at the start of each hunting season—the mayor in blaze orange and with a rifle by his side... Nicole, armed, drives to the resort and stows herself in Adam's BMW. She levels the gun and directs him to drive into the woods. Adam is sent off to his death and Nicole gets behind the steering wheel of the BMW, pulls up outside the clubhouse payphone—to call who to pick her up?"

"Paul?"

"Not Paul...her father. What choice does Troy Cooper have but to hurry over in his pickup, help stage the scene, and try to squash the story afterwards? His own daughter, carrying his grandchild. He can deal with the police, but there's a problem—Rosemary must have seen Nicole hide out in Adam's BMW. She demands money for her silence and the Coopers, father and daughter, pay up. Then Nicole overhears Rosemary bragging about the dinner with me, or the story makes its way to her ears some other way. Rosemary knows too much. She can't be allowed to speak with me. Again, Nicole acts without delay. Rosemary is surprised to see her, but not afraid, and turns her back. Nicole strikes."

Baker sighed. "It all fits. Why does it make me sad? We've found Adam's killer."

I glanced at the droopy sunflowers surrounding her form and decided practical was the way to go. "I better let Shane know what we dug up. He'll be wondering what's taking us so long."

I made a move toward the wall phone, then froze. A sound had come from behind the side door, the one we'd used to get in.

"Someone's here," Baker whispered.

We listened as a key slid into the door. As we'd left it unlocked, the intruder—the *third* intruder, given that Baker and I had no business being there—managed to lock it and so the door didn't open immediately. This gave us precious seconds. Baker set the letter and lockbox back in place while I dove across the room to turn off the lights. The choices for a hiding place were under the stairs leading to the restaurant above, or behind the connecting door to the pitch-black garage. We hurried into the garage, leaving the door open a sliver, and I clicked off the flashlight. Other than the soft glow of the glass-fronted refrigerator and the blink of the digital clock on the linen shelf, the basement settled into darkness.

Barely in time. A squeak of door hinges and a person stepped in, their tread strangely heavy on the concrete of the basement floor. A flashlight beam bobbed, altering the shadows under the door behind which Baker and I breathed silently.

The intruder paused to listen, as if they sensed our presence. The heavy footfalls approached. *Clunk, clunk.*

CHAPTER FORTY-FOUR

The footfalls stopped before they reached the door behind which Baker and I crouched. We heard faint beeps: phone keys being pressed. A familiar voice, male, cleared cold air out of a dry throat. "Cooper here. Yes, I know what time it is but *you* said twenty-four-seven. Look, I have something... Rosemary Moore's death was no accident, not accordin' to Chief Gus... Hold on, I'm getting there... Gus says Rosemary got struck on the back of the head—*with Adam's award*. And guess what they found at Clementine Baker's house?... Yup, that's what the police carried out... A dryer vent in the backyard... That's what I said, a *laundry vent*. Clementine Baker wanted Rosemary silenced and the award came in handy..."

Next to me Baker shifted and I elbowed her as a reminder to keep her temper in check. She elbowed me back. For my part, a low growl emanated from my pocket, making it tricky to hear parts of the conversation. There was a pause while the mayor listened to what the person at the other end of the line had to say. He came back with, "No, she hasn't been arrested yet. Soon, I expect." *Growl.* "And Jasper? Not a whisper of my family name. Make sure to get that into the paper, that this has *not a damn thing* to do with Nicole, you hear?... What?... No, I don't care about deadlines, just get it done! I don't want anything to ruin my daughter's day."

The handset slammed back into place, followed by more heavy footsteps, in the direction of the fridge. They stopped there.

Growl. I'd heard enough.

Lightly placing my hand on Baker's arm to signal that she should stay put, I stepped out from behind the garage door, switching my flashlight on abruptly as I did so.

Troy and I managed to blind each other temporarily. He barked, "Who's there?"

"Rodrick Gray."

"Gray? What are you doing here?"

"Investigating."

"Alone, I take it."

"Best way to break into a place."

He stood in front of the fridge with his daughter's wedding cake at its place of honor. He held the flashlight in one hand and a small glass jar in the other.

"I take it you overheard," he said conversationally.

"Every word."

His customary drawl was missing. "I snuck out of the house to make the call. Too many relatives around, and all of them nosy, loud and tipsy after the rehearsal dinner."

There was no reason not to be polite. "How did dinner go?"

"Nikki enjoyed it. The chef made banana bread for her... We've got a problem."

I agreed with him on that. "There's only one way you could know about the award being the murder weapon. About the laundry vent. And it's not because Chief Gustafson told you. He wouldn't disclose the details of an investigation that involves your family."

"He told Sheriff Doubek and the good sheriff passed the juicy tidbit along to me."

"No, I don't think so." I shone the light on the glass jar. There was some kind of whitish jelly inside. "What is that, lutefisk?

Gonna plant evidence, hammer another nail in Baker's coffin? A smudge of odd-smelling jelly on the gingerbread couple. Somebody's bound to notice. Paul is saved from having to be rushed to the hospital, Nicole's big day goes as planned, and the police are alerted. The jar is later found where, in the trash bin at Baker's house? Her vendetta against the Lindstrom family continues—and all of it leads the police further away from the real killer." I couldn't keep the triumph out of my voice. "Who is Nicole. You're covering up for your daughter."

"Why would my Nikki have done that, killed Adam and Rosemary?"

"I don't know that part," I conceded. "Perhaps you can tell me."

"You have it wrong."

Cooper stuck a hand in his pocket. The jar was gone and the barrel of a gun now gaped in my direction. I took an instinctive step back before remembering that I had extra lives.

He waved the gun. "Drop the flashlight on the floor."

I did so. It landed with a clatter and rolled a bit. "Nikki killed two people, didn't she?"

"Don't use her name."

Crou-crou. A squawk and a soft flutter in the dark above our heads.

The motive still eluded me. "Does it all have to do with money, trying to win the family fortune back? Would Adam have insisted that Nikki sign a prenup before marrying his younger brother—same as Tiffany did—and so he had to go? Let me have the gun and we can drive to the police station. It's the best course of action—for you, for your daughter."

"You can't resist inflicting advice on people, can you, Gray?" The folksy accent came and went. "Your father had an eye for readin' people too, but he put it to a different use. If I were you, I'd worry about my own hide."

"I'm not my father."

"He wasn't much of one, from what I remember."

If he meant for the dig to distract me, it didn't work. "Not like you, protecting a daughter who killed two people... Does Nikki remind you very much of your late wife?"

At my words, a willow grew tall and broad. I got it, then. The brash cowboy act of the man in charge of Two Lakes was just that, an act. Troy Cooper had a soft spot. A single one—but it left him wide open. Under the cascading willow branches lay rich, bare soil. Life-giving earth, every grain and speck a token of love. "Nikki is the spittin' image of Grace. The same smile. The same sparkle." His voice had cracked. Shadows hid his face above the flashlight but I thought I saw a tear roll down one cheek. He didn't bother wiping it away. "I'd do anything for her."

There was an ambiguity as to which *her* Troy Cooper meant.

But one thing was clear, I'd been wrong—Nicole wasn't the killer. "It was you all along. In the car with Adam that night. Waiting for Rosemary outside her door."

He didn't deny it. All pretense left him. "Yes. I killed them."

"Why do it?"

"Nikki asked me to."

Just four words. And behind them... Other than the willow for his late wife, Cooper's garden had become inhospitable to everything beyond Nicole's needs. His beloved child had asked. He'd provided. Ridiculous ice sculpture for a wedding, a great, big raven? Sure. Murder? *You betcha.*

He'd recovered his composure. "Wasn't hard. Nikki called me and I knew what I needed to do. I left the truck at home and skied over to the Toast to Adam dinner, my cowboy boots in a back-pack. The cold didn't stop me—I wore a visor and the snowsuit covered the rest. I'd done it before. Good for the mayor to be seen conquering the outdoors even if the business suit underneath ends up wrinkled—sixty-four years old and still goin' strong. At the restaurant, I stashed my ski gear in Adam's BMW—he never bothered locking it—then got a promise out of him to give me a ride back later because of the storm."

"A gamble—Adam might have mentioned it to another

person, and you risked being seen near his car. Is that what happened? Rosemary saw?"

"No one lingered in the parking lot, not with the windchill." He continued in an unrushed fashion, as if he had all the time in the world. And still it came, above us: *crou, crou*. "At the end of the night, I hopped into the BMW and waited while Adam helped Rosemary to her own vehicle. The skis between us sticking into the back seat, Adam drove and chatted about his future, oblivious. When we neared my house, I flashed my gun and made him drive past, turn into the woods. Ordered him to pull off to the side of the road and get out. The snow had started. I think he knew I planned to shoot him. I wasn't expecting him to fight back. He threw the award at my head—took it out of his coat pocket—and cut me right above the eye."

"Good thing you wear a cowboy hat," I commented, "or your injury might have been spotted."

"The bullet missed and he took off into the woods. Saved me from having to shoot him. Cleaner, anyways."

"You waited to make sure he didn't come back, then poured water in."

"He was hydrating, whatever that means, and had a water bottle in the car. That gave me the idea of emptying it into the gas tank. I ran the engine awhile, put my ski gear back on, and then—

"And then," I glanced from the gun barrel down to his ski boots, "you skied home."

"It's not that far from the woods to my house, a couple of miles, all downhill. The kitchen clock read one a.m. by the time I shook snow off my boots and skis. Nikki had long gone to bed."

No accomplice, no Y. Unless you counted the person who'd stayed safely at home that night, making calls to her bridesmaids.

I filled in the rest. "The storm erased your tracks but there was one problem—your blood was on the award, from where he hit you. You had to take it with you. Then another problem. You failed to foresee that Clementine Baker would keep badgering the police. Then there was Rosemary."

"Meddlesome women, both of them. Why couldn't they have minded their own business? What does Rosemary do? She spots bootprints in the fresh snow—cowboy boots, distinctive—leading from the restaurant to her boss's car at the end of the night. Leave it to Rosemary to file that bit of information away. She asked for a thousand dollars, instructed me to slip an envelope with the cash between some legal reference books. I had to come up with a pretense for being at the library. Research into family history. I tucked in the money, then made a show of peeling off in my pickup as if going home. I doubled back and parked in the alley behind Town Hall. I kept an eye on the library doors from my office window. That's how I figured out the identity of the blackmailer."

"Did Nicole overhear Rosemary blab about dinner with me and the pearls? I'm pretty sure Rosemary wasn't gonna tell me a gosh darn thing."

"Sooner or later she'd have talked to the police or a reporter. Money wouldn't have been enough. For some, it's about attention and Rosemary was that kind. Trust me, it takes one to know one."

"That—and you didn't want to keep paying."

He raised the weapon a smidge. "Well, sure. It was easy as pie. I waited outside her house, where the porch light didn't reach. She never saw it coming. After I made sure she wasn't getting up, I saw that letters had slipped out of her purse. I unsealed both and read them. One was addressed to Clementine Baker. I left it for the police to find. Even if I'd read the other letter beforehand, the one that told me she wasn't gonna talk—well, like I said, Rosemary got too greedy."

"Why not swap the letters, make it seem like she'd been blackmailing Clementine?"

"The money. Your gal, how much she have in the bank?"

"Right, no money to follow."

He scratched an ear. "You know, I'm not sure why I'm even telling you all this."

"People tell me things."

Crou, crou. "On the other hand, why not? It's not as if you're gonna live long."

He spaced out the words with deliberation. He wasn't just informing me of my fate—he was steeling himself for what he had to do, the beam of his flashlight exploring the floor and walls. Unaware that I wasn't quaking in my boots at the sight of the gun, he clicked his tongue. "Why did you have to butt in? I've killed two people. You'll be the third."

Crou-crou, now more urgent.

I looked up. A bird circled above us, its wings brushing against the low ceiling. Glossy black, it blended into the shadows, more of a movement than a creature. Same as the version chiseled out of ice and sitting in the freezer behind me, this bird wasn't made of feather and bone, but bits of soul. I'd heard the flutter of its wings once before, in the resort parking lot when Nicole chirpily chatted about the perks of the Oldehouse—such an abandoned, chilly place. The words had jolted a memory back into Troy Cooper. He'd left a human being to die in the cold of the forest. Invited the raven into his soul garden.

But I still had no idea why and it was eating at me. "Why did Nicole want Adam gone so badly? He was on his way out the door, with everything going to Paul. If it's not about a prenup..."

He didn't respond. Cooper's features had gone hard and ashen. He may have been doing this for Nicole, but it wasn't easy for him. He wouldn't be rid of the memory anytime soon, if ever. An odd moment for me to experience empathy, but there it was: my own likeness by his side in understanding that he had done this for his daughter. Only briefly, though.

Cooper clomped forward in his ski boots and bent down to pick up my flashlight, switching it on and doubling the beam in his hand. His folksy delivery, like a mask, was back. "You're goin' someplace cold."

Assuming he meant the freezer, I turned toward it but he poked me in the back with the gun. "In there."

In there was the garage. I didn't like this one bit. Might have been a mistake to barge out like that to confront him. I had no worries about my own safety. *Baker has only one life.* Cooper poked me again and I pushed the door open—no Baker. Good. She'd had the sense to hide.

Cooper selected a numbered key from a short line of hooks along one wall, the double beam bobbing on the three catering vans and the patio furniture stored around the perimeter. I caught sight of Baker's pants leg behind the stack of umbrellas.

Cooper gestured to the nearest of the vans. "Go on and swing the back open."

Was he going to shoot me and stash my body into the back of the van? I doubted it—the basement walls weren't thick enough to muffle the shot, even with the restaurant above deserted. And it would leave a mess. I floated a question meant to save me from having to wait long for rescue, so Baker would know where to send the police. "Is the plan to strand me in Lost Wolf Woods, same as Adam?"

"Take a long look around, 'cause from here on out, it's just you and the inside of that van. Now get in."

I climbed inside. *Time to ready a stone,* for when he did shoot me. I reached into my left pocket, my fingers trained by the calendar and familiar with subtle grooves in the stones. It was after midnight. Tuesday. Pain.

It happened in a flash.

A sudden movement in the dark and Baker jumped out to tackle Cooper, bellowing as she did so, "You are *done* harming people."

Cooper swore and dropped the pair of flashlights—they made a noisy clatter along the floor—and stumbled. "For heaven's sake, how many of you are there?"

The flashlights rolled to a stop, illuminating the action from below. The barrel pointed every which way as Baker and Cooper fought for control of the gun. She was nimbler on her feet, the mayor handicapped by the clunky ski boots but having the advantage of height and weight. The raven circled furiously, shrieking.

Inside the van, I hesitated.

Options, two of them.

Hang back, the mayor isn't going to shoot anyone in the garage, don't make a chaotic situation worse.

And...

Help Baker.

Jailbreak. Something pushed me out of the van—or maybe I rode it out. A she-lynx, sleek, graceful, muscular, its amber eyes alive with a wild intensity.

I hit the ground and grabbed the mayor's gun arm. He stuck a foot out and shoved Baker against the van's door. She scrambled back up. Creatures crowded the room as the mayor and I now fought for control of the weapon: the raven whipped around above us in tight, angry loops while a pair of large cats hissed and circled below. Mine and Baker's. I wanted to protect her, she wanted to protect me.

An almighty bang, then another—Baker gave a strangled shout—an object poked hard at my chest, sent me stumbling backwards. I landed spreadeagled in the van, my feet sticking out of it. Blood gushing out with my final heartbeat, I lay inside the gourmet food truck staring at its white ceiling, unable to move, not knowing if my childhood friend still drew breath.

CHAPTER FORTY-FIVE

The van rattled along Two Lakes' roads. In the back of it, Baker and I repeated the same words over and over, hers a stunned, "But I saw you die," mine a short, *"Ow."*

I broke the pattern by heaving a tremendous sigh of relief from where I lay, slumped against a mini fridge. "I'm glad you didn't get shot, Clem."

She was crouched beside me. "Never mind me. *How?* I saw you die." She'd managed to grab a flashlight, one that must have been part of the van's supplies, with its different grip color, electric yellow. Wide-eyed, she shone the beam at my chest, where my vest and shirt had been pulled open. "The blood. There's so much of it."

This was true. On my clothes, the floor, on Baker. She'd tried to stop the bleeding with her hands.

I let her talk, the Oversized Raindrop of Incredulity suspended in the air above us. "Your skin—it's pristine. The bullet hole is gone... Rod, *I saw the bullet hit you.* Watched the life drain out of you and I couldn't do a damn thing. You—you had no pulse. No breath, no heartbeat. Just before you slipped away, your eyes glazed over and you said something—"

"I did? What did I say?"

"You wanted me to hand you the stone you'd dropped. Oh, it's dissolved to powder now..."

An earthy scent permeated the van, for my nostrils only. Petrichor. Rebirth. The first bullet missed us both but the other had torn through my heart. Had I been a regular person that would have been it. Pain's stone had done its work, rewoven severed connections—I didn't want to think about it too closely—and had left behind warm ash in my palm. The pain, though. *The pain.* Being brought back to life is a rough process and I couldn't send the pain away, not anymore. I was inside the oak, one with it —my skin its bark, rough and abrasive, my insides gnarled, knotted, aged, rooted. Blindly, I let the ash fall on the van floor. I was dead for a brief chunk of time—*how long?*—and now I wasn't.

Through heavy branches, I saw Baker poke a finger into the hole in my shirt. She shook her head. "Am I hallucinating? Are we both dead? Ghosts?"

I hadn't considered this option before. "I don't think so. People can see me and respond to my voice. Look, I'll explain later." The piercing burn in my chest subsided a shade, the oak loosened its hold on me, and I sat up gingerly. "How long was I out?"

"I don't know, four or five minutes? It felt like a lifetime. I've always thought that was just an expression."

It *is* just an expression, of course, but I understood what she meant. The vehicle changed lanes, jolting us both to one side. I borrowed the flashlight from Baker and shone it around. The back double doors lacked windows. A bulkhead separated us from Cooper, wire shelving with catering supplies fronting it. On the lowest of the shelves, an emergency kit with band-aids and a thermal blanket gaped open, the source of the flashlight. I shone the light toward the catering supplies. "Any knives up there we can use as a weapon?"

"Only the plastic kind, sorry."

Also packed into the van was the minifridge, a grill, a prep station, folded chairs, and an upside-down stack of plastic emerald-green vases, for Nicole's tulips, I guessed. A spatter of dark red marred the vases. *Nicole won't be happy about my blood being on them.* Or maybe she would.

I pressed my wristwatch light. Four or five minutes dead, add another ten to fifteen which I spent getting my bearings and adjusting to being Gray the Fourth. "Did the mayor say where he's taking us?"

The matter-of-factness of my tone helped and color started to return to Baker's face. The raindrop vanished. She mimicked the fake drawl. "Now you make yourself comfortable, hon. And don't bother yellin', not a soul's gonna hear you from in there."

"You didn't happen to notice if we turned east or west out of the parking lot?"

"I was too busy trying to plug up the hole in the middle of your chest."

"Is he driving us to the abandoned quarry past Ostford?—no, not the quarry. If his goal is to abandon the van and ski back home, he can't take us that far. He must be making sure no one's following before circling back to where, Lost Wolf Woods? The Oldehouse? The mansion's empty and dark, with what's probably a very cold basement where no one would hear a gunshot. A bold move, given that his daughter is getting married there tomorrow —no, later today." It was past midnight. Another jolt as the tires lost traction briefly on a patch of black ice and the catering equipment clattered. I chided her. "Baker, you shouldn't have done it."

"Done what?"

"Pounced on the mayor like that. I understand why you did— he killed your lover. Nonetheless."

"That wasn't why. Besides, you didn't seem to be doing anything beyond meekly following his orders."

"I had a strategy."

"To what, let Cooper shoot you?"

"To be fair, A, who takes a gun with them on a cross-country ski to use a resort phone? And B, I didn't think he'd do it in the garage. You were supposed to call the police after we left."

"And what if the police didn't catch up with the van in time, Gray? All I could think of was, *not on my watch*." She added a dry, "This was before I found out you have some kind of magical power."

Cooper made a wide U-turn. Still sluggish, I twisted on my elbow. The bullet, after going through me, had left a hole in the side of the van. "What can you see through that?"

She put her eye to it. "We're on a two-lane road, no streetlights or houses. Dark trees. There's a light snow falling..." She pulled back abruptly and stuck her finger through the hole and wiggled it.

"What are you doing?"

"Signaling the car going in the opposite direction."

We tried slamming against the back doors with our legs, with no luck. The mayor had secured the handles, probably with a cord from one of the patio umbrellas. We proceeded to yell and bang on the side of the van until our throats went hoarse. I croaked, "I wish we had water."

"Yeah? I wish we had something stronger." Baker seemed struck by an idea. "Hold that thought."

She poked around and emerged with a third-full bottle of white wine. "Whenever there's extra left over from an event, the staff tucks it behind the fridge. They make sure the driver stays sober, so I always turned a blind eye."

She uncorked the bottle and passed it to me, rather as if we were toasting Gray the Fourth. I took a swig of the air-chilled wine to wet my dry lips, and Baker and I did a couple more back-and-forths. If we continued this way, I'd not only be achy from getting shot but drunk. On the floor, the sticky stains were starting to congeal, remnants of the previous version of Rodrick Gray. Disturbing. The Fern of Aversion to the Sight of Blood grew out of my knee, curling away from the stain, and I was glad Baker couldn't see it.

"Baker, can you pass me a couple of paper napkins?"

I splashed wine onto the napkins and was about to wipe the

blood off my neck and chest, but stopped. The mayor believed I no longer breathed and I wanted to keep it that way. "This is what we'll do. When the doors open, I'll play dead. The mayor will need help carrying my body down to the basement of the Olde-house—or wherever he's taking us. It must be why he hasn't shot you yet."

"How practical of him."

"I suspect the idea is to make it look like a murder-suicide, if our bodies are ever found. Your explosive temper drove you to shoot me. Then, in a fit of remorse and guilt, you shot yourself."

She winced. "Explosive temper?"

"It's just how the story is going to go. He'll make sure Jasper Jones gets it into the paper. Speaking of your temper..." The van had come to an abrupt stop, the engine still running. "Feel free to let it out. The mayor is a big guy and I'll need all the help I can get. A bullet hurts like heck. My chest is on fire."

"Right." Baker weighed the empty bottle in her hand, fingers wrapped around its neck, her back against the prep station.

I lay back down to play dead. We waited to hear the driver's side door open.

The van rumbled on. False alarm. Only a traffic light, which probably meant we were back inside Two Lakes proper.

We'd reached the forty-minute mark when the vehicle slowed for a right turn. The tires were now running over gravel. When they stopped, with the van facing downhill, the peephole to the outside world showed only dark and pine trees.

"What's he waiting for?" Baker asked uneasily, leaves whispering in the van.

But Troy Cooper did wait. Another half hour, with the engine idling and the lights off. None of his emotions seeped out through the material of the bulkhead, although I heard a soft *crou, crou* now and then. Finally a sound broke the silence—the driver's door opened, the engine still on.

Baker and I moved into position, ready to outsmart our kidnapper.

The back doors stayed shut. Nothing transpired for a blink, after which a whole lot happened all at once. The engine revved, shattering the hush of midnight. The van shot forward and rumbled down a slope, gaining speed. Baker and I held on. The van lurched onto level but noisier terrain, one that rattled and thumped beneath us for a few seconds. A moment of weightlessness followed, as if we were trapped in an elevator, and then an almighty *thunk*. The pair of us lurched along, the van skidded a good distance. Stopped. A hush descended. Then a groan arose from all around, an unearthly one, and Baker's nails dug into my arm.

CHAPTER FORTY-SIX

The right rear wheel broke through the ice first, tilting the van to that side. Baker and I grabbed hold of whatever we could to steady ourselves as everything not bolted down started rolling and catering supplies spilled from shelves. The remaining wheels still had purchase on the slick surface, but not for long. Water started to seep in through seams and joints and the bullet hole.

Another jolt. The left rear wheel.

"Gray!"

"Yes, this is suboptimal."

I did a quick calculation. My extra lives—now down to six— would buy me additional time. Drown, come back to life, repeat, maybe enough to find an exit and swim to the surface.

Baker has only one life.

We sprang into action. Baker smashed the wine bottle against the minifridge, sending glass flying. We attacked the bulkhead separating us from the driver's seat, the only way out. Baker sliced at the straps holding the wire shelving in place, I pulled. The shelf down, we attacked the padding. Baker slashed with a fury, I used my fists. Our hands would be bruised and raw if we escaped alive. All the while murky water poured in.

It hurt, the cold.

A front wheel lost its grip and the van jerked again. As we pushed and pulled and slashed, Baker spit out between jagged breaths, "Gray, I don't suppose you have any other magic tricks up your sleeve?"

"Wish I did."

The freezing water had gurgled up to our waists. If Baker lost consciousness—no, say it like it is, I told myself—*if she drowns*—I could pull her to safety. I'd read news stories about people resuscitated after falling through surface ice. *No villain is strong enough to defeat us.* A cheesy and childish slogan, maybe, and I was going to give everything I had to make sure it stayed true.

Baker cheered as the divider gave halfway and water seriously poured in—the mayor must have rolled down the side windows before taking off. She wedged herself into the space we'd opened and wiggled through to the other side, with me pushing on her soles. She stuck her arm back in to pull me up but my shoulders wouldn't fit.

"Clementine," I ordered, "go."

"Not doing anything of the sort, Rod."

"Get to shore." Water sloshed across the bridge of my nose and I coughed it out. Hunger in its stone meant I didn't recognize the taste—it was more of a familiarity, a homeful of sorts. "I'm pretty sure we're in Loon Lake—there's houses all around—get yourself to the closest."

"Move—ug—back."

The van now fully submerged, both of us holding our breath, she kicked at the bulkhead with her legs, I pulled at it. The gap widened, an exit opened, and I swam up, following Baker through the open window on the driver's side. I popped up at the surface, spit a mouthful of water out, and gulped air into my lungs. "Clem!"

"Behind...you."

With difficulty, shivering, we hauled ourselves up onto an ice floe no larger than a card table. The van continued its slow descent to the bottom. The churning waves settled down quickly, covering up all evidence of the large vehicle that'd been there moments before.

It was only then that we looked around. The light snow had stopped. The moon hid behind the clouds but this was my neighborhood and my lake and I didn't need to see more than contours of houses to confirm where we were. Cooper had driven the catering van onto the fishing pier that poked into the wide end of Loon Lake, by a small beach, part of a park bordered by pine trees. Across the water, at the reedy tip, 12 Nestling Lane awaited.

The closest houses, their windows unlit, slumbered in the night. We yelled but our voices didn't carry far enough. The pair of us were soaking wet, trembling in the frigid air on the unstable surface. My gloveless fingers throbbed and ached, and so did my toes in sloshy boots. Hypothermia and frostbite were probable, imminent. Between us and the shore lay a daunting path—cracked, unpredictable ice and narrow pools of dark, open water.

"I'm going to swim back to the pier and get help," I said without hesitation.

"I'll do it," she spit out between chattering teeth. "I'm a strong swimmer and you were shot not even an hour ago."

"I can return to life if I drown."

"Yeah? Again?"

"Not indefinitely, but..."

Six lives divided up between our unstable perch and the shore. It was possible. Hopefully the payphone at the beach park was in working condition. If not, I'd run to the nearest house and bang on the door. I wasn't about to let Baker die within view of the backyard where we had once played as children.

The ice creaked under us.

Baker wheezed, "Look."

A pair of lanterns on the shore. No, headlights, twinkling. A figure stood next to the car, jumping up and down and waving its arms, the voice muffled and low. I had to shake water out of my ears.

The figure gestured to a stack of canoes and cupped its hands. "Boss, I'm coming!"

CHAPTER FORTY-SEVEN

Around nine, I finished my second hot shower of the morning, then joined Baker in the kitchen. She was in my spare pajamas, a steaming mug of coffee in front of her, and projected a slumbering shadow onto the floor tiles. I had a slumbering shadow myself.

Neither of us had gotten a wink of sleep.

As Baker and I hung onto our icy perch, Shane had heaved one of the canoes off the rack of them, dragged it to the water and rowed over in a jagged line. Once we were safely onshore, he bundled us into Baker's Honda, which he'd left running with the heat on, and then put the public payphone to good use. I didn't have time to ask Shane what made him get behind the steering wheel, but I was glad he had. Baker and I shivered in the back seat under Hutch's blanket, with its dried muddy paw prints and fleece warmth, and watched vehicles with flashing lights arrive.

At the emergency room, no one noticed the round hole in my cardigan and shirt, the lake having washed off all traces of blood. The on-call doctor gave us the all clear and, in the early hours of the morning, offered Baker and myself a lift back to my house. The ruined clothing was now in the trash; after the second shower, I'd swapped my bathrobe for corduroys, a turtleneck, and one of the cardigan spares I kept folded on a shelf. I transferred the six remaining stones into its pockets.

Baker slumped forward, letting her forehead rest on the table. "Why can't I stop shivering?"

"Let's go."

"Where are we going?"

"For donuts. I'll call Shane, tell him we'll swing by to pick him up."

"Donuts, huh? I'll get my clothes out of the dryer."

The pain in my chest, where I got shot, had mostly dissipated. But elsewhere... My leg muscles burned with the night's effort as we walked the short distance out to the car. One of Chief Gustafson's officers had driven the Ford Falcon back from the resort and left it in the driveway, the keys on the dash. Andy probably, judging by the position of the seat. I adjusted it down to my height and we set a course for the diner. Bruises, purple and ugly, covered my hands as I steered—and Baker's hands, too. My nose ached with a runny redness. The tooth throbbed. Also, I had apparently at some point stubbed my toe without realizing it.

"You two look a little worse for wear." Ingrid ushered us into a booth and brought a pot of coffee and a plate overflowing with donuts.

Baker bit into a donut with relish, her Monster of Hunger practically bulldozing everything in its path—cheating death has that effect. I asked Shane how he knew where to find us.

"I've never been so glad to see anyone," Baker told him, her mouth full. The words came out muffled.

"When you didn't return or call, boss, I got worried. Officer Lewis had left for the night or I might have asked him for help. I finally decided I had to do *something*. I backed Clem's car down the driveway... Sorry, Clem, the left side mirror came off against the mailbox. I'll pay for it—and the damage to your mailbox, boss."

Strawberry jelly ran down Baker's chin. "You'll do nothing of the sort, Shane. You saved our lives."

"Or, at least, saved us from a risky and unpleasant swim to the shore. You can stop apologizing, Shane. Go on." Hunger's tentacles unrolled out of my own pocket and, too drained and weary to resist the jailbreak, I reached for one of the donuts.

Shane continued his story. "I arrived at the resort to see a van peel out, a pair of skis sticking out of the passenger-side window. Given the time of night, *totally interesting*, I thought. I *knew* that you had to be inside the van, both of you. I trailed it—a catering one, it had the resort logo—to Ostford and back. Clem's car kept losing traction on black ice, making me yelp every time. I dinged the front bumper against a stop sign—sorry, Clem."

She waved her third donut at him and dunked it in the coffee. "It's only a car."

"The van took Old Mill Way over to Loon Lake and turned onto the gravel road. Stopped at the rise, you know, where the slope starts dropping off. The driver killed the lights. Mine were already off—that's how the right side mirror went, against a tree. The driver—I assumed it was Chef Urban at the time—waited."

Our voices had not been exactly low and we'd started to acquire an audience. Ingrid's customers had draped themselves over the sides of the neighboring booths, openly listening. Monocles of Curiosity, a whole lot of them.

"Once the houses around the lake went dark, the driver jumped out and I saw that it wasn't Chef Urban after all." Shane absentmindedly picked up a glazed donut and chewed a largish bite. "Broader shoulders. Taller in the snowsuit. He took a quick look around and I saw his face before he slipped the visor on. Mayor Cooper. I didn't know what to do. Then I remembered..." Shane glanced around; the kitchen staff had come out to listen, agog and on their feet. "...something."

I could guess what. My extra lives.

"It was the right thing to do, hang back," I told him. "Cooper had a gun."

Screech. A real-life sound. Ingrid had joined the crowd, the Monocle of Curiosity distorting one eye, the legs of the chair she'd pulled up scraping against the floor. All conversation in the diner had ground to a halt.

"The mayor grabbed a single ski out of the van and propped the other at an angle down the driver's seat. Lodged it in against the foot brake, I'd soon realize. He spent a minute searching around on the ground—for a heavy chunk of ice, it must have been. He then leaned into the car and set the weight on the gas pedal—the engine revved. He slammed the door, pulled the wedged ski out the open window, and wham! The van lurched down the slope, built up speed as it barreled along the fishing pier —went airborne at the pier end—then rolled forward off onto the ice. *Wham!*"

This was met with audible gasps. Shane can tell a story.

"I may have yelped again. Can't swim." Shane put the donut down. "The mayor donned the skis and took off between the pines. I drove Clem's car onto the beach and waited. And there you two were, bobbing up, only a minute or so later."

"A minute or so?" Baker gave a shiver, not from the cold. "Felt like hours."

Shane filled us—the whole restaurant—in on the rest. Baker's Honda was still at the beach. He'd hitched a ride back from Officer Lewis and had a front row seat to the mayor's arrest. Chief Gustafson and his officers caught up with the mayor as he skied through sleeping neighborhoods, sweating in the snowsuit. Cooper pretended he was merely out and about getting some two a.m. exercise, but no one bought it. And when he heard that Baker and I had been rescued and were giving statements, there was no way out for him.

"Cooper tried to resist. Had to be bundled into a police car using the combined efforts of officers Lewis and Anderson," Shane said, resuming eating the donut, "all the while bellowing that he shot you in self-defense, boss, after Clem went berserk on him and you took her side. Good thing he missed, Chief Gustafson told him."

I met Baker's eye over my cup of coffee. "Good thing he did."

Ingrid got to her feet, shaking her head. "The mayor. Who'd have thought. Quite the lucky escape, Rod, almost getting shot and drowned." Then it came, the start of the slow clearing of my childhood friend's name. "And you too, Clementine... More coffee, everyone?"

CHAPTER FORTY-EIGHT

"Let's go crash a wedding," I said after the plate of donuts had only crumbs left on it and our audience had slowly dispersed.

"It can't still be on, can it?" Baker said. "With the bride's father arrested and accused of murdering the groom's brother."

"Only one way to find out."

Shane went upstairs to the agency to make a call at my request and Baker and I got back into the Ford Falcon. At the resort, we walked into a public scene in the lodge corridor.

"You *betcha* it's off." Clouds, bruise-purple and ominous, churned above Paul's scalp, matting his hair. "All of it. The ballroom banquet, the midnight ceremony at the Oldehouse—excuse me, you ordered me to call it the Old Cooper Mansion, soon to be the *new* Cooper-Lindstrom Mansion."

Nicole must have learned what happened before coming over, but she'd nevertheless donned a dress of ankle-length black silk. The matching veil was slung back and her crimson leather boots shone with polish. Heavy eyeliner encircled her eyes. Black lipstick. She clutched a Queen of the Night in one hand. A photographer, presumably there to take daytime photos of the wedding party, stood by uncertainly with a camera draped from his neck. Flanking him were four bridesmaids in emerald-green dresses. Tiffany wasn't among them.

Rounding out the group: Erin Lindstrom, Conrad Urban, Linda Bolander, and Todd West, along with a handful of other resort employees in their orange uniforms. Chief Gustafson and one of his officers stood nearby. It made for quite a crowd.

"Paulie, it's all lies, what they're saying about Daddy."

"My brother is dead. Your father killed him."

Nicole took a step back. "I'm sure Daddy didn't mean to, Paulie, must've been an accident..."

"Oh really. Your father *accidentally* sent my brother into the woods?"

Adam Lindstrom's widow arrived in time to hear this last statement. I assumed the police had contacted her but Baker whispered in my ear, "I called her while you were in the shower and left a message." Tiffany must have been in the middle of getting ready, as she wore the green bridesmaid's dress but not the gold shoes—just puffy boots, muddy.

"Troy Cooper, where are you?" Tiffany said, not quietly. She whipped her head around, searching for the white cowboy hat with the air of one who wanted to sink her manicured nails into the neck under it.

"He's at the station, under arrest," Chief Gustafson informed her. "How about we take this some place more private?"

Linda Bolander sent the photographer away and led a procession into the ballroom, where round tables were set up for the evening banquet. There was an empty platform where I guessed the ice raven was meant to go. Remaining on their feet, Nicole and Paul faced each other across the nearest of the tables. "Daddy —he'd never do such a thing—it must have been a misunderstanding."

We heard a door open and a wiry form slipped in. Shane had done his task, tracked down Jasper Jones. The reporter took a position by the wall. "Pretend I'm not here," he said and readied his reporter's notepad and pencil, then proceeded to make himself very visible. "So, is the rumor true? Has the mayor been arrested? Unless we're all here because someone has the wedding jitters."

"There'll be no wedding."

The chalkboard fence cracked and bent under the onslaught of her fiancé's storm. "Now, Paulie, you can't be mad at me. *I* didn't do anything wrong. I'm sure Daddy has a very good explanation if you ask him."

"Got a couple of witnesses here that say otherwise."

When Chief Gustafson speaks, people listen. He nodded at me and now faces turned to stare in my direction.

And I...froze. *I'm a safe ear.* I don't judge. A father had gone too far for his only child. A desperate act, one I could understand. Sure, he'd confessed, shot me in the chest, trapped Baker and me in a sinking van. Still. *I'm a safe ear.*

Baker sent me a glance and loudly announced, "Troy Cooper sent Adam to his death...*because Nicole asked him to.*"

"She's making stuff up to keep herself out of prison, Paulie," the mayor's daughter whined.

"No, she's not."

The Redwood of Determination was back by my side. I could understand even the most desperate act, but acts come with consequences—especially if you try to drown my childhood friend in icy Loon Lake. "Clementine's telling the truth. Troy confessed to killing Adam and Rosemary."

"Don't listen to them, Paulie, it's all lies. Daddy didn't know what he was saying. Why would I ask him to do such a thing? Adam *begged* you to take his place, Paulie. You phoned him and he said he'd considered Linda but in the end family's family, and all of it was yours. Right, Paulie?"

Paul had gone silent. An ashy tone settled on his features. He must have felt numb—there was nothing for me to see. Even Anger's storm had vanished.

I got it, then. This wasn't about a prenup. "You said no to your brother, didn't you?"

Paul nodded briefly. "Adam had been to visit Dad at the cemetery. Told me he'd asked for Dad's blessing to make the decision based on heart, not the bottom line. He wanted me at the helm. Sometimes people need a hand to pull them up, he said. Well, it wasn't what I wanted, to be pulled up. Adam had forgotten what Dad used to say, stand on your own two feet—he'd refused a job under his father-in-law as a young man... Adam didn't believe I meant it. Gave me twenty-four hours to think about it. I wasn't going to change my mind."

He stopped there. I filled in the rest. "After you got off the phone with him, you dialed Nicole and reached her where, the resort's front desk? No—the event coordinator office, her new assignment. She told you she was pregnant and you asked her to marry you. Then you made the mistake of mentioning Adam's decision—and your refusal."

"It wasn't what I wanted. I told her that."

"A test, that's what you meant it as!" A scent reached my nostrils, an unpleasant one, like pickled cabbage left outside in August. Nicole was desperate.

Paul was seeing things more clearly now. "Can you blame me? It may have crossed my mind. That if you said yes after I'd turned down the job and money, I could be sure you really loved me. That you weren't marrying me because my family is wealthy and you want to renovate the Oldehouse and live there."

"How did she take your refusal?" Chief Gustafson asked.

Paul answered, but he spoke to one person only. "You were mad about it at first, but then you said you understood."

"I *did* understand."

"Did you? Or did you dial your father's number as soon as you hung up?"

"Of course I didn't, don't be silly."

I may have been the only one to see wispy tendrils of silver fog rise up along her dress, clinging to the black fabric like ghostly fingers, but no one believed her. All along, a small part of Paul must have known that drawing attention to his fiancée and her father was best avoided. He'd pushed the concern away, come up with outlandish theories as to why his brother died.

"What I'm hearing is that Nicole got off the phone after talking to Paul and promptly called her father," Chief Gustafson said while Jasper Jones scribbled furiously. "There'll be a record of the call. But—" The chief looked from Nicole to Paul and back. "I'm unclear on one thing. Adam offered you the job. You passed. What changed when Adam died?"

Paul's shoulders sagged. The words came out reluctantly, as if he didn't care to have them out in the world. "Everything changed. My mother needed my help and so did the family business. No one had to pull me up—I stepped up. That's what it took, Adam dying."

The motive, finally. "And Nicole knew that," I said, "and so she asked her father for a favor, a big one. After which all she had to do was go home after work as usual and get cracking on calling friends to chat about bridesmaid dresses and come up with a theme for the hasty wedding—Gothic, how outrageous, never before seen in Two Lakes. Give 'em something to look at."

The cracks in the chalkboard fence widened. Behind it... Well, no one *feels* evil, even if they act like it or come across so to others. Fear closed in on Nicole—a dense forest hemmed her in, moving in beat by beat. And in the rotting underbrush, all around: statues, some chipped or broken, some fallen on their side, marble weeds. The Statues of Me, accumulated over the years, replaced by new ones as Nicole's image of herself matured—only not in a healthy way, but with each successive version grander, the pose more dramatic. The current one stood poised as if in the center of the universe, the marble blemish free, the chin lifted in a dismissive tilt, lips curled into a self-satisfied smile, the folds of the sculpted dress adding a regal touch.

Much packed the ballroom, climbed the walls, crowded the ceiling and the area under the tables. The Willow of Grief for Erin, who battled tears. Storms circulated above Baker and

Tiffany. Todd West picked at his sweater, anxiety's vines tight at the uncomfortable scene and growing from his torso up the wall he leaned against. Linda Bolander, with her tagalong windmill, had her arms crossed as if to say, *Let's get this over with so we can get back to work.* Officer Anderson once again sprouted a monocle. Conrad Urban had remained silent throughout, fiddling with an object in his apron pocket, engaged in some kind of private battle as he stood in the center of his ever-present moat. Even Chief Gustafson had succumbed to the situation and sprouted a thistle crown.

Every eye in the room was on Nicole. She took a step back and spat out at a still-numb Paul, "You weakling. He offered you the helm of his company, his half of it, his BMW. All you had to do was say yes."

"But I didn't and so you decided to do something about it?"

"I did nothing... Adam moving to San Diego or Key West or Hawaii, *none* of it would have been far enough. No spot on the globe would have been far enough for you to step up."

"And so, what, he had to go?" Paul inhaled, deeply. A free breath. "I meant it. I can't marry you now. I could never marry you. If the mayor had acted of his own accord—but to *ask* him... Unforgiveable. I'll be a responsible and joyful father to the baby, but that's all."

Nicole lifted her chin high up. Scrunched up her eyes. "There's no proof that I asked anyone anything. No proof—and there never will be."

She threw the Queen of the Night on the floor, stomped on it with a red boot, and left the room, trailing heads of iceberg lettuce —disappointment at her plans being thwarted—in her wake.

"Is that true?" Baker broke the silence after the door slammed shut behind Nicole. "What the mayor admitted to Gray—with me listening in—isn't enough to send her to jail along with her father?"

"Well, now." Chief Gustafson scratched his neck. "Troy Cooper did confess to the murders after we brought him in. Said he had a business beef with Adam. Apparently, way back, Fred Lindstrom paid a young town hall clerk to fudge the numbers on a wetlands report and allow the sale of town-owned land on the far side of Cooper Lake for pennies. Fred did the buying but the idea came from the clerk, whose grandfather had developed the marshy area between the lakes, also in a somewhat shady fashion. The bribe was paid and everyone moved on. Except years later, according to the clerk—who'd risen all the way up to mayor— Adam Lindstrom decided to come clean about what his father did. And so the mayor had to kill him. Cooper's been busy confessing to other bribes he's received over the years."

"That would have been, uh, before my time," Todd West chimed in, as if the chief had personally accused him of slipping a wad of cash into the mayor's pockets.

"If it's true, Fred never mentioned it to me." This from Chef Urban. "But then, he wouldn't have. I had my nose buried in the kitchen. It wouldn't surprise me—those were different times. Well, perhaps not so different after all. Did you know, Erin?"

She shook her head. "No."

"So Dad told Adam," Paul said, "but not me."

Adam had known—there was no way to be sure whether he intended to reveal all or not—and so did another person. When Rosemary wrote *I know all your secrets* in the letter with the herbal signature, she meant the Lindstrom family. The affairs, yes, but also Fred's secret from way back.

The ballroom slowly emptied, Linda instructing the staff still hanging around, "All right, show's over, people. Let's get back to work."

I turned to Jasper Jones. "Did you get all that?"

He flipped the notepad shut. "Clementine Baker, innocent. Wedding canceled. Troy Cooper confessed. A couple of you in this room seem to think Nicole egged her father on. Maybe she did and maybe she didn't, but the mayor has been taking bribes for years and it sounds like Adam was gonna talk. That pretty much sum it up?"

Chief Gustafson and his officer left, Jasper Jones trailing in their wake, still lobbing questions, the windbreaker swishing with his stride.

Baker watched them go. "That's it? Nicole gets off free?"

"Her father will never give her up."

Erin had said the words softly. Earth. It's unyielding when it needs to be. When it came to Troy Cooper, the police could dig and dig, but they'd never find anything.

Then again, maybe they would. I was the only one who saw, but I rather thought I saw the chief reach into his pocket and press the OFF button on a voice recorder as he left. I like to think the recorder belonged to Adam, that the chief borrowed it from the evidence room.

People and their emotions lingered. Erin stood by her younger son's side, a she-lynx under a willow tree: protectiveness of Paul sharing territory with grief over Adam. "I'm sorry you were ever suspected, my dear," she said to Baker.

Linda Bolander ran a harried hand through her hair. "What a mess. I don't think we can fire Nicole over this and give you your old job back, Clementine. As she said, there's no proof."

"It's all right. I don't want my old job back."

Linda looked at our small group and made a couple of executive decisions. "I'll help Paul run things as best I can. I won't hold a grudge that I might have had the big office if Mayor Cooper hadn't intervened. I've given twenty years of my life to this place —did you know I started out cleaning rooms?—and I plan to give it twenty more... And Erin? I was thinking the other day that it would be nice to have art classes on offer for guests who aren't into outdoor sports."

Erin glanced around as if searching for a nonexistent glass into which to dump the cigarette she didn't have in her hand. "I think more than that is called for, my dear friend. Paul's not happy where he is. I thought *I* might give it a try—with your help."

"Then we'll do that."

"Ms. Bolander, should we still set up the refreshments for the photo session?" Ellie Gackle had walked in, teetering under a stack of clear-lidded trays loaded with mini quiches and crab puffs. She glanced around uncertainly.

"Better put it back in the fridge, Ellie. No use in setting up for a wedding that won't take place."

"Ellie, hold up." I'd remembered something. "When you told me the other day that it's been tense under the new boss, whom did you mean?"

Todd West quietly moved over and took over the trays from Ellie. She beamed at him, causing him to almost drop the trays. "I meant Ms. Cooper. Now that she's in charge, she's kind of mean. She's always finding reasons to chew us out. You're either on her good side—or watch out."

"Ellie, I had no idea." Linda shook her head. "Next time, knock on my door. It's usually open... All right, I should call the Oldehouse caretaker and let him know the ceremony's canceled."

"Hold that thought."

The words had come out gruffly. Chef's hat in hand, Conrad Urban stepped in front of Erin. A redwood crushed the moat he'd surrounded himself with willingly all these years to watery bits. Conrad proceeded to announce the undisclosed ingredient in Erin's Cake to everyone within earshot. "Fred and I were desperate for the resort to take off. Sounds like we both made mistakes the other didn't know about. He paid a bribe, and I... In a moment of madness, I melted bacon fat into the batter. Just like that, the cake became a hit. Best cake in the world! I should've come clean years ago." The lie had become so ingrained that there'd been no silver fog for me to see. "I didn't want you to think badly of me, Erin, and so I said nothing. Kept my shame to myself." A whole lot of people stood around listening but the speech was intended for an audience of one. "Will you accept my apology for lying about your cake all this time, Erin? For thinking it mattered?"

"Connie, I wouldn't have cared. We all make mistakes."

"You forgive me?"

"I forgive you."

"Then..." He dropped down—on one knee. This produced gasps all around, though it was obviously just a marriage proposal. Proposals happened every day. The floor wasn't even particularly hard under his knee—the chef had rolled out soft earth of his own. *A troublesome tooth, now that's out of the ordinary.* The pain elsewhere in my body had settled to a dull ache but the tooth twinged sharply. I'd have to make that appointment as soon as possible. Dentists, not proposals, are to be appreciated. *Dentists and aspirin.*

Conrad produced an object out of the pocket of his apron, a plastic ring. He held it aloft toward Erin. "It's only a cake topper, but will you marry me?"

Erin spoke. A single word. "Yes."

"Today? I know an abandoned mansion may not be your style..."

"I don't care about that at all, Connie. Not one bit. But maybe we don't wait until midnight?"

The ring fit her finger.

I glanced at Baker. "Why are you crying?"

"Only a robot wouldn't be, Gray."

And so there was a wedding after all, Tiffany announcing to anyone within earshot, "If I have to wear this green horror, I better be *somebody*'s bridesmaid."

She was. No one wanted to go to the Oldehouse, so we put to good use the *Closed For a Private Event* sign on the ballroom doors, a priest was found, and it made no difference that the formal paperwork would be filed a day late. The happy couple stood in earth of their own making and there were doves, too, a quartet of them. Paul shook off all his troubles and served as the best man, carrying a soul-garden sunflower on his lapel, one of many in the room.

At the banquet afterwards, I deviated from my schedule yet again—I hoped this wouldn't become a regular thing—and uncorked Hunger for the occasion. The kitchen had redecorated the cake, with its black frosting and bacon-infused velvetiness, with whipped-cream roses.

After the proceedings, the newlyweds drove off on an impromptu honeymoon to Niagara Falls—fifteen hours each way, but something told me neither party would mind.

CHAPTER FORTY-NINE

With the case over, I ignored the message Baker left on Wednesday, hoping she'd forget about seeing me die and be reborn.

On Thursday, I aired out Anger and the storm found a target. Baker's wild speculation about the second letter, the fact that she ended up being correct...well, let's just say it was seriously irritating.

On Friday, I chatted with Chief Gustafson over the phone and asked him whether what he recorded was enough to send Nicole away, along with her father.

"Noticed the recorder, did you? Whether she's charged is up to the district attorney. I expect a jury'd feel sorry for her—the baby, for one—but we'll try. Maybe we get justice, maybe we don't. You know how it is."

I did. I told the chief I wouldn't see him at the gym this week —Shane had set up a Saturday morning dental appointment for me as, apparently, what they called "mild to moderate" pain wasn't enough to be considered an emergency to get me in sooner —and then went to my weekly date with the Joy & Humor stone at the bench in Cooper Lake Park. Sometimes—like when I built the snowman—these dates leaned toward the happiness half; other times I found everything unbelievably funny. It turned out to be Joy's day. I found my eyes moist at the recollection of Conrad proposing to Erin and that quartet of doves.

So. *Not a robot after all*. I merely took longer to get there.

CHAPTER FIFTY

"You owe me an explanation," Baker reminded me.

We were in her Honda. I'd finally returned her call and she'd offered to drive me to my dental appointment. I'd managed to be evasive on the way over but the procedure, a new filling, had rendered the world unsteady from under the brim of my fleece hat. My face felt lopsided, my tongue clumsy and oversized from the Novocain. "No chance you could forget what you saw?"

"You returning from the land of the dead? How could I forget that?"

Not only was Baker's car dinged here and there from Shane's adventures, the heat was slow to come on and we were both bundled up. A vehicle cut her off and she rolled down the window to send an angry gesture after it with a gloved hand. I recognized the driver. "Wade Gackle. Don't mind him. He's in a bad mood and I know why."

"Gackle... Ellie's husband?"

"Not for long. They're divorcing." I hadn't meant to reveal client information but, having already said that much, it didn't hurt to add, "It's his own fault."

"Good for her. I heard she asked Erin for a loan to buy the

Oldehouse and turn it into a B&B, now that Paul doesn't want it anymore... You're trying to distract me. It won't work, Gray."

I took a deep breath and proceeded to tell her everything, or most of it, anyway. By the time I finished, she'd pulled up the driveway of 12 Nestling Lane and was idling the engine in front of my garage. A gloved finger hovered an inch from my face. "You can see feelings?"

"And touch, smell, and hear them. There's this thing called synesthesia, where people see colors when they listen to music, or taste flavors when they read certain words. I seem to have ended up with a supercharged version of the phenomenon."

"And you have extra lives, like a cat?"

"Exactly like a cat—nine of them. You don't think a cat stumbled across one of these things—a meteorite—millennia ago?... But yes. I lost my original life in the knife attack—another when I got hit by a car; I'll tell you about it sometime—and a third one when Cooper shot me. Three gone, six remain."

She gave a small nod, as if this made perfect sense. "It's cold and I have more questions. Can I come in?"

I offered her coffee but she only wanted answers. I filled a glass of water for myself, dug up a straw, and we sat down at my kitchen table. Emptying the left pocket of my cardigan, I arranged its contents in a circle, a mini Stonehenge. "That one's Hunger. A monster lives in it."

"I don't see anything."

"Only I can. I let the monster out of its jail cell at dinnertime on Wednesdays. The one next to it is Anger. There's a storm in the stone. That one is Joy & Humor—sunflowers and polka dot balloons. Save your jokes until Friday so I get them... Today's is this one. Envy & Embarrassment."

She picked up E&E and turned it over in her hand. "Which one are you, envious or embarrassed?"

"Neither yet. I'd planned to air it out later."

"Great, I want to see you do it."

"Uh, well, let's see." I took a long slurp of the water. "Ask me how I feel about being completely wrong about Chef Urban."

"How do you feel about being completely wrong about Chef Urban?"

"I tried my best, that's where the facts and his moat pointed to, and I'm not perfect."

I double-tapped the stone. The fig leaf draped itself over my front, cutting an outline into my clothing, leaving the rest of me bare—to my eyes only, thankfully. "Now ask me again."

"How do you feel? You don't look any different."

"I feel foolish—quite a bit foolish." I could feel the heat in my good cheek. "Conrad Urban agreed to make the cake for Paul and Nicole's nuptials not to poison him, but out of respect for Paul's mother."

"You were half-right. Somebody *did* intend to mess with the cake, only it turned out to be Cooper."

I bent my head over the glass. "There's more. I didn't antici-pate that Paul might have said no to his brother—and Nicole's reaction—and what her needs meant to a loving father."

She shook her head. "That's not love. It's something warped."

The day's edition of *The Bee* sat between us. The mayor's arrest had taken over the front page for the fourth day in a row. Other than the wedding being called off, Nicole wasn't mentioned in any of the articles and most of the quotes were from Sheriff Doubek and not the local police station. Today's article was no different.

Ahead of his upcoming trial for murder, Troy Cooper has been coming clean about his financial crimes, including the one that ultimately led him to take the life of Adam Lindstrom and Rosemary Moore. *The Bee* has learned from Sheriff Doubek that a list is being compiled of all the bribes Troy Cooper has admitted to receiving. The district attorney, Gideon Nema, has told this reporter that the evidence is overwhelming...

Baker tossed the empty E&E stone from one hand to the other. "Rosemary wasn't wrong—Adam's death is on me. If I hadn't come back to Two Lakes, none of it would have happened. No farewell speech by Adam. Nicole wouldn't have watched Paul refuse the money, or begged her father to intervene. Adam and Rosemary, they'd be alive. The mayor wouldn't be sitting in jail, awaiting trial for murder..."

We'd been here before. "You're not responsible for the criminal behavior of others. And it was only a matter of time. Nicole knew that for Paul to be jolted out of his safe orbit, Adam had to go."

I'd counseled Paul to ask for full custody of the child, when it came. Whether Nicole went to prison or not, I was confident she'd agree to the arrangement. As to Baker, not a single gargoyle surfaced in the dentist waiting room and I even saw even a friendly nod or two. I said, "Pretty sure no one thinks this is your fault."

"Lorna from across the street stopped by to apologize about the brick. She said it was an accident—don't ask me how she might have accidentally lobbed a brick through my window—and that she hoped the Bundt cake she'd brought would make up for it." Baker shook her head. "I still can't believe it. Two murders... Wait, three! I forgot that he killed you too."

"Well, it didn't stick."

She glanced out the kitchen window at Loon Lake and gave a shiver. "I don't think I'll ever look at the lake the same way."

"It'll pass. Besides," I said, reaching for the glass, "if you hadn't returned to Two Lakes, love wouldn't have blossomed."

Water dribbled down my chin and I wiped it off, then looked up to find Baker staring at me. A roll of barbed wire had unfurled between us. *Ah, she'd misunderstood.* Pushing out of my mind the moment in the basement of The Cork when Hunger had almost gotten the best of me and I'd—absurdly—almost kissed her hand, I clarified. "Chef Urban and Erin. So something positive did come out of all this. In fact, let's count the number of people helped.

You, of course. Paul—better for him to know the truth now than after the rings were exchanged. Erin and Chef Urban. Tiffany. We got justice for Adam and Rosemary..."

"And Nicole's baby?" she said, a furrow on her brow. "Did we help the child?"

"I wish I knew. There's no easy answer there. The child will have a good father in Paul, and a devoted grandmother. That's more than some people get." A complaint slipped out, muffled by my swollen mouth. "By the way, that was a very lucky guess, Baker, about the second letter. Without any rational basis whatsoever, you managed to—"

"Whoa, Nellie. I had a reason."

"Yeah?"

"Where there's one, there's another. I doubted I was Rosemary's only target." She nodded at the mini Stonehenge. "And the remaining two stones?"

"Sundays I spend half an hour being sad. Hanging moss; if it rises to the level of sorrow, it morphs into a willow tree. Monday is... Well, I used to think the stone held nothing, or maybe gut feeling. Now I'm not so sure." Thumbing the stone in my palm, I pondered the window that had recently opened in the cloudy film. Things shifted when I watched my childhood friend wrestle with Troy Cooper for control of the gun. In a single breath, a jailbreak—by the Forest of Fear and the she-lynx who lived within— and I'd hurled myself at the mayor. All along I'd assumed that fear had stayed bonded to me after the knife attack five years ago, but never reared its head for a simple reason, the usual one: Given my extra lives, what did I have to be afraid of? But there it was, trapped in the stone. I sipped water through the straw and studied the tiny, eerie forest with the even tinier she-lynx roaming inside. Was there more in there?

Baker was browsing employment ads without paying much attention to them.

"Baker... Sorry."

"What for?"

"For not telling you everything in the first place. For it not being fair that I should have these extra lives and you don't."

"To be honest, I'm not sure it would be worth it, Gray. This business of keeping your feelings stowed away sounds like a lonely, dimmed version of a life. No offense. But I suppose that's the trade-off for it to work—what did you call it, supercharged synesthesia?"

I didn't correct her. I was almost sure that I'd still have my gift, even if I emptied all the stones and welcomed the feelings back. From a practical point of view, I didn't need my own inner world tangling up what I observed in the vicinity of clients. And yeah, maybe I liked not having to feel too deeply anymore. "Look on the bright side. For one thing, you don't have to tiptoe around my feelings."

The tongue-twister *tiptoe* had sent water dribbling down my chin again. A sunny laugh reverberated around my kitchen, sending balloons upward. "Yeah? That mustache is about a decade too stale."

"You're the second person to comment on it this week. I'll shave it off. See how easy that was?... How do you feel?"

"I thought you could see that."

"Only what's there in the now. I meant how do you feel in general, with Adam's murderer caught?"

She pulled her shoulders in, as if a sudden draft had entered through the closed window. "Raw, like a bulldozer passed over my life and I find myself standing atop rubble."

"Ah. I call it the winter wind." I didn't add that in my experience, it took clients months, sometimes years, to emerge into sunshine.

Baker gave a start. "What about murder's mark? What did it turn out to be?"

I'd drawn a fresh entry into the sketchbook. The raven had made an appearance in The Cork's basement when Troy Cooper aimed his gun at me. A day earlier, I'd heard its wings in the resort parking lot—after Troy had been reminded of sending Adam to his death in the cold; Nicole had been speaking of the Oldehouse and the word *chilly* had done its thing. I'd visited Cooper in jail and listened to the slow flutter, a presence he'd never be rid of. The raven would nest in his soul forever.

And, it struck me, in the soul of the killer of Gray the First, who'd vanished into the night.

I explained about the raven. "I've settled on a name for murder's soul mark—I'm going to call it Murdermore."

"I get it—like in Edgar Allan Poe's poem. Quoth the Raven, 'Nevermore,' isn't that how it goes?"

"I read it a while back. There was a line I was trying to remember—I ended up going to the library to look it up." I turned the notebook toward her. I'd copied the line down next to the sketch of the bird, words Poe had penned about his raven: *And his eyes have all the seeming of a demon's that is dreaming.*

It felt odd to be talking about these things in my sunny kitchen. Baker asked, "Are you going to take murder cases from now on?"

I'd given it some thought and in the end taken down the sign outside the agency doors. "I figure it's my duty to do so, now that I know what to look for." I doubted it'd be that straightforward and easy; not much in people's soulscapes is. Baker threw another disinterested glance at the employment ads and I made a suggestion. "How about a pastry shop? One of your ancestors way back must have been a baker."

"Because of the name? Won't work. One, I have no money to open a shop and buy supplies and equipment. And two, I don't know how to cook. But I'm glad you asked. I did rather enjoy being a Crime Knight, breaking into a restaurant after midnight."

"And almost getting killed?"

"Even that." She folded *The Bee* back to the front page, with its shouty headlines about the former mayor, and rose to her feet. "I should head home, Hutch needs his afternoon walk. What time do you want me at Soul Garden Investigations on Monday?"

A moonless night—of confusion—enveloped me; to Baker it

must have appeared as if I were staring at her blankly. "I already have an assistant," I said.

"But not a partner. Listen, Gray, you're just going to have to trust me when I say that if you did have gut feelings, your gut would tell you to snap me up in a jiffy."

"You don't mind me being able to see your mood? All the time?"

"I'm hardly one to hide my emotions."

I reached for Ike.

"Really, the coin?"

"The coin."

"Go ahead, then."

I went ahead. *Heads, Baker joins the agency. Tails, she doesn't.* The dollar landed face down on the kitchen table. I stared at the eagle landing on the cratered Moon.

Homeful. *For her, or for me?*

I pocketed the coin. "Welcome to Soul Garden Investigations, Baker."

ABOUT THE AUTHOR

Author's Note: Did you enjoy this book? Get bonus content! Unlock the Meet Cute scene from Shane's screenplay and receive updates about future books by signing up for my author newsletter, neve.substack.com. I send these out about once a month and will never share your email address with anyone. (If you're already on the list, thank you for your support—starting January 2026, you'll find the Bonus Content Link at the bottom of your newsletter.)

Neve Maslakovic writes mysteries set in speculative worlds. She's been published by 47North and under her own banner, Cosmic Tea Press. In her books, no place is safe from the criminal element — including an academic time travel lab (*The Incident Series*), a parallel universe (*Regarding Ducks and Universes*) and a Seattle of the future (*All the Whys of Delilah's Demise*). Her newest project is a genre-bending mystery series set in the 1980s, starting with *That Murder Feeling*.

Neve's life journey has taken her from Belgrade, Serbia to a PhD at Stanford University's STAR Lab to her dream job as a writer. She lives in the Twin Cities with her husband, son, and high-spirited goldendoodle. Find out more at neve-maslakovic.com.